Craving

Redemption

By Nicole Jacquelyn

Visit my Facebook page at www.facebook.com/authornicolejacquelyn

Dedication

To the woman who was my safe haven.
You taught us that we don't have to agree with someone's choices to
love them,
family is important,
and food can be a sign of love.
You fed us constantly.
I love you and miss you Gram.
This one is for you.

Contents

Prologue

Callie

I'd gotten a call from my baby brother almost three months earlier, telling me he'd been shot, but not to worry. *Who did he think he was talking to?* I'd been taking care of him since the day they brought him home from the hospital—that wasn't likely to stop just because he was doing God knows what in some town in Oregon. I'd never stop worrying about what was going on with him, just like he'd never stop standing between me and the world. That was why he was in this mess in the first place—why he gave up his education at one of the most prestigious universities in the country and joined a motorcycle club—leaving me all alone.

I hadn't had any say in the matter. He'd left with Asa that day a year ago and I'd been too wrapped up with holding myself together to be able to stop it. I'd been such a mess—in shock and trying to figure out how it had played out the way it had. But I was no longer that broken girl who allowed herself to be patted on the head and told that everything was going to be okay. I was going to bring my brother home, no matter what I had to do.

When I pulled up to the gate, there was a man leaning against the fence outside. When he saw me, his shoulders stiffened for a minute before relaxing again as if he wasn't overly concerned about what I was doing there. That was his first mistake. Then he grinned at me, checking me out and staring at my chest as he started toward my car. That was his second mistake. His third mistake was to walk up to my window and lean in, never even glancing at my hand that rested in my lap.

If he had seen me as a threat instead of staring at my boobs, he wouldn't have been so surprised when I pressed the Taser against his chest.

Once he was down, I got out and rolled open the gate in front of my car. I was glad, but a little baffled, that there was no lock on the gate. They must have trusted whoever was guarding the gate to keep intruders out. *Their* mistake.

I started back for my car, skirting around the man lying on the gravel. I wanted to just leave him there. I really did. But the light was fading, and I was afraid if I left him lying there in the middle of the driveway someone would drive right over his ass. So instead of hopping in my car and heading down the road before someone could catch me, I leaned over and grabbed both of his ankles. It took me forever to drag him to the side of the road, and by the time I got him settled he'd begun to twitch as if he was waking up. I needed to get the hell out of there.

I once again walked toward my car, grabbing his phone off the ground as I passed it. If he woke up before I got to the big house, or whatever the fuck it was called, I didn't want him warning anyone I was coming. I didn't need them waiting for me. The only thing I had going for me at the moment was the element of surprise.

I pulled the car through the gate, but my conscience wouldn't let me just leave things as they were. Jesus, I needed to stop having such a freaking bleeding heart. I left my car running and quickly ran back to shut the gate before heading down the road. They weren't going to be thankful that I knocked out their guard, but at least I didn't leave the gate open. That had to *somehow* work in my favor.

When I pulled up to the huge building, I could see there was some sort of gathering going on, but it didn't stop me. Not once did I think I should come back or wait until a better time. I was on a mission to get my brother the hell out of there and nothing was going to stop me.

I knew it was a bad idea—knew the entire trip was one step away from a clusterfuck—and as soon as I saw Asa I took that final step. I was so consumed by rage; my vision had darkened at the edges. It was *his* fault. All of it; from the son I had at home in some shitty worn down apartment, to the fact that my brother was living in some biker compound in the middle of goddamn nowhere ruining his life and ultimately getting shot. It could all be traced back to Asa. *The bastard.*

There was a couple standing outside when I pulled up, but before I could even get my rental car's door open, the man was shouting toward the building. I couldn't understand what he was saying over the pounding in my ears. I was finally there; I knew it from the leather vest that the man was wearing. It was almost identical to the one Asa had worn for as long as I'd known him.

I knew I looked like a crazy person, but when men started swarming out of the club, I used the only protection I had and started waving the Taser around. I was hoping they wouldn't be able to tell what it was until I could figure out what the hell I was going to do. I hadn't thought things through very well. I'd been so anxious to get there that the ramifications of driving into a Motorcycle Club's compound uninvited had barely crossed my mind.

Just as I was beginning to get really scared, I saw Asa walking through the group and all the anger inside me wiped away any fear I had felt. That's when I started screaming.

"You fucking *dick*!" I yelled, my voice sounding tinny and quiet in my ears, though my throat was aching with the power behind it. "Where the *fuck* is my brother?"

He started walking toward me, and the look on his face had me retreating. "The fuck are you doing here, Callie?" he yelled back, running his fingers through his hair. "You're outta your goddamn mind!"

I wasn't thinking straight. I was scared that I wouldn't see my brother in the sea of faces before me, afraid that he hadn't been telling the truth when he'd told me he was fine. It had taken months of eating ramen noodles to save up enough money to come get him, and I was terrified that I was too late to help him.

I was still taking backward steps toward my car as I screamed at Asa, searching the crowd for any sign of my baby brother and finding none. He wasn't there. Oh God, he wasn't there.

I'd started to panic by the time Asa reached me and didn't hear much of what he said as he pried the Taser from my fingers. My heart was so loud in my ears, and my breath was coming at such a fast pace, that I knew it was only a manner of minutes before I passed out. It had happened once before, and though I tried to beat it, I just couldn't get enough air in my lungs. *Oh God, where was Cody?* Why wasn't he there, in between me and Asa, making peace and wrapping his arms around me? He had to have heard us yelling; if he were there, he would have come for me by then.

When Asa tossed the Taser to the ground, effectively disarming me and making me completely defenseless, I snapped. Completely and utterly lost it.

I swung my fist at his face, grazing his jaw as he twisted to dodge it. I didn't stop there, though. I was on autopilot, using every single move I knew to hurt him. I wanted him to hurt as much as I hurt. I wanted to punish him and I set out to do it with a single-minded intent that would have scared me, had I been thinking clearly. He let me hit and kick him for a few seconds before wrapping me up in his arms and lifting me off the ground. When I swung at his face again, he pressed it into my neck where I couldn't reach, so I pounded on his back instead. My mind was completely blank beyond the need to hurt him, my throat making little sounds of distress that I wasn't even aware of.

The harder I struggled, the gentler he became; his arms more comforting than punishing, even though I was acting like a crazy woman. When I ran out of options and my arms and legs felt like lead, I made a last ditch effort to punish him and bit down on his shoulder as hard as I could, tasting blood but refusing to let go.

His voice broke through when my body became too exhausted to fight anymore and my mind finally began to clear.

"It's okay, baby. He's fine. He's fine. It's okay. Shhh," he told me quietly, rubbing my back softly even though it must have hurt like hell where I had my teeth clamped down on the muscle of his shoulder. My breath caught on a sob as I finally relaxed my jaw and let my body go limp, instinctively knowing he would never let me fall. I tilted my head back and looked up at him through my tears, silently begging him to fix things. He brushed my face gently, rubbing at the blood on my cheeks as my entire body jerked with silent sobs.

"Fuck, baby, what were you fuckin' thinkin'?" he asked me before sliding his mouth down over my nose to my lips.

While surrounded by angry bikers, with his blood on my mouth and tears running down my face, he kissed me for the first time in three years.

God, I loved him.

Chapter 1

Callie

5 years ago…

I shouldn't have been at the party. It had been a bad idea from the very beginning, and that was *before* my ride had vanished into the upstairs of the house to have a drunken one-night-stand with a guy who had more acne than facial hair. It wasn't my scene. I'd prided myself on being the wild child of my high school, but nothing had prepared me for that part of town. I didn't know the names of the drugs that were spread across the coffee table, and I didn't *want* to know—I didn't even want to be near them.

I had decided to flip my parents the bird by going out with a friend that I knew they thought very little of. They'd grounded me the night before for breaking curfew by a measly ten minutes, but then they did me the favor of going out to dinner with my dad's boss, leaving me all alone and full of teenage spite. I called Mallory to pick me up, and within fifteen minutes of their departure, I was on my way to Chula Vista with a girl who smoked pot while she drove and carried a flask around with her at school.

When we arrived, I stuck close to Mal, practically holding her hand as we walked through the house full of people who were both older and harder than anyone I'd partied with before. High school house parties, where we'd stolen our parents' liquor and spent the night with kids we'd known since grade school, hadn't prepared me for what we walked into. Mal seemed to blend into the crowd. She laughed at jokes I didn't understand, and nonchalantly nodded her head to the music blaring through the speakers, while I stuck out like a nun at a Rob Zombie concert.

I'd dressed to impress, pairing low-waist jean shorts with a skimpy tank top that showed a sliver of my belly. I felt almost reckless when I left the house, as if I'd turned into a sluttier version of myself as a final *fuck you* to my overly strict parents. But when we got to the party, my version of slutty was a joke compared to what the other women were wearing. And they *were* women—older than us by at least a couple of years in age and hundreds of years in experience. It was mortifying, like we were playing at being grown-ups.

I was hell-bent on proving a point to my parents; I could do what I wanted. I wasn't going to be treated like a child when I was practically an adult. So, even though all of my internal warning systems were screaming, I accepted a cup of some sort of alcohol from a man I'd never met. Then I smiled how I'd practiced—with my mouth closed tightly over my teeth and my left cheek showing off a dimple.

The house was full of people dancing, drinking, and yelling over rock music that I'd never heard before. It's not that I didn't listen to rock, I listened to everything really, but this was angrier than I preferred. I couldn't even understand the words—where was the fun in that type of music? I was sitting in the corner, on an ottoman that had been pushed aside to clear the floor, and trying to be as unobtrusive as possible. I wasn't feeling rebellious anymore. I wasn't angry at my parents and I was no longer trying to prove a point.

I just wanted to go home.

Whatever I'd drunk when I first arrived was making me feel really sick to my stomach, but I was too afraid to go to the bathroom. I didn't want to stand up and be noticed. These guys were not the kind I was used to; the ones I could wrap around my finger with a flip of my hair and a wide smile. They were big, and tattooed, and they passed around the women as if they were Fireball whiskey and they needed a shot. I'd seen one woman leave the room four separate times with different men, and each time she returned looking dazed, unkempt, and strangely satisfied. I knew what she was doing, but having it play out in front of me made my face heat in embarrassment. I was *so* out of my element it wasn't even funny.

I just wanted to get the hell out of there, but unless I wanted to call my parents for a ride home, I was stuck.

I was sixteen. I would have rather run home barefoot through broken glass than called my parents to have them pick me up from a party. It was bad enough that I'd gotten braces during my junior year of high school, pretty much ensuring that I wouldn't smile with my mouth open for the entire year—I didn't need my mommy picking me up from a party, too. There was no way in hell that my mother would just quietly pull up to the end of the driveway. Even with my dad trying to calm her down, she'd be at the front door yelling and chastising in Spanish, making me look like a twelve-year-old.

So, I sat in that corner for over an hour as my stomach grew worse, until finally, I thought I would pass out or vomit all over the carpet. The thought of puking in front of all the people around me was enough to push all my fears aside. I had to find a bathroom. As I stood up, the world began to spin, and I leaned my hand against the wall to get my balance. *Shouldn't that drink have worn off?* It had been hours since I'd had anything. It shouldn't have been getting worse, but it was. I'd only felt that way once before—my parents had been out of town and I'd raided their liquor cabinet with my baby brother. God, I wished I were home with him. He would've seen the problem and gotten me to a bathroom. Hell, he would have put me to bed by then.

I took a couple steps away from the wall, and that's when I grabbed the attention of the room. I felt eyes on me as I made my way across the floor, shuffling my feet across the carpet. My legs felt heavy and unsteady as I reached the entryway to the house. My head was spinning as I tried to decide if I should make my way out the front door that was so close, or to the bathroom at the end of the hallway. I turned slowly toward the front door, thinking that would be my safest bet. I only took a couple of slow steps before there was a guy behind me, both hands holding me steady and making my skin crawl as his fingers pressed into my belly through my tank top.

"Where you going? The party's in here, sweetheart," he told me, pulling my body toward the living room again.

I couldn't seem to get my legs to stay put, and the heels of my Vans squeaked on the wood floor as he pulled me back. My fingernails were digging into his forearms, but doing little damage as I stuttered and squeaked, trying to get him to let me go.

"I need—I'm going to be sick," I groaned desperately, cringing as he started chuckling.

I wasn't sure what was happening, but I knew I didn't want the man touching me. His free hand was roaming all over my thighs and breasts, and my heartbeat roared in my ears when I realized he really wasn't going to let me go. My struggles seemed to make him bolder and I whimpered as his hand started to slide up my shorts.

I was looking longingly at the front door, my heart in my throat and praying for deliverance, when all of a sudden it came. But not in the manner I would have ever envisioned.

The door burst open quickly, and the man behind me paused at the entrance of the living room, giving me a glimpse of the men stomping into the house. They were huge, all of them, and they were covered in tattoos and matching black leather vests. They didn't seem happy.

There was a clear hierarchy in the group that even *I* could catch in my fuzzy state, and the leader was one of the most gorgeous guys I'd ever seen. He had to be over six feet tall and his shoulders were massive. He had full-sleeve tattoos wrapped around his arms, and I wondered vaguely how I could find him attractive when his face was covered in a full beard. If I hadn't been ready to crawl out of my skin at the arm encircling me, I might have smiled. But the vibe in the room had changed when the men walked through the door and I just wanted to get as far away from the situation as I could. I was just a high school student from Mira Mesa; I just wanted to go home.

"Jose," Beard Guy nodded to the man holding me, his body coiled tight. "We got business. Why don't you let her go and we can talk."

"Eh, this one's mine for the night. Grab a beer while I bring her upstairs. I'll be with you in a minute," he replied with a forced chuckle.

When his arm tightened to move me, I whimpered and tried again to pull his arm from around my waist. I knew if he got me upstairs, I wouldn't be going anywhere that night, and saliva pooled in my mouth as I envisioned what that would entail. My head had dropped forward, feeling too heavy for my neck, and I slammed it backward, trying to hit anything I could. It felt like I was moving in slow motion, and I guess I was, because my head landed ineffectually on his shoulder. I left it there, too tired to fight.

Beard Guy raised his eyebrows as he finally got a good look at me, and I could only imagine what he was seeing. My tank top had risen with the arm wrapped around me, my hair was falling out of its ponytail, and my mouth was slack, showing off my braces with little purple rubber bands. For the first time that night I hoped that someone would see me as I truly was—a scared sixteen-year-old girl with a mouthful of orthodontia and makeup covered pimples.

Before I could speak, four men who'd been at the back of the house joined us in the entryway, and the energy in the room went from tense to electric. The man holding me let go and I dropped to the floor in a heap of arms and legs. As I scurried to get my limbs under me to crawl away, I heard the men arguing above me. Beard Guy never raised his voice, but the way he spoke was much scarier than Jose's screaming in Spanish. I couldn't figure out what they were arguing about, but at that point I was too concerned with myself to care. I got to my hands and knees and crawled toward the men in the vests. They *had* to take me with them. I didn't care what their problem was with the guys at the party; they couldn't leave me alone with them.

When I reached the leader, I kneeled at his feet and slowly wrapped my arm around his thigh. He was warm and he smelled good and I wanted to rest where I was for just a moment, so I closed my eyes and laid my head on his thigh.

"What the fuck?" I heard him rumble above me as his hand weaved through my hair. "You fuckin' drug her?"

He sounded pissed off, but I couldn't tell who his anger was directed at, so I leaned my head back to look up at his face. He wasn't looking at me, so I pulled on his pant leg to get his attention. He didn't look away from the guys across from him, and just when I thought he was going to completely ignore me, he looked down and his brown eyes met mine.

I didn't think he would help. I was tired and disoriented and afraid, but I knew I had to try one last time to get away from there. It didn't ever dawn on me that I might be exchanging one bad situation for another.

"Please," I whispered, but my word was lost in the sound of a gunshot. He shoved me sideways to the floor as another shot rang out, this one closer to us. I whimpered and tried to crawl away, but he held firm to my hair, pressing my face into the floor.

I wondered detachedly if that was my punishment for disobeying my parents, and then everything went black.

Chapter 2

Callie

I woke up on a scratchy comforter, and as soon as I opened my eyes, I squinted at the bright lamp in front of my face. *Where the hell was I?* It looked like a hotel room, but I couldn't remember going to a hotel. The last thing I could recall was walking through the house party on Mallory's heels, trying not to bring any attention to myself.

I lay there quietly, trying to catch my bearings, when I realized I wasn't alone in the room. I could hear two men's voices, one deep and the other raspy.

"You fucked up the meet, man. Slider's gonna cut off your balls," the raspy one joked.

"Shut the fuck up. Jose was gonna cause problems and you know it. Had nothin' to do with the girl," the deep voice replied, sounding frustrated.

"Yeah, but it wouldn't have been a fuckin' gun fight if you woulda kept your head."

"I kept my head. Someone starts fuckin' shooting at me, I shoot back. It's fuckin' common sense. Jose's low level, no one's gonna miss him or his men."

Then, another voice joined the discussion.

"Dude, it's gonna look like you took Jose out over a piece of ass," he said quietly.

"Then you'll have to explain matters, won't you?" the deep voice warned.

"Not sure what I'll be explaining. You took them out and then grabbed the bitch and left. Looks pretty cut and dry to me…"

"Brother or not, I'll fuckin' drop you where you stand."

"Fine."

I tried not to panic as someone grabbed a hold of my foot at the edge of the bed and shook it.

"Grease, man, it looks like your girl is waking up," Raspy Voice said to someone else in the room.

I lay there silently, begging to be anywhere but in that fucking hotel room waiting to see what would happen. My head was starting to throb with the beat of my racing heart, and when someone spoke from right behind me, my whole body jerked.

"Get your fuckin' hand off her foot," the deep voice growled. "Don't fuckin' touch her."

The tone of his voice was enough to clear all the cobwebs from my brain. Before he even finished speaking, I had pulled my legs up and pushed with my heels until I was sitting, curled into a ball against the headboard of the bed. As soon as I was as small as I could make myself, I jerked my head up to see what I was dealing with.

There were four men in the room—*really big men*—and when I saw them I whimpered a little in the back of my throat. Three of the men were wearing matching black leather vests, tattoos covered their arms and they all had beards. They looked like they belonged in a Hell's Angels documentary, and I swallowed hard, knowing they belonged to some motorcycle club. *Motorcycle Clubs were full of criminals, weren't they?*

God, if I had just stayed home like I was supposed to, I wouldn't have had to deal with any of the mess I had created for myself. My eyes raced around the room, taking all of them in, and I was surprised when I saw the fourth man. He wasn't wearing a vest, and his clothes seemed similar to the ones I saw every day at school. The only thing setting him apart from my peers was the Mohawk on his head and the tattoo that wrapped around his left hand. He didn't seem scary until I looked at his face. He was scowling at me and his eyes were empty.

I didn't know what the hell I was doing there, but I knew it was bad. They looked scary. None of them were smiling, and for the life of me, I couldn't think of one good reason that I would be in a hotel room with four men. My clothes were still intact—I even had my shoes on—but I was afraid they had been waiting for me to wake up.

I eyed the door, but there was no way I could get off the bed and through it before one of them caught me. They were sitting and standing throughout the room, and one of the guys in a vest seemed to be standing guard in front of the door. *Why would he be guarding the door?* Oh God, I was in so much trouble.

The second I was about to panic—crying and screaming for them to let me go—the man closest to me sat down on the edge of the bed. He was extremely good looking, and probably not that much older than I was, though he had a full beard covering the lower half of his face. When he reached out to lay his hand on my knee, I squeaked in fear and pulled my legs closer to my body. God, I didn't want him to touch me.

"Hey, not gonna hurt you," he told me quietly. "You passed the fuck out and we had no idea where to take you. Now that you're awake, you can call someone to come and get ya."

His voice, so different from the tone he'd used earlier, calmed me down enough that I was able to look up into his eyes. As soon as I saw them, I remembered the night in a rush of clarity. He'd saved me. He'd taken me out of that house with the disgusting guy that was trying to pull me upstairs. Before the thought was even finished in my mind, I'd launched myself across the bed and into his lap sideways, wrapping my arms tight around his neck.

"Thank you. Thank you," I told him over and over again, pressing my forehead into his neck. I didn't realize that he hadn't touched me until his hands gripped my upper arms and pushed me away from him.

"The fuck are you doing?" he asked me, his eyebrows furrowed.

"You took me out of there. Oh my God, thank you," I told him again, straining against his hold.

"Babe, I'm not sure if whatever you were on just hasn't worn off yet, or if you're fuckin' naïve as hell, but you can't sit on my fuckin' lap," he mumbled as he pushed me onto the bed.

My face blushed beet red as I realized what I had done. The man wasn't a policeman or a fireman. He wasn't a family member. Shit, he wasn't even like the guys I knew from school. He was big, strong, and completely rough around the edges. I'd been so thankful to be out of the house, I hadn't grasped the actual situation I was in. I was surrounded by men that I didn't know from Adam, and they were all staring at me as if I'd just sprouted horns.

"I'm, uh, sorry," I whispered, worried about what would happen next.

"No need to be sorry. Just need to get you home. You got someone you can call?" he asked as he walked toward the dresser with a cell phone sitting on top of it. He tossed it to the bed, and I reached out quickly to grab it. I needed to get home, but my stubborn pride wouldn't allow me to call my parents. I wasn't sure what to do, but he was treating me like an adult, and for some reason I didn't want to look like a kid in front of him.

I should have been scared as hell, but I wasn't. I was just … worried. I wasn't sure what would happen next, but the guy didn't set off any alarm bells. He'd protected me, and that's what I felt—protected. I was pretty concerned with how things would play out, though. I couldn't just sit there on the bed indefinitely, looking at the phone, while the men in the room watched me in silence. The man in the corner made my skin crawl a little, and though my protector seemed to be in charge, I knew with the slightest provocation that the man in the corner would make his play.

"Um, I don't have anyone to come get me tonight," I told The Protector, "But I'll call my Gram. She can come get me in the morning. She can't drive at night," I hurried to explain before running my tongue between my braces and my lips. My mouth was dry from whatever I'd drunk at the party, and my lips were starting to stick to the little metal brackets in my mouth.

"Yeah. Call her. But tell her I'll bring you home," he grumbled, staring at my lips.

"But—," I started, but he cut me off.

"No. You're not staying the night in my goddamn motel room. Not gonna happen. Call your fuckin' grandmother, or a friend, or your fuckin' priest, but you're *not* staying here."

His voice was so sharp that I felt my breath catch in my throat. I mean, I knew I was a nuisance, and I could tell that they didn't know what to do with me, but he didn't have to be so mean about it.

I flipped open the phone and dialed the number from memory as The Protector went to stand against the wall, his eyes never leaving me. After only half a ring, she answered.

"Hello?"

"Hey, Gram. What are you doing up this late?" I put my hand to my forehead in embarrassment as one of the guys chuckled quietly at my attempt of small talk.

"Callie? What's going on? Where are you? This isn't your number."

"Yeah, I lost my phone." I looked up to see The Protector swinging my purse from side to side across the room. Okay, I guess I didn't lose my phone. "Well, I mean, I couldn't find my purse."

"Your purse? Why aren't you at home?" she asked, and I could hear her leaning forward in her creaky recliner.

"It's a long story, Gram. I'm on my way—I have a friend bringing me to your house. If Mom calls can you tell her I'm there and I'm asleep?" I asked, crossing my fingers. Asking Gram to cover for me was hit or miss, I wasn't sure if she would help me out.

After a minute of silence, she answered slowly, "Yeah, I'll tell them. But if you're not here in an hour, I'm calling your dad."

I'm not sure what she heard in my voice, but she knew I needed her to help me out, and for once she wasn't going to give me shit and leave me hanging 'for my own good'.

"Thanks, Gram. I'll see you soon. Love you."

"Love you, too. Get your ass home," she told me and then disconnected.

When I looked up at the room, eight eyes were watching me closely, and it looked like the man who'd saved me had gone pale. I looked around the room, trying to figure out what the problem was, when the man by the door barked out a sharp laugh.

"Holy fuck, Romeo. You decide to play fuckin' knight in shining armor, and the bitch you bring home is jailbait."

Chapter 3

Callie

The Protector didn't say anything as he moved around the room. He pulled two hoodies out of a duffel bag at the foot of the bed and handed me one as he pulled off his vest.

"Put that on. It's gonna be cold on the bike," he instructed, most of his words muffled as he pulled the sweatshirt over his head and then threaded his arms back through the vest. When he lifted his arms, his black Metallica t-shirt raised just enough that I could see some sort of tattoo across the bottom of his stomach. I quickly looked away before he could catch me staring.

I put the sweatshirt on and took a deep breath, noticing it smelled like him. His scent was a mixture of leather and surprisingly, Armani cologne. It was almost ironic, those two scents mixed together. Who *was* this guy?

As soon as I had the sweatshirt on, I stood up and he handed me my purse so I could sling it over my shoulder. I knew that I should check my cell phone for messages, but I just didn't think I could take any more drama. I decided to wait and see who had called once I was safe at Gram's; I'd deal with everything then.

I was lost in my head, trying to decide how I was going to explain everything to my parents when the Protector's voice cut through the silence in the room. Half of his mouth was pulled up in a smile, his eyes were crinkled at the corners when he looked at me, and I just knew I'd been thinking out loud.

My face burned in mortification as they watched me, but I

straightened my shoulders and tilted my chin up as if they hadn't just heard me talking to myself.

"I'm Grease," he mumbled, lifting his arm out to shake my hand. As soon as I took hold, he gestured with his other to the men in the room. "That's Dragon by the dresser."

"Hey," Dragon called out quietly, busy messing with the phone in his hands.

"His voice isn't usually like that," Grease shared, a genuine full-blown smile on his face. "Got strep-throat from some chick with kids."

"Shut the fuck up," Dragon spat back, looking up from his phone.

With a smile in his voice, he introduced the last two in the room. "That's Tommy Gun by the door. The guy with the Mohawk is my brother Deke."

The men both lifted their chins at me, watching me from their sides of the room, but didn't say a word.

He stopped talking as I nodded to the guys around the room, but he never let go of my hand, and I didn't try to pull away.

"I'm Calliope. Callie," I replied nervously, wondering if I should have given them a fake name. It's not like Calliope is a popular name, it wouldn't be hard to find me if they were looking. Then I realized that Grease would be driving me to my Gram's house, so it's not like giving them my real name would've mattered anyway.

"What kind of name is Grease?" I asked as he pulled me out of the room, following the other men as they strode down the stairs to the back parking lot. He was pulling me quickly, and my legs weren't quite up to the pace he was keeping, so I kept stumbling over nonexistent dips in the concrete.

"Only name you're gonna get," he answered, pausing for a

second so I could catch up with his long strides.

As we made our way out to the bikes, Grease never let go of my hand. I thought that maybe he was afraid I'd take off if he didn't have a hold on me, but when I glanced up at the expression on his face, I knew differently. I wasn't sure what happened in the room that I didn't notice, but the hand-holding was for the men's benefit, not mine. He was staking his claim.

"Stand right here. Don't move," he ordered, placing me next to a big black Harley.

"Um, okay..." I answered, wondering why we weren't getting on the bike.

He answered the question in my voice by walking six feet away to where the rest of the men were huddled at the far end of the bikes. I couldn't hear a word they were saying, but the body language of Dragon and Tommy Gun led me to believe that they weren't happy with whatever Grease was telling them. When my eyes moved to Deke, I noticed he was watching me, completely ignoring the conversation going on around him. When he smiled at me, his entire face changed and I smiled back, wondering why he'd given me such a weird feeling before. He seemed nice enough.

Grease caught our little interaction and slapped Deke on the back of his head, breaking our eye contact. After a few more words, he broke away from the group and walked toward me.

While I stood waiting for him, I finally grasped how very bad this could potentially go for me. I was climbing on the back of a motorcycle with a man I'd never met before. The whole night had turned into some after school special, a warning for kids who disobeyed their parents and drank alcohol. My hands started to shake, so I stuffed them in the front pocket of the hoodie that was hanging down covering my shorts. If there was any question about how I could handle myself against these men, the fact that the sweatshirt I borrowed hung to the middle of my thighs gave a pretty clear answer. If any of them decided that I was easy pickings, they would be correct. I was completely defenseless.

Before I could open my mouth to tell Grease I'd just call my parents, he spoke, and my apprehension started to fade.

"You ever been on a bike before?" he asked, pulling a helmet off the back of the bike and putting it on my head.

"No. My uncle had a motorcycle when I was little, but he died before I was old enough to ride it," I overshared, watching his face as he scowled at the helmet. Suddenly, he pulled it off my head, causing my hair to fly in all different static-filled directions.

I startled when his hands came up to both sides of my face, but stilled when he gently began pulling my hair back. He brushed it with his fingers, grabbing it in his fist before pulling a hair tie off his wrist. He tied it back and then ran his hands down my neck as I stopped breathing altogether. His eyes weren't on my face, they were on my throat, and the look in his eyes was one I'd never seen before. I couldn't decide if I should pull away or not, and before I could make my decision, his hands had made it to the nape of my neck and he was pulling the hood of the sweatshirt over my head.

He acted like he hadn't been just ogling my neck—he was all business as he plopped the helmet back over my hood-covered head and buckled the strap.

I took the time while he was situating the helmet to explain where my Gram lived and asked if he needed directions, but he seemed to know the area pretty well. I wasn't sure where he was from, but I wasn't about to ask him if he lived in San Diego. If he did, I would have to decide whether I wanted to try and see him again, and if he didn't, I would have to deal with the disappointment. I didn't want to do either.

"Helmet's still a little big, but that should help a bit," he told me with a nod before he started messing with his bike. I just stood there like an idiot, wondering if that look he'd given me had meant something. *Was he into me?* It was a ridiculous question, I knew he was older than me and completely out of my league, but I couldn't help but feel like he'd been checking me out.

He climbed on to the bike, settling in, and I just stood there staring. He had long hair. *How had I missed that before?* It wasn't super long like the guy on the front of Gram's romance novels, but it was long enough to put in a hair tie at the back of his head. Normally, I would've laughed at a guy with long hair, I mean, really? But he worked it. The fact that he didn't seem to care how long it was, and the ponytail was more of a completely tangled bun than a slick ponytail... it was hot.

His back was slightly toward me, giving me a good glimpse of his broad shoulders and his jeans pulled tight across his thighs in a way that made my heart speed up. *Holy shit.* I'd never even *noticed* a guy's thighs before. They were just a part of someone's legs, right? No big deal, nothing particularly special about them. But for some reason, looking at this guy's thighs made my stomach clench.

I was snapped out of my perusal by the clearing of his throat. When I cut my eyes quickly toward his face, I knew he hadn't missed the way I'd been staring at him. Half of his mouth was pulled up in a grin and his voice was laced with humor as he spoke.

"Well? Climb on."

Chapter 4

Callie

I made it onto the bike with little trouble, though I thought for sure I was going to wipe out. I sat with my hands wrapped around his waist and my cheek against his back for most of the ride. I could tell he loved it—the wind and the open highway—because his whole body seemed to relax once we were on the road. He made riding seem so easy, his movements fluid and graceful, and the ride would have made it to the top ten best moments of my life if not for one thing.

I was fucking freezing.

The wind cut through the sweatshirt I was wearing, and at first it didn't bother me much, but as soon as we were on the freeway, the wind felt like little shards of glass cutting into my skin. My legs, completely uncovered in the shorts I'd thought were so risqué earlier in the night, almost felt sunburned from the cold air. It was miserable.

The first time I shivered, I didn't think he noticed, but when my teeth began to chatter against his back I felt him tense. His shoulders only tightened for a moment before he dropped one hand off the handlebars and reached down to rub my thigh briskly, running his fingers as high up as he could reach and then back down over my knee to my shin. He did this over and over before switching hands and rubbing the other thigh the same way.

At first, it didn't seem to matter what he was doing, my legs continued to burn and I counted the seconds until we would make it to Gram's. But less than five minutes later, I was burning up for an entirely different reason.

When I started to squirm behind him, he paused with his hand on my knee. I was afraid he was going to stop what he was doing, but instead he reached even further back and grabbed my hip, scooting my body toward his until there was no space between us. Once he was sure I was done moving around, his hand found my thigh again, his pinky sliding under the side of my shorts before sweeping down my leg slower than he had before.

He let go of my leg as we took the exit we needed and I shuddered once before getting control of myself. I felt my face heat as I thought of the way I must have looked, practically purring as he warmed up my legs, and I was happy as hell that he couldn't see me make a complete ass of myself when he was only trying to warm me up.

Gram lived only a couple blocks off the exit in a small trailer park that I knew would have been silent at four o'clock in the morning if it weren't for the roar of his motorcycle. Thankfully, the people who lived there were closer to my Gram's age than mine, so the possibility of waking them up sans hearing aids was pretty slim.

I let go with one arm as we neared my Gram's trailer, digging the fingers of my other hand into his stomach even though we were going less than fifteen miles per hour. I'd made it the entire half an hour trip, I didn't want to fall off the bike when I was so close to making it home in one piece. I used my free hand to point him in the right direction, but as we glided closer I realized that he would've known where to go anyway. It was the only trailer in the park that was entirely lit up and Gram was standing on the front porch waiting for us as we pulled to a stop.

I hopped off the bike as soon as we were stopped, wobbling and tripping like an idiot as I got my feet back under me. Gram was backlit by lights so I couldn't see her face, but all of a sudden, whatever bravado

I'd had on the ride over was completely gone, and I was anxious to get in the house before she laid into me for being out so late. I was fumbling and pulling at the strap of the helmet, trying like hell to pull it off when I realized Grease was climbing off the back of the bike.

I felt my eyes go wide, the universal 'stop what you're doing' look, but he completely ignored me and took a few steps forward. Gently pushing my hands away from the helmet, he slowly unlatched the buckle as if my Gram wasn't giving us the evil eye from the porch.

"I programmed my number into your phone back at the hotel, Sugar," he rumbled quietly. "None of this shit should blow back on you, but you need me for anything, you call."

I stood there staring at him, not sure what my reply should be, until Gram's voice broke through the quiet night.

"Well? You two coming in?" she asked, causing my head to jerk around in surprise.

"I better get going, ma'am," Grease called out quietly.

"Bullshit. You just brought my girl home. You're probably hungry. Come on in and eat, I've got breakfast ready."

"Gram—" I tried to reason with her, but she cut me off.

"Callie, get your butt in this house. Bring your friend with you," she told me, turning back to walk in the door.

I spun around to Grease to tell him he didn't have to stay, but he was already at my side. He placed his hand on my lower back to lead me inside, and I sputtered as I walked toward the porch steps.

"Sugar, your grandmother asked me inside. I'd be an asshole if I just took off. I'll eat and I'll leave. No problem," he assured me as we reached the porch.

When we got to the front door and could see Gram's kitchen table covered with food, I heard Grease chuckle in my ear. He leaned close until I could feel his breath at the side of my neck.

"Your grandma always cook full meals in the middle of the night?" he whispered, a smile in his voice.

I snorted and answered him, "More times than you could possibly imagine."

We sat down at the table as Gram moved around the kitchen, washing dishes and putting things away. She was wearing a nightgown that covered her from neck to toes and an apron wrapped around her waist. I watched for a few moments as her nightgown billowed out behind her legs as she walked, wishing I hadn't gotten her out of bed to deal with my mess. She'd never complain; to her it was just what family did. If someone needed you, no matter what time it was or why, you stepped up and did what you could.

I handed Grease one of the plates that was stacked in front of me and started to dish up when Gram came and stood behind me.

"Thanks for bringing my girl home. Not sure what she got herself into, or how you're a part of that… but thanks for getting her home. I'm Rose," she told Grease as she squeezed my shoulders. I felt tears hit the back of my eyes as the ramifications of her words set in.

She wasn't going to ask. It didn't matter where I'd been or how I'd gotten there. I was home safe, and that was enough for her.

Grease's eyes looked back and forth between Gram and me as he finished chewing, and he took his time wiping his mouth with a paper towel before he replied.

"Asa," he said quietly, half of his mouth tipping up as he noticed the look of surprise on my face. "And it was no problem, ma'am."

"Well, you two fill up. I might as well go get dressed."

I was staring at *Asa*, trying to get my bearings, when Gram stepped away from me. Before I could ask her to stay, Asa was standing and moving around the table. My body tensed as I watched him, but I relaxed into my chair as he gently grabbed Gram's elbow and guided her back to the table, speaking quietly in her ear.

"You got up and made us this huge breakfast. I'd feel a whole lot better if you'd sit down and eat with us before it got cold."

"Well, I guess I can do that. Where are you from, Asa?" she asked him as she grabbed a plate off the table and began to fill it.

"I'm from Oregon."

"Oh yeah? I've got a sister up there. I try to get out to see her at least once a year, but it's getting harder and harder to do. Got a sister down here, too; much easier to see that one. These old bones don't take to flying very well anymore."

They talked for an hour, occasionally pulling me into the conversation, but mostly leaving me to chime in when I felt like it. The past eight hours were really catching up with me and I felt like I was in the Twilight Zone, watching the big biker speak to my Gram as if she was The Queen of England. He never once swore, though my grandma did, and his table manners were impeccable. *Who was this guy?* I'd thought I'd had him pegged by the time we'd left the hotel room, but he wasn't acting the way I'd expected him to.

My head began to ache, but I was too enthralled to leave the table, so I just laid my head down on my arms and let their voices wash over me. After a while, I found myself in that place between wakefulness and sleep where I could hear everything going on but I wasn't quite conscious. I felt the table move a little under me, and seconds later I felt Gram's gnarled hands sifting through my hair.

"She's had a rough night. There anything I need to know about?" she asked quietly.

"No. She should be fine after a couple hours of sleep."

"Don't do that. Don't act like nothing happened. I've buried two sons. I've watched three of my children go off the deep end, and I've stitched their wounds myself after bar fights and car accidents. My granddaughter walked in here looking shell shocked and scared and I want to know what happened," she told him shortly, her voice leaving no room for argument.

"Far as I could tell, she went to a party with a friend and got left there. Not sure what happened to the friend, but she was alone when I saw her. Looked like she'd been drugged—not sure with what. She passed out, but woke up about two hours after I'd gotten her out of the house," he replied, sighing loudly at the end.

"You were at the party? Why'd you need to take her out of there? Why didn't you take her to a hospital?"

"I wasn't at the party. I had... business with one of the men there. She looked like she could use the help, so I took her with me."

There was a long pause before Gram spoke, like she was sifting through his words in order to decide whether to believe him or not.

"She... they didn't?" she whispered, her fingers tightening slightly in my hair.

"No ma'am. She was downstairs and fully dressed when I found her. Even had her purse draped across her chest."

I heard a small gasp above me, almost a sob, as Gram's hand came down heavy on my shoulder. My head was beginning to lose that dreamlike quality that I'd been enjoying and I started to move, but I froze when I heard the way Gram's breathing grew ragged before she brought it under control.

"Thank you," she told him strongly, her voice once again at a normal level. "You'll always have a place at my table. You're in town, I expect you to come see me, you hear?"

When Asa rose from the table, his chair scraping across the linoleum, I raised my head to watch him with bleary eyes. I wasn't sure how much longer I could stay awake, but I didn't want to miss saying goodbye to him. Gram started bustling around the kitchen again. It was the way she coped with too much emotion, but I knew she was also trying to give us some semblance of privacy though she wasn't ready to let me out of her sight.

"Thanks for bringing me home," I rasped at him, my voice scratchy with sleep as I stood up from my seat. Once I was standing, the world tilted a little, so I braced the flat of my hand on the tabletop to get my balance. It didn't seem to help, though, and I was swaying like a drunken sailor when Asa called out to Gram and reached for me, lifting me up like a baby into his arms.

He carried me in and laid me in Gram's bed, kissing my forehead gently before walking out. I waited, listening to the sound of his motorcycle start up and drive away. The last thing I was aware of was Gram climbing into bed behind me and wrapping her arms tightly around my waist.

Chapter 5

Grease

I'd had an entirely fucked up night.

I was in California trying to hash out a distribution disagreement that my club was having with a gang in San Diego. I hadn't been a member of the Aces Motorcycle Club for that long—only a couple of years—but my pop had been a member my entire life, and that gave me a little more clout than the other brothers who had gotten their cuts around the same time as me. I was happy to do what I could, but the whole fiasco had irritated the fuck out of me since I rolled into San Diego three days before.

The men I'd met up with were big fish in a small pond and they'd been pissed from the very beginning that Slider, my President, hadn't at least sent the VP to deal with them. The entire thing had turned into a goddamn pissing match that they had no chance of winning, but that hadn't stopped them from trying to piss the farthest and the longest. It was a fucking joke. The Aces controlled the gun trade over pretty much the entire western coast of the United States, and these jokers covered about a quarter of San Diego county. Comparing the two wasn't even like comparing apples and oranges—it was more like apples and fucking maize.

Fuck, I have absolutely no problem with Mexicans. I don't. I've met a lot of different Hispanic people that I liked a fuck of a lot. My half-brother is even a part of the Jimenez gang, which is part of the reason Slider sent me down there in the first place. Dear old Dad spent some time in California about twenty years ago, and when he came back he left a pretty little Mexican girl brokenhearted and knocked up. He took care of her until he died, and he took me down to see my brother Deke whenever he had the chance. We didn't grow up close, but he was my brother—it was as simple as that. I had his back and he had mine.

So when we started having some payment issues with the Jimenez gang, Slider thought it would ease some minds if I went down to collect the payment. It wouldn't look like we were trying to strong-arm them, even if that *was* our intention. It was a friendly reminder from the brother of one of their members; a warning to get us what we wanted.

Everything had gone down relatively well if I didn't count the president of the gang beating his chest and trying to exert his dominance whenever I was in the room. The man was like five-seven and had to weigh less than a buck-sixty. I could've snapped him in two, but instead, I was fucking diplomatic and did my job. I wasn't going to get pulled into some bullshit fight when my entire club was a good eighteen-hour ride away.

I had Tommy Gun and Dragon with me as back up, but Dragon was a fucking prospect and I'd known Tommy since birth and he wasn't the sharpest tool in the shed. I trusted them to have my back, but I wasn't about to put them in a situation where they would need to—it was the first meet I was in charge of, and I wasn't going to fuck it up.

I thought I was free and clear. I'd been stoked to be headed home with money in my saddle bags, and I was looking forward to the long ride with nothing to worry about but piss breaks and truck stop food.

When El Presidente asked me to stop by and handle some business with Jose, saying he had a quarter of the money they owed in his house safe, I was irritated as hell, but I went anyway. Apparently, Jose had been dealing for the gang, and he'd just come into a shitload of cash, but he hadn't yet paid up. It was supposed to be just a quick stop on our way out of town, but when we pulled up to the house I *knew* shit was going to go down.

The dude had a fucking house full of people when I knew he'd been told we were coming. I didn't know if he was feeling squirrely, or if he just didn't care who knew he was doing business, but I wasn't pleased with either scenario. It was business, and I was getting tired as hell of these fucking dicks acting like they were hot shit and not giving us the respect we deserved.

We parked our bikes by the road, and my brother Deke pulled in behind us in his little rice-grinder car. I wasn't sure why Deke felt the need to follow us, but the hair stood up on the back of my neck when he told me he was coming along for the ride. I never ignored that feeling, so I just slapped him on the back before I climbed on my bike. I met Dragon's eyes before we took off and I knew he was feeling it, too. Something was off.

The house was as full as it appeared from the outside, with people everywhere when we walked inside. I kept my guard up, but lucky for me, the dick I was looking for was standing in the entryway when we showed up. He had his arm around a woman who seemed to be having a hard time standing up, but I just barely registered her as I took everything in.

I didn't see her as a threat, but I should have.

I glanced around the house and looked back at Jose just as the woman dropped her head back against his shoulder and I got a good look at her face. She was gorgeous. Nice tits, tan skin, and light blue eyes; a weird mix that seemed to work on her. But those weren't the things about her that were the most apparent. She wasn't a woman; she was a girl. Her cheeks were still a little chubby, and when her mouth went slack I could see braces in her mouth with little purple rubber bands. It made my stomach clench that Jose, who was at least ten years older than me, was groping the girl, but it wasn't my problem, so I deliberately looked away from her face even though it fucking killed me to do it.

There was something about her. I'd been around a lot of bitches in my life, whores and good girls, but this girl was different. She didn't fit the situation. She was like a colored puzzle piece mixed in with a black and grey puzzle. It bugged the shit out of me—but I couldn't let it break my focus. Whatever she was doing there had nothing to do with me.

I started talking to Jose, telling him we had business to discuss, when four of his boys showed up from somewhere in the back of the house. As soon as they were close, Jose dropped the chick he was holding and I knew shit was going to get bad. *Really bad.* Three of his boys were packing, and what had seemed like an easy pick-up suddenly turned into something I hadn't seen coming. I was trying to assess the situation, wondering why Jose was being an idiot instead of just handing over the money, when the girl he'd been holding crawled across the floor and grabbed a hold of my leg.

It only took a second.

I looked down at her when she grabbed a hold of my thigh, her fingernails scratching across my jeans, and that was enough of an opening for the fuckers. The pulled their pieces, and before I could say a word, started firing.

When people are shooting at you, it isn't like the fucking O.K. Corral. You don't stand there and shoot back and hope you don't get hit. You get the fuck down and *then* you shoot back. So that's what I did. I dropped hard on top of the girl as I reached for my piece in the back of my waistband.

When all was said and done, there were people all over the house fucking screaming and running, but Jose and his men were dead. My boys may have been new—or in Tommy's case, completely fucking stupid—but they'd done their job. I climbed to my feet as people rushed out the back of the house and started to step toward the front door, but the look on Dragon's face stopped me. He was staring at the floor, and that's when I remembered the girl.

She was completely out of it, sprawled out on the hard wood. She wasn't wearing revealing clothes, nothing that a normal teenager wouldn't wear, but the way she was sprawled out on the floor made her short shorts and tank top look fucking obscene. Her legs were spread wide with the legs of her shorts gaping, one of her arms was crossed over her chest and the other was close to her face. With the way her hair covered everything from the neck up, it almost looked like she was sucking her thumb. She looked so goddamn young that I felt like I'd been punched in the throat.

I couldn't leave her there like that—alone and vulnerable to any dick that came across her.

So I took her with me.

Getting her on a bike wasn't going to happen, so I stuffed her into the back of my brother's car before we headed to a motel by the freeway. We'd been staying further south, but after that mess with Jose I wasn't going to stay where we'd been. The gang had to have known within minutes what had gone down and I wasn't about to be ambushed for something that wasn't my doing in the first place. Their boy had decided he felt froggy and was going to stiff me the twenty-five grand he owed us. *Bullshit*. He took the first shot—fucking bad luck for him that he didn't make the last one.

I wasn't thinking straight. The adrenaline was flowing, and I was trying to figure out why I hadn't just left that girl behind, so when we got up to the motel room, I was blindsided by the fact that I actually had a teenage girl in our room and my brother was pacing the floor, mumbling to himself. When the shit hit the fan, I hadn't thought about what that would mean for Deke—he'd been put in a really bad position.

"Deke, man, follow us up. I can get you a meet with Slider, no worries," I reassured him, but he wasn't interested.

I tried to convince him to leave it all behind, but he wasn't having it. He seemed to be under the impression that he wouldn't have any problems, and he was a grown-ass man, so I wasn't going to argue. If he wanted to stay, that was on him. Even though I was older by a little less than a year, I couldn't tell him what to do. He'd been taking care of himself for a hell of a long time.

We were arguing about what had gone down, and the fact that I had a chick we didn't know in my bed, when the girl woke up.

Everything after that was like some sort of fucked up version of *The Twilight Zone* that I couldn't escape. She was as young as I'd thought when I saw her with Jose, but it wasn't just that. She had to be around seventeen or eighteen in age, but Christ, in experience? She was a ten-year-old. She had no sense of self preservation and she thought I was some kind of hero for saving her ass from somewhere she shouldn't have been in the first place. I knew she was young, goddamn, but when she climbed into my lap I felt myself growing hard underneath her.

It's not like I was much older than she was, I was only twenty, but I'd stopped fucking girls her age when I was fourteen. There was a huge gap in life experience that made anything I wanted from her impossible, which was proven when she told me she had to call her grandmother and spoke to her like she knew she was going to be in trouble. When we introduced ourselves to her, she wrinkled her nose in confusion and I could tell the wheels were turning in her head as she gave us her name. For a split second, I thought she might have given us a fake one, but I could tell by looking at her face that she hadn't—and she was kicking herself for it.

I made plans to meet the boys about an hour north of San Diego and took Callie to her grandmother's. There was nothing else I could do. She was fucking jailbait, and even if she wasn't, there was no way she was staying the night in my motel room. The girl had fucking braces on her teeth. She came from an entirely different world.

When I got her home, I thought I'd feel relief, but I didn't. She'd spent the entire ride rubbing up against my back, with her little hands clenching and releasing my chest like a kitten, and her not quite innocent actions had me hard as a rock. I wanted her. Bad.

I'd programmed my number into her cell phone back in the motel room, but I didn't see any reason why she'd ever need to call me. So when her grandma ordered me in for food, I took her up on her offer. I told myself that I just wanted some home cooked food, that I didn't want to ride with my jeans strangling my dick, that I wanted to make sure she was okay from whatever she'd been given earlier in the night— but none of those reasons were the truth. I just didn't want to leave her yet.

She was so sweet—the way she looked at her Gram, the way she served up my plate without even asking what I wanted, and the way she smiled with her mouth closed, trying to hide her braces. I'd never been around sweet like that before—I fucking loved it. She didn't talk a whole lot, but I figured that might have been because of whatever she still had in her system. Her Gram was watching her with an eagle eye while we sat at the table, but Callie didn't seem to notice. By the time we were done eating, she'd passed out at the table.

It fucking killed me to leave her there, but I knew that her Gram would take care of her and it really wasn't any of my business. I had gotten her home safe and sound and I'd look like a jackass if I hung around too long—not to mention the fact that I probably had forty Mexican guys gunning for me.

I needed to get the fuck out of there before I did something stupid and got myself killed.

Chapter 6

Callie

I woke up alone in Gram's bed to bright afternoon sunlight shining through the lacy white curtains. My head was throbbing, and my mouth tasted like something had crawled in there and died. I tried to roll over, but gave up with a groan when my entire body protested the movement. It only took a few seconds for me to go from wondering why I was so sore, to remembering *exactly* why I felt like shit.

My mind raced over the events of the night before, and I was completely baffled by everything that had happened. Shit like that just didn't happen to me. I rarely got into trouble, and when I did it was for normal things, like talking back to my parents or staying out past curfew. I couldn't have imagined the night before if I'd tried.

I was busy sifting through my memories, trying to catch the elusive ones, when Gram came into the bedroom to wake me up.

"Oh, good. You're up. I'm heading over to Aunt Lily's and figured I'd drop you off at home on my way. How you feeling?" she asked me as she walked around the room, pulling on a sweater and a pair of tennis shoes.

"Eh. Like I got ran over by a truck. My mouth is dry like the freaking Sahara."

"Yeah, well getting drugged by some piece of trash will do that," she told me with a glare, sitting down beside me on the edge of the bed. "I know you were just having fun, Callie, but crap like that has a way of getting out of hand. I took care of things for you last night, but something like this happens again and I'm calling your dad myself. You put me in a hell of a position."

I felt like shit when she was through talking, but had to hide my smile at her subtle guilt trip. *Sneaky old lady*. I forced my achy body into a sitting position and wrapped my arms around her waist, cuddling up to her as I apologized. "I'm sorry, Gram. I won't ever do something like that again. I don't want to get you in trouble with Dad."

She wrapped her arms around me and rubbed my back for a minute while I relaxed into her, knowing I was forgiven. It was amazing what one simple hug could do to soothe us both. Before I could grow too comfortable or fall back asleep, she pulled back, jarring my throbbing head that was resting on her shoulder.

"Callie, I love you, baby, and we're fine ... but your breath smells like shit. Go brush your teeth," she grumbled with a wrinkled nose and a smile.

I loved my Gram.

I pulled myself out of bed and went to brush my teeth, sliding by Gram at the kitchen counter and rubbing her back lightly as I went. She was making sure her "billfold" and keys were in her purse, just like she'd done every single time we'd left the house for as long as I could remember. She always checked and re-checked her purse for everything she needed and it had been like a treasure trove of goodies when I was younger. There was always a little notebook and pen if I was bored at the grocery store, a hair tie if she needed to pull back my hair, or a Band-Aid if I scraped my knee. Gram's purse could solve any problem, no matter where we were.

As soon as she made sure she had everything she could possibly need, we climbed in the car and took off for my house. We didn't usually chatter much in the car, but that ride was significantly quieter as I thought about the night before. I was so relieved that my little ordeal was over. I was lucky—I was going home safe and sound, when I could've been dead. The thought of that man touching me, or the way the gunshots sounded in the entryway of that house had me shuddering in fear, and I quickly turned my mind to my parents and what I'd be facing when I got home.

I wasn't sure what Gram told my parents, but whatever it was had calmed them down enough that they weren't calling my phone over and over like I'd been expecting. I was glad for the reprieve, but I knew it wouldn't last long. I'd been missing for hours between the time when they would've been home for dinner and when Gram called them at 3 am. They were going to be livid—especially my dad.

Gram was my dad's mom. She'd raised three boys with a drunk for a husband, and she'd pretty much seen it all. Unfortunately for my brother and me, my dad knew every trick in the book because he'd used them, which meant we rarely got away with anything. All of Gram's sons were hellions while growing up, but somehow my dad had pulled himself off the road they'd been on and was living on the straight and narrow. My uncles hadn't been so lucky.

I remembered my uncles as fun and a little crazy, but I'd only seen them once a week for the family dinners that Gram had established to keep us all connected. They would tease me constantly by pulling my braid and calling me 'little senorita', and I'd loved the attention even though my mom's mouth would tighten every time they did it. I hadn't understood until a few years later that my parents saw it as a dig at my dad for marrying a Mexican woman. I didn't know if I agreed with my parents' assessment, but soon it hadn't mattered anyway.

I'd viewed them with a sort of hero worship, never understanding why we saw them only at my grandmother's and only for a couple of hours at a time. My parents had kept me out of the day to day drama, but when I was ten they'd been unable to shield me and my brother Cody any longer when both uncles were killed in a bar fight in Los Angeles.

I'd been too young to understand the implications of their deaths; I just knew that I'd lost two people who I thought had hung the moon especially for me. My parents, however, saw all too clearly that my dad's brothers had died the way they lived—with a blatant disregard for the law and a recklessness that they'd wanted no part of. I'm not sure what happened—my mother must have said or done something during those few weeks after Gram lost her boys—because we never again went to family dinners and my mother and Gram never spoke again.

When we pulled up to my house, I unbuckled my seatbelt and turned toward Gram whose hands were tense at ten and two on the steering wheel. She didn't put the car in park, just sat there with her foot on the brake, waiting for me to hop out. It didn't surprise me, though, I knew she'd never step foot in our house if she could help it—not even if I needed her to run interference.

"Thanks, Gram!" I told her with a kiss on the cheek. "I'll call you this week—I have Thursday and Friday off from school so maybe I can come spend the night."

"Sounds good, baby girl," she replied with a tight smile. She was anxious to leave, nervous that she'd have to interact with my mom if she came out of the house.

I pushed open my door and climbed out, leaning back in to give her one more smile. I hated leaving her even though I knew I'd see her again soon.

"Love you!"

"Love you, too. Get on inside," she ordered with a nod as I shut the door behind me.

I knew Gram wouldn't pull away from the curb until I'd walked in the front door, so I jogged to the front of our two-story house and let myself inside. It was quiet, almost eerily so. I slid my shoes off and dropped them into a basket by the front door and walked further into the house, finding my parents sitting in the living room waiting for me. My mom was on the couch facing the wide doorway, and when I met her eyes, she stood up and started toward me.

I couldn't tell what she was thinking—her face was completely blank—so I stood there stupidly as she got closer, and I didn't even flinch when she raised her arm. I wasn't prepared for her to slap me across the face before my dad, who'd jumped out of his recliner, could stop her. She was screaming in Spanish about what a horrible daughter I was, and all I could do was stand there in shock while she berated me. I could feel myself crying, tears were rolling off my chin and my cheek was on fire, but I was too stunned to do anything.

She'd never hit me before.

Finally, my dad pulled her away from me and took her place, speaking in a low but furious voice.

"We got a call from one of your friends this morning. I'm pretty sure I told you to stay away from Mallory, but according to her, you two went to a party together last night," he hissed, clenching his jaw. "She was worried when she tried to leave and couldn't find you. She said she called your phone over and over, and when you didn't answer she decided to try and call us. Funny thing about that, I thought you'd been at your grandma's last night."

"Dad—" I tried to explain but he cut me off with an angry movement of his arm that had me jerking away from him.

"Don't even try it, Callie! Obviously, you can't be trusted and neither can my mother. I'll call her when I'm done with you," he stated menacingly, causing guilt to rush through me at what I imagined my Gram would go through. "You're grounded. I'll let you keep your phone on the off chance that Cody calls from school, but I'll be monitoring when you use it. Don't use it," he told me, his voice icy.

I stood, frozen, not sure what I should be doing after I got caught in the biggest lie of my life. I'd never been in so much trouble, and I couldn't wrap my head around how angry they were. The night before had been a huge mistake, but I didn't know how to tell them that I'd learned my lesson without getting into the details I knew would only piss them off more.

My mom stood behind my dad with her arms wrapped tight around herself as she shook, and both of them were staring at me like they didn't even know who I was. I shifted my eyes between them, trying to figure out what to say, until my mom snapped, and with the veins in her neck bulging and her face turning red, she screamed at me to get in my room.

I bolted.

I spent the rest of the day cleaning my room and finishing up the homework that was due on Monday, quietly listening to music in my ear buds. My mind raced back and forth from the night before to the scene I'd walked in on earlier in the day; I had a hard time concentrating on anything else. One little decision and I'd completely screwed myself.

At around seven o'clock, I was lying in my bed reading when my mom came into my room carrying a plate full of food and a soda. I sat up quickly as she placed the soda on my nightstand and sat on the side of my bed. When she handed me the food, she started speaking, and my stomach tied in knots when I heard the tremble in her voice.

"You scared me, mija. I called and called when we got home last night and no answer. So I call your friends, none know where you are.

Your father had the phonebook out to call the hospitals when your grandmother calls and says you're with her," she told me in a calm voice, sniffing as she spoke. "We knew something was not right, but I knew if she said you were with her, then you were safe and we could deal with it when you got home today."

"I'm sorry, Mama," I apologized quietly, and it had never been so true.

"Well, you are home safe now," she commented with a shrug, as if that was all that mattered. "I brought you dinner, so you can eat in your room. Your father, he's not so ready to see you yet. Maybe tomorrow, okay?"

When she finished speaking, I lurched into her arms, anxious for forgiveness. She wrapped her arms around me tightly, and as she kissed my head over and over, I knew how much I'd scared her. When she finally relaxed her arms, I held on to her, loathe to let her go—but she didn't make me. She smelled so good, like a mix of fried food and Paris Hilton perfume that she'd received as a Secret Santa gift the year before and had worn every day since. For the first time in almost a year, I wasn't secretly embarrassed that she was wearing a perfume made for teenage girls. She smelled like home, and she didn't let go of me until I was ready.

After she was gone, I ate dinner and got ready for bed. I was a little afraid of what my dad would be like the next day, but he was usually gone before I got up for school, so I knew he'd have an entire day to cool down before I saw him again. He never stayed mad for very long, so I was confident that by the time he was home from work, we'd be back to normal.

If I'd known what would happen, I would've acted differently. I wouldn't have relaxed in the shower. I wouldn't have taken the time to shave my legs or paint my toenails. I wouldn't have let him stay mad or let things go unsaid between us.

I would have marched downstairs and made things right with him, and then I would've curled up next to him on the couch like I had as a little girl—content to watch boring television just so I could spend time with him.

But I didn't—and I had to live with that.

Chapter 7

Grease

I met up with the boys and headed out of town before we had to deal with any more problems. The open road calmed me like it always had, and by the time we hit Sacramento I'd finally stopped thinking of her. She was just another girl in a long line of girls I'd wanted to fuck—nothing more and nothing less. I convinced myself that there wasn't anything special about her.

We were a few hours from the Oregon border when I signaled the boys to follow me off the freeway. My phone had been blowing up in my chest pocket for the better part of an hour, and while I felt justified ignoring one or two calls when I was riding, something felt off. The hairs on the back of my neck were standing straighter with each call, and by the time I shut off my bike, I was ready to strangle whoever had messed up my Zen.

I scrolled through my missed calls, seeing about fifty of them from both Slider, my club president, and Deke. My mind was racing with possibilities, but before I could call my prez back, Deke called again.

"Grease, man, Poet's been calling my phone. Didn't even realize it—want me to call him back?" Dragon called out to me from a few feet away. He was still sitting on his bike, but the relaxed posture of the last few hours had faded and his body was tight. He was feeling it, too—whatever it was.

It was bad.

I nodded my head at Dragon as I connected with Deke.

"Deke, what's up, man?" I asked him cautiously. He was my

brother and I loved him, but I would have preferred to talk to Slider first. If they were both calling non-stop, it was nothing good and I'd need my boys at my back. Deke might be family, but he was also a Jimenez.

"Grease. Boys down here weren't real hot on how things went down with Jose," he told me haltingly, pausing at the end and pissing me off that he wasn't getting to the point.

"Yeah, brother. I figured. I'm fuckin' hours away from there. Can't do shit to me now, and once I'm home they can talk to Slider—"

"No," he interrupted me, and the next words out of his mouth were like a punch to the chest. "They're going for the girl."

"The fuck are you talking about?" I roared into my phone, causing Tommy Gun's head to snap toward me. I glanced to Dragon, wondering what the hell Poet had said, and the look on his face confirmed what I already knew.

I'd unknowingly left her to the wolves.

Deke starting scrambling, "It's probably already over. I started calling you hours ago, man. Nothing you can do about it now. She was nothing—but they don't know it. I didn't tell them she wasn't yours. So now it's equal brother—" He was actually trying to explain how a fucking drug dealing gang could justify going after an innocent sixteen-year-old girl. I couldn't deal with him. I flipped my phone closed and stood staring at Dragon as he got off the phone.

"It's a warning. No need to call Slider back—Poet says they just wanted you to know what was going on." He paused and ran his hand over his beard and then nodded once. "Said to tell you, next play's up to you. We can head back to San Diego or get to Oregon and deal with it from there."

I just stood there, my mind racing. I was goddamn *hours* away from her. There wasn't anything I could do. I could feel every muscle in my body tensed in preparation of heading back to San Diego and killing those fuckers myself—but it wouldn't do anything but get the three of us killed. We'd be in their territory, and without back up it would be a suicide mission. But, God, I wanted to go back and get her. I wanted to go back to twenty-four hours before and shoot to fucking wing Jose instead of hitting him with two in the chest. I wanted to tell Callie's Gram to lay low for a while. I wanted to have never left her there without protection.

Goddamn it—I'd been so fucking concerned with getting away from her jailbait ass that I hadn't considered the possibilities of leaving her. That was on me.

I reached my hand up and pulled the rubber band out of my hair, pulling it out of my face to give me a few more seconds before I had to make the hardest decision of my life. I had to fucking leave her down there, possibly alive and hurt, or lead my boys into a situation that none of us would come out of. It was a fuck of a decision—but I wasn't going back.

I started to slide my phone back into my pocket, opening my mouth to let Tommy and Dragon know what was up, when my phone rang again. I didn't know the number, but with all the shit going down, I answered it anyway. Thank fuck I did.

"Grease?" she whimpered in my ear, her voice so quiet I had to plug my other ear with my finger.

"Yeah?" I thought it was her, but she was so fucking quiet, I wasn't sure. Fuck, could they be playing me? Trying to get me back to San Diego?

"Asa? I'm scared." she sobbed quietly—and I knew it was her. No one called me Asa.

"Baby, you okay?" I asked her gently, climbing back on my bike and nodding to the boys whose faces had hardened.

"I'm hiding," she whispered.

The last twenty-four hours had turned into a long list of complications and bad decisions—and it looked like I was going to make one more.

Fuck the consequences.

"Stay where you are and keep quiet, sweetheart," I ordered her as I strapped my helmet on. "I'm coming to get you."

Chapter 8

Callie

I was startled awake in the middle of the night, and it took me a second to figure out that someone was banging on the front door. My heart started racing as I hopped out of bed, my feet tangling in my sheets when I reached for my phone that was charging on my nightstand. Any knocking in the middle of the night signaled bad news, and my mind sifted through scenarios of policemen telling us someone was hurt.

I scrambled to the door of my room, meeting my mom in the hallway as I saw the back of my dad as he walked down the stairs. His bare shoulders were straight and tense, like he was preparing himself for whatever was on the other side of the front door, but his hands were loose at his sides. It took a lot for my dad to lose his composure.

My mom reached out and grabbed my hand as we watched him, but neither of us moved to follow. She was in a robe that was tied at the waist, and the hand not holding mine clutched the lapel in what was both a nervous gesture and a way of keeping the fabric covering her breasts. I was a little grossed out that both of my parents had dressed in a hurry, but I didn't focus on that because most of my attention was at the front door. I wasn't ready to face whatever was happening, and naively believed, for just a moment, that if we stayed in the hallway time would stop and I'd never have to find out what was going on.

Time slowed as we waited for my dad to reach the door, and we stood quietly listening to the turn of the deadbolt and the snick of the latch.

When he opened the door, I heard him say, "What the hell?"

before gunshots tore through the quiet house. I stopped breathing, my confusion and horror paralyzing me. *What was happening?* I couldn't seem to wrap my mind around what was going on until my mom squeezed my hand tight and jerked me to get my attention. She was wearing an expression that I'd never seen before, and in my haze it took me a minute to interpret it. Fear—all consuming, unrelenting, hope stealing fear.

Fear, but not panic.

Then time sped back up.

"Escóndete en el closet detrás de las decoraciones de Navidad. Te quiero. No salgas," she whispered, her voice so low that I had to watch her lips.

Get in the storage space. Behind the Christmas decorations. I love you. Don't come out.

I tightened my grip on her, shaking my head frantically as she wrapped her arms around me in a quick hug. I didn't want to let go, and I tried so hard to drag her with me as we heard the men moving around on the bottom floor of the house, but the minute they sounded on the stairs she pushed me hard, causing me to stagger across the hallway.

"*Go!*" she mouthed to me before turning her back and facing the stairs.

I raced into my parents' bedroom, scrambling to the wall. There were storage areas beneath the eaves that we kept Christmas decorations in, and I quickly slid one of the little doors open, put my phone between my teeth, and scrambled inside. My hands were sweating so much that I had a hard time getting the door closed behind me, and I bit down hard on my phone, sobbing silently as my fingers tried to find purchase on the smooth wood.

It only took me seconds before there was no light shining from my parents'

bedroom, and I crawled silently behind the boxes of Christmas ornaments as quickly as I could. Cody and I had used the storage areas as hideouts when we were little, playing hide and seek and pretending that we were hiding from bad guys. Little did I know how an innocent game would end up being the thing that saved me.

I was shaking hard, my teeth clenched to keep them from chattering, when I heard a man yelling at my mother in the hallway. Whatever he was saying was muffled, there were too many boxes between us for me to hear clearly, but the gunshot wasn't. It was as clear as if he were standing right next to me.

I bit my arm as hard as I could to muffle the screams in my throat when I heard a loud thump in the hallway. I was hyperventilating, rocking in small movements back and forth, my mind spinning. My chest felt like it was cracking open, like any minute it would just spontaneously split apart, but still, I stayed silent.

I heard the men come through my parents' bedroom, tearing apart the bed and lifting the mattress up off the frame before dropping it loudly. They were calling me by name, telling me to come out from wherever I was hiding, and somewhere, behind the mind numbing fear, I was mortified because I felt myself peeing my pants.

I don't know how long I sat there after they left, shaking. It could have been minutes or hours, but I was afraid they were just waiting for me to make a move, so I did nothing. I just sat there in my own mess, with my head on my knees and my fingers twirling slowly in my hair—a habit I thought I'd grown out of when I stopped sucking my thumb in kindergarten.

When I finally felt safe enough to do something, I slowly reached my hands to the floor around me, searching for the phone I'd lost in the darkness. When I found it, I took a short breath of relief until it fell out of my shaking hand with a loud clatter, startling me and causing me to curl into a tighter ball of fear. I didn't hear anyone, but I waited a few moments before reaching out with both hands and grabbing the phone again.

I knew I should call 911, and that was my intention, but when I accidently pushed send with my trembling fingers, I didn't hang up when I saw the name 'Grease' come across the screen. He didn't say anything right away, and it took me a couple of seconds to realize that the phone had stopped ringing.

"Grease?" I was whispering, terrified that my phone call had somehow alerted the men in the house and any second they'd slide open the door of my hiding place.

"Yeah?" he answered in his gruff voice, and I was instantly filled with a choking feeling of both relief and terror.

"Asa?" I asked again, desperate to know it was really him. "I'm scared."

When he spoke again, worry lacing his voice, I felt like I could finally breathe. I quietly informed him that I was hiding, and when he told me he was coming to get me, I believed him. *He'd saved me before, hadn't he?* So when he told me to stay where I was and keep quiet, that's exactly what I did. I never called the police, and I didn't leave my hiding spot. I did exactly what he told me, because I was afraid of what would happen if I didn't.

I didn't answer when I heard people walking around, yelling that they were police, and asking if anyone was still in the house. I didn't call out when they searched through my parents' room and called back and forth to each other. And I didn't make a sound when they talked about my dead parents as if they were science projects. I couldn't be sure they were safe. Without seeing their faces, I didn't know if it was all a game they were playing to try and find me. So I stayed hidden, waiting for Asa, until finally, the house was silent once again.

I sat there, curled in a ball, and I thought of my mother and why she hadn't hidden with me. We would've had time, and there was space enough for the two of us. I rocked and rocked, my sleep shorts growing clammy and chafing my skin as they dried.

Asa texted me throughout the day, asking me if I was okay and still hidden. I replied with one word, "Ok," to every single one of his texts, no matter what he sent. I was busy replaying the night over and over in my head, trying to figure out what I'd missed, trying to see how I could've done things differently. I couldn't seem to think of any other words to type—my mind consumed with what ifs—until I received a text asking me where I was. For some reason, the thought of telling anyone where I was hiding made me feel like I was crawling out of my skin, and he had to send the question seven times before I could make myself reply, "crawlspace."

The last time I'd seen my mom, she was standing with her shoulders back, her robe tied tightly around her waist, showing off her hourglass figure. Her back was to me, so I hadn't seen her face, but I knew which expression she'd worn with that body language. She was bluffing. The raised chin and rigid posture I'd seen whenever she felt uncomfortable was in full view as I'd left her.

She'd stood her ground for one reason. If they'd known who we were, or even if they hadn't, they would've expected to find my mom somewhere in the house—but a teenage daughter could be absent without raising any red flags.

If my mom would have followed me into the crawlspace, they would've known there was somewhere to hide and would have searched until they found us.

So instead, she'd faced them like a lioness, fiercely, and with absolutely no reservation.

I wasn't sure about the passing of time, and it didn't matter—not really. Because the moment I figured out why my mother hadn't hidden with me, I shut down and retreated into my own mind—effectively blocking the outside world and anything with the potential to hurt me further.

Chapter 9

Callie

I was yanked out of my quiet place by a loud hammering coming from my bedroom. I'd been so out of it that I hadn't heard anyone come into the house, and my heart started racing like a scared rabbit's when my phone lit up beside me with an incoming call from 'Grease'. I didn't answer it, like I hadn't all day, too afraid to make any noise. The pounding grew louder, and I heard someone cursing, when all of a sudden I got a new text message. "We're here," was all it said, and I was hit with a surge of relief mixed with panic. I wasn't sure what to do, and my thoughts were so jumbled that I just sat there, staring at the screen as the cursing and pounding became louder. Was he here as in my house, or here as in San Diego County? I couldn't be sure if the noise in my room was him, or someone ransacking the house. I couldn't be sure of anything.

While I sat staring at the screen, I heard the sounds move to the hallway, and I froze in terror as they came closer. Just then, another text came through, and I almost dropped the phone from my shaking hands as I checked it.

"Where are you?"

The voices came into my parents' room and started knocking as I slowly pushed the reply button and typed a message back. "There's some1 in the house". I tried to listen closely to the voices on the other side of the wall, but my mind was racing so quickly I couldn't interpret what they were saying. I started rocking again, my hand in my hair, but the movements were jerky and short as I tried to be as silent as possible.

The voices in the room grew louder after my text, and I started hyperventilating when I realized that one of the words they were using was my name.

Still, I said nothing. I just waited; staring at my phone like it was my last link to sanity.

The pounding came closer and closer as I tried to slow my breathing, and eventually it stopped right above the little sliding door of my hiding place. Someone called out, and I whimpered quietly in the back of my throat as the door of the crawlspace slowly slid open.

I watched in terror as the boxes closest to the door were moved out of the way, slowly dismantling the only thing that had kept me safe. I kept my eyes on the opening and the arms reaching inside as I used my heels to push myself tightly against the wall, curling into myself. I vaguely registered when Asa's voice filtered into the space, but I couldn't understand why I was hearing him.

Man, it smells like piss in here. You sure she said the crawlspace? It just looks like a bunch of Christmas shit.

She's there. Keep going.

Fuck, man. If she's in here then why the fuck isn't she saying anything?

A dark haired man slid the last of the boxes out of the storage, and once he had a clear view I saw the whites of his eyes as they opened wide in surprise. I couldn't really see his face, his back was to the light, but I could hear the glee in his voice as he called out behind him, "Yup! She's here!" before crawling further inside. When he reached me and lifted his arm as if to pull me forward, I kicked out with one of my heels, smashing it into his chin like a karate master.

"What the fuck?" he yelled at me, causing me to retreat back into my corner as he scrambled back out the door. "Bitch just kicked me in the face!"

"What the fuck did you do?" a voice I recognized roared.

In the next second, broad shoulders wedged themselves through the door, and a familiar face was gazing at me in the sliver of light coming through the small gap between his chest and the doorway.

"Hey, Sugar. You okay in here?" he asked me gently as his eyes ran up and down my body as if checking for himself.

I wanted to answer him. I'd been waiting so long for him to come get me, but once the moment was there, I was still frozen in my little corner, silent and unable to move. It wasn't safe out there. I knew that now. It wasn't safe in my house, it wasn't safe anywhere. If I moved, they could find me, whoever those men were. I was too afraid to do anything but stare at him.

"Callie, sweetheart, I can't get in there. I'm too fuckin' big." He watched me closely as I silently twirled my hand round and round in my hair. "You're gonna have to come to me, baby."

I jerked my head once and began rocking again, the nervous habit forcing my body back and forth as he watched, unable to reach me.

"Calliope, I'm not gonna let anything hurt you, but we gotta get out of here. There's still crime scene tape on the door—" he stopped when I flinched at his words.

He was leaning on one elbow, and the arm that had been resting on the floor reached up into his shirt pocket and pulled out a cell phone. I watched in confusion as he typed something out on it and then set it back in his pocket. I jumped when my own phone went off in my hand. I looked between the phone and him a couple times before reading the text. "You gotta come out of here. I promise I won't let anything happen. Come to me."

The text message brought everything back together and my eyes snapped up to his. It was as if the tornado in my mind had come to a complete stop and left one single thing undisturbed. One thing to focus on. One thing to count on. This was the man I'd been waiting for. This was the man that had saved me. Grease. *Asa.*

I slowly crawled toward him, my knuckles scratching on the unfinished floor because I refused to let go of my phone. But he didn't move out of the way so I could climb out of the storage. When I reached him, he gently lifted his hand and slid it across my cheek and behind my head, pulling me to him so my face was resting against his neck. I scooted my knees under my body and knelt on the floor, letting him soothe me with whispered promises and a gentle hand running through my hair.

I'm not sure how long we sat there, but eventually a voice outside our cocoon told us we needed to go. Asa pulled back and started scooting his big body out the door, moving his hand from resting on the floor to grip my thigh, never severing the connection between us. When he was mostly out the door and on his feet, he slid his hand up my torso and down my arm, never once letting go, in order to grip my hand tightly.

"Okay, baby. Almost there—come on out," he told me gently, watching my face closely.

I scooted to the doorway, wincing as the waning sunlight coming through the windows hit my eyes. I closed them tight, shuddering as I tried to make my way out. I couldn't do it. I couldn't make myself get out of the space. Fear slammed into me with the power of a freight train, and I whimpered as once again I was unable to make my limbs move. My hand went limp in his, but before I could scoot back into my safe haven, Asa had made a growling noise in his throat and grabbed a hold of me under my arms, lifting me like a child.

I twisted once, trying to pull away, before he jerked me to his chest and put his mouth to my ear.

"You're okay, sweetheart. You're okay. Just hold on, I'm not gonna let anything happen to you," he told me over and over again until it finally pierced the paralyzing fear in my head. I wrapped my body around him like a monkey, and he wrapped his arms under my thighs to support me, finally leaving us in a somewhat comfortable position.

I was holding on to him as he turned to leave, when another voice spoke up in the room, jolting me from the little comfort I was feeling.

"Man, she's gonna fuck up your leathers. Girl stinks to high heaven," the voice warned, instantly reminding me that I had peed my pants and causing me to let go of Asa as I tried to scramble off him. I started crying again, like a baby, and for one minute I wasn't thinking about how very afraid I was.

"Shut the fuck up, Tommy," Asa growled in a voice I hadn't heard him use before, his chest expanding as one of his arms wrapped around my back to hold me in place. "She's fuckin' fine where she's at."

He walked out of the room as I quietly cried and buried my face in his neck, afraid to see the hallway where I'd left my mom. He walked me straight through my room and into the connecting bathroom without stopping, pausing only once to switch on the light and shut the door before he loosened his arms around me. He let go completely and set me on my feet, but I was too embarrassed to look at his face as he studied me, instead watching my brightly polished toes.

"Hey, pretty girl, look at me, yeah?" he mumbled gently, running his hand up the side of my face and into the hair by my ear, gripping it so he could tilt my face up. "You ain't got nothing to be embarrassed about. Anybody'd stink after being stuck in a fucking storage closet for eleven hours. Coulda been worse, baby, what if you'd shit your pants?" he asked with a smile, trying to tease me.

"I'm sorry," I whispered, my voice raw from disuse.

"Fuck that, Callie." His grip tightened in my hair. "Nothing for you to be sorry about. You coulda been covered in shit and vomit and I still woulda carried you outta there. I got you, Sugar, nothing's gonna change that."

He waited until I nodded, acknowledging his words, and looked around my bathroom. "You need to take a shower and get dressed. Can't get on my bike the way you are," he informed me, embarrassing me again before clarifying, "shorts and a tank top ain't gonna work. You want me to grab you some clothes?"

"Yes, please."

"Okay, you get in and I'll bring them to you," he mumbled into my forehead, kissing me there before letting go and walking out.

I stood there for a second, watching him leave, as my body started to shake. Once he was out of the room and the door was closed, I walked to the shower and turned it on, my hands trembling so badly that I didn't even worry about trying to change the temperature. I got undressed and climbed in, trying to blank my mind as I quickly washed off, but it wasn't long before the memories assaulted me and I lost all feeling in my legs, sliding to the shower floor in a heap.

Chapter 10

Grease

She was taking a long-ass time in the shower.

I went through her shit, finding all sorts of sexy underwear that I hadn't expected, and finally picked the least appealing ones for her to wear. She was a mess, and I didn't want to be thinking about how badly I wanted to see her wearing a lacy pink pair of boyshorts with little half-moons of her ass hanging out the bottom—but I was twenty years old; most of the time I was thinking with my dick. I grabbed a bra, hoodie, and some jeans and set them on the bathroom counter, thinking I should probably say something, but I didn't. I didn't want to scare her any more than she already was by letting her know I was in the bathroom while she was showering.

Fuck, but I had no idea what I was going to do with her. I couldn't be her bodyguard, I didn't fucking live anywhere near her—but I couldn't just leave her, either. It was my shit—Aces shit—that got her into this mess and I had to find a way to get her out of it. I found a messenger bag full of school shit, reminding me how young she was, and dumped it onto her bed. Ignoring the pencils and assorted mess, I started stuffing a couple changes of clothes into the bag. I had no idea what she'd need, but she wasn't going to be able to come back, so I figured anything would help.

Dragon and Tommy were standing by the door talking quietly, but I ignored them as I looked around her room, trying to decide if she'd need anything else. As I grabbed the charger for her phone and her iPod off the nightstand, Dragon finally raised his voice.

"Grease, man, what's your plan? We're fuckin' sittin' ducks here."

"Not sure. Gonna take her to her grandmother's and figure it out from there. Just need to get her outta this fuckin' house first," I answered him distractedly.

"This ain't our problem, man. We can just fuckin' drop her off—"

I cut him off, turning my head in his direction as anger made my muscles tighten. "It is my fuckin' problem. You're too pussy to have my back, then fuckin' kick bricks."

He stared at me for a moment then nodded once, "Always have your back, brother."

Tommy usually kept to himself, never getting in the middle of arguments and steering clear of drama, but for once he spoke up, ending the stare down between us. "Brother, she's been in there a long-ass time. Need to get outta here—you better go check on her," he advised, being the sound of reason for the first time since I'd known him.

I'd been trying to give her some time to herself, but obviously I'd waited too long, because when I opened the door and called her name she didn't answer me. I turned and tossed the bag in my hand to Dragon and went in the bathroom, leaving the door cracked a bit as I made my way to the shower. I said her name a few times but she never answered me or made a sound, and I could feel my heart starting to beat a little harder as I got to the shower and drew open the curtain.

She was on the floor of the shower, her knees raised to her chin, giving me a glimpse of her ass and hair between her legs that I quickly averted my eyes from. Her hair was a scraggly mess around her shoulders, only half wet, and as I pulled the curtain wider to shut off the cold water pouring down on her, she raised her head to look at me.

The look on her face was like nothing I'd ever seen before.

I knew a lot of men who could keep their emotions in check. Their faces showed no indication of what they were thinking or feeling; it was impossible to read them. Shit, *I* was one of those men, but this was different.

Her face reminded me of that—no emotion, completely clear. But her pretty face wasn't just completely free of emotion; it was like a blank slate.

It was … nothing, like she was completely oblivious to the world around her.

I turned the water off and crouched in front of her, waiting to see if she'd acknowledge me, but she just sat there not moving—not even shivering. Grabbing a towel off the rack, I pulled her up, swallowing hard as she stood up completely unconcerned with her nakedness. Fuck, she was built like a goddamn pinup and I was having a hard time keeping my eyes off her tits as I wrapped the towel around her.

I wasn't turned on, I'm not that much of a dick, but she was beautiful and naked and I'm a man. It was inevitable that I'd take a good look.

I took her out of the shower and dried her off while she stood there quietly, but thankfully she moved her arms and legs to help me get her dressed. Taking a bra off was something I'd mastered at sixteen, but getting one on was a hell of a lot harder. I felt like I was squeezing the circulation out of her tits as I wrapped it around her chest, but she didn't make one noise in complaint, so I soldiered on and finally got her shit together.

It only took about ten minutes from beginning to end, but by the time I was finished I could feel sweat soaking the armpits of my t-shirt. Jesus Christ. I was *not* cut out to be nursemaid to some comatose girl—

but I couldn't stop myself. I needed to take care of her.

She was mine—and goddamn if I could change that.

I needed to get my fucking head checked.

Dragon called through the opening of the door, and my chest expanded as if I could block Callie from view if I could just make myself big enough. I didn't want that fucker to see her like this, even if she was dressed. It was the most raw I'd ever seen a person, and I was sure as shit going to protect that. Even from a brother.

"Grease, we gotta go. Been here for half an hour already— you're fuckin' pushin' it," he grumbled.

Callie gave a start when Dragon spoke, and when my gaze snapped to hers, she was back. She didn't say anything, but she was finally seeing me.

"Gimme a second, man," I called back to him, never looking away from her face. "Gotta put up her hair and we'll be out. Close the fuckin' door."

The door slammed shut and Callie flinched, so I leaned down and kissed between her eyebrows. I wasn't sure how to comfort someone—it'd been a long time since my mom died—but I knew that whatever I was doing helped, because as soon as my lips met her head she sagged into me.

I grabbed a brush and ran it through her snarled hair, but I didn't have time to get the tangles out, so I just pulled it back into a ponytail as it was. It looked like shit, but it'd keep it out of her face on the bike and that was all that mattered. I moved to walk toward the door, but she wrapped her arms around me like she was afraid to let me go, so instead, I grabbed the back of her thighs and lifted her up. Fuck, I was going to be carrying her to the john when I had to take a piss.

I nodded at the boys and headed to the hallway when she

whispered in my ear that she needed something from her mom's room. It was the first time she'd really spoken to me since I'd gotten there, so I wasn't about to remind her we needed to get the hell out of dodge. I probably would've strapped a fucking futon to the back of my bike if that's what she'd asked for.

When we got to her parents' room, she stopped breathing, and I had to rub my hand up and down her back for a few moments before she dropped her legs and started toward the dresser. Sitting on top was a generic jewelry box, and when she reached it, she almost knocked it to the floor because her hands were shaking so badly. She reached in and grabbed something I couldn't see before racing back to me. She was jumpy as shit—not that I could blame her. She gave me whatever she was holding and turned around so her back was facing me. It took a minute for me to figure out what the hell she was doing.

She'd dropped a thin gold chain with two pendants on it into my hand. One was a St. Christopher medal, and the other a tiny gold cross. She stood there quietly as I wrapped it around her neck and fumbled with the tiny-ass clasp. That shit was not made for my bear paw hands, but I eventually got it on her.

She spun around as soon as I was finished and climbed back up into my arms—was she fucking joking? But fuck if I cared. I couldn't lie and say that I didn't want her there. She was a tiny little thing, and the way she molded to my body with her face in my neck was not anything I'd ever get tired of.

We made our way through the house, passing the bloodstains in the upstairs hallway and the entryway as I held her face against my neck, ensuring she wouldn't look. She wasn't moving, just quietly breathing into my throat, but I didn't want to take any chances that she'd see the fucking huge puddles of blood that covered the floor. I didn't want her to go blank again.

When we got to my bike, I tried to figure out a way to make her get down, but I shouldn't have worried. The minute I told her I was taking her to see her Gram, she completely let go of me, the weight shift almost making me drop her before I could set her on her feet. I was in the process of changing out my smelly t-shirt for a clean one in my saddlebags when she spoke up.

"She's not dead?" she asked, looking at me like I'd just invented the fucking moon.

I reached up and put my hands on both sides of her face. I knew it was fucked up, but I loved the way she was looking at me. Like I'd give her anything. I was sure I was going to hell, and the whole situation was total shit, but I was soaking up the fact that she needed me. Shit, no one had *ever* needed me like she did right then—and I knew it wouldn't last long, but for just a few more minutes she was completely mine. I put my face close and ran my nose up the side of hers, wanting to kiss her but knowing it sure as fuck wasn't the right time.

"No, baby. She's waiting for you."

Chapter 11

Callie

The ride to Gram's house was a blur of anticipation and apprehension that I had a hard time remembering. After Asa grabbed a clean shirt from his saddle bags and slipped it on, we left my house behind. I didn't realize it would be the last time I'd ever step foot in the house I'd grown up in, but even had I known that I wouldn't have looked back. Any good memories I had there couldn't overpower the almost twenty-four hours of horror I had gone through.

Being out in the open on the back of a bike was the very last thing I wanted to do, but Asa said he'd protect me, and for some reason I believed him. I clutched his waist with my arms, my nails digging into his hard abdomen the entire way, but he didn't make any complaints or ask me to loosen my grip. Every once in a while he'd rest one of his hands on mine, rubbing it softly before putting it back up on his handlebars. I timed the ride by the motion of his hands, waiting patiently for him to do it again and again until we got to Gram's.

When we pulled up to the house, I felt the blood drain out of my face as I noticed a large black SUV sitting in the carport behind Gram's little Mazda. Asa's hand went back to mine as we rolled to a stop, watching as Gram and four scary looking men walked out her front door to stand on the little porch. It took me just seconds to realize that they were wearing the same leather vest as Asa, but that didn't calm my anxiety at all when I saw the way they were standing around my grandmother.

Asa lifted his chin to the men as he turned off the bike and the two men with us climbed off of theirs. He sat patiently, waiting for me to climb down so he could follow me, but I didn't move except to push my face into the leather on his back. I didn't think I could face any more, I'd reached my limit hours before and I was barely hanging on to any semblance of sanity.

I didn't see Gram take a step toward me, or the man with the long silver beard put his hand on her arm to stop her. I didn't see him lean down to whisper something in her ear, and I didn't see her glare at him but stay where she was. The only thing I was aware of, the only thing I could focus on, was the man in front of me gently petting my hand and talking in a low voice before he tried to climb off the bike.

He pried my fingers from his shirt and swung off the bike before I could grab a hold of him again. I wasn't prepared to lose the connection, and I made a desperate noise deep in my throat as he moved away. I reached for him, scrambling for purchase as I scratched the leather of his vest, but it was only seconds before he turned and wrapped his arms around my waist, pulling me toward him. In my haste to get to him, I pushed off on the bike, almost tipping it over before his dark haired friend caught it. I was oblivious to the chaos I was causing in my rush.

By the time I was wrapped securely around him, my heart had stopped beating in my ears like a drum, and I felt like I could breathe again. I hated myself for being so afraid, but there was nothing I could do about it. It was so overpowering that I couldn't feel anything else. I wanted Gram so badly. I wanted her to rock me and tell me that everything was okay, but the thought of going anywhere near those men surrounding her made me feel like I might lose control of my bladder again.

Thankfully, Asa must have known that going any closer would

completely unhinge me, so he stayed standing by the bike, rubbing my back and speaking softly in my ear.

"I know you're scared, baby, but those are my guys. Nobody here is gonna hurt you. They're here to protect you. Understand, Sugar? You're safe. Safer than you've ever been," he soothed me, never moving except to nuzzle his nose against my ear. "You wanna go inside, sweetheart?"

I tightened my legs around his waist in reply, and he used one hand to boost me higher on his chest before speaking again.

"I won't put you down. But you gotta tell me what you need. Can't stand here all night, sweetheart." He paused, waiting for a reply. "What d'you wanna do, Callie?"

"I want my Gram," I whimpered, understanding what he was telling me but still unable to let go of him and go to her myself.

"Okay, baby. You just hold on to me. I'll bring you to your Gram," he assured me, squeezing once before starting toward the front door.

"Poet!" he called out above my head. "You're scaring the fuck outta her. Take a step back so I can get her in the house, would ya?"

I felt him moving, but refused to open my eyes as he carried me into the house. His chin bumped into my head as he nodded at someone, and before I knew what was happening, he had unwound my legs from his waist and flopped down hard on the couch so I was straddling him. When the couch shifted, telling me that someone had sat down beside us, I lifted my head and met the eyes of my grandmother just inches from mine.

I fucking lost it.

I was off Asa and between the two of them in an instant, my head buried in my Gram's chest and my arms wrapped around her waist, sobbing like a child. I was so filled with relief that I was finally with her that I couldn't even catch my breath. I knew then that everything would be okay. She was the comfort I needed when my entire world was falling apart, and as much as I was thankful to Asa, he could never give me what I gained in one second with her. I was her baby and she loved me without reservation, giving me the strength to finally all at once snap out of the fog I'd been in.

"Gram—" I moaned into her chest.

"It's all going to be okay, darlin'. Everything's gonna be just fine now. I've got you, sweet girl. I've got you," she told me as she rocked, tears streaming down her face.

When I'd finally calmed and was resting quietly in Gram's arms, I let my mind wander to where I hadn't let it go all day. I'm not sure how I'd kept myself from rolling it over and over in my head, but I think, maybe, the human brain can only take so much before it just stops. It's a defense mechanism that when available, can stop a person right at the edge of sanity, keeping them from falling off the edge. Once I'd selfishly given Gram some of my grief, there was finally room for me to think of it. There was finally enough courage for me to wonder and ask for answers.

"Gram," I called, my body bracing as if preparing for a blow, "is Cody okay?"

Chapter 12

Callie

Once Gram had calmed my immediate fears about Cody, I was able to pull myself together a little and sit up. I hadn't consciously realized that Asa had pulled my legs onto his lap as I was cuddling Gram, but when I pulled away to set my feet on the floor, I was instantly aware of the absence of his hands rubbing my calves.

He'd been rubbing my legs the entire time, and I felt a little off kilter that I hadn't noticed his touch until it was gone. It was bizarre. I'd seen my parents do it, little touches on the back or leg that the other didn't even seem to notice, but I'd never reached that point with any of my boyfriends. I'd always felt their touch keenly, as if I was waiting to jump out of my skin at the lightest brush of their fingers. I knew him so little, yet it was almost like I expected his touch, feeling out of sorts when we weren't connected. I told myself it was the situation we were in and tried to ignore the panic and guilt that flared in my belly.

I needed to get my shit together, but still felt like I was seeing and hearing things in a fog when Gram stood up and pulled me to the kitchen table. She was so much more comfortable in the kitchen that I didn't protest when she sat me down and started puttering around. As she pulled ingredients for whatever she planned on cooking out of the fridge, she explained how she'd talked to Cody's school that morning on the phone and was waiting for them to call her back with his flight information. My brother was coming home for the first time in months, and the thought of him walking into the mess I was in made me feel like ants were crawling all over my skin.

She was still talking to me in her no-nonsense voice, getting things done even though it felt as if the world was crashing down around us, when the men in the living room started migrating to the kitchen table. Exactly where I was sitting. My body froze, the hand scratching the invisible ants pausing with my nails still embedded in my skin until I felt a familiar hand at the back of my neck.

"Stop scratching, Sugar," he whispered into my hair as he reached down to pull my hand away from my arm. He leaned down until his lips were close to my ear, and I closed my eyes as I felt his breath. "You're gonna make your arm bleed. Nothin's crawling on you, nothin's itching. Keep those hands off your arms."

I felt him stand up straight behind me, so I opened my eyes and stared at the table, trying desperately to keep my hands from scratching.

"Rose, I know you got a lot of shit—excuse my language—a lot of stuff going on right now, but we gotta figure out how we're gonna keep Callie safe," Asa rumbled behind me, sliding his hand across my neck as he sat down in the chair to my right. "She's not safe here."

"Well, you boys are here now, right? Your friend Poet here said we were fine as long as you were here," Gram replied, turning from the biscuit dough she had on the counter to face Asa.

As they spoke, the men sat around the table, filling up three of Gram's six white chairs until only the one closest to Gram was empty. The other three leaned up against the walls, watching the scene unfold with little expression on their faces.

"That is true," the man across from me answered Gram, his accent startling me into looking up. When my gaze landed on his face, he was watching Asa and me with an expression I couldn't decipher. "But we're not from around here. Can't stay here forever."

"Asa—" I asked in a panic, swiveling my head to look at him.

The man across the table choked on his coffee at my outburst, his eyes shifting between Asa and me.

Both Asa and Gram started to reply, but the man waved his hand in the air as if to cut them off, and surprisingly, even Gram stopped speaking. I wasn't sure what about him garnered such respect, but I could tell that he was the leader of the group. He had to be a little older than my dad, judging by the white beard that hung down his chest, but he definitely wasn't as old as my Gram. There was something about him, though; something about the way he held himself, or the look in his eyes that told me he'd seen a lot of the world and very little of it was pretty.

"Before you start bitchin', give me a chance to introduce myself," he told the room before moving his eyes back to me. "I'm Poet. Sorry to meet ya under these circumstances, but not sorry to meet ya," he said gently, and his face transformed into something so tender that I felt a lump form in my throat and had a hard time keeping my tears at bay.

"Now, I'm not saying that we're going to leave you to the wolves here, darlin'. I can see that you and Grease have something going on and I doubt he'd leave ya even if I told him to. But he can't stay here and neither can you."

His words were like a bomb dropped in the middle of the room, and for a minute everyone was silent. I was trying to grasp the implications of his words, but I just couldn't figure out what he meant. *I couldn't stay there? In Gram's house? In San Diego? What was he trying to tell me?*

Gram eventually found her voice, and when she spoke, it was harder than I'd ever heard from her before. "What do you mean she can't stay here? She's sixteen years old! Where else would she go?"

"I mean that it's not going to be safe for her in San Diego. These boys don't mess around, and they're just enough of a pain in the ass that we have to keep an eye on them," Poet replied calmly, not diffusing the tense situation at all.

"She's mine," Asa finally spoke up, his hand tightening on the back of my neck. "They won't touch her if I claim her. Not if we make sure they know she's off limits."

The faces around the room showed shock as what he said sunk in, but I didn't understand the weight of his words. It seemed as if I was the only one waiting for a punch line, or an explanation, because even Gram had an understanding look on her face as she watched Asa closely.

"Boyo, you sure you wanna go there? You need to think this through," Poet warned in a low voice, further confusing me. "Even if she's yours, accidents fuckin' happen. She'd still need to go north, if not to the compound then at least to Sac where we've got boys."

"I'm fuckin' sure," he answered, his words almost echoing in the silence of the room. It was then that I understood that something big was happening, even if I wasn't sure yet what it was. Asa had used a swear word without once apologizing to my Gram.

He didn't sound like my Asa.

He sounded like the man they called Grease.

Chapter 13

Grease

Callie was practically falling asleep at the table after dinner, but refused to go to bed no matter how much Rose bitched at her. It was kind of cute how she squeezed her lips into a stubborn line and refused to leave my side, but her eyes were so swollen and red from crying all day that it looked painful to blink. I was trying to figure out how I could get her to go to bed when Poet cleared his throat from across the table and motioned with his head for me to follow him outside. Problem solved. I thought maybe if I wasn't sitting right next to her, she'd at least get some pajamas on. *Shit, did I even pack her pajamas?* I stood up from the table, putting my hand on Callie's shoulder when she tried to follow me.

"You stay here, sweetheart," I told her as I shook my head. Shit, she was looking at me like I'd kicked her. I wasn't sure how to keep her from freaking out—she looked like she was ready to climb me like a tree again—so I pulled her chair out and crouched down in front of her. Her hands were folded in her lap, and looking down I could see that her knuckles had turned white from how tight she was gripping them. *Poor baby.* It was going to take a long fucking time before she felt secure, if she ever did again.

"Gotta talk to Poet for a minute—you go get ready for bed and I'll be back in a couple minutes, yeah?" I told her softly, rubbing her cheek with my thumb. She wasn't wearing any makeup, and for the first time I saw that she had a few little zits on her chin. For some reason that little imperfection, a sign of her age, made her even sexier. "Go get ready for bed, baby," I repeated, watching her face until she gave a little nod.

Outside with Poet, I pulled a pack of smokes from my pocket and lit one up. I loved the first scent, that first deep inhale of a freshly lit cigarette. There wasn't anything better. Poet was standing at the end of the trailer, leaning against the metal siding while he smoked his own cigarette, and I braced myself as I walked toward him. He wasn't pissed, I could tell that much, but he also wasn't happy with what was going down. Before I even reached him, he started speaking.

"That little girl is beautiful, I'll give you that," he told me with a nod, not even looking in my direction.

"It's not about that. But yeah, she is." I wasn't sure where he was going with the conversation, but I didn't want him to think my decision was about ass. I wasn't sure why I felt the need to take care of her, but it went far beyond trying to get in her pants.

"You're young, boy. You got your whole life ahead of ya, and so does that girl in there," he rumbled, and by the tone of his voice I knew to keep my mouth shut because he was just getting started. "Girl's not even seventeen years old. I know she's got some sort of savior complex going on, and I get it. It's not uncommon; I've had to deal with that shit a few times in my life. But changing your life for her, claiming her when shit's out of control the way it is—it's not gonna end well. She's gonna get over this. She's gonna move on with her life, and where's that gonna leave you?"

"I don't know," I replied quietly, his words something I'd thought of already.

"You're an adult. I'm not gonna tell you what to do, I just want you to think with something other than your dick for two seconds and tell me where you think this is going."

"Can't explain it, Poet. There's something about her. I know she's young, and shit is insane for her right now—"

"She's not the only one who's young, boyo."

"I know that, too. But whatever the fuck this is, it's strong. She's mine. She's been mine since she crawled across the floor and grabbed a hold of me at that party. It just *is*." I had a hard time explaining what was going through my head because *I* couldn't even figure that shit out. I wanted to take care of her, and as fucked up as it was, I wanted her to need me.

"Brenna's mom wasn't much older than Callie when we hooked up," he mumbled, looking up at the sky. "I knew she was too young for me, but fuck, when she looked at me I felt like a fuckin' superhero. So I took her, in more ways than one. I soaked that shit up, reveled in it. She wasn't the most beautiful woman I'd ever seen, but fuck, the way she looked at me?" he shook his head. "It was like nothing I'd ever had before. So I get it. What you're doing. Just be careful, yeah? Woman like that's got the power to fuck up your life."

"Not sure how careful I can be," I admitted, putting out my smoke on the bottom of my boot.

"Yeah." He paused for a moment before casually putting out his cigarette with his fingertips. *Fucking crazy bastard.* "How the hell did you get into her house? I figured cops would be swarming the place."

"We just rode right up. No one was fuckin' there. Crime scene tape on the doorways, blood all over the floors, but not one fuckin' cop. Idiots."

"I'm guessing Jimenez has more pull than we'd originally thought. Houses are usually full of cops for at least twenty-four hours after a murder, taking prints and staging shit." He looked deep in thought, and I didn't ask how he knew police procedure so well. He was remembering something, and his past wasn't any of my business.

"I'm gonna get back to Callie. She's probably climbing the

walls."

"Yeah, I'll be in there in a bit. Let the boys know to get their shit off the bikes and outta the Yukon. Gonna need bedding—we're staying here for the night. Something's not sitting right."

I wasn't sure what he meant, but I was glad they weren't headed to a hotel. I sure as fuck wasn't leaving Callie and Rose and I was glad Poet had the same idea. Unfortunately, Rose's trailer wasn't very big and it was going to be a tight fit, even with the boys sleeping on the floor. I knew Poet was gonna take the couch, which left me with the tiny-ass loveseat.

When I got back in the trailer, Callie was sitting at the edge of the couch with her knees pulled up to her chest. The boys had made themselves comfortable around the table playing cards with Rose, so I let them know to get their shit and then I headed toward my girl. She was wearing a long-ass nightgown and I couldn't help but smile at how innocent she looked. It was a big difference from the tiny-ass shorts she'd been wearing when I met her.

She scooted into my side when I sat down beside her, and tension I hadn't noticed seeped from my shoulders. Yeah, the girl had completely fucked me.

"Gram gave me a nightgown," she muttered into my armpit as I wrapped an arm around her.

"I see that. It looks… cozy," I told her with a smile, glad she was talking without crying.

"Shut up," she huffed. "I look like I belong on fucking *Little House on the Prairie*."

Her words were like a punch to the chest and I chuckled, wheezing like I couldn't catch my breath.

I'd seen her relieved, and I'd seen her embarrassed, and I'd seen her confused and scared. But I'd never seen her confident or sarcastic. Up until that point, I'd wanted her. I'd wanted to take care of her, pamper her, and make her feel safe. But her dry tone of voice had an entirely different effect. It made me want to bend her over the damn couch we were sitting on and fuck her. Hard. *Holy shit.* I readjusted my suddenly tight jeans and settled more comfortably in the couch before saying anything else. That was all I fucking needed—for Rose or one of the boys to see me tenting my jeans like an asshole.

A couple hours later, Callie fell asleep and I carried her into Rose's bed for the night. The boys were setting up the sleeping arrangements and I didn't want them to wake her up. The girl looked tired as hell even when she was actually sleeping. Once I had her settled, I grabbed a blanket from Rose and got situated on my tiny-ass bed for the night. My back was going to kill me in the morning.

It wasn't too long after the house had fallen asleep that I woke up to someone moving around in the living room. When I opened my eyes, I saw Callie quietly making her way through the guys on the floor. She was stepping around them when she could, and over them when she had to, walking on her toes as if that was going to help. I could see that most of them had woken up—men didn't get far in this life if they let their guard down, and they would have felt the shift as soon as she came out of Rose's room—but none of them moved or made a sound.

As she was stepping over Hammer's chest, one of the brothers that came down with Poet, I saw his eyes open and his head move slightly as if to look up her nightgown. *Fucking prick.* I didn't want to startle her by saying anything, but when his hand moved as if to grab her, I'd had enough.

"Touch her and I'll fuckin' gut you, brother or not," I growled, my voice raspy from sleep.

Callie squeaked and jumped, almost falling into the men sleeping on the floor. She barely caught herself and ran to me, stepping in any open space she could find between the bodies. When she got to me, she dove, landing sprawled on my chest and almost clipping my nose with her chin. I grunted as her knee came really close to my balls, and quickly moved her legs so one was between me and the back of the loveseat and the other pulled high on my waist. Fuck, even with her landing on me like a ton of bricks, my dick still sprang to attention.

"I thought you left," she murmured quietly in my ear. She'd straightened out one of her arms so it was lying down our sides, but the other was across my stomach and bent with her hand on my bare chest. I should've left my goddamn shirt on, but it was hot as fuck in the room with so many people in it and I hadn't wanted to sweat through the only clean one I had left. I was seriously reconsidering my choice when she started kneading my chest, like she was making sure I was actually there. When her hand strayed close to my nipple, my dick practically jumped in my jeans and I quickly grabbed her hand and held it in the middle of my chest.

"Not going anywhere," I reassured her with a kiss on her forehead. I thought about telling her to go back in with Rose, but I knew she wouldn't sleep if she did. I had a feeling the minute she thought I was asleep, she'd be on her way back out, waking up the men on the floor again.

"I'm sorry I'm being such a pain in the ass," she whispered, relaxing her body into mine. "It scares me when I can't see you."

I wasn't sure what to say to that, so I didn't say anything. I just listened to her breathe until a little snore came out of her mouth. Her nightgown had ridden up, so her bare inner thigh was pressing against my stomach, and the heat in the room was making our skin sweat and stick together. Fuck me; I was never going to be able to sleep. I took a deep breath, pulled the thin blanket Rose had given me over us so the boys didn't catch a peek of her ass, and tried to get my dick under control.

I must have finally fallen asleep, because I woke up to a bit of sunlight shining through the windows and Rose standing over us with a soft look on her face. It took me a second to figure out where I was, and I almost relaxed, but it was then that I realized that while one of my arms was innocently draped over Callie's back, the other was beneath the blanket gripping her thigh, my hand so high up that my index finger was just barely inside her underwear and resting on hot, soft skin.

Chapter 14

Callie

I woke up the next day alone on the loveseat. I felt like an idiot for climbing in with Asa, but when I'd woken up in the dark my instinct had been to find him. I lay next to Gram, trying to force myself to stay put, but I couldn't. My anxiety had built and built until I'd finally crawled out of bed and went to find him.

Now I couldn't see him anywhere. The house was really quiet, a big change from how crowded and noisy it had been the night before. When I sat up and started to fold the blanket I was using, I noticed two men out of the corner of my eye. They were sitting casually at the table, turned toward me, and the dark haired one I'd kicked in the face gave me a little smile.

"Your Grandma went with Poet to get your brother from the airport," he informed me, watching closely. Knowing that I must have looked like a basket case the day before, I met his eyes calmly and nodded nonchalantly, as if to prove that I wasn't going to start screaming and running around the house like a lunatic.

I'd caught some kind of second wind, and the weak little girl I'd been the day before was pushed to the back of my mind as I stood up slowly and turned my back to him. I was afraid, that feeling wasn't going away, but somehow in my sleep I'd formed some sort of a barrier between my emotions and my actions. I wasn't panicking. The fear was a throbbing mass in my belly, constant but controllable.

I focused on cleaning up my sleeping area and quickly walked to Gram's room to get dressed before I asked where Asa was. I was trying to act relaxed, but it felt like I was going to jump out of my skin. I knew Gram wouldn't have left me alone with those guys if she didn't trust them, but I was still uncomfortable that they'd been in the room while I slept. The longer I was awake, the more aware I was that I hadn't seen Asa, and by the time I was dressed, I was almost in a full-blown panic. I guess I wasn't as calm as I'd thought. I knew it wasn't rational. I knew that I was acting like a freak, clinging to him when I barely knew him. He was probably irritated as hell that I wouldn't leave him alone. But I couldn't stop myself; it felt like he alone could protect me from the outside world.

I stayed in Gram's room for as long as I could, straightening her bedding and going through the bag I'd brought with me. Asa hadn't packed much, but at least he'd remembered the essentials. I found my iPod at the bottom of my bag and held it to my chest, thankful that he'd thought to pack that small piece of technology. It was silly, but it felt like one piece of normalcy in my suddenly upside-down life.

When I couldn't stand it anymore, I took a deep breath and made my way out into the living room. The men were still sitting at the table, and I stepped as close to them as I could make myself, stopping six feet away. I battled with myself whether or not to ask where Asa was when he suddenly walked into the kitchen from the small hallway leading from the bathroom. He was fully dressed, his hair wet, and he held a towel up to his beard, rubbing it from side to side.

I stood in silence until he noticed me, running my tongue over the cuts in my mouth to keep me from speaking. I catalogued where my braces had rubbed against my cheeks and tried to focus on remembering if I had wax in my purse or not, acting as though I wasn't waiting for him to acknowledge me. I refused to be the one who spoke first or to run to him like I wanted to; I needed him to come to me.

"Hey, sleeping beauty. These boys wake you up?" he asked me with a small smile, walking slowly toward where I was standing. The men at the table hadn't noticed that I'd come out of the bedroom, and both their heads swiveled around quickly in surprise.

"No, they didn't wake me," I replied, begging him silently to come closer.

He seemed to understand what I needed, or maybe he needed it too, because he came right to me, wrapping his arms around my waist and lifting me up in a bear hug until my feet were dangling off the ground. His beard tickled across my neck and I grasped his shoulders tighter in response. It was exactly what I needed.

I was disappointed when he let me down, but he kept his hands on my hips once my feet were safely on the floor. He was about to say something, but I'd never know what it was, because just seconds later the front door banged open. The noise startled me so badly that I jumped up, knocking my forehead into his chin as I wrapped my arms and legs around him. I wasn't tall enough, so I ended up lower than I'd wanted and ended up pulling and scratching my way up his chest until his hands gripped the back of my thighs and hoisted me the rest of the way.

It must have only taken seconds, but by the time I was safely in his arms, I heard my brother yelling.

"Who the hell is *he*? What the fuck? Let go of my sister!"

I wanted to go to him. His voice was so strained it was cracking like it hadn't done in years, and I knew he would be embarrassed, but I was too wrapped up in making myself breathe that I didn't have the capacity to comfort my brother.

"Cody, that's Callie's friend. You just leave them be a minute and she'll come talk to you," Gram told him in a no-nonsense voice I'd heard before.

"Screw that! That guy's like forty years old! What the hell is going on?" he yelled again, his voice once again his usual deep tenor.

They argued some more, but I didn't catch what they were saying, because all of a sudden we were moving and Asa was speaking quietly in my ear.

"It's all good, baby, but you need to climb down. Your brother's about to stab me with one o' your Gram's kitchen knives and she's gonna be pissed," he told me in an amused voice, his hand rubbing soothingly up and down my back.

I'd finally gotten my breathing under control, so I slid my legs down the outside of his body and stepped away, mumbling, "Sorry," before I faced my brother.

Cody and I faced each other across the room, both of us uncomfortable with our audience. Any other time, we would have already been hugging and pushing each other around, but we were so far out of our comfort zones that we just stood there staring. He didn't want to seem like a pussy to the men who filled the house, and I was embarrassed that he'd just seen me wrapped around Asa, so neither of us made a move until I finally found my voice.

"I don't think he's forty. Maybe thirty," I told him with a small grin.

That was all it took.

We met in the middle of the room, wrapping our arms around each other as he swung me around slowly. It was what we always did when we saw each other for the first time during his visits. A few years before, he'd grown taller than me, and to prove that he was bigger he'd swung me around, teasing that he wasn't the little brother any longer.

Having my brother near always made me feel like the world was right again, but this time I knew it was just an illusion. Nothing would ever be right again, and breathing in my brother's familiar scent reminded me in a flash that I was the reason we'd lost our parents.

How I'd managed to put it from my mind, I didn't know, but the minute he set me on my feet, I stumbled to the side as if hit, hearing the voices of the men who killed my parents inside my head.

They were calling me by name.

He reached out for my arm, an alarmed look on his face, but I pushed him away, unable to bear his comfort.

"It's my fault," I told him, surprised. "Oh, my God. It's my fault they're dead."

His face drained of color as he watched me, but I didn't see anything else because I was running for the bathroom with my hand over my mouth as if to hold in the vomit that was pressing at the back of my throat.

Chapter 15

Callie

I wasn't sure if I should be thankful that I didn't actually throw up or disappointed that I hadn't purged the nastiness in my stomach. I rinsed my face over and over with cold water, filling my mouth with the cool liquid—but nothing could take away the bitter taste of bile in the back of my throat.

A knock at the door warned me that someone was coming in before it opened. When Gram pushed her head in and walked inside, I wished for a moment that I would've taken the time to lock it. She was pissed.

"Calliope Rose Butler, what in God's name was that all about?" she hissed at me, crowding me into the space between the countertop and the bathtub. "If I didn't know you were hurting so bad, I'd slap your mouth for spewing crap like that to your brother!"

I don't think she expected me to answer her, but I felt the need to defend myself, so I stood up tall and answered her.

"They were calling my name, Gram," I told her, sucking in my breath with a deep sob, "I could hear them!"

I clenched my eyes shut, the pain of those words seeping through my body as I lost all sense of control. I couldn't hold it in anymore; my voice was making god-awful noises, like the barking of a seal. I couldn't hold them back.

Gram reached for me as I started to slide to the floor, wrapping one arm around my waist and the other at the back of my head.

"You are absolutely *not* to blame here, Callie. Not at all, sweetheart," she whispered into my hair. "You got caught in the wrong place at the wrong time. That's all it was. Those men weren't after *you,* baby."

The tone of her voice had me raising my head as I tried to understand what she was alluding to. She wasn't giving away anything with her expression, but once she knew I was keeping it together, she pulled me by my waist out of the bathroom and down the hallway.

Once we reached the kitchen, she sat me down at the table and walked to the fridge where her apron was hanging on the handle. It reminded me of a suit of armor as she tied it on; it was a way to protect herself.

"Poet, Asa, and Cody!" she called to the guys sitting in the little living room. "Get in here. We need to clear some things up."

As the men made their way to the table, she started pulling things out of the fridge and setting them on the kitchen counter. That's when I knew that the conversation we were about to have wasn't going to make anyone comfortable—Gram was cooking.

As Asa walked into the kitchen, he stopped behind my chair and rested his hand on my shoulder for a second before sliding it across my collarbone and up my neck. When he reached my chin, he tilted my head back so I was looking at him upside down.

"You okay, Sugar?" he asked me quietly. Once I nodded my head, he leaned down and kissed the spot between my eyes slowly. "Okay, I'm gonna sit over by your Gram so your brother can sit here. You need me, you just rub that spot between your eyes, and I'll get you the fuck outta here. Okay, baby girl?"

When I nodded again, he swept his hand back down my throat and moved to the other side of the table. He was so gorgeous; I couldn't help but watch his movements, but when Cody sat down next to me I had to stop myself from cringing in guilt at the train of my thoughts.

"Hey, sister. You okay?" he mumbled, his eyes sliding between Asa and me.

"Yeah—" I cleared my throat and tried again. "Yeah, I'm fine. Sorry," I told him, my eyes locked on his face. It seemed like every time I didn't see him for a few months, his cheeks became more chiseled or he had just a little more scruff on his face. He was growing into a man, and I wasn't sure I was comfortable with that.

He opened his mouth to speak when Gram interrupted him, her voice rising above the noise of pots and pans clanging as she searched for the one she needed. "Poet and Asa, Callie is under the impression that those men were there for her. Apparently they were calling her by name. You boys want to explain that to her?"

If I hadn't turned to look at Asa when Gram started talking, I wouldn't have noticed the color leach out of his face before he stood abruptly from the table. "Callie—"

"Grease, sit your ass down," Poet called with no inflection in his voice, and it was scary, because Asa immediately sat.

"Girl, none of this was your doing. If anything, you were in the wrong place at the wrong time." *Why did people keep saying that to me?* "We had business with Jose—the man who had you at the house. When Grease went to take care of that business, Jose decided to be a dick. You with me so far, darlin'?"

I nodded slowly as I waited to hear the rest of the story. I needed to know.

"When Grease took you outta that house after—well, let's just say they put more importance on you than they should have." I flinched at his words, and that little movement had Asa on his feet again.

"What the fuck, Poet?" he roared. "Watch what the fuck you

say!"

Cody reached down and grabbed my hand as we watched the men across the table stare each other down. The tension was so thick that even the guys in the living room had turned toward us and were watching with wide eyes. A few of them were shaking their heads.

"Grease, I'm telling it like it is. No disrespect to your woman—" he stopped and turned his head to the living room as a couple of the guys made noises of astonishment. "Like I said, I wasn't being disrespectful. Now, sit the fuck down and show me some goddamn respect before I fuckin' drop you."

He was calm. He never raised his voice or gave any inflection to the words he was using.

It made his little speech infinitely more terrifying.

"Like I said, Calliope, they thought you were important to Grease, so they were using you to get to him," he finished with a nod.

I tried to act calm even though my insides were quivering. There was more to the story that I didn't understand, but I'd honestly heard enough. I was trying to sort through the memories of that night and the new information I was just given, but Asa's voice pulled me out of my reverie.

"Fuck, Callie. I'm so sorry, Sugar—I thought you knew. If I thought that you were blaming yourself I woulda set you straight right away. It was my bad, darlin', I fucked up when I took you outta that house." He sounded weary as he confessed to me, and he wasn't even looking at my face, but at the table in front of me.

I squeezed Cody's hand once in apology before pulling away and standing up. Gram had stopped all movement at the stove and was watching me out of the corner of her eye as I walked toward Asa. When I stood behind his chair, I ran my fingernails through the hair at the side of his skull and tilted his head back like he'd done to me just minutes before.

"So you fucked up by saving me from being raped?" I asked him gently, playing absently with a piece of hair that had fallen out of the messy ponytail at the back of his head.

He reached his long arms behind him, wrapping his hands around the backs of my knees and squeezing them gently before he replied. "No, baby. I'd do that again. I'd do that a thousand times. But I should've known; I should've seen that shit a mile away and known to stay with you until it blew over."

"I shouldn't have been there in the first place. I was grounded. I shouldn't have even been out at all," I told him flatly, trying to ease the guilt I saw in his eyes.

"You're sixteen, Callie. I know my life hasn't been the most normal, but even *I* know that sixteen-year-old girls go to parties without their parents' permission. You did nothing wrong, Sugar." He squeezed the backs of my legs in emphasis.

The look in his eyes was sincere, and I knew that he believed what he was saying, but I couldn't let it go.

"I shouldn't have been there, Asa," I whispered while curling my body down and around his—forgetting for a moment that there were others in the room with us. My eyes filled with tears, and one slowly ran off my cheek and onto his lips. "If I would have just stayed home—"

He cut me off by letting go of my legs and standing from his chair. As soon as he was facing me, his hand came to my cheek, but before he actually touched me he must have remembered the people watching us because he grabbed my hand and turned to Gram.

"We need a minute, Rose." His comment was both a question and a warning.

"Go on into my room," she told us with a small nod of her head.

As we made our way out of the kitchen, I heard Cody tell Gram, "This is bullshit," and Gram replied that he wasn't too old for her to wash his mouth out with soap. Normally, I would've laughed at the exchange, but my chest was tight with an emotion I couldn't name as I followed Asa into the bedroom and watched him close the door.

He sat on the bed and pulled me with him until I was standing in between his spread knees, looking down at him. He was so tall that his face wasn't far from mine, and I watched him closely as he swallowed, and then swallowed again.

"Had to get outta there—they were watching us like fuckin' bugs under a microscope," he told me, rubbing his hands up and down the outside of my legs. I hadn't had that impression at all, but now I was alone with him and I wasn't going to argue.

"Okay," I mumbled back, waiting to see why he'd brought me in there.

"I don't want you thinking it's your fault, Callie. Okay? I don't wanna hear that shit come outta your mouth ever again." His voice had taken on a stern quality, his fingers digging into the skin of my hips. "It was *my* fuck up. I should've stayed where I could protect you. I should've seen that shit coming. This is on me, not you," he told me harshly, giving me a small jerk.

He was sitting there taking the blame on his shoulders, but I knew it was both of our faults, or maybe no one's fault at all. I'd gone to what I thought would be a party like I'd been to a hundred times before, and ended up in way over my head. Grease had been there to do whatever sort of business he did, and ended up saving a girl with braces on her teeth from being raped by a guy twice her age. Neither of us had planned how things went down. Neither of us could've anticipated the events.

I felt so much for him right then, my chest was burning with it. I wasn't sure what it was—not love, it couldn't be love—but something so close and consuming that it made my heart race.

"You saved me," I whispered as I put my hands on his head and pulled the rubber band out of his hair. When I started to run my fingers through the strands, he groaned low in his throat.

"Callie, you gonna start crying again, Sugar?" he asked, scooting himself back on the bed and pulling at my knees so I was straddling his lap.

"No," I answered him, wondering at the question as I wrapped his hair around my fingers and softly outlined one of his ears.

"Good, 'cause I'm gonna kiss the fuck outta you."

Chapter 16

Grease

I knew that all the shit that had happened to Callie was on me. It was my call to pull her out of that house, and my call to leave her helpless when I'd finished my business. They were both bad decisions, but there was only one that I would've changed.

There was no way I could have left her passed out and alone on the floor of that house. The longer I knew her, and the more time I spent with her glued to my side, the more I knew that the decision to keep her safe had been the right one.

It was the decision to walk away that hadn't been right.

At some point, Callie was going to realize that her fucked up life was entirely my fault. She was going to blame me and hate me and wish she'd never met me.

But at that moment, in her Gram's bedroom, she wasn't doing any of those things. Instead, she was standing in front of me, pulling the rubber band out of my hair far more gently than I ever had, and running her fingers through my hair.

I wasn't a fucking saint.

I asked her if she was planning on crying again, mostly because I wasn't sure where her head was at, and when she told me no, that was it.

I pulled her onto my lap, on her grandmother's fucking bed, and I kissed the shit out of her.

I was so distracted by the taste of her that I didn't notice her whimper at first. It wasn't until the taste of blood filled my mouth that I ripped my head back to see what the fuck was going on. She had blood pooling in the corner of her lip, and for a second, I was afraid I'd fucking bitten her or something.

She wiped at the blood, swallowing thickly as her face turned beet red.

"I'm sorry! My mouth's just—well, my braces…" she stuttered, looking at me apologetically.

"Holy fuck! Did I just do that to you?" Shit, I kissed her and drew blood. My thoughts were completely self-centered until she started trying to pull herself off my lap.

"No. Um, yesterday my mouth was really dry—and I wasn't being careful." She tried to lift her leg over me to crawl off the bed, but I grabbed both of her thighs and pulled her tight against me, effectively ending her squirming as her breath caught. "My braces cut a bunch of little sores on the inside of my cheeks. Totally not your fault."

"Ah, sweetheart, why didn't you say anything?" I asked her quietly, finally understanding what was going on. I'd never been with a chick with braces, and I couldn't remember any of the kids at the club having them growing up, either. But it wasn't hard to see how having metal fucking brackets in your mouth could fuck your shit up.

"Let me see, Sugar." I hoped that the damage wasn't bad enough that she'd need stitches or something. *Fuck. That was all we needed.*

She pulled her lips out on the sides and turned them a little inside out so I could see the little red sores in her poor mouth. The things must have burned like hellfire, but she hadn't said a word about them until I'd fucking attacked her.

"You got something you can use to fix it?"

"I've got wax in my purse I think. I forgot it here at Gram's the other night." She gave me a small smile. "It won't help the cuts, but it'll keep the little fuckers from making them worse."

The bravado in her eyes from dropping an f-bomb mixed with the little goddamn dimple in her cheek had me smiling back at her. I couldn't even help myself. It was so fucking...cute. I knew at any minute she was going to remember—she was going to get lost again in grief and guilt, and those few minutes where it was just her and I would be over.

Instead of talking to her, rubbing her back, or getting up so she could go find some of that fucking wax she needed for her braces, I lifted my hand and wrapped it around the back of her neck so I could bring her mouth to mine again.

I was careful, but I still tasted blood when I licked her lower lip.

"Ugh. Gross. I'm sorry. My mouth's still bleeding," she told me quietly, but her hands were still threaded through my goddamn hair. *Christ, that was hot.*

"Don't fuckin' care," I mumbled before pushing my tongue between her lips.

No one could ever accuse me of being a good guy.

Chapter 17

Callie

For a few moments, I was just a normal sixteen-year-old girl again.

He kissed me over and over, careful of the braces, but completely unconcerned with the way my mouth still tasted vaguely of blood. He tasted like tobacco and the gum that was tucked into his cheek, and I practically inhaled him as he tried to keep the kiss light. It wasn't until we'd reached the breaking point and I was beginning to rock against the thickness in his pants that he finally pulled away.

"Pretty sure this isn't what your grandma expected us to be doing in her bed," he told me gruffly, using his hands on my hips to push me back until I was standing by the side of the bed.

"Ha! I'm surprised you care what my Gram thinks we're doing," I answered ruefully, still a little dazed as I ran my fingers through my tangled and greasy hair. *Yuck, I needed a shower.*

His head snapped up at my joke and his jaw was clenched as he stood up from the bed, putting his own hair back into a ponytail.

"Baby, we're in her house. She's cooking for us, letting us crash here, and she's your grandmother. Woman deserves respect," he chastised, making me feel like a jackass.

I nodded once and then dropped my head to the side, pretending to look at something on Gram's dresser so I didn't have to make eye contact. He made me feel like a child. Getting away with something was a common game among my friends, with each of us detailing to each other how we'd snuck around. It had been exciting, doing the forbidden. Now, though, it just seemed immature and stupid.

I was trying to look anywhere but at him, but he wouldn't let me hide for long. His smile was tender as he wrapped his hand gently around my throat to tilt my face toward his.

"Calliope, we're under your grandmother's roof. Not gonna disrespect her and I'm too old to be sneaking around and keeping quiet when I'm with my woman," he told me, leaning down to give me a deep, wet kiss. "We weren't here? You'd already be naked and making so much fuckin' noise you'd be waking up the neighbors."

He winked at me before turning and opening the door, waving me through.

Whatever universe I'd been in, or part of my mind I'd shut off when I'd realized that he was feeling guilty and I'd needed to comfort him, rushed back with the speed of a freight train when I walked back out into the living room.

Gram and the men were talking quietly at the kitchen table, crowded around almost uncomfortably in the small space, and I didn't have to wonder why.

My baby brother was sitting on the couch, bent over with his elbows on his knees and his head in his hands.

He was crying. Quietly. Privately.

I glanced up at Asa, who nodded, and then went to Cody. Sitting down next to his hunched back, I draped myself over him, wrapped my arms around his waist, and laid my head on his shoulder.

"Hey, brother," I whispered, giving him a squeeze.

"Hey," he sniffed once, rubbing his hand underneath his nose. "This fucking sucks, Callie. What are we gonna do? Gram just got off the phone with the funeral parlor and she's making all of these arrangements and shit," he swallowed loudly, using his thumb and fingers to dig into his eyes. "I don't know what the fuck I'm supposed to be doing right now."

"You don't have to do anything. Let's go talk to Gram and see what the plan is, okay?" I pulled him from the couch and dragged him into the kitchen, stopping directly in front of Gram.

"What do you need help with? Anything we can do?" I asked her forcefully. It may have come out a little more abrasive than I hoped because Poet huffed at the end of the table in amusement. I glared at him, causing his eyebrows to raise in response, and then turned to Gram again. "We don't want you to have to do all of this by yourself, so tell us what the plan is."

Gram smiled up at Cody and me then stood and wrapped her arms around us. "How'd I get grandkids like you? Huh? Best of the bunch, I tell ya."

"Gram," Cody replied, his voice muffled by her shoulder, "I'm reasonably sure that we're your *only* grandchildren."

"Reasonably?"

"Well, Uncle Tommy and Uncle Charles got around…" he told her with a laugh, jumping away before she could swat him with a towel.

"That's okay! Run away now… I'll remember this far longer than you will, my dear," she told him with a twinkle in her eye.

I was grinning at them both, my head whipping from side to side, when Poet spoke up from his place at the table, effectively ending our lighthearted moment. God, I was smiling and laughing. *What the hell was wrong with me?*

"Rose, I know that the funeral is important to you guys, but we're gonna have to figure out what Callie's doing. Time's running short—I got shit to do in Oregon and my boys can't stay here babysitting."

"Callie, sit down, darlin'. Time to talk," Gram told me grimly.

"You too, Cody."

The men sitting around the table backed off, a couple going into the living room and the others heading toward the front door, pulling cigarettes out of their chest pockets. Only Gram, Cody, Asa, Poet, and I were left in the kitchen when Gram sat down heavily.

"Baby girl, you're gonna have to move," she told me wearily, running her fingers over her bottom lip in a nervous gesture I'd seen a million times. "It's not safe for you here."

I watched in silence as she seemed to think over her next words carefully, and for a moment it looked like she wasn't going to say anything else. When I was about to speak up, she started explaining what was going to happen.

"Grease is gonna take you up to Eugene. That's where they live and they can keep an eye on what's happening. As soon as I get all of your parents' legal stuff and Cody's school stuff taken care of, I'll follow you up there."

I felt my eyes start to water as I thought about moving all by myself, but swallowed hard and kept it together. Moving to Oregon was the least of my worries. It shouldn't have been such a big deal, but the idea of being so far away from the only family I had left was a daunting prospect.

"Okay," I answered her, my voice breaking a little.

"Gram…" Cody looked between us, his skin pale and his eyes worried. "What about me?"

"Well, you'll go to school. It'll be the same as it was before, except you'll fly to Oregon to be with us on your breaks," she reassured him.

She turned back to me and opened her mouth to give me more details when Cody's voice broke through the quiet again.

"I can't!" he told us, looking back and forth at our faces as if gauging our reactions. "My scholarship—the one that pays for school? It's for exceptional students in *San Diego County*. They won't pay for school if we live somewhere else."

Gram and I both burst out with words of denial, but halted mid-sentence when Asa's dark haired friend, Dragon, opened the front door and leaned inside.

"Poet! Grease! We've got a situation."

Chapter 18

Callie

Poet and Asa hopped up from the table like it was on fire and moved toward the front door after Dragon slammed it shut—both reaching for guns I hadn't noticed in the waistbands of their jeans. I'm not sure if it was the thought of cowering like I'd done before, or the thought that Asa could be in danger, but when Gram grabbed my arm I shrugged her off and followed them outside.

When I crossed the threshold, I couldn't see anything at first. Gram's house stayed shaded inside during the day in an attempt to beat the heat, so walking into the waning sunlight had me raising my hand in front of my face to shield my eyes. When I'd acclimated to the change, my hand dropped limply to my side as I registered what I was seeing.

There were Hispanic guys all over my Gram's driveway and two silver SUVs with spinning chrome rims blocking our vehicles in. For some reason, I couldn't look away from the rims of those SUVs. I'd never understood why people chose them for their cars, and the way they kept moving, even though everything else was still, felt like an omen.

"Javier," Poet rumbled from a few steps ahead of me. "What brings you out for a visit?"

"Eh, you know, just taking a little survey in the neighborhood. It seems your neighbors don't like having bikers clogging up their parking spaces," one of the Hispanic men answered, causing my eyes to shift toward the group on the ground.

Our guys were standing in a semi-circle around the front of Gram's trailer, their bodies tensed and ready, but the Hispanic men weren't in any sort of formation. They were standing around the driveway, some leaning on the vehicles, looking like they were out for a casual stroll. There were so many of them, though, that their appearance was deceiving. Even if they didn't look like they were ready for anything, their sheer numbers were enough to cause a tightening in my stomach.

Wait, when had I started to think of those bikers as 'ours'?

"Well, you took your survey, now it's time to leave. I'm feeling... mellow, today. And I doubt Rose'd like my boys using up a fuck-load of water cleaning blood off her driveway," Poet growled back, making the hair at the base of my neck stand up.

"Your boys killed three of my men. It's not something that can go unpunished. You know this," the man answered back almost gently.

Poet scoffed, "Three? I thought it was four? Well, fuck me. Looks like you left one breathing," he said, barely turning his head in Grease's direction.

"Cabrón! I'll have blood for this. Hand over the girl and we're even." The man spit on the ground, and for the first time, looked at me, causing me to sink back.

"Not gonna happen, you little Mexican piece of shit," Grease growled, stepping sideways so I could no longer see what was happening. "Get the fuck out of here."

The man started spouting off in Spanish, and I wished for one minute that I didn't understand the language of my mother. His words cut off when Gram stepped out from behind me, almost shoving Grease aside as she started using Spanish words of her own. I was so surprised that she was fluent, that it took me a minute to register what she was actually saying. It wasn't until she started using English that everything became clear... or at least, less confusing.

"I've got contacts of my own, you little cocksucker. If my boys were alive, you'd already be dead for what you've done to my family," she hissed, yanking me fully behind her as she raged. "You leave my granddaughter alone or I'll see you in hell!"

"Rosa," he looked surprised, but spoke respectfully, "who does she belong to?"

"She belongs to *me*! That's all you need to know."

"Ah, senora, that's not the way this works. You know this. She belongs to Tommy or Chuck, well, that's one thing. If she belongs to Daniel, that's an entirely different matter."

Watching him over my grandmother's shoulder hadn't prepared me for his words, and I gasped as he said my uncles' names… and then my father's. His eyes flickered to me for a moment, but were drawn back to Gram as she straightened her slightly curved back, making her almost as tall as I was.

"She belongs to *me*," she told him again, slapping her chest in emphasis.

"Well, now, I know that's not true. Imagine my surprise when I heard that she lived at the address of an old friend. It was jarring, really, to hear that name again."

He looked as if he was remembering something for a moment, but quickly snapped back to the subject at hand when Gram tried to speak again. He cut her off with a wave of his arm and spoke.

"Due to our history, and my history with your sons, I'll give you two some time together," he told her kindly, his voice like that of someone talking to a child. "But she'll be mine, one way or another."

He gave a nod to his men and started toward the vehicles when Grease's incredulous voice boomed out from beside me. "You forgetting something?"

"No, I'm not." The man shook his head, "I'm not concerned with the Aces. You may be here now, but you won't be here for long." He waved his hands dramatically as his face broke out in a smile. "Once you ride back to that rainy hellhole you call home, well, I'll be here... fucking your girl, and then killing her."

Poet grabbed Grease as he lunged, and both of them almost tumbled down the porch stairs as the Hispanic man laughed and closed the SUV's door.

When the men drove away and all was quiet, my mind was once again reeling with the new information flooding in. *What the fuck had just happened?* And more importantly...

How in God's name did my Gram know those men?

Chapter 19

Callie

For the next few hours, we discussed our plans, arguing and debating the merits of each idea over and over again. If an idea sounded good to me, Gram disagreed with it, and if we both thought something was a good idea, Poet or Asa shot it down. It was frustrating as hell trying to figure out how we were going to get me out of the mess I was in. The guilt ate at me as the sun dropped from the sky, and by the time Gram had dinner on the table, my stomach was so tied up in knots that I couldn't even eat. I was also too anxious to ask about my uncles' connection with the men that were after me—the questions I had just didn't seem as important as getting far away from them as fast as I could.

Cody was willing to drop out of his expensive prep school in order to move with us to Oregon, but I could tell that the thought of leaving was causing him a lot of anxiety. He was adamant that the school wasn't important, but I knew it was. He'd been away at private school for two years, and the thought of having to start over was scary for my introverted baby brother. He'd already had his parents and his home ripped from him because of my stupid decisions, I absolutely refused to take that from him, too.

The situation left Gram in the position of choosing between us.

If she moved with me to Oregon, Cody would have to leave school. If she stayed in San Diego, I had to move up North all alone.

There was no right answer.

So I didn't let her choose.

I chose.

"I'll move up North on my own," I finally stated, my heart racing in my chest. "I'd be going to college soon anyway. It's not like I can't live by myself eighteen months earlier than planned."

"Callie, you can't move all the way to Oregon by yourself!" Gram replied sharply, looking at Poet for backup.

"Rose, not sure what you'd like me to say," he answered her look, "not a whole lot of options open to ya."

"That's ridiculous," she snapped. "She'll be all alone in a new town and she hasn't even graduated from high school!"

"Gram, it's fine. I can do it. Really. I'll just get a little apartment and finish school out there. I'll be fine."

"Callie," Gram sighed wearily, looking at me with an apology in her eyes, "baby, I can't afford to get you an apartment. I'm barely living here, I can't support two houses."

Her cheeks tinged red at the confession and I felt like a complete asshole. Of course she couldn't afford to pay for another house. While I'd been psyching myself up to convince her to let me move alone, I hadn't even thought about the money situation. Gram was on a fixed income, and even with her social security benefits and my grandpa's pension, there wasn't a whole lot of extra cash left after she paid her bills.

Before I could reply, Asa spoke up from where he was sitting beside me with his hand on my knee.

"I'll take care of her," he told Gram before his eyes moved to me, "I'll take care of you."

I opened my mouth to say something back, but I looked like a guppy as I closed it and opened it again. I had no clue what I was supposed to say in a situation like that. He'd take care of me? *What the hell was he talking about?* He'd been watching out for me physically and emotionally from the minute we met, but for some reason, paying my bills seemed like a much bigger deal. It was like the difference between letting a neighbor borrow a cup of sugar and buying them a car. One of those was a completely understandable sacrifice, the other just seemed crazy.

"Asa, you're a sweet boy, but I can't let you do that," Gram stated kindly from across the table.

"I'm a man," he rasped, looking between Poet and Gram. "I'm a man and I take care of what's mine." His voice was solid. Resolute.

I sat there dumbly as they argued. They were talking about me, and yet I couldn't think of one thing to say.

"You've known her for less than a week. She's not yours. *She's sixteen years old, goddammit!*" Gram responded, slapping the table with her hand, frustrated with the entire situation. I think the way Asa looked at me had finally sunk in for her because she looked like she was beginning to worry as she glanced between us. There was a difference between how a teenage boy felt about his girl and a man felt about his woman.

A teenage boy may speak strongly in defense of his girl, full of piss and vinegar and grand dramatic vows of how he'll protect her—but that only lasts until the boy meets with odds that are no longer on his side. But a man? He'll make it clear that he stands between his woman and the world, no matter what the consequences are. And then he'll prove it.

Asa wasn't making grand promises, vowing to slay dragons or sweep me off my feet. He was making a very serious gesture of commitment, and it was freaking me the fuck out.

"I don't want to go all the way to Oregon," I blurted, breaking into Asa and Gram's staring contest. "I don't want to be so far away that

Gram can't drive up and visit me."

All the heads at the table had been watching the interaction between Gram and Asa, but they all swiveled toward me at my declaration, so I decided to keep going.

"Can't I just go to Sacramento or something? I mean, that should be far enough away, right? That way, Gram can drive up and see me on the weekends sometimes. And I wouldn't have to leave California, so all of my school stuff would transfer fine..." my voice trailed off at the end as I ran out of steam.

"That wouldn't—"

"That doesn't make—"

Asa and Gram's arguments were cut off by Poet's raised voice.

"Now *that* doesn't sound like such a bad idea," he told me with a nod. "Children need their elders around. Moving Callie so far away that her grandmother couldn't visit, well, that would be a shame."

He turned his head to Gram and convinced her with only a few words. "She'd be alone, yes? But we have a chapter in Sacramento that would look after her. And, well, Grease wouldn't be able to live with her in Sacramento, would he?"

Asa sputtered across the table, realizing that his plan wasn't turning out the way he'd hoped. He wanted me with him; it was clear by the way he was speaking. And to be completely honest, I wasn't opposed to that idea, either. I didn't feel pressured by Asa's wish to move in together, and at that point, I couldn't even imagine being without him for five minutes. All of a sudden, the thought of living with Asa didn't scare me as much as the thought of living all alone.

"Boyo, you understand Callie's reasoning, yeah? Girl wants to be close as she can to her family and can't say I blame her," he said quietly to Asa who still hadn't said a word. "Question now is how that affects *your* decision."

Not one person around that table anticipated the answer Asa would give, because none of us saw a twenty-year-old man supporting a sixteen-year-old girl who wasn't related to him—especially if she wasn't even going to be living with him.

"I take care of what's mine. Doesn't matter where she lives," he told us, giving my knee a squeeze before standing up from the table. He kissed my head gently as he passed by me, mumbling in my ear, "Be right back, Sugar. I need a smoke."

He walked out the front door as if what he'd just promised was of no consequence at all.

Chapter 20

Grease

I wanted Callie with me. I wanted to come home to her at night, in an apartment away from the clubhouse where I'd had a room for the last three years. I wanted a fucking place of my own where I didn't have to listen to bitches squealing and brothers fighting at all hours of the night. I wanted a goddamn living room that I could sit in with a beer in front of a big-ass TV.

I wanted a *home,* for Christ's sake.

I'd been sacking away money since I started getting paid, so I wasn't hurting for cash, but there was no way I'd be moving from the clubhouse anytime soon if I was paying for an apartment for Callie. I wasn't making *that* much money.

Taking care of Callie would set me back in a big way, but I couldn't see any other option. She needed me. She needed to be out of San Diego, and I saw the guilt on her face when her brother was trying to bluff his way through giving up that fancy-ass school he went to. He didn't want to give it up but he was willing to. I respected the fuck out of him for that. But if he gave it up, that would be one more thing she felt responsible for, and the guilt was already so heavy on her shoulders...

Fuck it. I'd handle it. She was only a couple years away from being eighteen, and then she could take care of her own shit. I was hoping by then she wouldn't want to; that she'd be so wrapped up in me that she wouldn't want to be living eight hours away. At least that was what I was counting on.

I felt like a selfish asshole when they'd looked at me like I was crazy—like I was so fucking selfless because I wanted to pay her way.

Didn't they see that I wanted her to *owe* me? I wanted her fucking dependent on me, and I'd do anything to make that happen. I couldn't figure out what the fuck was wrong with me—I just knew that the minute she didn't look at me like I was saving her, it would gut me.

I didn't know how fucked up it would make our relationship. It would be years before I saw how resentment builds from one person being totally dependent on the other and how the beginning of our relationship started a cycle of guilt and blame that would fester and flame out of control.

Chapter 21

Callie

Once the decision had been made, things happened fast.

The next morning, Poet got on the phone with someone from the Sacramento Chapter and set things in motion up there.

Gram called the funeral home where my parents would be sent and tried to move up their service.

Cody slept in.

Asa left for an hour and came back with an empty moving truck.

And while everyone moved around me in preparation, I sat quietly and tried not to cry.

I missed my mom and dad with a depth so overwhelming that I thought if I started crying again I'd never stop. I'd never understood the word sorrow until then. The thought of never seeing my parents again was almost too much for me to handle. Throughout the past few days, I'd known that they were gone. I'd cried and panicked and worried, but I don't think it had sunk in. It was finally sinking in, and all I felt was... sorrow.

It was such a small word for such a huge emotion.

My parents would never see me graduate from high school or college. My dad would never walk me down the aisle at my wedding. I'd never again sit with my head on my mom's shoulder after a bad day, or hug her tight while she was cooking dinner. I'd never see her eyes light up with love for me again. And I'd never get to make peace with my dad after the awful fight we'd had.

I'd lost almost everything in one single night and I didn't

understand it. It was so hard to comprehend the magnitude of changes in my life that I'd gone into shock, and as I sat on my grandmother's couch, I was finally coming out of it.

Without the need to plan or worry, I was finally able to grieve.

I did it silently and without fanfare. I let myself break apart, feeling the heaviness in my chest and the trembling in my fingers, but not allowing anyone to see it.

It's a common phenomenon to see a child get hurt while away from their parents and then walk stoically to them to be patched up. It's almost as if they know instinctively that no one will hear them, so they don't cry right away. Yet, the minute they see their parent, they burst out in sobs, as if the crying wasn't necessary until they had someone to hear it.

I was in pain, but I no longer had a parent to hear my cries.

So I stayed silent.

I stayed that way, turned inward and grieving, until Asa sat next to me and wrapped his arm around my shoulders.

"Hey, pretty girl. How you holding up?"

"I've been better," I answered him with a sniffle, unable to hide the frog in my throat.

He pulled me closer to him until I wrapped my arms around his waist and laid my head on his shoulder. His hand came up to lightly run his fingers up and down my arm, and the motion had me relaxing into his body in relief.

"It'll get better, baby. I promise. This fuckin' sucks, and if I could take it away from you, I would. Nothing about this situation is okay. Not one goddamn thing. But it'll get better," he mumbled into my hair.

"It hurts, Asa," I whispered back.

"I know it does, sweetheart," he told me with a kiss on my head, "lost both my parents, too."

I jerked at his words but didn't speak. I didn't want to ask what had happened. It felt insensitive to ask about it. What if they'd been killed the way my parents had? I couldn't imagine having to explain it to anyone.

"Yeah. Mom died when I was fourteen in a car accident. One minute she was there, and then she was just… gone. Fuckin' worst day of my life." I felt him shake his head above me. "Dad died last year. He was sick for a long-ass time before that, though, so it was different."

He spoke the words in a matter-of-fact tone, but I couldn't imagine that he felt nothing, so I looked up at his face to gauge his mood.

"I'm sorry you had to go through this twice," I told him quietly, lifting my hand to push back the hair that had fallen in his face.

At my gesture, he moved his face toward mine until our noses were almost touching. "Calliope, what I went through ain't *nothing* like the shit you've had to deal with. It doesn't even come close. And I'm so goddamn sorry." He leaned down further until our foreheads were touching and ran his nose against mine. "But I'm gonna take care of you. I'm gonna make all of this shit seem like a bad fuckin' dream. Nobody is gonna take anything from you again. I fuckin' promise." He tilted his head so he could touch his lips to mine before pulling back to look me in the eyes again. "Do you believe me?"

His eyes were so dark I could see myself in his pupils, and I swallowed hard before answering. "I believe you," I whispered back, and I meant it. This man, so different from me and anything I'd ever known, would walk through fire for me. It didn't make any sense. He didn't love me. He didn't even *know* me. But for some reason, he'd claimed me. And when everything else around me was spinning crazily out of control, he was there, steady and unmoving.

He made a noise deep in his throat and moved in again, taking my mouth in a wet kiss that had me holding my breath. It was deep and sweet and exactly what I needed.

Our lips broke apart, but his arms didn't leave me when Gram walked into the family room, worrying her lip with her fingers.

"The funeral parlor doesn't know what the hell is going on," she told us as she paced. "They don't even know when they'll have Danny and Angie. It's up to the police and the coroner, and they haven't said a goddamn word to me!" Her steps sped up as she walked from one end of the living room to the other and then she stopped suddenly in front of us, looked at me with fresh grief in her eyes, and told me quietly, "Apparently, it could take weeks. I won't be able to lay my baby boy to rest for *weeks*."

I stood from the couch and wrapped my arms around her. I didn't know how to comfort her—her loss was so different than mine. She'd grown my father in her belly, nursed him, and watched him grow into a man. He *was* her baby, her last baby, and now he was gone. So I just stood there, with my arms wrapped around her bent shoulders and let her sob, while tears ran slowly down my cheeks.

I'm not sure how long we stood there before she calmed down enough to move away, but by the time it happened, Poet had walked into the house from wherever he'd been and Cody was sitting on the arm of the couch.

"Rose," Poet called softly, "I know this is a shit time. And I know you don't wanna hear this—but Callie ain't got weeks here. We've got two days at the outside before she's gotta be outta town. Any longer than that and we're asking for trouble."

Oh fuck. Oh fuck, fuck, fuck.

I was going to miss my parents' funeral.

I thought, *How much worse could my life get?* before I quickly erased the question from my mind. My life could be infinitely worse and I didn't want to make the mistake of asking a question, even in my head, that I didn't want to know the answer to.

It was as if Poet's statement had lit a fire under my Gram's ass, because the show of grief evaporated like mist and she turned into a human tornado—tearing apart the house.

She raced around, packing up what little I kept at her house into two small suitcases while I watched in horror. When she was done, she gave them to Asa to put into the moving truck as she packed us sandwiches and drinks for the road. But she didn't stop there. She grabbed a black garbage bag and started stuffing kitchen utensils and pots and pans inside as she explained what each was used for. It was like she was trying to impart years of wisdom into an hour of feverish activity, refusing to stop and allow it to sink in that I was leaving.

"Gram?" I asked anxiously as she tried to tell me the recipe for her stuffed pork chops, "I don't have to leave yet. Right? Poet said I had a couple days!"

She stopped mid-sentence and took a deep breath as she moved away from the cupboard she'd been pulling supplies from. "I know what Poet said, Callie. And I'm not trying to scare you, baby girl. But these men? They aren't going to wait. I was stupid for thinking we'd have more time. I know better, and so does Poet. He was being kind, darlin'. We don't have days." She laid her hand on my cheek. "We have *hours*."

She was right.

Less than two hours later I found myself hugging my baby brother goodbye.

"I've got my phone, and Gram says she's going to figure out all the paperwork and shit, so it should be good for a while at least. If I have to get a new one, I'll call you, okay?" I asked him as I clutched him tight around the waist.

"Yeah. Call the dorm and someone will pick up. I'm not sure what I'll do if the cell phones get cut off…"

"Don't worry about it. If I need to, I'll send you a new one, okay? Call me all the time. I want to hear about everything you're doing."

"I will," he told me with a squeeze. "Be careful, sister."

With one more squeeze and a kiss on the top of my head, he let me go and I faced Gram. Her chin was high and her shoulders were straight, but the sheen in her eyes told me she was having a hard time keeping it together.

"You call me when you two get there. Asa says he's going to head straight through to Sacramento, so you should be where you're headed by late tonight." Her voice quieted as she spoke directly into my ear, "That boy feels something strong for you Callie. I don't know what happened between you two that I didn't see, and it's not my business… but I've been around a lot of men in my life—enough to tell the good ones from the bad—and I'll tell you one thing, baby, this man's as good as they come. You trust him, okay? He'll take care of you." She pulled me into a hug, but it wasn't long before she was holding onto my arms and pushing me away. "I'll be up in a few weeks to help you get settled. You call me if you have any problems, you hear?" She pulled me back in for a kiss and then pushed me lightly toward Asa. "I love you, Callie Rose."

Asa wrapped his arm around my shoulder and helped me into the moving van that carried his motorcycle and my pitiful four bags before climbing in and starting the engine. I waved as we pulled away and couldn't help the sob that left my throat when I watched Cody stand next to Gram, setting his arm around her shoulders.

Asa's friends, Tommy and Dragon, were planning on escorting us north on their bikes and then continuing to Eugene once we'd settled in my new place. We wouldn't need the extra protection once we met up with the crew in central California, and Asa had explained that it would give him more time with me if the guys didn't stay with us. I wasn't sure why their itinerary had anything to do with us, but I didn't ask about it either. I didn't care what they were doing as long as Asa could stay as long as possible before leaving me behind.

Poet and his group were going to stay with Gram for the next week to make sure things went smoothly, but they didn't seem too concerned. The Jimenez gang was only interested in me, and according to Poet, with me out of the picture, they'd lose interest. I think that Poet may have stayed for another reason entirely—to make sure that Gram had everything she needed as she took care of the enormous responsibility of going through my parents' things and putting them to rest. I was glad that he chose to stay for her when I couldn't, but it didn't help the burning in my chest when I thought of her doing those things without me, so I made an effort not to think about it.

I was getting pretty good at not thinking about things.

By the time we hit the highway, I had controlled my tears for the most part, but I was staring out the window, refusing to look at Asa. Being alone with him for the first time was awkward and uncomfortable, and the fact that he was going to be paying for my entire life made things infinitely worse. Did I say thank you? It seemed so ridiculous to say thank you for such an enormous thing, like the word just didn't encompass enough to fully express my gratitude.

I was busy feeling uncomfortable, with stray tears running down my face, when he reached out and rubbed his hand up and down my thigh.

"Hey, Sugar. Look at me, would ya?"

I turned my face in his direction, not planning to meet his eyes, but he caught me with them anyway.

"It's me and you now, yeah? You remember my promise?" he waited until I nodded before looking at the road again. "Why don't you lay down? It's been a long fuckin' day already and we've got a long way to go." He patted his thigh, raising his arm to lay it across the back of the seat and run his hand over the back of my hair.

I thought about saying I wasn't tired, or spouting something sarcastic about him telling me what to do, but his hand gently smoothing the hair at the back of my head reminded me that he was just taking care of me like he'd promised. I was sixteen years old, alone, and moving away from the only life I'd ever known... and I wanted someone to take care of me. I wasn't ready to stand on my own two feet, no matter how weak that made me.

So I laid down, my head in his lap and the seatbelt digging into my hip, and I quietly cried myself to sleep as he ran his fingers through my hair and drove us to my new life.

Chapter 22

Callie

My memories of the first few weeks in Sacramento aren't very clear. They're mostly a blur of setting up my new place and registering for a new school, but every single one of them has one clear focal point. Asa.

Poet had made some calls while we drove north, and there was an empty apartment waiting for us by the time we'd arrived. The complex was owned by one of the members of the club they belonged to, and according to Asa, the guy had given him a *smokin' deal.* He refused to tell me how much he was paying, but when I saw it for the first time, I couldn't help but think that whatever he was paying had to be too much.

It was clean, but old and small and completely unlike what I was used to. The house I'd grown up in wasn't a mansion by any means, but my dad had kept the appliances updated, and my mom had taken pride in the way our house was decorated. Needless to say, the avocado green sink, toilet and bathtub set in my new bathroom and the fridge in my new kitchen that made a loud humming noise whenever it kicked on, were a far cry from my old home. But I didn't say a word.

What was there to say?

I wasn't about to bitch about the apartment not being up to my snobby standards—it would make him feel like shit. Asa was paying for an apartment that he wouldn't even be living in, and I had no room to complain, not really. All the appliances appeared to work, there was a lock on the door, and most importantly, it was clean. And if, when I saw my new home the first time, I had to pretend to use the bathroom so I could lock the door and let a few tears escape—well, I'd never admit to it.

The first night we were there, we had to drive to Wal-Mart for blankets and toilet paper, but we were too tired to shop for anything else and ended up sleeping curled up on the floor of the bedroom wrapped in my new blue and yellow comforter set.

Sleeping was a very loose term for what I'd done that night.

The arrival in my new apartment had not only marked the beginning of a new life, but also the start of nightmares that would plague me on and off for the next few years. It was also the first time Asa wrapped me in his arms and calmed me down afterward, but it wasn't the last.

Our first week was spent outfitting the new apartment with anything and everything I could need, from shampoo to barstools for the kitchen counter. I tried to be as frugal as possible, knowing that even if my parents had some life insurance policy no one knew about, I still wouldn't be able to pay Asa back any time soon. Asa, however, insisted on buying anything he could get his hands on while I tried to bite my tongue and sneak odds and ends back onto the shelves without him noticing. He didn't let me get away with it, though, and we ended up backtracking, more often than not, for the items that I'd placed haphazardly around the stores.

I finally snapped in one of the kitchen aisles at the local IKEA.

"We don't need a freaking orange peeler! Who uses an orange peeler? It's ridiculous!" I was griping at him, waving the offending peeler in the air while he watched me in amusement. "People have been peeling oranges for hundreds of years, and *they've* never needed one of these stupid things!"

"Not sure why a ninety-nine cent peeler has got your panties in a twist, Sugar," he mumbled at me quietly.

"Because it's a *waste*! Ninety-nice cents here, two ninety-nine there—it freaking adds up, Asa! I'm never going to be able to pay you back for all of this!" I hissed in frustration as I willed tears of embarrassment to stop forming at the back of my eyes.

"I didn't ask you to pay me back," he told me, his jaw tight and his eyes angry. "Never *once* did I tell you that you were paying me back for a goddamn thing."

"I know that," I replied, "but you just keep buying things that I don't really need and it's making me crazy! I don't *need* a coffee table. God, I don't even need a *couch*! I can just sit on my bed when I'm home…"

His voice was still slightly pissed off as he reached up and grabbed my chin, lifting my face so he could look directly into my eyes as he spoke, "We need a couch because I wanna sit on the fuckin' couch when I come home."

"Home?"

"Yes, *home*. I might not be living there full time, but me and you? We're making a fuckin' home. With a comfortable couch, that we will *not* be buying here because these couches are too fuckin' small, and a big-ass TV that I can watch Westerns on. And we're gonna buy anything you need to cook and organize shit the way you like it. Because, baby? I'm gonna be gone a lot, and I want to know that when I'm gone, you're going home to a fuckin' comfortable house where you can relax and feel safe."

I stared at him for a moment, sifting through everything he'd just said and trying to find an appropriate response, but the only thing I could think of was, "Westerns?"

"Really? That's all you got?"

"Are you sixty-five?"

"Shut the fuck up."

"Do we need to get one of those denture containers for you to put your teeth in at night?"

"Callie…"

"I think we need to go a few aisles back for something like that…wait, do we need to call AARP and make sure they've got your change of address?"

I squeaked as he moved toward me, trying to scoot around the cart so I could use it as a barrier, but I couldn't escape him. He was too quick, and soon I was in his arms and he was tickling my neck with his beard.

"You think you're so funny," he grumbled into my throat, his chin digging into my shoulder.

"Westerns!" I hooted, pushing at his shoulder and gaining the attention of the shoppers around us.

My hoot made him redouble his efforts and we knocked into shelves as we scrambled into a position that left little room between our bodies. One of my arms had pushed up his chest and over his shoulder while the other wrapped around his trim waist, my fingers clenched into the back of his belt. I was breathing heavily, and I couldn't decide if I wanted to pull up on his jeans and give him a wedgie, like I would've done if he was Cody, or take the safer route of dragging the gray beanie from his head in an attempt to annoy him.

It was all giggling and growling until he opened his mouth against my neck and bit down playfully.

My breath caught in my throat and I froze mid-wiggle. I was suddenly hyperaware of every place our bodies touched, the scrape of his beard on my collarbone, and the heat of his breath on the side of my neck. I no longer thought anything was funny, and by the way his growl turned into a deep moan and he bit down harder and start to suck, he didn't either.

Then I wasn't thinking of anything.

His arms tightened around me as I felt my eyes falling to half-mast, barely registering a couple starting down the aisle only to quickly move the other way. He pushed his foot in between mine, never letting up on the suction at my neck as he positioned us so that I was just barely straddling his thigh. I was trying to find my balance in our new position, holding back whimpers in my throat and trying to remember why we shouldn't be doing what we were doing in a very public store when he used the hand at my hips to rock me against him and the one on my back to catch my hair and tilt my head back.

I won the fight against whimpering and stayed silent—but I couldn't stop my hand from sliding away from his neck and into his beanie, gripping his hair tightly in my fist as I took over the rocking motion with my hips.

I'm not sure what would have happened if an employee hadn't interrupted us, asking us to cease and desist or she was going to call security. I stumbled back slightly in embarrassment, my face burning as I gaped at Asa's smug face.

"No need to call security, ma'am. I think she's learned her lesson," he told the employee dismissively, grabbing a hold of our cart and sauntering away.

He freaking *sauntered* away.

I didn't saunter. I shuffled … with my proverbial tail between my legs.

We were quiet as Asa grabbed the last few things he wanted from the store. I was still completely mortified, scanning the area around us for the employee who'd verbally bitch-slapped me from my Asa fog.

God, I never wanted to see her again. *How humiliating.*

It wasn't until we were emptying our kitchen utensils onto the check-out belt, and I turned to Asa with a glare, holding not one, but *two* orange peelers, that he finally spoke.

"Westerns are American history brought to life. Those fuckers were badasses, Callie," he told me with a smirk. "Plus, John Wayne's the fuckin' shit."

I shook my head at his smirk and continued emptying the cart, "I'll take your word for it as long as you don't make me watch them."

"Fuck that. You're sitting through every single one…"

"I'll just read or something," I told him distractedly as I watched the numbers on the register move higher and higher while biting the inside of my cheek.

I wasn't prepared for him to move in behind me and settle his hand low on my belly.

"I'm pretty sure you're gonna watch them, Callie," he whispered in my ear, pushing his hips lightly against my ass.

"Oh yeah?" I replied, trying to sound dismissive but ending up breathy like Marilyn Monroe.

He didn't answer back right away because he was busy swiping his credit card and gathering his receipt from the clerk, so I moved slightly away from him, thinking the conversation was over. I was surprised when, instead of grabbing our bags, he moved to me and slid a hand into my hair at the base of my neck, tilting up my face for a quick peck on the lips.

"Yeah, baby. You've got a hickey the size of Texas on your neck that tells me you're *not* gonna be tellin' me no."

He chuckled once and let me go, slapping me on the ass before picking up our purchases and walking toward the exit.

I should've been annoyed but I wasn't. His words had flipped a trigger, and my mind grasped on to one simple fact.

Almost every minute I was conscious, my mind was consumed with grief and guilt. It was burying me slowly in a depression that I had no idea how to deal with. It just kept beating at me, never letting a smile cross my face or a feeling of gratefulness sink in before I felt like shit for enjoying anything when my parents were dead.

But when Asa was touching me, I wasn't thinking about anything else. Not one single thing.

It was a heady feeling—knowing I'd found my oblivion.

Chapter 23

Callie

Once I realized that Asa was expecting to share the house when he could, it was easier for me to pick out the things I thought we'd need, like an electric slow cooker. Sure, a slow cooker wasn't a huge purchase—or even really important in the greater scheme of things—but my mom had taught me how to use one. I had a ton of recipes that I knew were really good, and I wanted to make them for Asa. So for the first time, without his prodding, I'd bought something. A freaking electric slow cooker.

I had no idea where Asa was getting the money for our huge shopping spree, but he seemed to be unconcerned with the grand totals as we made our way through different stores.

I thought the big TV he wanted would be our largest expense, but it was nothing compared to the cost of all the small things we had to buy. It was daunting, trying to remember everything we needed. At one point, I had to try to remember a pad of paper and a pen just so I could write a list of all the other things we'd forgotten as we made our way through store after store.

We drove the moving truck around town as we picked up our supplies, and we must have looked like idiots putting seven bags of groceries into the empty cargo area. Asa refused to return the truck until we'd found the bed and couch we wanted. And by *we*, I mean him. The couch and bed *he* wanted. If it had been up to me, we would've bought the least expensive ones we could find, no matter what they looked or felt like. However, Asa was adamant that we get furniture that were both comfortable and appealing, so he eventually stopped asking my opinion after I told him a lime-green couch with bright orange flowers looked nice. In my opinion, the nicest thing about the couch had been the bright red clearance tag hanging off its arm.

By the second week in the new apartment, we'd completely settled in. I hadn't been sure about, well, *anything* to do with Asa, but the longer we spent time together, the more comfortable I became with him. It didn't help my anxiousness, however, when we set up the new furniture, or the thoughts racing through my mind the entire time I got ready for bed.

We hadn't discussed what the sleeping arrangement would be.

Since the day we'd left San Diego, Asa hadn't done anything beyond stealing a kiss or two and leaving the massive hickey on my neck—even though we'd been sleeping together on the floor every night. It was cozy and comforting sleeping wrapped in Asa's arms, and the thought of waking up after a nightmare alone didn't appeal to me—but sleeping in the bed seemed so much more intimate than camping out on the floor. It was a situation that I had no idea how to handle, but once again, I didn't actually have to handle anything. Asa just stepped in with little fanfare and made the decision for me by stripping down to his boxers and climbing into my bed before I'd finished brushing my teeth.

I felt my hands grow clammy as I took in his broad shoulders and inked skin against my pale blue sheets. Since the hickey incident at IKEA and the subsequent light bulb that went off in my head, I'd been trying to get the courage to start, at the very least, a heavy make out session. Many nights, I was falling asleep with a splitting headache from controlling my emotions all day. I was a mess. It wasn't helping my nightmares because every time my headaches were at their worst, I was waking up in a cold sweat halfway through the night.

"You coming to bed, Calliope?" he called from the bed, breaking me out of my thoughts but never looking away from the phone in his hands.

I drug my feet across the ugly-as-shit brown shag carpet as I made my way to the bed while I tried to psych myself up. We were just sleeping like we had for the past eight days, right? It was nothing to get all bent out of shape about. Just me and Asa, camping out... but this time with a pillow top mattress and five hundred thread count sheets.

Fuck.

I wasn't a virgin, and I wasn't worried about that aspect of our relationship. I also wasn't freaked out because we were sleeping together—we'd been doing that for over a week. It was the mixture of sleeping together in an actual bed, surrounded by household goods that we'd bought together, and the knowledge that we'd never have to be careful or sneaky about what we were doing. For the first time, I was completely without guidance or rules—and for some reason that made me anxious. Beyond anxious.

"We're not having sex," I blurted out as soon as I'd climbed into what I guessed was now "my side" of the bed. *Fuck, it was getting weirder by the minute!*

"Uh, did I ask for sex?" he asked with raised eyebrows.

"No. I mean, well, you seem like you want to and everything, but, no, not tonight. You haven't said anything tonight," I was babbling, trying to get my point across, and I was doing what my dad would call a "piss poor" job.

He scooted down in bed and set his phone on the floor, mumbling about how we needed bedside tables, before rolling back toward me and gesturing with his hand.

"Come here, Sugar."

"Why don't I just stay here?" I asked, my spine straight as a ruler against the headboard.

"Calliope, it wasn't a question," he rumbled back, his voice coming out deeper than it had before.

With a huff that I made sure he heard, I hopped out of bed and shut off the light, then crawled in next to him. As soon as I was within reach, he rolled me to my side and spooned his body against the back of mine.

"We're not having sex anytime soon, Callie," he told me gently, and then squeezed his arm around me as I tried to bolt.

"Baby, I've got blue balls like you would not believe." He moved his hips against my ass, grinding for a second until I could feel him, and I held my breath as I waited for what he'd say next, hoping he would keep moving. "You've had a ton of shit happen in very little time, Calliope. We're not gonna add fuckin' each other's brains out to that long list of shit."

He couldn't see me as I opened my mouth to argue, but he must have felt my head move, because he cut me off before I could say a word.

"Let me finish. I want you like hell on fire—I see you bending over to put shit in cupboards and my dick gets so hard I can't fuckin' think straight. But, baby, I don't wanna fuck you up worse than you've already been fucked. Shit is crazy for you right now, and you're sixteen years old. *Sixteen.* I've known sixteen-year-olds that live with their man and they're happy as hell with that life—but those girls came from shit lives that they were trying to get away from and they were more grown up than most middle-aged men. That's not you. Less than two weeks ago you were fuckin' grounded for staying out past your curfew. You had parents that loved you and coddled you."

By the time he finished speaking, I was pissed. I rolled over and got in his face to bitch at him for making me seem like an immature brat—but I hadn't counted on the smell of his minty and smoke flavored breath or how close our faces would become. Instead of pitching a fit like I'd intended, I found myself diving toward his mouth as if to prove him wrong.

I licked into his mouth and was instantly wrapped in his arms and rolled so I was on top of him. I thought he was only rolling me off the arm that had become trapped underneath me, so he could use both arms to push me away, but the minute I was on top of him I moved my knees up his sides until I was straddling and grinding into his hips.

I felt the moment he gave up the fight.

It was the same moment that I gained the euphoric feeling of oblivion from everything else.

He growled down my throat as his hands began to move over the curves of my body. One hand slipped inside the t-shirt I was wearing to wrap around my breast and the other slid to the bottom of the shorts I wore to bed. My hands were braced above his shoulders, holding my weight, and I groaned, my elbows almost buckling when his fingers found my nipple and pinched it lightly.

I was a frenzy of movement the more turned on I got, and I arched my hips even harder into his, trying to get the friction I needed—then he made a sound in his throat like I'd punched him. His hands slid out of my shirt, causing me to whimper and push even harder, but he suddenly grabbed my hips and practically shoved me back, ripping his face from mine.

"Jesus Christ, Callie! You're gonna push my balls into my throat!" he winced, gasping for air.

I'd had sex in that position before, and I thought I knew what I was doing, so his words were like a splash of ice water to my face.

I sat back hard on my heels in shock before shame swamped me and all I wanted to do was get as far away from him as I could. I thought it was dark enough in the bedroom that I had a little protection—but he must have seen the look of horror on my face, because before I could make my legs move to scramble off him, he sat up straight and wrapped his arms around my back.

"Where you going?" he rasped, trying to get a good look at my face as I tucked my chin into my chest. I didn't answer him. I couldn't. Because unfortunately, I was feeling so embarrassed that I could feel a lump forming in my throat.

"Hey, look at me. Where'd you go, baby?" he asked quietly, trying to force my face up with a careful hand.

"I'm sorry," I mumbled pitifully to his chest, wishing I was anywhere but there.

"Sorry for what? What am I missing here?"

"For, you know, attacking you. Pushing your, uh… into your throat," I told him, cringing.

He barked out a laugh, startling me enough to have me raising my head.

"Baby, you wanna attack me, you feel free," he told me with a wide smile. "Nothin' you did was wrong. You obviously needed somethin' and you were tryin' to get it. Ain't nothin' wrong with that."

"Okay, well, okay," I replied stupidly, "I'm gonna just go to bed now."

"You've gotta be fuckin' kidding me, Callie," he replied incredulously. "Get over here and kiss me."

I leaned forward to get it over with, as I didn't see him letting me go if I didn't, but the peck on the mouth I had planned turned into something else when the minute I got close, he bit my bottom lip and pulled me toward him.

"You needed somethin' and you weren't getting it, Callie," he told me against my mouth, the words separated with little bites. "I'll give it to you."

His hands quickly stripped my t-shirt up and over my head before I could process his words, and my hands flew to his hair as he arched my back and pulled one of my nipples into his mouth. My head fell back and my hips twitched, but I was too worried about moving wrong to let them rock the way I wanted to. If I was doing it wrong before, I wasn't going to magically know how to do it right then. So, against everything my body was yelling at me to do, I stayed still.

His mouth pulled away from my breast with a small popping noise, and he looked at me in confusion before his face cleared. His hands moved to my hips and started rocking them. I concentrated on the movement until I was sure I could replicate it, but it wasn't doing anything except getting me wetter than I already was. I felt swollen and needy, but I wasn't going to say anything. Everything he was doing felt good, and by far surpassed anything I'd gotten out of past encounters.

He watched my face intently as he let go of one of my hips and ran his hand along my body to my breast. When he pinched my nipple again, my hips jerked down into his, and he nodded slightly and let go of my other hip.

"Keep moving, Sugar," he ordered, sliding his hand down my belly and into the front of my shorts. When his thumb hit my clit, I jerked again and he gave a small shake of his head.

"You keep moving the way I showed you," he growled, circling my clit over and over with his thumb. "It feels so good. You're so fuckin' wet; I can feel it through your shorts." He paused in his dirty talk for a moment, watching my body move against him, before capturing his train of thought again. "You're not gonna be able to get off from this angle," he explained roughly, "so you were pushin' and pushin' and it was just getting you more frustrated. And with our clothes on, you were fighting a losing battle."

His breath hitched as I rode him, his fingers tightening on my breast before he continued.

"You need me right here," he rasped, pushing his thumb harder against my clit. "This right here is going to push you over that ledge."

He dipped his thumb farther down and when he pulled it back up, my entire body clenched. It was winding tighter and tighter as he whispered to me, and when he sucked my nipple hard into his mouth and pushed down hard with his thumb, I came with a high pitched moan.

He held his thumb where I needed it as I rode out my orgasm, but as soon as I finished, both hands went straight to my hips to move me faster over the length of him. He latched onto the inside of my left breast as his breathing grew more and more ragged, sucking hard as he came and groaning into my skin until finally stopping the movement of my hips.

"Holy fuck, Callie," he mumbled, as he fell backward on the bed, taking me with him. "Shit, when I get you naked you're gonna fuckin' kill me."

I lay there on top of him, blissed out and relaxed, until he made me get up so we could clean up and use the restroom.

More than an hour passed before my mind grew dark again.

Chapter 24

Grease

Our second week in Sac started with a bang, and shit didn't settle down after that. Callie was hot on my dick—pushing for us to have sex—and after the night we set up the bed, I was having a hard time telling her no. Fuck, that was an understatement. I had a feeling I was grinding my back teeth down to nubs with the strain of holding back. The idea that I was the one telling her no was fucking ridiculous, but I was trying to do the right thing. I didn't want her freaking out afterward—it's not like she had anywhere to go if she lost her shit.

We were fooling around—that didn't stop. We weren't doing anything beyond what most kids her age were doing— hands and all that shit. But *holy hell*, I wanted her. I'd made the mistake of cleaning off my fingers with my mouth after one of our rounds, and *goddamn* if my mouth didn't water now every time I got anywhere near her. It was a joke. I was being a fucking pussy and I knew it. She didn't have any reservations about fucking, and thank god she wasn't a virgin, but there was something...off. Something I couldn't put my finger on.

She was almost desperate for it—my touch. And as much as I wanted to strut around like I had balls made of gold, I knew her craving for it was too extreme.

We took her in that week to sign her up for school, and I swear to Christ, the secretaries in that piece of shit high school kept looking at her belly. The fact that some tattooed guy brought her in to get her shit taken care of confused the hell out of them. I guess the conclusion they came to was that I'd knocked her up. It was so far from the truth is was fucking funny, and she elbowed me about fifteen times as I rubbed on her belly. The secretaries could suck my dick. They'd better not give her any shit when I wasn't there.

We set it up so she could start school the following week, and that afternoon we picked her up a little car that I'd bought from one of the brothers. The Aces Sacramento Chapter was pretty small, but it had some good guys in it. Several of them were close to my age, and I'd partied with them quite a bit whenever I was in town, but I was fucking dreading introducing Callie to any of them. I'd claimed her, and I knew they wouldn't touch her, but fuck if I wasn't jealous of any time they'd get to spend with her—especially after I headed back to Eugene. I didn't want them even looking at her. I knew where they'd been. Shit, I'd *seen* where they'd been. I didn't want Callie anywhere near that shit.

The clock was ticking down on my time with Callie, and it was wearing on me more and more each day. I got her the car so she'd have a way to get around when I wasn't there—I was worried that she'd hole herself up in the apartment if she didn't have a way around. It didn't seem to matter, though. She didn't want to go anywhere without me.

Every time I asked her to run to the store or pick us up some dinner, she'd come up with some excuse so she didn't have to do it—she wasn't feeling well, she'd just gotten comfortable on the couch, she wanted to cook something herself. It was never fucking ending, and by the end of the week, her neediness was getting on my last fucking nerve.

"Callie, get off your ass and go to the fuckin' store!" I sniped at her. We'd been arguing about shit we needed, like fucking milk, and once again she was outright refusing to leave the goddamn house. I was going to lose it. I was still into her. That hadn't changed, and I fucking loved taking care of her, but it felt like I was turning into her freaking parent.

"I can't, Asa. I don't have very good night vision," she told me with fucking doe eyes. Since I'd met her, those eyes had been able to get me to do anything for her, but right then, they just pissed me off more.

"Calliope, I'm paying for your fuckin' apartment," I hissed as I pulled her off the couch. "I pay for your fuckin' shampoo and your makeup and your goddamn toilet paper."

I pulled her through the apartment by her arm, ranting at her the entire way. If she wasn't going to pull her weight, I'd make her do it. I wasn't asking her to milk a cow, for God's sake; all I asked was for her to go to the grocery store only two blocks away. When we got to our dresser, I picked up her purse and shoved it at her, letting go so it would fall if she didn't reach up to grab it.

"I'm fuckin' done with this shit," I mumbled as I pulled her keys out of my pocket and put them in her hand.

I drug her back out to our living room and pushed her out the front door before I turned to walk back inside. Before I could take one step, I froze at the sound of her hiccup.

Then I kept going.

When I turned around to close the door, she was standing there, shaking, with tears running down her face—but I wasn't about to coddle her. This shit had to stop.

"We need milk, Callie. We also need toilet paper, coffee, and some fuckin' fruit or something. Bank card is in your wallet," I told her before shutting the door in her face.

I leaned against the door and listened to make sure she left. I waited there for ten minutes and there was no sound except for an occasional sniffle. When I'd finally reached my breaking point, feeling like shit for what I'd done, I heard her walking down the stairs outside.

My gut clenched.

I fucked up. I knew it.

I should've done shit differently.

She was fragile and sweet, and still trying to figure out her new life.

I knew she was scared; I held her after her screaming nightmares woke us both up in the middle of the night.

But I had to do something.

I had three days before I had to head north.

If she couldn't even go to the store when my ass was sitting on our couch waiting for her—how the fuck would she survive on her own?

Chapter 25

Callie

When Grease left me on the doorstep, clutching my purse and wearing pajama pants and slippers, I was stunned.

I knew I was being a pest, following him around like a lost puppy, but I couldn't seem to stop myself from doing it. He made me feel safe, and it wasn't something I'd ever willingly give up. So, yes, I knew what I had been doing, but it wasn't until that night that I knew it was bothering him.

The foundation of our relationship was based on my need for his strength and his need for my weakness—but apparently my weakness was no longer something he wanted.

Unfortunately, I was still weak.

I stood outside the door, waiting for him to open it back up and tell me it was all a mistake. That he didn't really expect me to go to the grocery store all alone, in the dark, and with my boobs hanging out of the thin tank top I was wearing without a bra. I waited, but he never came.

I eventually made my way to the car, jumping at every noise, and jerking my head from side to side as I tried to watch my surroundings. I felt exposed, like at any minute, someone would drive up and it would all be over. My eyes searched the backseat before I unlocked my door and climbed inside and my mind raced with scenarios of someone hiding back there, lying in wait for me to leave the house.

I knew it was ridiculous, but the shock of Grease pushing me out the door, and the lingering fear that the gang in San Diego would find me, were the making of a perfect storm for my imagination.

I turned the car on and drove to the grocery store, but once I parked I couldn't make myself get out of the car. I sat there, hyperventilating and crying like a lunatic for over an hour before I finally snapped and turned the car back on.

He'd said that he was done.

Done.

I was in a car that didn't belong to me, in an unfamiliar town, and I had nowhere to go.

So I followed the signs that lead me to the interstate, and I started driving south.

I was two hours into my drive when I remembered that I hadn't called Gram yet that night, so I pulled my purse toward me and started shuffling through it, finally pulling out my silenced cell phone. I'd called her like I promised I would the night we got to Sacramento, and since that first call we'd talked every night. It grounded me to know she was there, waiting until the day she could move north to live with me, and I think it gave her a little peace of mind to have me calling to check in.

There were missed calls, but I didn't look through them before I dialed Gram's number.

"Callie?" she answered on the first ring. "Thank God! Where are you? Are you okay?"

"Yeah," I told her, baffled at the worry in her voice, "I'm fine. What's wrong?"

"Where are you, Callie? We've been calling you for hours! Asa called me, worried as hell that you hadn't come home!"

"I'm fine, Gram," I reassured her, pissed as hell that Grease had called and worried her. "I'm on I-5 South."

There was a slight pause before she spoke again, her voice calm, "Why are you on I-5, Callie?"

"It's not working out up here. I need to come home," I told her stupidly. I knew I couldn't go home. I didn't have a home any longer.

"Baby girl, you need to turn around. Take the next exit and you turn right back around," she replied in a soothing voice normally used on small children.

"I can't," my voice caught in my throat, "I don't have anywhere to go."

"Calliope Rose, you've got a man searching high and low for you right now, what do you mean you don't have anywhere to go?"

"He pushed me out of the house, Gram," I told her on a whisper. "He said he was done because I didn't want to go to the grocery store."

I knew I wasn't being fair. Grease's issue was a lot bigger than the fact that I didn't want to go to the grocery store that night. He was fed up with me—but I didn't want my Gram to know that. She was telling me to turn around, and I was hopeful that if I painted him in a harsh light, she'd tell me to come home.

I just wanted her to take care of things.

I didn't want to be an adult anymore.

"Baby, he's been frantic. He's called me no less than ten times asking if I'd heard from you yet. Whatever happened between the two of you can be worked out, I promise. Now turn around."

I took the next exit and pulled into a gas station. I didn't need any gas yet, but I needed a minute to decide whether I should keep going or start back. My mind was a jumbled mess of emotion, half of me happy that he was worried about me and the other pissed enough to not care that he was worried. He'd kicked me out of the house. He swore at me and pulled me around the house like a rag doll.

Fuck him.

"Okay, Gram. I'm heading back," I told her calmly, though my chest was burning with righteous anger. "If he calls you, tell him I'll be back in a few hours."

"Good God, Callie. How far south did you get?"

"I'm only two hours south, but I have to stop at the grocery store on my way back," I explained as I pulled back onto the freeway.

"Okay, baby, I'll tell him... are you sure you don't want to call him yourself?" she asked me, sounding relieved that I'd gotten my head on straight.

"No, I really shouldn't be talking on the phone as I drive," I said, though it had nothing to do with the reason I wasn't calling Grease.

We said our goodbyes, but before she hung up, I had one last thing to say.

"Hey, Gram? Make sure you tell him not to worry," she took a deep breath in relief, but I wasn't finished. "Tell him not to worry—that I'll be stopping at the store for his toilet paper and milk."

Chapter 26

Callie

When I walked in the apartment later that night, I was surprised that Grease wasn't waiting by the door. Gram had made it seem like he was crazy with worry, but I saw no indication of that as I juggled the bags of groceries and locked the deadbolt behind me. The place was quiet as I walked through the living room, but when I flipped on the kitchen light his voice startled me.

"Where the fuck have you been, Callie?" he asked quietly from where he was sitting on the couch. He was leaning forward with his elbows resting on his knees and a beer bottle dangling from his right hand, and the unnatural stillness of his body must have been the reason I didn't notice him as I'd walked in. I continued into the kitchen as if I was unconcerned with his presence.

"Went grocery shopping," I told him flippantly as I started emptying the bags on the counter. "The big store wasn't open, so I stopped by the 24-hour place. They didn't have a wide selection of fruits, so you're gonna have to wait until tomorrow for those."

I pushed the milk into the fridge as I spoke, and when I turned around I was startled to see that he'd followed me and was standing in my space.

"It's almost three o'clock in the morning, Callie. Where the fuck have you been?" he asked again, his voice controlled but the veins in his neck bulging.

"Wow, it's getting late. I'm going to put these groceries away and then I'm heading to bed," I told him flatly, ignoring his question as I scooted around him.

I knew I was pissing him off, but I didn't have it in me to care. My anger had faded the further I'd driven, and by then I was just feeling... empty. He may have worried about me, but it was *his* decision to push me out the door.

When he grabbed my shoulder gently and spun me around, I didn't even fight it. I just let him maneuver me until we were standing almost nose to nose. Whatever he saw in my expression must have caused the reign on his temper to dissolve, because within a second, he was tossing his beer bottle across the room where it shattered against the living room wall.

I didn't even flinch at the movement.

"Where the fuck have you been, Callie?" he roared in my face, searching my eyes and obviously not finding what he was looking for.

"I went for a drive."

"You went for a drive?" he parroted.

"Yeah. I went for a drive," I answered him, my voice never changing from the monotone I'd used since I walked through the door. I crossed my arms under my breasts and his eyes shifted down my body, taking me in.

"What the hell are you wearing?"

He frowned at me, taking in my hard-soled slippers and flannel pajama pants before coming to rest on my breasts. His jaw was clenched, but the veins in his neck had disappeared, indicating that he'd calmed down a little.

"I'm wearing the same thing I was wearing when you pushed me out the door," I reminded him, refusing to meet his eyes. I was so exhausted after the hours in the car and the emotional drain of the evening that I didn't even have the energy to give him the fight he was so obviously looking for. I just wanted to go to bed.

"What?" he whispered in disbelief.

My eyes snapped up to his, but the apology I saw in them wasn't enough for me.

"I tried to find a sweatshirt or something in the car, but there wasn't anything in there," I told him quietly, the bravado I'd been feeling finally leaving me. I crossed my arms higher on my chest, blocking my breasts from view like I'd done as I'd picked up the groceries at the store that night, my cheeks flushing a little as I remembered the cashier's leering gaze.

I tried to step away from him, but his hand slid up my shoulder and behind my neck effectively holding me in place.

"Baby…" he whispered gently, trying to pull me forward into his chest.

"I just want to get some sleep, okay?" I told him, finally pulling out of his reach. "It's been a long night." I shook my head once and then moved toward the hallway. "I got you some TV dinners that you like. I wasn't sure if you'd had dinner."

I heard him make a noise in the back of his throat, but I didn't turn around. I kept walking toward our bedroom, only pausing for a second when I heard his fist punch the kitchen wall.

He didn't come to bed for another hour; I knew because I hadn't been able to fall asleep. I'd been so tired when I got home that I could barely keep my eyes open, but the minute I'd crawled under the blankets, I was wide awake.

I didn't know how to navigate this new territory we were entering. Our interactions had always consisted of me cowering in his shadow, and now that I knew I couldn't count on him for protection, the entire situation had tilted on its axis. I couldn't trust that he would protect me—that was clear. But it wasn't as if I had completely stopped trusting him. I knew that he would do his best to live up to his promises; however, I could no longer lean on him for my security. I had to find my *own* security.

In order to do that, I had to distance myself from him as much as I could.

I tensed when I heard him crawl into bed next to me. I wasn't sure if I should tell him that I was awake, or pretend to sleep so I didn't have to deal with anything else that night. But when he wrapped his arm around my waist and pulled my back against his front, he must have known I was awake, because he started speaking in a quiet voice aching with apology.

"God, Sugar," he groaned into my shoulder, "I shouldn't have pushed you outta the house like that."

"It's okay," I told him, even though we both knew it wasn't.

"No. I fucked up." His head shook briefly. "I just wanted you to use that fuckin' car I bought you. I wanted you to get outta the house by yourself, so I knew you could do it when I left. Do you understand? You gotta be able to stand on your own two feet, Callie—I'm not gonna be here most of the time, and you have to be able to fend for yourself." He squeezed his arm around my waist and kissed my neck as if the whole episode was over.

I wasn't sure what I was supposed to say to that. Thank you? Please throw me out of the house in pajamas again the next time you need toilet paper? All is forgiven?

I settled on the safest bet and whispered, "I understand," before closing my eyes and trying to relax my body.

But I didn't fall asleep for hours.

Because I *didn't* understand.

Chapter 27

Callie

I woke up the next morning ready to put the whole mess behind me. A good night's rest had always helped me put things in perspective. I was already feeling stronger as I got out of bed and got ready for the day. I should've known that I was going to have to suck it up and take care of myself at some point, and I probably would have figured it out for myself, but the hardest part of the night before was having that truth thrown in my face without warning. I hadn't had time to prepare.

I ran it over and over in my head as I took a shower, and by the time I was drying off, I knew that Grease had been right. The fact that he was leaving was something that I'd pushed to the back of my mind so I didn't have to deal with it. We only had days left before he had to leave, and if I made myself think logically, I knew that I had only been postponing the inevitable.

I really was on my own.

It was silly to depend on him for everything.

We were going to one of his friend's houses for a barbeque that day and I was a little nervous about it. I wasn't afraid, I knew Grease wouldn't put me in danger, but the thought of meeting a bunch of new people who knew I was living with him was disconcerting. I didn't want them to think I was taking advantage of him.

The morning passed uneventfully while I puttered around the house sorting laundry and washing dishes. I'd expected there to be tension or something when I woke him up but there wasn't. It was like every other day we'd been together, except for the fact that I didn't let myself stay near him too long. I didn't want to come across as needy again, so for the most part, I stayed out of his way.

As I walked through the apartment, I could feel his puzzled gaze on me, but he never said a word, so I just smiled whenever we made eye contact. I hoped that he was noticing my change in demeanor. I wanted him to realize that I wasn't going to hang on him anymore. First, I wanted him to know I got the message and second, I needed to ensure that he wouldn't kick me out for real the next time.

We were getting ready to step out the door when I realized I couldn't find my phone in my purse. I ran back into our room without saying a word, but I couldn't see it anywhere so I called out for help.

"Grease, have you seen my phone?" I bellowed, flipping the comforter and sheets down the bed in case it had fallen between them.

I was just about to kneel down on the floor to check under the bed when he walked into the room and the air felt electric.

"You don't call me Grease," he told me adamantly, meeting my eyes from the doorway.

"What?"

"You don't call me Grease. You call me Asa," he answered, stepping into the room. "You and your grandmother are the only people on this earth who do."

I wasn't sure what the big deal was, so I just nodded my head and started looking for the phone again. I'd dropped to my knees on the floor and was starting to bend over to look under the bed when I heard him curse behind me and lift me up by my armpits.

He tossed me on the bed and I bounced once before coming to a stop with his body covering mine.

"I don't think you're hearing what I'm saying to you. You're the only one who calls me by the name my mother gave me, Callie. The *only* one. You say it when you're frustrated, and when you think something's funny, and when you're coming all over my hands."

My breath caught at the fire in his eyes, and as he shifted against me, my heart started to race.

"You can be pissed as hell at me, call me a dick or an asshole. You can scream at me, throw shit, and stomp around the house." He nuzzled my neck as he spoke, and my hands lifted involuntarily to his hair to anchor him to me.

"But if I hear you call me Grease again, I'm going to spank your ass," he whispered, gripping one of my ass cheeks in his hand to force my hips into his.

God, I'd been thinking and overthinking things in my head for the last twelve hours, and all I wanted to do in that moment was get lost in him again. I wanted to get to that place where the only thing that mattered was where his body was pressing against mine. I made a noise and tilted my head back to give him easier access to my throat, but it didn't give me the response I was looking for. Instead, he planted one of his fists on the bed and used his other hand to pull his phone from his back pocket. He flipped it open and pushed a button, never looking away from my face, and I felt my breathing speed up as he started to slowly rock his hips into mine.

"Hey, man. We're not gonna make it today," he growled into the phone, his voice deep and guttural. "Got some other shit that came up... yeah, I'll let you know."

He closed his phone with a snap, and I heard it thud against the carpet as he threw it off the bed, but I was too busy looking at him to see where it landed. He leaned back onto his knees and was pushing my shirt up my stomach, licking and biting at me on every inch he exposed. When I finally had enough of his teasing, I reached down and tore it off, going for his vest next and pushing it off his shoulders.

We wrestled and rolled until our clothes were strewn across the bed and my chest was heaving with exertion. Asa was a huge guy. I knew he allowed me to push him around the bed because he easily weighed a hundred pounds more than I did. But he let me scratch and bite at him, taking everything I gave him as my frustrations poured out of me. His skin turned red across his chest, and there were fingernail marks covering the length of his back where I'd scratched him as he kissed me. I'd also left a fat hickey on his neck and a bite mark on his shoulder—almost as if I was marking my territory.

We ended upside-down on the bed, my bare feet sliding under our pillows, but he made no move to right us. He was too busy staring between my legs as his fingers rubbed and pulled and pinched at my flesh. His eyes were so dark they looked almost black, and his eyebrows were furrowed in concentration as he suddenly stopped, causing me to whine out my annoyance.

"What's my name?" he asked me gruffly, moving his hips back as I tried to reach him.

"Huh?" I was in a fog of arousal and didn't understand why he was talking instead of touching me.

"Who am I, Callie?" he asked again, rubbing his fingers softly across my skin. "What do you call me?"

"Asa!" I cried out as his fingers finally hit the spot where I needed him.

"That's right, Sugar. Say it again," he demanded as his fingers started up a rhythm that had me squirming.

"Asa. Asa. Asa," I murmured over and over. I didn't care at that point; he could've asked me to call him Sergei the Snake and I probably would have screamed it.

By the time I came back down from my orgasm, he'd shifted us on the bed so we were cuddled under the blankets. It took me a few minutes before I realized that he hadn't come. Normally, when we were messing around, I'd use either my hands or my body to get him off, but I'd been so blissed out I hadn't even tried. I reached down to the waistband of his boxers, running my nails across his skin the way I knew he liked, but before I could dip my hand inside, he grabbed my wrist and pulled it back up between our chests.

"It's fine, Callie," he told me sleepily, "that one was all yours."

I lay there for a few minutes thinking over his words when I finally decided to ask him a question that had been bothering me for days.

"Why won't you have sex with me?"

He choked a little from surprise, and then situated himself more comfortably next to me with his arm curled up under his pillow.

"We've had this conversation," he told me bluntly, closing his eyes as if to end it.

"Yeah, but that was before. We're practically having sex already, what's the big deal?" I asked. His logic was completely asinine in my opinion, and I was wondering how he would try to explain it.

"Callie," he huffed out in annoyance, but when he opened his eyes and saw how serious I was, his expression changed. "It's gonna happen. Probably sooner than later. But, fuck, I'm leaving in two days. You're gonna have a hard enough time with me gone, living your own life and going to school and shit. I'm not gonna take it all and then leave you, baby."

"Pfft! You act like I'm asking you to marry me or something. Don't act like you don't sleep with chicks and then bail all the freaking time," I scowled back, completely irritated with his explanation.

"You and me are different."

"What the heck does that mean?" I raised myself up on one arm and had to push his face up to look at me when he seemed to be mesmerized by the breast that was peeking out of the blankets.

"It means that you're living in my house and sleeping in my bed. Those other bitches aren't relationships, and I don't give a flying fuck what they think about. I don't care before I hit it, and I sure as hell don't care after."

My jaw dropped.

"That's a dick thing to say!" I exclaimed, my eyebrows practically touching my hairline in surprise. "What the hell?"

"Callie, don't look at me like that, Sugar," he scowled, "those chicks know the score. Not one of them is looking for a happily ever after, and when I'm with them I treat 'em with respect."

"Oh, yeah. You sure sound respectful."

"Like I said, they know from the beginning they're only getting one thing." He sighed in exasperation, "How the hell did we get on this conversation?"

"I was asking why you wouldn't fuck me, even though apparently, there are *loads* of women that you *will*."

"Baby, I ain't looking at nobody but you. Alright?" he said as he leaned forward to give me a soft peck on the lips. "But we're waiting until I get back."

I lay there silently as he fell asleep and thought over what he'd said. I knew logically that he was trying to look out for me, to keep things as easy as possible as I made my transition to living alone.

I was just afraid with the unspecified status of our relationship; he wouldn't have a problem with having sex with someone he *didn't* care about.

I was suddenly glad that I left reminders of me all over his body.

Chapter 28

Callie

Asa left me for the first time on a Monday morning.

We'd spent the weekend lying around the house, watching Westerns and debating music. Yes, Westerns. I'd been expecting the old-fashioned John Wayne movies, and there were a few of those, but he'd also introduced me to *Lonesome Dove* and *Tombstone*. Those two had me at the edge of my seat, giggling and biting my nails. The longer we watched, with Asa's running commentary, the more I realized that he didn't watch them for the men in the white hats—he identified with the men in black.

A few of his friends stopped by the house on Sunday, introducing themselves as Echo, Chucky, and Michael. Asa seemed more relaxed around them; it was a side of him that I'd never seen before. He laughed more often. It was a quiet rumble, but it was there, and it was a beautiful sound.

Their visit also seemed to make him breathe a sigh of relief. He was worried about leaving me on my own, and I knew that it was causing him to lie awake at night while we both pretended we were sleeping. I wouldn't have known the extent of his worry without witnessing his relief when it eased a little. He'd wanted to be sure that I had people in my corner when he left, and he'd set out to make sure that happened.

They were all rough around the edges, and no one I'd want to meet in a dark alley, but my association with Asa made them treat me as if I were one of them. After sizing me up for the first thirty minutes of their visit, they'd relaxed into a type of big brother mentality, teasing and joking with me as if they'd known me for years.

But none of them ever touched me. Not even to put a hand on my shoulder or to brush past me on their way to the kitchen.

It was almost blissful, those last couple of days, and I could have lived that way forever.

But reality had a way of reaching out and pinching you—a sharp reminder to pay attention.

I woke up Monday morning to Asa tracing his fingers over my back, running them down to where my sleep shorts rested on my hips and back up to the nape of my neck. I lay there for a minute, dreading the day, and pretending to sleep. I didn't want him to leave.

He didn't let me play possum for long, though, and as he rasped that he knew I was awake, he tilted his head and bit the side of my neck. It instantly made my blood run faster in my veins and I tried to roll over to face him, but instead he wrapped his arm around my hips and pulled me in against him so we were spooning.

"Don't wanna get outta this bed," he grumbled into my neck, his hand sliding up my torso until he was holding one breast in his palm. "Don't wanna leave you."

He continued to run his hands over my body as I bit my tongue so I didn't beg him to stay. I'd tried to get him to move in with me permanently, but the conversation hadn't ended well and I hadn't brought it up again. He was loyal to the men in Eugene and couldn't imagine moving away from them—and he got pissed whenever I'd mentioned it. Also, I was trying to be less needy. I didn't want him changing his mind about me because I didn't get my shit together, so instead, I hid it.

I hid the fact that I wanted him near me every second, I hid that leaving the house alone still terrified me, and I hid the fact that I was afraid the minute he left, I'd finally break into a million pieces.

Everything was hidden.

I arched into his hands as he started grinding against me, his arm under my head curving down to fondle a breast. The other hand slipped beneath my sleep shorts and I jolted as he went directly to my clit, plucking and rubbing it.

"You're mine, yeah?" he whispered into my ear as he played my body. "Not gonna let any of those pimple-faced high school boys in here, are you?"

He didn't seem to need an answer, because he just continued on—staking his claim and making my body sing as he whispered reassuring and dirty words in my ear.

By the time we were finished, his alarm had already sounded and we didn't have time to cuddle in bed like we usually did. He had to hit the road, and I had to get ready for my first day of school.

God, I didn't know how I'd ever be able to go back inside a high school again. I felt so much older than everyone there, the thought of gossiping and dances made me curl my lip in disgust. I knew, though, if I wanted to be able to support myself I had to at least get my diploma.

I wished that I didn't have to start school that day. I needed a day to get myself together when he left, but I think that leaving on the day I started school was his plan from the beginning. He was hoping it would give me something new to focus on, a specific reason to get out of the house instead of wallowing in our bed.

He stayed with me as long as he could, but by the time I was ready for school, I could tell he was anxious to get going. We left the apartment quietly, both lost in our own thoughts, but I'd barely reached my car before he was in my face, kissing me hard.

My back was against the cool driver's window, his hips snug

against mine, when he spoke.

"You're gonna have a good day, Sugar. Meet a bunch of new people, get outta the house for a while, learn some shit. I know you're nervous, but there ain't nothing for you to be worried about, okay?" he told me gently, rubbing his thumb across my cheek.

I couldn't understand why he was talking to me about school. Who cared about that? He was leaving me there all alone, and I'd already started to miss him as I looked into his warm brown eyes. School was an afterthought. An annoyance.

"Be careful, okay? Call me when you stop. I'm sure I'll be bored as shit all day," I told him with a small smile, the best I could do under the circumstances. I didn't want to make him think that I couldn't do it without him. I had to pretend.

"Yeah, I'll text you. Doubt they'll let ya answer your phone in class." He leaned down to kiss me again. "I'm gonna follow you to school and then I'll take off. Call me when you get home—doubt I'll pick up, but I wanna know you got home safe."

"Got it," I assured him, standing up straighter and pulling back my shoulders. "You better get going or I'll be late. Not the impression I want to give on my first day."

He nodded once before taking my mouth again in a wet kiss and then pulled away. When he climbed on his bike, I had to dig the fingernails on my left hand into my palm to keep myself from calling out to him that I needed one more minute. Just one more.

Instead, I called out playfully, "Why do they call you Grease?"

"Depends on who you're talkin' to," he answered with a mischievous smile, storing a few belongings in his saddle bags as I watched him. "Dad thought it was funny to call me that as a kid because I was so worried about staying clean. Minute I got done doing something

I had to wash my hands. Didn't matter what I was doing."

I smiled widely at him, imagining him as a persnickety little boy.

"Poet calls me Grease for a different reason." He finished buckling the bags and looked at me, taking in the jeans and sweater I was wearing. "Said he couldn't figure out how I was picking up chicks so easy—had to be that I was greased."

"What does that mean?" I asked, puzzled.

He chuckled a little as he climbed on his bike.

"Didn't have to do anything, just slid right in like I was greased."

I still didn't get it. And then suddenly I did, and I wished that I had something I could throw at his arrogant ass. I scowled at him before flipping him off and getting into the car, hearing his roar of laughter even after I'd slammed my door.

He followed me all the way into the parking lot of the new school but he didn't stop. We both knew that if we had to say goodbye again, I'd never be able to make myself go inside the ugly brick building. I watched as he waved his hand at me before taking off, and I had to hurry out of my car before I started crying.

The school was pretty easy to navigate, and I had no problems finding my classes, but for the first time in my life, no one talked to me. I hadn't been the most popular girl in my old school, but I'd had a solid group of friends and I'd always easily made new ones. It was different in the new school, though. People barely even looked at me, and when they did they walked right past me.

It wasn't until I'd finished two classes, and was sitting down in the last one before lunch, that I had any interaction at all.

"Hey, new girl!" a pretty blonde girl called to me, setting her bag next to mine on the floor and taking a seat next to me. She was one of the most beautiful girls I'd ever seen, and I wanted to turn and look behind me to make sure she was talking to me, but I didn't. Her hair was set in a huge bump at her forehead then smoothed back into a ponytail, she had a piercing above her lip on the right side like a beauty mark, and she was wearing the most flawless makeup—including bright red lipstick—that I'd ever seen on anyone. I think I may have drooled a little.

I'm not sure if I said hello, or just kept staring at her, but she smiled genuinely at me and I found myself smiling back.

"So here's the deal," she told me, as she put her elbow on the table and leaned her chin on it. "Everyone saw you and your escort this morning—he's smokin' hot by the way—and everyone around here tries to keep their distance from shit like that. It's easier if they just pretend that the Aces don't exist, know what I mean?"

I was nodding stupidly as she spoke, trying to wrap my mind around the fact that people were actually scared of Asa, so I barely caught what she said next.

"—so we can hang out, if you want to."

"What? Sorry, I didn't hear you," I told her, feeling like an idiot.

"Dude. I'm sitting right in front of you and you're watching me talk. Pay attention," she told me seriously. "My mom's screwing one of the Aces, so I know how you feel. People barely talk to me around here and I grew up with them. They've known me for years. I get it. So if you want to hang with me—the offer's open."

I was trying to process the fact that Asa was scary and her mom was screwing one of the guys he worked with, so I didn't say anything back. When she finally huffed out a breath like she was annoyed and went to stand up, I grabbed her forearm to stop her.

"I could definitely use a friend around this place," I answered her ruefully.

"Great! We can have slumber parties, and paint each other's

nails, and do each other's hair..." she told me dreamily, her eyes going unfocused as she thought about it.

For a split second I looked at her in horror, wondering what the hell I'd done.

"Ha! I'm dicking with you!" she giggled infectiously at the panic on my face. "We'll just smoke pot and watch 'Dazed and Confused' and you can tell me all about the hot dude that followed you to school today."

And that's how I met Farrah.

Chapter 29

Callie

The first night without him was the hardest, and the fact that he was busy as hell didn't help matters much. I lay in bed that night, listening to every creak and thump in the apartments around ours, and tried not to crawl inside the closet so I could get some relief from my racing heart.

I'd like to say that the next night was easier, but it wasn't.

The third and fourth nights weren't any better.

But on the fifth night, something finally clicked—or my body was just too tired to stay awake any longer, because when I got home from school, I fell asleep on the couch. I didn't wake up until sunlight hit my face through the tiny window in the kitchen.

I hopped up from the couch and ran to the bathroom. Sleeping for sixteen hours was no joke when it came to matters of bodily functions. I didn't even think about the fact that I'd been radio silent for all that time until I picked up my phone and my heart sank in my chest.

I had forty-seven missed calls and one hundred and four text messages. All of them from Asa and Gram.

I called Asa first.

"Are you okay, Sugar? Where are you?" he roared into the phone. I pulled it away from my face so he wouldn't burst my eardrums, and when I heard him quiet down a little I brought it back.

"I'm so sorry!" I told him anxiously, "I fell asleep after school and I just woke up!"

"What do you mean you fell asleep after school? It's Saturday," he asked , his voice an ominous rumble that made the hairs on the back of my neck tingle.

"I know it's Saturday, I'm not stupid. I fell asleep yesterday after school and didn't wake up until today," I answered, enunciating every word.

"Are you seriously lying to me right now? What the fuck, Callie? That's like twenty-four hours of sleep."

"No it's not. It's sixteen, and I'm not lying," I snapped back. I was starting to get a little peeved at that point. I knew he was worried, so I would let him get away with a little pissy behavior, but I couldn't believe he was accusing me of lying.

"Why the hell would you need to sleep for sixteen hours?" he scoffed back, as if I was being completely ridiculous.

"Because I haven't slept since you left, you jackass!"

My hand flew to my mouth at the confession, and I berated myself silently as I realized what I'd done. I'd played the happy-go-lucky, well-adjusted girlfriend on the phone that week, and all of the lies and assurances I'd given him were wiped out in an instant.

"Aw, Sugar. I'm sorry you're not sleeping," he crooned quietly, his bad attitude completely vanished. "What's keeping you up? You scared or are you having a hard time shutting your brain off?"

"A little of both, I guess," I confessed, "but it's getting better."

"Shit, Callie, I wish I could be there," he complained. "I've got some shit going down the next two weeks, but I may be able to come down for a couple days the week after."

"Okay, that sounds awesome!" I exclaimed, and the excitement in my voice had him laughing quietly. "Hey—I better get off of here and call Gram. She's been blowing up my phone all night."

"Yeah, I bet. I called her last night," he warned, and then I heard him sigh, "I was getting ready to get on my bike and come looking for you."

"Well, damn," I huffed in mock annoyance. "I should've slept for another hour."

"Not funny, Calliope. I'll call you later, yeah?"

We said our goodbyes as the background noise on his phone got louder, and once we hung up I wondered what he was doing. It sounded like he was surrounded by people, but I wasn't confident enough to ask about it. I didn't want him to think I was checking up on him or something ridiculous like that.

My phone call to Gram sounded eerily similar to the one with Asa, but thankfully, Gram said that she would be headed up to check out my place later in the week after she dropped Cody at the airport. It filled me with relief that she was coming to see me, but it also made my stomach drop to know that Cody was headed back across the country and what that meant.

The coroner had finally released my parents' bodies and my parents were getting their funeral.

On one hand, I was glad that they were no longer being poked and prodded in some sterile lab, but on the other, it was gut-wrenching to know that their time was finally coming to a close. Soon they'd be buried in the ground, and I struggled with the fact that I wouldn't be there to say my goodbyes.

I'd never gotten to say goodbye.

It also made me sick to my stomach when I thought of the way I'd been so focused on Asa and my new life. I'd pushed my parents' gruesome death to the back of my mind so I could just get through each day, and I'd latched on to new problems in order to hide the old ones. Because of this, I'd been projecting all of my angst onto things that weren't impossible to change. I could never get my parents back, they were completely lost to me—but I could change the situation with Asa even if I was refusing to do so.

Knowing that the things I was upset about could change if I wanted them to gave me a sense of control—the control I'd lost when I took that drink at that party. If I just kept my mind on matters that were easily rectified, I could lock the door on things that I knew could never be fixed.

Missing my boyfriend, and choosing that to be my solid focus, made me feel normal in a life that was far from it.

So that's what I did.

I got up that day, did my laundry, and took a shower. I went along living a life that I'd never envisioned for myself, and pretended not to know that my parents were being buried just three days later.

Instead, I thought about Asa, what he was doing, and why there were so many people with him when I'd talked to him on the phone.

It wasn't until I was in bed that night, lying in the quiet, that I thought about my parents and how much I missed them. Then, once I'd pulled the blankets up and over my head, I let the tears and gut-wrenching sobs envelop me.

Sorrow was such a small word for such a huge emotion.

Chapter 30

Callie

I woke up Tuesday morning with a feeling of dread.

Holy God, my parents were going to be buried that day and I wasn't there. I wondered if they knew what was happening, if they'd understand why I wasn't there for Cody and Gram. I had a feeling that they'd be relieved that I was out of danger even though they wouldn't be too pleased about my living arrangements. I curled further into my blankets and let quiet tears run over the bridge of my nose and into the hair at my temples. I missed them—even their overprotectiveness that had plagued me for as long as I could remember.

I didn't move when the alarm went off beside my bed, letting the grating beep go on and on until it finally quieted. I wasn't sure what time it was, but it didn't really matter anyway—I wasn't getting out of bed. If the day of my parents' funeral wasn't cause for a day off, I wasn't sure what was. Instead, I reached under my pillow for my cell phone and sent off a quick text to Farrah.

"Not going to school today"

"Y?"

"Sick"

"Bullshit! Just saw you yesterday."

"Text you later"

"WTF?"

I tried to fall back asleep, hoping that it would make the day pass quickly, but thirty minutes later there was a pounding on my front door. My heart raced and my entire body froze. I couldn't think of any reason that someone would be at my door. Only Asa's friends knew where I lived and I hadn't seen them since he left.

I opened up my phone quietly to call Asa when I heard a familiar voice yelling.

"I know you're in there!" Knock. Knock. Knock. "Open up, Callie! I better see vomit!"

Farrah's yelling and knocking escalated as I stumbled my way into the living room. I wasn't sure how she found out where I lived, but I wanted to hug her for showing up.

I opened up the door, almost getting punched in the face as I caught her mid-knock.

"Damn, girl. You look like shit," she told me as she pushed her way inside. "But you're not *sick*."

I shut the door behind her, flipping the two deadbolts I'd begged Asa to install before he left. I'd never again be caught unaware by someone coming into my house.

"So, what's up? That Ace hottie drop you?" she asked me, dropping onto the couch.

I laughed a little at her guess; little did she know she was sitting on his furniture.

"No, he's fine. Still in Oregon, though," I replied, walking into the kitchen to brew some coffee. If I was going to be staying awake, I needed a boost.

"Well, what's the deal? You look like someone kicked your dog," she asked in an exasperated tone, following me in and taking a seat at one of our barstools.

"My parents' funeral is today," I answered quietly, deciding to just rip of the metaphorical band-aid. If she was staying, she'd have to know eventually. I didn't think I'd be able to keep it together for long.

She was silent behind me, and I gave her a minute to let the news sink in before turning around to face her. By the time I was looking at her again, she'd wiped all surprise off her face but was looking at me with sympathetic eyes.

"A gang in San Diego broke into our house and shot them while I hid in the closet," I explained, not sure where the verbal diarrhea was coming from, but feeling an immense sense of relief from just saying the words out loud. I hadn't been keeping it a secret, but it felt like one.

"Dang. Tough break," she told me seriously, and I couldn't help the snort that made its way out of my nose. Tough break? God, she was so unflappable.

I think that's why I'd chosen to tell her. She'd seen pretty much everything while living with her mother.

We spent the day watching movies and eating everything in the house. The movies didn't keep my mind off what was happening, but the marijuana she'd brought with her did a pretty admirable job. By mutual agreement, we didn't discuss my situation with Asa. She had to have been really curious, but she didn't ask. I think she was used to not being able to ask questions about things—living occasionally with her Ace quasi stepdad made sure of that.

However, by the afternoon, I was dying to discuss stuff with her. I wanted to know her opinion on everything—my relationship, the weird living arrangement, and Asa's job.

"So, he just... claimed you and then moved your ass up here?" she asked lazily, rolling her head against the back of the couch until she was looking at me.

"Yup. Just like that," I replied, trying and failing to snap my fingers in emphasis.

"Yeah, he fucked up." She nodded slowly.

"What's *that* supposed to mean?" I gasped, offended.

"Not about you, idiot." She waved her hands in front of her. "He never shoulda left you down there in the first place. He shoulda made sure you were safe first."

"Well..." I paused, thinking over her words and then answering strongly, "he couldn't have known what would happen."

She watched me closely for a few seconds and then turned her face back toward the TV.

"Sure. You're right," she stated, already focusing on the movie.

"Do you think it's weird, me living here and him just coming to visit once in a while—even though he's paying for everything?" I asked, pulling her attention back to me.

"I wouldn't know. I mean, we only see Gator once in a while... but he's got a wife," she replied distractedly, not realizing that each word she spoke was like a slap in the face.

I took a minute to control my facial expression, fiddling with the blanket I'd dragged off my bed to cuddle with. I didn't want her to see that I felt like shit at her comment. Did Asa have a wife? He seemed too young for it, but he could easily have a girlfriend in Eugene. Or... an old lady. That's what the guys had called their significant others when they'd visited.

There wasn't any way to become emotional without making it seem like I thought Farrah's mom was a slut, so I made myself think of other things.

"Your mom's boyfriend is named Gator?" I asked her, with a small laugh.

"Yeah, how fucking stupid is that?"

A few hours later, she had to leave to take her car home so her mom could drive to work. I wasn't sure what her mom did for a living, but I'd seen her once before and I wouldn't have been surprised if she was a stripper. The fact that Farrah stayed home alone most nights made me feel even more connected to her. We were two teenage girls that had to play grown-up every day when school got out, and knowing that she was living a similar life made me feel less alone.

I straightened up the house a little and made myself a pizza pocket while I waited for and dreaded my nightly phone calls. Gram called every night if I hadn't called her by eight o'clock. It was reassuring to know that she was checking up on me, but that night I was on pins and needles waiting for my phone to ring.

For the first time since I'd moved, I didn't want to talk to her.

When she finally called, my phone startled me by vibrating on the kitchen counter. I walked over to check the caller ID, but didn't even pick it up. I was afraid that if I did, I wouldn't be able to stop myself from answering, just to hear her voice. If it had been any other night, I would have relished the phone call. But, I knew if I picked up the phone I'd be able to hear the grief in her voice and I didn't think I could handle it. So I just stood there, staring at it until it stopped vibrating, not even checking the voicemail that she'd left.

As I got ready for bed, I carried my phone around with me. I was planning on avoiding Asa's call, too, but oddly I didn't want to miss it. I was too raw, and I was picturing him in Oregon with a whole other family, my imagination running wild. I didn't think I'd be able to talk to him although I wanted to hear his voice just as badly as my Gram's.

It wasn't until I was in bed, surrounded by the comfort of my blankets, that I worked up the courage to listen to Gram's voicemail.

Hey, baby girl. I'm sure you're having a hell of a day… just text me and let me know you're all right. Okay? I can't figure out this damn phone to text you back, but I'll be able to see if you send me one. If you don't, I'm gonna worry... I dropped your brother at the airport this afternoon and he seemed okay—but you might want to call him in the morning. He's missing you like crazy... Okay, well, I'm gonna get off of here. I'll be heading out bright and early in the morning—so I should be up there around dinner time. I love you, Callie Rose.

I listened to her voicemail twice before pulling the phone away from my face and texting her that I loved her. It felt like years since I'd seen her, and I couldn't wait for her to get there the next day. I even giggled a bit at her complaints about not being able to work her cell phone.

As I lay awake that night, listening to the sounds of the apartments around mine, I felt calmer than I had in days. I'd successfully made it through one of the hardest days of my life.

But when I finally drifted off to sleep, my heart ached.

And Asa never called.

Chapter 31

Callie

Gram showed up half an hour after I got home from school. I'd barely set down my messenger bag and stuffed my dirty laundry into my bedroom closet before she was knocking. I practically skipped to the front door and swung it open hard after I'd unlatched the locks.

She didn't even make it past the threshold before I was in her arms.

"Hey, baby girl," she whispered into the side of my head, giving me a kiss before she pushed me away so she could look me over.

"Well, you haven't starved to death," she commented as she pushed her purse higher on her shoulder. "But you look skinnier."

"That's what happens when you don't eat fried food every night," I joked before stopping short.

"Hey, now, none of that," she said forcefully as she poked me in the side and walked past. "Can't be careful of everything you say, baby. Things are different for you now, no use pretending otherwise."

I closed the door and locked it before following Gram to where she was standing in the middle of the kitchen.

"What?" I asked nervously. She was just standing there, her eyes darting from the floor to the cabinets above the sink.

"You cleaned up since you moved in?" she asked as she dropped her purse on the counter.

"Yeah," I looked around in confusion, "I straighten up before I go to bed at night."

"Callie, you actually have to *wash* things," she told me in exasperation as she turned on the water in the sink, pulling the little metal strainer thing out and reaching in with her fingers to clean out the drain.

"I *do* wash things!" I snapped back, embarrassed.

"Your mother did you no favors by following you around and cleaning up your messes," she mumbled, shaking her head.

My back snapped straight at her comment and my stomach began to churn.

"Don't talk bad about my mom," I growled at her, causing her head to whip toward me.

"I'm not talking bad about anyone," she answered, her eyebrows raised. "I loved your mother, Callie. Don't you talk to me like I'd ever say a word against her."

"You didn't even *talk* to her! You wouldn't even come to our *house!*" I practically screeched back at her, my hands trembling. I didn't know where it was coming from, but I couldn't stop the words spewing from my mouth. "She wasn't welcome at *your* house! Dad had to visit you by himself!"

She raised her hand as if to smack me, but dropped it back down at her side as she took a step away from me. We were both shaking by then, my awful words hanging like a dark cloud above our heads.

"I loved your mother, Calliope. As if she were my own child," she told me quietly, her words thick with tears. "When your father brought her home, I couldn't help but love her."

She sniffed quietly and started messing with the sink again as I leaned heavily against the counter.

"She told me that my boys deserved what they got," she whispered, never looking away from the bottom of the sink. "I knew she was hurting. We all were. But I couldn't look at her after that. Every time

I saw her, that's what I thought of—those awful words she said to me after the funeral."

She was quiet for a few more moments before saying something that was so quiet, I had to strain to hear her. "I loved your mother, and I refused to see her for years. That's my cross to bear."

My anger fled in a puff of smoke and remorse instantly took its place. I walked up behind her, wrapped my arms around her middle, and rested my chin lightly on her shoulder.

"What do you mean, when dad brought her home?" I asked, giving her a little squeeze and teasing to lighten the mood. "Did you guys live together? One big happy family?"

I'd been joking, so when she nodded her head, I was stunned.

"What? Why?" I asked, my voice high in surprise.

"Well, she was young. Just eighteen when your dad found her—
"

"*Found* her?" I squeaked, my voice growing even higher.

"Ugh. Sit down, Callie, before you hurt yourself," she said in exasperation, all traces of our argument absent from her tone. She pushed me toward one of the stools and slapped a wet washcloth on the counter, nodding her head at it as if to tell me to get started.

As I started cleaning off dried juice and what looked like Easy-Mac off the counter, she told me my parents' story.

"Your dad was… eh, about twenty-three when he brought her home. Poor thing was black and blue, and your dad wasn't much better." She shook her head at the memory. "I cleaned 'em both up and put your mama to bed. I'll never forget the look on your dad's face when he informed me quite strongly that she was staying with me. He didn't have his own place back then, but he was rarely at my place, either."

She paused to search for the broom, then once she started

sweeping, continued with the story.

"Well, I wasn't having none of that!" she chuckled quietly in her throat. "Made your dad explain as much as he was willing—which wasn't much. But from what I pried out of him—your mama was from a little town in Mexico. She was real smart, so her parents were hoping to send her to a college up here in the States, you know, give her more opportunities than she would have had back home."

"So my dad met her while she was in college?" I asked her, becoming impatient by the slow way she gave me the facts.

"Stop interrupting me if you want me to finish!" she warned, as she lifted the broom off the floor and swatted my legs with it from across the room.

"Okay, fine!" I giggled back, pulling my legs up in front of me.

"Well, her parents made a deal with some boys from up here, promising that they'd get her into a school and whatnot." She glanced at me, giving a small shake of her head. "They didn't. The Jimenez brothers—"

"Jimenez!" I gasped, dropping the wash cloth onto the floor.

"Yup, same ones. Pick up that washcloth and get a new one. This floor is filthy," she ordered, brushing dirt into a dustpan I didn't even know I owned.

"Anyway, they brought her up here, didn't plan on helping her do anything, and that's where your dad came in. He took one look at that girl and had to have her. I'm not sure what happened, but your uncles backed him up and he took her home with him."

"Why didn't he send her home?" I asked, fascinated by this story that I'd never heard before.

"Couldn't send her home—then she'd be right back where she started," she told me offhandedly, as if it was a simple thing to understand.

I finished up the counter, which was pretty much spotless at that point, and started washing down the front of my cabinets quietly. I needed a few minutes to process the new information I'd been given. I never asked my parents how they'd met, it hadn't seemed important, but I suddenly wished that I had.

"It's history repeating itself," I murmured to myself.

"What?" Gram called out from the corner of the kitchen where she'd started to mop the floor.

"It's history repeating itself," I said again, my voice carrying across the kitchen.

"Well, I wouldn't say it's *repeating* itself, but it does seem pretty similar," she answered distractedly as she scrubbed a stubborn spot on the floor with her foot pushing on the head of the mop.

"Is that why you let me move with Asa?" I asked as I stood, stretching my back.

"Your Asa looks at you the same way my boy looked at your mother," she told me seriously, pausing in her mopping to look me directly in the eye. "And your father would have never let anything happen to your mother if he could stop it."

My throat burned with tears I refused to let fall, but instead of acknowledging her words, I bent down and started cleaning the front of the oven.

Later, I followed her around the house, helping her clean and burning in embarrassment when she opened my closet full of dirty laundry and gave me an equally dirty look before scooping it into her arms.

"This is disgraceful, Callie!" she told me with a disgusted sniff, dropping the laundry in the middle of my bedroom floor.

"I was in a hurry!" I griped back.

"I'm gonna make you a list," she huffed as she stripped the sheets off my bed. "Things you have to do every day, things you need to do twice a week, and things you can get by with doing only once a week. You follow my list and you won't have to live in a pit."

"It's not a pit!" I argued, my hands on my hips as I watched her wrestle with my comforter.

"It's a pit."

I helped Gram remake my bed before we headed out for dinner with her grumbling that she was too tired to cook. I felt like shit that she'd driven all day and then cleaned my house all afternoon, but I also knew that she'd loved it. She lived to take care of her kids, and in a weird way I think my living in a pigsty made her feel validated. I really *did* need her—at least to help me clean up my shit.

After we curled up in bed that night, on sheets fresh out of their packaging, we talked for hours about everything and nothing. I fell asleep as she ran her fingers through my hair and spoke about the latest drama in her trailer park. I didn't have nightmares at all that night.

Gram's visit was over before we knew it, and I had to say goodbye once again. She was able to stay with me for nine days, and it had been blissful having her there when I got home from school each day. She'd brought up garbage bags full of my clothes, four loaves of freshly baked banana bread, and an entire box full of homemade jams and canned fruits with her. It was like heaven having all of it at my disposal.

But the best part of having her there was just... her. She made me feel like a kid again, and I soaked it up like a sponge.

While we were having our visit, Asa only called twice. He didn't even seem to notice that something was off—but he still told me that he'd let me have time with Gram without "interruptions". I wasn't sure if he was being thoughtful, or if he was grateful he didn't have to babysit me long distance. I was able to ignore the feeling nagging in my gut that something was off while Gram was there, but it seemed as if the minute she left for San Diego I was hit with a massive force of anxiety.

Why wasn't he calling?

Chapter 32

Grease

When I left Callie in Sacramento, I was anxious as fuck to get away from her. I'd wanted her dependent on me, and I loved the fact that she looked at me like she needed me… but the reality of that was a little more than I could handle. Part of me had wanted to stay with her and take care of her, and the other part of me wanted to just get back to where my fucking world made sense.

By the time I'd pulled up to the club, I was fucking beat. I barely said hello to the boys before slamming into my room and passing out on the bed. I didn't want to move for at *least* twenty-four hours.

The next day, Slider called me into his office to get a rundown on the nonsense down in San Diego, and I had to wait through his ranting and raving before I could try and explain. I knew Poet had already called him, and he was just trying to make a point, but I still walked him through the entire episode. I thought his head was going to explode when I told him about Jose trying to fuck us over, and when I described the Jimenez boys showing up at Rose's I saw a vein on his temple throbbing above his clenched jaw. He was pissed.

The rest of the week was pretty uneventful until Callie went radio silent on Friday night. Since I'd arrived at the club on Monday, I'd been giving her a call every night, but doing whatever the fuck I wanted the rest of the time. I wasn't going on any runs, and the mechanic shop we ran as a legitimate business was pretty dead, so I didn't have a lot of work to do.

I was enjoying my freedom, barely thinking about Callie at all, when I called her phone Friday night and she didn't answer. There were a shit ton of people at the clubhouse that night, so I got distracted for a while, waiting for her to call back, but about an hour later I realized I still hadn't talked to her.

I spent the rest of that night pacing my room like a pussy, getting angrier and angrier that she hadn't answered her phone or called me back. It was like as soon as I couldn't get a hold of her I missed her like hell on fire.

At one point, I even called the boys down in Sac to drive by her house and make sure her car was there. Knowing that it was didn't seem to make a difference because my saddlebags were packed and ready before Slider pulled me aside and told me to suck it the fuck up.

They'd been watching me lose it the entire night, and they were all laughing at what they called my 'hysterics'. *Fucking pricks.* I knew that if it were Vera who wasn't answering her phone, Slider would be climbing the walls or already halfway to Sacramento by then.

When I finally got a hold of her, I was pissed as hell. If I had been in the same room as her, I don't know what I would have done.

She calmed me down with that sweet voice of hers, but when she told me she was having trouble sleeping, my anger disappeared. I wanted to make it better for her, but I wasn't sure how. She wasn't willing to move where I was, and I sure as shit wasn't going down to the Sacramento Chapter and leaving all my brothers behind.

Our options were pretty much nonexistent because of her stubbornness, and when I got off the phone, my frustration over being away from her—turned into being frustrated *at* her.

So even though I knew it was an asshole move, I distanced myself.

I didn't call as often as I had before.

I ignored the voice in the back of my head telling me that I missed her and she sure as hell was missing me.

On Monday, after I talked to her, I volunteered for a run.

I completely forgot to call her the day of her parents' funeral—which made me feel like a complete dick and distance myself even more.

I didn't know what the fuck I was doing.

I just kept fucking up, and I kept waiting for her to call me on it—almost wishing she would bitch me out.

But she didn't. She just took what I gave her and didn't make a single noise in complaint.

And that pissed me off even more.

It was no longer enough for her to need me. I wanted her to be willing to *fight* for me.

Chapter 33

Callie

A week went by with only sporadic calls from Asa, and I was starting to wonder if I'd done something to piss him off. It's not like I expected him to be calling me every hour on the hour, but what was once a phone call a night had turned into once a week. By the time that Friday rolled around, I was on pins and needles wondering if he was going to show up like he'd said he would.

He hadn't mentioned visiting again, but I was hoping that he was just going to surprise me. It was lame, and I knew it, but I held out hope that even though he was practically ignoring me, he still wanted to see me.

When I got home from school on Friday afternoon, I felt a small bit of panic flutter in my chest as I took in the apartment. Farrah had spent almost every day with me after school and the place was trashed. There were food wrappers stuffed in the couch, unidentified dried liquids all over the counter and the floor, and there was a weird but disgusting smell coming from the garbage bag that I'd been too lazy to take out.

I couldn't let Grease see how horrid I'd let the apartment get, so I threw my bag onto the couch and raced toward the bedroom to change clothes. I got about halfway down the short hallway before shaking my head frantically and going back to pick up my bag so I could hang it on the end of my bed where it belonged. If I was going to clean up, I couldn't leave shit lying around.

It took me two hours and what felt like five buckets of sweat to clean the apartment, but by the time I was done it looked almost as good as when Gram had cleaned it. I wanted it to be sparkling, and I knew it wasn't—but I just couldn't figure out what the hell I'd missed. Gram was a freaking magician. God, I wished I knew where her list was. She'd left it on the fridge, but I had no idea where it had gotten lost and I had a horrible feeling that it was in the disgusting trash somewhere.

There was no way I was rifling through that nastiness. When I took it to the dumpster, I'd found out that it had seeped into the bottom of the garbage can and started fucking fermenting. I'd had to clean the bottom of it with an entire container of disinfectant wipes, and the whole time I was reaching in the can—up to my waist—my heart was pounding. I just *knew* that Asa was going to walk in while I was hip deep in a freaking garbage can.

He didn't.

He also didn't show up when I took a long shower to clean off the sweat and garbage juice, or when I spent half an hour blow drying my hair.

He didn't show up when I was making dinner, or eating, or cleaning up.

And he didn't show up while I worked on what little homework I had while trying to watch a movie.

He didn't show up at all.

When I finally crawled into bed at midnight, my belly felt... hollow. I berated myself for imagining that he'd show up to surprise me, but I'd been so sure that if he hadn't been able to get away, he would have called. Those thoughts—the silly thoughts that convinced me that he'd never stand me up, had my heart racing in fear. I started imagining him getting into an accident on the way to see me and how awful I was for thinking the worst.

So I called him, just to make sure he was okay.

"Hey, babe," he answered on the third ring, sounding just fine.

"Hey, I was just… calling to say hi," I lied. I couldn't tell him that I'd been waiting all day for him, or that I'd been thinking he was dead on the side of the road somewhere. He hadn't even mentioned coming to see me in weeks, and I didn't want to look like a jackass for assuming.

"Oh, okay. Everything all right?" he asked gently, and then my stomach became one huge knot because I could hear him covering up the phone while he talked to someone else.

"I'm fine. I just thought you'd be visiting soon," I answered him, immediately slapping myself on the leg as I realized how needy I sounded.

"Yeah, shit's been pretty crazy around here. I haven't been able to get away. You know how it is…" his words trailed off, but I could hear people speaking in the background and then he chuckled.

That small laugh hit some sort of trigger, because all of a sudden I didn't feel like an asshole for calling him. All of a sudden, *he* was the asshole.

"Hey, Grease?" I called sweetly to gain his attention.

I knew the second he realized what I'd said because he inhaled harshly into the phone.

"The fuck?" he growled, almost giving me the reaction I was hoping for.

"The next time you tell me that you're going to be here, could you please let me know if you're not *actually* going to be here?" my tone hadn't changed, but there was no way he could miss the bite in my words.

"I didn't tell you I was coming down there, Calliope," he growled again, frustration evident in his tone.

"Yeah, you did. Before Gram came up—when you had your panties in a twist that I didn't answer my phone for a few hours. Remember? You were all fired up to see me and then you just disappeared off the face of the earth," I told him calmly, my heart racing.

"Ahhhhh FUCK! I forgot," he groaned, "I'll come down as soon as I can, Sugar. Okay?"

He was trying to apologize, but I was done with his bullshit. He'd left me in Sacramento, full of promises to visit, and he couldn't even be bothered to call me very often. *Fuck him.*

I took a deep breath, listening to him apologize and tell me he'd visit as soon as he possibly could. He said all the right things, and I wanted to believe him—but I didn't. I was just biding my time, and as soon as he paused to make sure I was still on the phone, I dropped my bomb.

"Don't bother coming back," I told him flatly and slid my phone closed as I heard his pissed off voice calling my name.

That was the reaction I'd been hoping for.

I lay awake again that night, but for once it wasn't because I was crying. Instead, I was making a list in my head of the things I needed to do.

First on the list was to party with Farrah, and anyone else I could think of, in Grease's apartment.

Second was to find a job and move the fuck out of there.

And third was to never stop moving or planning, so I didn't have to notice the ache in my chest.

Chapter 34

Grease

I was at a party at the club when I got Callie's call. Shit, every night at the club was some sort of drunken get together—but this one was different and I was thoroughly enjoying watching the women in the room. There was a clear hierarchy. It was one of the only times a year that sluts and old ladies would be anywhere near each other—the party for a new member—and it was fucking hilarious. I was waiting for a catfight to break out.

Dragon had gotten his cut earlier in the day, and he was weaving his way around as different brothers patted him on the back. Poor fucker had a massive healing tattoo on his back—but dealing with that shit was tradition. All of us had gone through it and survived—he would, too. I was looking at him when he stopped dead, staring across the room. When I followed his eyes, all I saw was Brenna and Vera—so I couldn't figure out what the hell he was looking at. He had the stupidest fucking look on his face, almost dazed— and I wondered what the hell he was doing. As soon as he started across the room, my phone rang in my pocket and I lost sight of him as I tried to make my way through the crowd to answer Callie's call.

By the time she hung up on me, I was in my room, and the whiskey and beer I'd downed at the party were like dead weight in my gut.

She was pissed, and I fucking *knew* she was going to do something stupid.

I had to get to Sacramento.

I stood up from my bed to find a bathroom and pack my shit, and the room fucking spun.

Great.

I stumbled my way to the door, trying to decide if I should just try and drive my bike down there—or wait until the morning when I knew I'd be sober enough that I wouldn't lay down my bike somewhere and fuck up the paint job.

I started calling Callie again, but every time I did, she sent me to fucking voicemail. I made it into the hallway just in time to see Dragon leading—fuck—Brenna into his room. Did he have a death wish?

I tried to stop him. I really fucking tried.

But I was so goddamn preoccupied with Callie's shit and just trying to stay standing that he bitched a little and I dropped it. The stubborn-as-hell look on his face told me he wasn't listening to a goddamn word I said anyway, and Brenna didn't even look at me as he pushed her gently into his room.

He wanted to fuck around with Poet's daughter?

Fuck it.

And why the fuck wasn't Callie picking up her phone?

I didn't remember making it to the bathroom, but I must have—because when I woke up the next day, at two in the goddamn afternoon with the mother of all hangovers I hadn't pissed myself.

Chapter 35

Callie

I looked around the apartment full of people with a small smile.

I'd set my plan into motion that morning, and so far it had worked perfectly.

I'd driven around our small neighborhood watching for 'help wanted' signs, and within fifteen minutes I'd found one in the window of a local fast food place. After giving them my application and doing an interview with a greasy guy not much older than I was, I had the job. I wasn't sure how they'd chosen me so fast, but I hoped it was because I was the only one that applied and not because the skeevy manager couldn't stop looking at my boobs. Either way, I'd walked out with a job that started the next week.

The next thing on my to-do list had been even easier to arrange. One call to Farrah and I'd been promised all the booze and weed I could handle. I left it to her to spread the word, and she hadn't disappointed. She showed up at seven o'clock that night and by nine, the entire apartment had been filled with people.

So, by nine-thirty I was sitting on my couch with friends of Asa's that heard about the party from Farrah's stepdad. I couldn't even *begin* to understand that type of fucked up parent-child relationship, but instead of worrying about my friend, I told myself it really wasn't any of my business. I was enjoying being social for the first time in months, and the male appreciation for my shorts and wide-necked white shirt wasn't anything to scoff at, either.

When Farrah walked by to grab more drinks, I pulled her onto my lap.

"I love you, Farrah," I told her dreamily.

"Ha! Okay, drunky," she answered back, patting me on the head.

"I'm not drunk." I gave her a squeeze, "I'm just happy I have a friend like you, who throws me awesome birthday parties."

Her eyes widened and her head snapped toward me.

"It's your birthday?" she asked me in confusion, and I couldn't help but laugh at how she wrinkled her nose.

"Yup!" I took a drink of the screwdriver she'd mixed for me. "Seventeen. Woo fucking hoo."

From the side of the couch I heard someone mumble, "Holy fuck. She doesn't *look* seventeen," and then what sounded like a thump before Michael warned, "Hands off, she's Grease's."

I ignored them both, my eyes still on Farrah.

"When's your birthday?" I asked her, trying to get her attention away from where Echo was standing across the room.

They'd been eyeballing each other the entire night, but I knew how Farrah felt about bikers. After watching one after another come into her mom's life—and bedroom—she had little respect for them. I knew she wanted a normal guy with a normal family, at least in her head. It seemed her hormones wanted something entirely different.

"Earth to Farrah!" I called, my voice rising above the music.

"Oh, what? Sorry. It was last month," she answered distractedly, her eyes darting between me and Echo.

"Dang. You're already seventeen?"

"No, I just turned sixteen," she told me with a shrug, "I got moved up a grade."

Michael stood up, pulling a cigarette out of his pocket, and she immediately slid off my lap and into his vacant seat. I couldn't help but tease her about her age as she eyeballed Echo who was flirting with some girl in the kitchen. He was way too old for her, but it's not like I could bitch at her about it. I didn't think I had any room to judge, especially when the front door slammed open and Asa stood in the doorway.

I wasn't surprised when he showed up—my last comment to him had been the equivalent of waving a red scarf in front of a bull. I just hadn't been sure if he'd cared enough to take the bait.

"Get the fuck outta my house!" he roared, throwing his helmet across the room, barely missing some guy who had passed out sitting on the floor.

Most of the people shot out the front door, and someone actually grabbed the passed out guy and dragged him out. Within seconds, the only people left in the house with us were Farrah, Michael, and Echo. Farrah had reached for me when Asa started yelling, and by the way her nails were digging into my thigh, she was scared out of her mind.

"It's fine, Farrah," I told her, never taking my eyes off Asa. "He's just pissed he wasn't invited."

I stood up and started picking up beer cans and garbage as everyone looked at me in shock. I wasn't sure if they expected me to be scared, or if they themselves weren't sure what to do, because no one moved.

"Everybody out," Asa rumbled again, his voice lower but no less menacing.

Farrah hopped off the couch and looked around her as if she wasn't sure what to do. I recognized the look of panic in her eyes, and I instantly felt like shit that I'd put her in the middle of our drama. At the very least, it had to be really uncomfortable for everyone.

"Hey, guys," I looked at Michael and Echo with weary eyes, my fight pretty much gone, "can one of you drive Farrah home?"

Echo offered to drive her, and I almost opened my mouth to argue, but one look at Asa had me shutting it again. I knew that Echo wouldn't let anything happen to Farrah, and I had to let that be enough. Asa wasn't going to wait much longer to have it out with me and they needed to get out of the apartment.

It was strange, but at no time was I afraid that Asa would physically hurt me. He'd protected me in so many other important instances that I couldn't even *imagine* him putting his hands on me in anger. However, words? He could definitely cut me with those.

Chapter 36

Callie

Once Farrah and the guys had left, it was completely silent in the apartment. Asa stood watching me as I cleaned up the beer bottles and garbage, but he didn't speak. I wasn't sure what to say to him, and I felt like anything I *did* say would be like poking a rabid dog—so I kept quiet. I swept and dusted and wiped down every surface I could until both the kitchen and the living room were spotless, but still, he said nothing.

When I was finally finished and putting the broom away, I heard him take a step behind me, so I spun toward him. He was standing away from the wall and had raised his arms until his hands were entwined behind his head, his elbows pointed toward the ceiling. I watched his biceps flex as he pushed his head back against his hands and my mouth went dry.

"What are you doing here?" I asked quietly, running my tongue between my lips and braces where they'd stuck together. "I thought you were busy this weekend."

"You knew I'd be here." He scowled at me, "You practically *begged* me to come."

I almost gasped in outrage but took a deep breath in through my nose instead. I wasn't going to turn into some screaming psycho, even if that's exactly what I wanted to do.

"I told you not to bother," I sneered back, crossing my arms over my chest.

"Yeah, you did. What the fuck was that about?"

"You don't want to be here—don't come. It's pretty simple," I answered flatly.

"I told you I had shit going on! That's my fuckin' job, Callie. How do you think I'm paying your fuckin' bills?" he thundered back, a vein in his neck bulging.

"Funny thing about that…. You sure showed up pretty fast even though you had shit to do," I answered, tilting my head to the side in mock confusion.

He raised his face and roared at the ceiling, his entire body tight with frustration.

When he finally dropped his head back down, I'd controlled my facial expression from the horror his explosion had caused, and was glaring at him with my brows raised.

"You done?" I asked calmly, as if my heart wasn't racing.

"Bitch, I'm paying for your shit. The food in your belly is mine. The power in your electronics is mine. The fuckin' gas in your car came from me! The fuck is your problem?"

Bitch?

I snapped.

"You can keep it, you fucking prick!" I screeched at him, grabbing a bunch of bananas off the counter and throwing them at his head. "I got a job! I don't need you! Fuck you!"

He ducked the bananas, but the apple that I threw right after hit him square in the jaw. We both stopped for a second, stunned, and then I was darting around the counter so we had a barrier between us.

He was stomping toward me, his chest heaving, but when I lifted my hand between us, he stopped instantly.

"You didn't even call me on the day of my parents' funeral," I told him quietly as a lump formed in my throat. "I needed you."

"Fuck, sweetheart. I'm sorry," he answered, rubbing the back of his neck. "I was on a run and I forgot."

"You forgot?" I asked incredulously.

"I know the world revolves around you Callie—"

"What?" I yelled, cutting him off.

"Fuck, that didn't come out right. But, shit, girl. It's not like I'm in Oregon sitting at a desk in some office! I've got people depending on me up there to keep their asses alive—I can't stop to call my girl because she's having a hard day." He ran a hand down his face. "I'm not explaining this very well."

"No. You pretty much just sound like an asshole at this point."

"Sugar, I was in the middle of something important and I fuckin' forgot. No excuse," he told me, lifting his palms out in front of him and then dropping them down at his sides. "I'm sorry as shit for it."

He *was* sorry. I was sure he'd fuck up again, but at that moment, I knew he was sorry for being so distant. His face was soft in a way that I'd seen before, watching me as if I'd break.

I couldn't comprehend what he was doing in Oregon that was so important, but he obviously felt strongly about it, so I wasn't going to question him. I didn't want to know about that part of his life. However, I was still freaking about one other thing in Oregon.

"Do you have a wife?" I blurted, mortified, but not willing to take back the question.

"What? No!" he laughed, looking at me like I was crazy.

"Well, Farrah's mom sees a guy named Gator and *he* has a wife!" I griped back, annoyed that he was laughing at me. "She only sees him once in a while! It sounded pretty fucking familiar!"

"Wait, you're friends with a club whore's kid?"

"Her name is Farrah, and don't call her mom a whore," I replied snottily.

"Gator's bitch? Wait, Natasha?" he asked, his voice raising an octave as his face paled.

"Yes. That's Farrah's mom," I answered with a nod, daring him to say anything further. "She only sees Gator once in a while because he has a *wife* and *kids* he has to get back to."

"Sweetheart, I think you're forgetting something," he told me in amusement.

"I'm pretty sure I'm not."

"I'm pretty sure you are," he said back, imitating my voice. "Only reason you aren't living with me is because you refused to move to Oregon." He laughed again. "Sugar, you're my old lady—not a whore on the side."

"Oh," I sighed, my doubts fading.

His words gave me a sense of calm even though he was laughing as he spoke. But I wasn't sure that I wanted to be considered anyone's 'Old Lady'. My mouth lifted in a small smile at his laughter. I couldn't help myself. His laugh was beautiful.

But even though I wasn't feeling the need to maim him with fruit, I still wasn't fully ready to forgive him. He'd pretty much ignored me for weeks and then showed up acting like *I* was the one who was in the wrong. *Um, no.*

"I'm going to bed," I told him dismissively, ignoring the shocked look on his face as I gave him a pat on the stomach, effectively ending our conversation. "I'll see you in the morning."

I knew I wouldn't get far.

I barely made it into the bedroom before he was wrapping an arm around my waist and pulling my back against his chest as he slammed the door behind us. His arm squeezed tight—almost to the point of pain—before he was using his chin to brush my hair away from my neck.

"You didn't tell me it was your birthday," he rumbled against my throat, placing sweet kisses there.

"How?"

"Michael was outside when I showed up," he answered, kissing me again. "You shoulda told me."

"It wouldn't have made a difference," I mumbled bitterly, pushing at his arm on my waist.

"Yeah, Sugar. It would've." He walked us to the bed, flipping me over onto my back before lying down on top of me, his forearms on each side of my head. "You have to tell me this shit, Callie. How'm I supposed to know if you don't tell me?"

"You knew about the funeral," I pointed out, tilting my head.

"Are you gonna keep throwing that shit in my face?"

I ignored his comment as if he hadn't even spoken.

"And when exactly was I supposed to tell you? The two fucking times you've called in the last three weeks when you barely spoke and couldn't wait to get off the phone with me?" I sniped back, raising my head from the comforter until our noses were practically touching.

"Don't gimme that shit, Calliope! The phone works both ways," he growled back, lowering his head until mine dropped back down to keep us from touching. "Only time you seem to call me is when your ass is in trouble!"

My eyes opened wide as I stared at him, stunned.

"*You* never seem to want to initiate contact, but you're pissed as fuck when *I* don't call. It's fuckin' bullshit, Callie," he growled at me, his brows drawn in frustration. "What the fuck do you expect?"

He was waiting for an answer, but I didn't have one. Instead my eyes closed in disbelief.

He was right.

"Fuck," I whispered, feeling like an insane bitch.

"Yeah, Sugar. 'Fuck' is right," he grumbled, dropping his forehead against mine.

We lay there silently, our breath mingling for long moments before he whispered against my mouth.

"Can we just drop this shit?" he asked me quietly, rubbing his nose along mine. "I fuckin' missed you."

Every emotion I'd been feeling since he'd left me instantly bubbled to the surface and I made a sound deep in my throat. I reached up to grab the back of his head, but I didn't have to pull him down because his mouth was already covering mine, his tongue pushing between my lips.

He tasted like mint and smoke and I couldn't get enough.

I slid my fingers into his hair and worked out the rubber band holding it back, making him groan as he slid us farther onto the bed. When we'd almost hit the other side, his lips ripped from mine and he leaned back, searching my face.

Whatever he saw there had him slowly pulling the wide neck of my t-shirt down my shoulder until one of my breasts was popping out the top, covered in a plain white strapless bra.

"Fuck me," he whispered, a grin forming on his face. "Is it wrong that I'm glad as fuck that you had a bra on out there with those assholes?"

He laughed hard as I punched him in the stomach, but his face quickly turned serious as he used my squirming to pull my shirt over my head. He didn't take the time to undo my bra, just pulled it down to my waist, but I didn't care. I was too busy watching his face as he undressed me. It didn't take long before I was completely naked, and I shook as his eyes took me in.

His nostrils were flared and his jaw tense as he ran a finger from my collarbone to my navel.

"Look at you. So beautiful," he whispered, running his fingers lightly over my nipples. "You scared? You're shaking, sweetheart."

"No, just wondering if you're going to be a prude again," I joked uncomfortably as I pushed at his vest with the tips of my fingers. "Are you finally going to get naked, too?"

That was all the prodding he needed to stand up from the bed and start stripping with a small smirk on his face. It took less than a minute for him to get completely naked, and he paused for a moment, completely unselfconscious to let me stare. His body was huge, with wide shoulders, a thick chest, and a lean waist that tapered down to heavily muscled thighs. He didn't have the steroid look that I'd seen so many times in Southern California—his body came from being naturally large and honed to perfection. *Holy shit.*

"Naked enough for you?" he said quietly before climbing onto the bed and pushing my legs apart. When he was braced above my body, he grabbed my thighs and pulled them up his sides so he could nestle between them.

"You're already wet," he mumbled into my throat, sliding his hands from behind my thighs to the slick skin between them. "Fighting turn you on, Sugar?"

"Shut it," I moaned back, arching into his hands.

"Ain't nothing wrong with that," he told me with a chuckle. "I was hard as a rock the minute you started spoutin' off in the kitchen."

He rubbed his fingers over me in a slow stroke and I felt like I was going to shoot off the bed. It had been so long since the last time he'd touched me—I was starved for him.

He stopped rubbing where I needed him and I made a sound of protest, but he cut it off with his mouth before moving his lips south.

"You had a party in my fuckin' apartment," he growled at me.

"Your friends were here!" I gasped, trying to move against his fingers, but failing to get what I needed.

"Doesn't fuckin' matter," he told me, biting me not so gently at the top of one of my breasts. "You don't have a bunch of fuckers in our house when I'm not here."

"Okay. Okay," I whimpered as I reached down to push at his hands.

"There were a lot of men out there, thinking they might have a chance at this," he rumbled into my skin, grabbing my wrists in one of his hands and moving them between our chests, causing my skin to break out in goose bumps. "So I'm gonna make sure they know."

I ran my hands around his chest and dug my fingernails into his back as he sucked hard at my neck, one of my heels involuntarily rubbing down the back of his thigh as I moaned.

"Know what?" I gasped, trying to stay at least a little coherent as my body arched again.

He moved his lips down my chest to the inside of my breast and bit down again, making me screech as he sucked hard at my skin. Once he was done, his eyes rose directly to mine.

"You're mine. Nobody touches you but me."

I was nodding my head in agreement, trying to pull him up my body, but he continued to move lower until his head was between my thighs.

"One more," he told me quietly, and my entire lower body froze.

"Asa..." I squeaked nervously, trying to close my legs even though his wide shoulders were holding me open.

His head snapped up at the fear in my voice and his eyebrows furrowed in confusion. "You think I'd hurt you, Callie?" he asked me, his voice a deep rumble that made my breath catch in my throat.

"N-No," I stuttered back, my hands fisted in the comforter.

"Then lay back and relax your legs," he ordered, his jaw tensing when I didn't immediately comply. "Relax, Callie."

When I'd finally relaxed enough that he could go back to what he was doing, my heart felt like it was going to beat out of my chest. I waited for the hard suction I was coming to expect, but I was completely startled when he latched onto the inside of my thigh as he pushed two fingers inside of me.

I came so hard, my body curled into a sitting position, my stomach muscles tightening to an almost painful level.

By the time I came down, he was kneeling between my legs with a condom in his hand.

"Put it on me," he ordered quietly, his voice still so deep it was almost unrecognizable.

"Okay." I reached for the condom and tried to roll it on him, but it wasn't working.

"It's inside out, Sugar. Turn it around," he told me patiently, running his fingers through my hair as I grew flustered.

I fumbled with it, turning it back and forth before finally pushing it down his length. As I finally got it into place, I heard what sounded like a deep breath of relief from above me.

"You could have just done it yourself," I snapped at him, tucking my chin into my chest and lying back like a sacrificial virgin. I was embarrassed and inept, and I hated how stupid he made me feel.

"Look at me, Calliope," he rasped, positioning himself before pausing to lift my chin so we were eye to eye.

"You're fuckin' gorgeous. You know that?" he asked as he slowly but firmly pushed his way inside.

He stopped halfway, grimacing, and I tried to relax as much as I could.

"Fuuuuck," he groaned, sweat rolling down his chest. "You're tight as hell, Callie."

"I'm sorry," I moaned as I rocked my hips against him. "I've only been with two other guys and neither was as big as you."

He paused and lifted his weight off my chest, wrapping his hand around my jaw.

"Shut the fuck up," he told me gently.

"I was just—"

"No. I don't ever want to hear about that shit. I sure as hell don't want to fuckin' hear it when I'm balls deep inside you."

"You're not ba—"

My words stopped on a sharp inhale as he pulled back and slammed back in, this time bottoming out inside me.

I arched my neck and back, relishing the feeling, but only seconds later he'd wrapped his fist in my hair so he could tip my head back toward him.

"You put the condom on me because I want your hands on me," he explained slowly between thrusts. "I want you touching me every goddamn second we're in the same room."

He let go of my hair and wrapped his hand gently around the side of my neck so his thumb rested beneath my chin. The other hand had moved down my thigh and was holding my knee forward until it was inches from my chest.

"You don't know how to do something? Then I'll teach you," he growled, leaning down to bite my lip. "You got the basics down, but

Sugar, when it's me and you? Only we know what we like together. And there ain't no way to figure that out unless we're actually doing it."

I grasped his hair in one hand, pushing it away from his face, and used my other hand to hold him against me, wrapping it tight around his back as his thrusts became faster and harder. I was groaning and sweating, making noises that he seemed to enjoy, judging by the grip of his hand on the underside of my knee.

"You feel so good," I smiled up at him, running my nails down his back.

"Yeah, Sugar. You too," he told me with a grin, leaning down to run his tongue over my bottom lip.

His hand slid from my knee and he leaned up a little so he could push his hand between our straining bodies. Zeroing in on my clit and pinching it with two fingers, he used the momentum of his thrusts to slide his hand up and down. "You're so fuckin' perfect," he groaned, his hips picking up speed. "You love it when I leave my mark on you. Don't you—?" his words broke off with a low groan as my hand tightened in his hair.

I was coming again, and my back arched completely off the bed as all of my muscles tightened and a low keening came out of my throat.

Between the clenching of my pussy, my nails digging into his back, and my fist pulling at his hair, I tipped him over the edge with me.

I was still catching my breath as he pulled out and laid his head flat on my chest between my breasts.

"I love it when you put your fingers in my hair," he sighed, lazily sucking a nipple into his mouth as I ran my fingers through the hair in question. "Feels so fuckin' good."

His eyes closed for a while as his breathing slowed, and I realized that he had just driven all day. He must have been exhausted. I closed my eyes, and was seconds away from falling asleep when his head popped up from my chest and he quickly rolled off the bed.

I pulled the blankets back over me, intent on falling asleep, when I felt cool air rush over me, followed by a stinging slap on my ass.

I twisted my head to him with a startled look on my face, but he just raised one eyebrow at me.

"Told you not to call me Grease," he chastised, pulling on his boxer briefs. "Go in and go to the bathroom, yeah?"

I watched him, confused as hell as he walked out of the room, and then I could hear him checking the locks on the front door. I hadn't moved while he was gone, and when he realized I was still lying in the same spot, he looked at me in exasperation before pulling me out of bed to stand on my feet.

"Go to the bathroom," he ordered seriously.

"I don't have to go. What the heck is wrong with you?" I asked, shaking my head in confusion.

"I take care of you, yeah?" he asked, kissing my forehead. "You need to go to the bathroom after you're done with sex. Just trust me on this."

I stood silently for a moment before a vaguely-remembered conversation with some girls at school popped into my head. When realization dawned, my face blushed a deep red.

"Callie," he called from where he was propped against the headboard, "I figure that's probably something a chick learns from her ma. Didn't know if she had that talk with you. Stop overthinking it and go."

He checked his phone and then slid down the bed with a sigh as I walked toward the bathroom.

But I couldn't help overthinking it.

He was right—my mom *hadn't* had that talk with me.

I wondered what other conversations I was going to go without before pushing it to the back of my mind where everything else was hidden.

I finished following his directions and climbed back in bed with him. When the heat of his body sank deep into my back, I closed my tired eyes—ignoring the sounds of the apartments around ours.

"Happy Birthday, sweetheart," he whispered with a kiss to the back of my head.

I slept through the night for the first time in three weeks.

Chapter 37

Grease

It felt good to wake up with Callie. It felt even better that she hadn't put any clothes on before climbing back into bed the night before.

She was sprawled out on her belly with one hand on my chest and her knee raised up where it was digging into my hip. She'd been restless as she slept, but she hadn't woken up in the night, and I wondered when her nightmares had stopped. The nightmares were one of the things I'd worried about while I was gone, and the guilt over not being there to take care of her afterward was another reason I'd distanced myself.

I rubbed my hand over my beard. I'd been a dick.

Half of me was irritated as hell that she refused to move and the other half felt guilty for leaving her ass in Sacramento while I did my shit in Oregon. The whole situation was a fucking powder keg, and I knew at some point it was going to blow. We couldn't keep living like we were. Neither one of us wanted to be away from the other—but it didn't look like anything was going to change in the near future which meant I was going to have to get my shit together.

I was going to have to figure out a way to make it work, because I sure as hell wasn't going to give her up.

Her mouth was open as she slept, and I got a good look at the way her braces were pushing her lips away from her gums. They looked like some sort of medieval torture device in her mouth. I wasn't sure how she smiled with that shit, but only seconds after I thought about it, she was doing just that as she woke up.

"Hey," she whispered, her eyes opening into slits.

Fuck she was cute when she just woke up. How had I forgotten shit like that?

"Morning, Sugar."

"Do you have to leave today?" she asked me, straightening her legs so she could curl into my chest. "You had things going on this weekend."

She lowered her eyes as she spoke and her body was stiff against mine.

"Nah. I moved some shit around. I need to be back up by Monday—Tuesday if you give me a reason to stay," I mumbled, distracted by the way her body softened against mine.

Her tits were pressed up against my side, one of them practically resting on my chest. I pulled my hand from behind my head and went straight for it, pinching it lightly as her leg slid up my thigh.

"I'm freaking awesome. There's your reason," she told me lightly, her hand sliding down my chest to run over my stomach.

"You're not lying," I agreed, letting go of her nipple and pushing her face up to mine. Just as I was about to kiss her, her eyes opened wide and her chin hit my chest hard making me grunt. "The fuck?"

"I haven't brushed my teeth!" she mumbled, barely opening her mouth.

I barked out a laugh at her and shook my head when I realized she was serious. "Neither have I. Now kiss me," I ordered.

She shook her head and opened her mouth on my chest, biting down lightly on my nipple and then sucking it into her mouth. I groaned, reaching down to pump my dick once before sliding my hand up her leg.

"Well, fuck, Sugar. If you aren't gonna kiss me then do something else with that mouth," I groaned as she ran her hand further down my stomach and underneath my boxers.

She pushed her body up until she was sitting on her feet by my side and leaning over me, pushing my boxers down my hips clumsily with one hand, the other hand still rubbing up and down. When I saw her lean down, I grabbed her hips and pulled her over me before she could make contact. She made a startled shriek as I situated her ass above my face, and immediately started squirming. Her tits pushed into my stomach as she tried to lift her hips, so I slapped her ass in warning and she froze.

"Stop moving, Callie," I warned, "you knee me in the face and we're gonna have problems."

I ran my hands up the backs of her thighs, my thumbs finally meeting right over her pussy, and she moaned deep in her throat, dropping her face against my hip.

"I need a shower," she whispered against me. "Let me take a shower first."

"You don't need a shower," I told her, running one of my fingers over her and watching her grow soft and wet.

"Yeah. You can't—" she paused on a quick inhale and then started jabbering again, "Your face is—"

She wasn't worried about a fucking shower. I laughed lightly. She was self-conscious about the goddamn angle.

"Baby, I've seen you. Ain't nothing I'm seeing now any different than what I've seen before," I reminded her gently. Shit, I could practically feel how hot her face was. My girl and her blushes—cute as fuck.

I didn't give her any more time to worry.

I used my thumbs to pull her apart, tilted my chin up, and ran my tongue over her clit. She tasted good, and I ran my tongue all over her, taking it all in. When her legs started shaking, I pulled away, using my teeth to pull at her lips.

"Put your mouth on me," I growled at her, squeezing her thighs in my hands.

I heard her inhale sharply, but less than a second later she was pushing up with her hands until she was braced above my hips. It made her back arch, and I knew she finally wasn't thinking about how she looked from this angle. *Christ, what a view.*

I waited until I was in her mouth, her tongue wrapping around me before I started in on her again. It didn't take long before she was outta her mind, sliding her knees away from my shoulders and riding my face while she sucked and bobbed her head, her fingernails digging into my thighs.

When she came, she moaned against my dick and brought me with her.

As soon as she was done, she rolled off me, embarrassed, and I laughed weakly. Shit, she may have sucked all of my energy out through my dick; my legs felt like Jell-O.

She scrambled off the bed, jostling me, and I rolled over to watch her stumbling out of the room. Her ass was round and flexed every time she moved, and my mouth watered until I noticed it had a perfect red handprint on it. *Whoops.* I hadn't meant to slap her that hard, but I smiled a little when I saw it. I wasn't sorry—it'd gotten me what I wanted.

I stretched when I heard her turning on the shower and hopped out of bed to join her.

She screeched when I pulled back the curtain and shampoo started rolling down her face and running into her eyes. She was slapping at me blindly as I climbed in, and I couldn't help laughing as bubbles ran into her mouth, making her gag.

"Rinse that shit out, crazy!" I told her, pushing her back into the spray.

"You scared the shit out of me!" she griped, still spitting and sputtering.

"You knew I was here," I replied, running my hands over her wet tits as she rinsed her hair.

"I didn't know you were going to *follow* me!"

"You're wet and naked, I'm there," I told her seriously, reaching my thumb up to wipe gently at the huge hickey on her neck. "Look at you, with my bite marks all over you."

"Yeah, that doesn't look trashy or anything," she grumbled, rolling her eyes.

"I don't give a fuck. You have my mark on you—men think twice."

"Yeah, well, I wanted to find an orthodontist this week and I start my job. I'm going to look like an idiot."

"What the fuck is that about?" I asked her as I gently pushed her out of the way and pushed my head under the spray. I had to bend my knees to get under it, twisting my body awkwardly.

She laughed a little as she self-consciously lathered up her legs and started shaving, her back toward me like she could hide what she was doing.

"I want to get these braces off."

"They ready to come off? I thought you had like six more months?" I asked as I soaped up my beard.

"Four more—but it's expensive as hell to keep them on. My teeth are fine without them."

"I'll pay for them, Callie. Don't act like I don't take care of you."

"I'm not saying that." She shook her head as she rinsed off her razor, coming so close to my balls with it that I felt them drawing up as I scrambled backward.

"I'm not gonna get you," she snickered at me, waving the razor around. "It'll cost like, thousands of dollars to finish out the next four months with no insurance."

My gut burned and I said nothing as I finished soaping up the rest of my body. There was no way I could pay for that shit.

"It's not a big deal, baby," she told me, dropping her razor on the side of the tub and raising her hands to my face. "My teeth are straight, I don't need them."

No matter what she said, I knew that she needed those four extra months, but there was nothing I could do about it. It pissed me off.

"Sorry," I told her roughly, pushing her arms off me and turning my body away from her to rinse off.

She was silent for a moment before wrapping her arms around me from behind and squeezing. "Not a big deal, Asa," she told me quietly before climbing out of the shower.

Chapter 38

Callie

Asa was quiet for the rest of the day, and I knew it bothered him that he couldn't pay for my braces. I wasn't sure how to snap him out of the funk he was in, so I didn't say anything more about them. It was stupid; I didn't want them anyway. They made me look like a twelve–year-old, they got food stuck in them, and they cut the shit out of my cheeks if I wasn't careful. Besides, it hadn't been *my* idea to get them in the first place. My teeth hadn't been that bad—the top ones had a little gap between them and the bottom ones had been a little crooked, but it hadn't bothered me. It was my parents who'd decided that they suddenly had enough money for orthodontia, so I *had* to get them fixed.

I wished I hadn't even brought it up to Asa; I could've just had them taken off and then told him I didn't need them anymore. Unfortunately, there was no way for me to get the appointment without telling him I needed around five hundred dollars to pay for it. I hadn't gotten to that part before he'd gone weird, and I hadn't wanted to say anything else. I decided to wait on that conversation, hoping to talk to my Gram and see if she could pitch in before I said anything more about it.

Instead, I walked on eggshells around him that day and jumped him at bedtime.

By the next day, things were back to normal—well, normal for *us*.

We spent the weekend like an old married couple and I loved it. We went to the grocery store and bought a ton of food, rented a Western

TV series from the movie store, and spent the rest of the time curled up on the couch watching it when we weren't fucking on every surface in the apartment.

I didn't answer my phone except to let Gram know that Asa was with me for the weekend and to let Farrah know that he hadn't killed me and dumped my body somewhere—her words not mine.

The only downsides to our weekend were the discussions about my job. Asa didn't want me working—though his reasons changed with each conversation until he'd compiled a list that was as long as my arm. I'd be out late on nights I had to close. School was more important. I'd have to work when he or Gram came to visit. I'd come into contact with tweekers and who knows what else. People robbed fast food places all the time. He'd even tried to say that I'd get sick more often because I'd be coming into contact with too many people—which made me comment that maybe I shouldn't be going to school, either—*that* shut him up for about ten minutes.

I worked my first shift on Monday night after school while he sat at a table in the front of the restaurant, glaring at anyone and everyone. It was funny, and a little embarrassing, but having him there also settled my first day nerves so much that I dreaded when he wouldn't be there anymore. I also began to understand his argument about working while he was visiting. I resented the time I had to spend away from him at school and work when I had so little time with him to begin with.

Our disagreement never came to a resolution before it was time for him to leave, but we were both unwilling to make it a huge deal. The fight that had goaded him to visit had given both of us perspective, and neither one of us wanted to end the weekend on bad terms. We didn't know when he'd be able to visit again—and having a tantrum wasn't going to get the same reaction the next time. He couldn't just drop everything to deal with me, and it wasn't fair of me to expect it.

On Tuesday morning, we stood outside while he stuffed a few things into his saddle bags. The scene seemed eerily familiar. It made my stomach turn as I remembered how he'd acted after he left last time. My arms were wrapped around my waist, and I was trying not to cry, but my throat had a huge lump in it and I could feel my nose tingling with repressed tears.

"Hey, Sugar," he called gently, pulling me against him with a hand at the back of my neck. "I'll be back as soon as I can, yeah?"

"Okay," I answered, tucking my face into his chest. "You'll call, right?"

"Yeah, baby, I'll call." He pulled my face away from him and kissed my forehead, then reminded me, "You call, too. None of that bullshit like before."

I snorted, and then started giggling as his brows rose in surprise.

"Did you just snort?" he asked me with a grin, wrapping his arms around my waist and lifting me off the ground. "Like a little piglet?"

"I'll call!" I screeched as he swung me around, his beard tickling my neck as he pressed his face in.

When he finally put me down, we were smiling, but it didn't last long before both our faces fell. I wasn't sure how I looked, but his jaw was tense and his eyes stony as he reached over to grab his helmet.

"Call me tonight and let me know you got there, okay?" I asked softly.

He gave a nod, watching me closely. Suddenly, his hand shot out and grabbed my jaw tightly, pulling my face to his. He kissed me hard, biting at my lips urgently while his hands grabbed and pushed at my clothes. I ran my hands through his hair softly as he practically inhaled me, trying to calm him down, but as soon as he grabbed the backs of my legs and lifted me until they were wrapped around his waist—I lost my calm.

We were frantic. One of his hands fisted the back of my shirt while the other went up the front, ripping the cups of my bra down so he could pinch at my nipples. I fisted his hair in response, causing him to groan, and reached the other hand down the back of his hoodie so I could dig my nails into the only skin I could reach. It didn't matter that we were standing in front of the apartment complex where anyone could see us—we were desperate.

He started back toward the stairs while we kissed, but he hadn't made it to the first step when his phone started ringing and vibrating in his pocket.

"Shit," he mumbled into my mouth, sliding his hand out of my shirt to pull the phone out of his pocket.

I moved my mouth to his neck as he answered.

"Grease," he barked, tilting his head to the side and squeezing my ass with his free hand.

"Dragon, don't do anything stupid." He paused for a few moments while I continued to grope him. "Brother, I fuckin' warned you who she was."

He was quiet for a moment, and in the silence I bit down hard on the skin where his shoulder met his neck. He inhaled sharply and started rocking me against him, stumbling backward until his back met the wall, and then groaned deeply as I started to suck.

"I'm on my way. Don't do anything fuckin' stupid before I get there," he snapped before closing his phone and stuffing it back into his pocket.

"Fuck me," he groaned, pulling me harder against him as I used my teeth again.

He grabbed the back of my hair and pulled me away from his neck, tipping my head back so far that I had to look down to see his face.

"You're fuckin' trouble, you know that?" he rasped, squeezing his fist so my hair pulled sharply again.

"Let's go back upstairs," I whimpered, pulling against his hand so I could get my mouth on him. "I'll ride you so hard."

I wasn't even sure what I was saying, but I didn't care. I'd say or do anything at that point, I was so turned on. My hips were frantic against him, sliding and rubbing but never hitting the right spot to get me over the edge.

"Sweetheart," he groaned, stilling the movement of my hips with his hand, "I gotta fuckin' go. Shit's about to hit the fan in Oregon."

My mouth dropped open and my eyes popped wide as he pushed at my legs. When I dropped them down, I almost tripped as I tried to move away from him.

"Seriously?" I griped at him, slapping at his hands as he tried to catch me.

"Fuck, Callie!" he roared, grabbing one of my hands and pressing it against his very hard cock. "It's not like I want to ride my goddamn bike like this!"

"Well, then don't!" I snapped back, trying to pull my hand away.

He let go of me, but quickly wrapped his arms around my waist before I could storm off.

"Sugar, I've got a friend that fucked up. His shit is so fucked up, he's lucky if he sees daylight again," he told me seriously, the tone of his voice causing me to pause in my struggle. "I gotta get up there and help him figure his shit out."

Dammit. He wasn't going to stay.

I slumped against him dejectedly and hit my head against his chest repeatedly as he rubbed my back, calming down my overheated body. Once both of our heartbeats had slowed, I tilted my face up to him, still pouting. He immediately swooped in for a kiss with a small smile on his face.

The kiss was sweeter and deeper than it had been before. It wasn't full of lust and desperation.

It was a kiss goodbye.

"It's you and me against the world, yeah?" he whispered, smoothing my hair away from my face. "We won't be doing this shit forever. Just gotta be patient."

He let me go, and it took all of my willpower not to beg him to stay just one more day. One more day wouldn't have helped anything, and I knew that we would have to go through the exact same thing all over again. So I gave him a trembling smile and got in my car, unable to say a word past the lump in my throat.

This time when I drove away, he didn't follow me to school. His mind was already focused on whatever was happening to his friend, and I was thankful for it.

I cried the whole way to school, but as soon as I got there, I wiped off my face, pulled up my big girl panties, and acted like I was fine.

Eventually, I was.

Chapter 39

Callie

Asa was true to his word and called whenever he had the chance. He never brought up the problem with his friend and I assumed that he had gotten it all straightened out. I was the queen of burying my head in the sand, refusing to deal with anything outside of my own little world.

Thankfully, there had been a little left over in my parents' bank account when it was transferred to Gram, so she'd been able to pay for me to get my braces off. She drove up to visit me when I had my appointment even though she didn't agree with what I was doing. It was silly, I didn't mind going by myself, but I think she was afraid that I'd feel bad that my mom wasn't with me. Even though I hadn't kept them on as long as I should have, we still celebrated with caramel apples and popcorn—two things that had been forbidden—once they came off.

Gram knew just how to cheer me up without even trying. With my parents gone, she was the one person who knew me better than anyone else. She knew what my reaction would be before I did, and she went out of her way to make sure that nothing within her power had the opportunity to upset me. Thus, the visit when I had my braces taken off. The braces that my parents had saved up for and been so proud of. I hadn't been able to brush it off like I'd pretended.

After her visit, Asa came to see me again and was able to stay an entire week. He had something going on with the Sacramento Chapter, so he was gone a lot of the time, but I didn't care. Knowing that he was just minutes away for an entire week had me practically dancing through work and school. Even the drama with Farrah that week hadn't brought me down.

Farrah's mom had a falling out with her man, and apparently had gone off the rails. She was partying like it was the end of the world, and Farrah had to deal with junkies and drunken assholes pounding on her locked bedroom door at all hours of the night. There must have been a breaking point—something must have happened—because soon after, Farrah was hot and heavy with Echo and staying with him more than she was home. I tried to talk to her about it, but she was shut up tighter than a bank vault. She'd just roll her eyes and tell me she couldn't deal with the drama, changing the subject before I learned anything worth knowing. I was a shit friend, because when she changed the subject? I let her.

Because I wasn't willing to upset the life raft I was on by taking on her problems.

I was an asshole.

That time, when Asa left, I wasn't as lost. I'd made a pretty steady life for myself in Sacramento, and I was finally comfortable in my surroundings. I knew the neighborhood I was living in, I had a best friend that hung out at the apartment almost every day, I had a decent job that gave me a little bit of spending money, and I knew that Asa and I were solid.

I got good at paying bills and taking out the trash. I figured out which Laundromats always had wet clothes in their washing machines for hours on end and which ones were the cleanest. I figured out how to buy groceries on a budget without living on ramen noodles, and I cut coupons and filled a box in my bedroom closet with free toiletries that would take me years to use up.

I figured out how to take care of myself.

I finished out my junior year of high school, and instead of taking a break, decided to take a few classes that summer. I'd taken extra credits in San Diego, and it left me with a surplus that, with the help of a few summer classes, had me graduating a full year earlier than I was supposed to. Farrah was irritated that I wasn't going to be able to spend the summer laying out by Echo's apartment complex's dilapidated pool, but I knew if I had too much time on my hands, my carefully constructed life would crumble. I couldn't allow myself to slow down for fear that I would start thinking about things that were better left forgotten.

Once she realized that I couldn't be swayed, we settled into a life not unlike the one we'd had during school. She was usually at my apartment by the time I got home, and hung out until I had to go to work. I ended up making her a key, and a lot of nights I'd get home to her sleeping on my couch. She rarely went home anymore—the only time she made herself go there was during Asa's visits, which left me feeling both ecstatic that he was there and guilty that she wasn't staying.

My life became a monotonous schedule, broken up only by my graduation from high school and Asa's visits. I planned everything around them, eventually making every visit an event that I spent weeks planning for. I began waxing my legs, armpits and girly bits the week before I knew he was scheduled to come. I cleaned the house from top to bottom and filled the fridge in preparation for another person sharing my space.

We became more and more comfortable with each other, bickering about stupid things and feeling free to vent our frustrations. "The Fight", as I remembered it in my mind, was slowly forgotten as we settled more into our relationship. I was no longer worried that he would forget me once he was in Oregon, and he no longer stressed about how I was handling life alone. We turned into a couple like any other long-distance couple, spending time every day to talk or text each other, and fucking like rabbits when we were in the same zip code.

Over time, my life became measured by how long it had been since I'd seen him. It was a sequence of, "two weeks until Asa comes" or "only two days since Asa left".

My world revolved around him, even when he was hundreds of miles away.

If I still woke up occasionally from nightmares, I pretended like I didn't. When Cody called and didn't sound right, I bolstered him until he sounded normal, and when I hung up I pushed the conversations to the back of my mind. I didn't think of my parents, or the worst twenty-four hours of my life. I didn't wish for things I couldn't have.

I refused to worry about how deep Farrah was falling in with Echo.

I refused to get upset when Gram visited and she had to go back to San Diego, leaving me alone once again.

And I *absolutely* refused to acknowledge that over the course of that year, Asa's visits became further and further apart.

Chapter 40

Callie

My eighteenth birthday began like any other day of the year. I had a hard time making a big deal out of becoming an adult when I'd already been one for so long.

I'd been promoted to manager of the restaurant I worked at right after I'd graduated. I thought the owner was an idiot for making a seventeen-year-old a manager after a few months, but I wasn't about to argue with him. The boob ogler had been caught grabbing the asses of other employees and was fired, and I think the owner just didn't want to deal with hiring someone older. All of the employees were in high school, or drop outs, and I was the cream of the crop—as sad as that was.

So I spent my birthday at work, figuring out time sheets for the coming weeks. It was a freaking headache to do. This girl wanted certain days off to go to school functions, that one wanted to only work Tuesdays and Thursdays because she had church shit on the others. It went on and on until figuring out the schedule was like putting together a puzzle that never quite lined up.

By the time I arrived home, I had a headache from hell and I was sweaty from the drive since my car's air conditioning was busted and Asa hadn't visited in almost three months to fix it. I was irritated and tired and I just wanted to strip down to my underwear and pass out with a fan pointed at my bed.

I almost missed the motorcycle parked at the end of the parking lot.

Almost.

I ran up the stairs, cursing that while I'd had my monthly waxing session the week before, I hadn't cleaned up the house or packed the fridge. My heart raced as I opened the door, and my jaw dropped when I saw the amount of people in the apartment… and the other shit.

There were streamers crossing the ceiling, posters on the walls, and balloons hooked to anything heavy enough to hold them from flying to the ceiling. It looked like a party store threw up.

Farrah.

I stopped in the doorway, and no one noticed me as I searched the crowd for Asa. Farrah was sitting on Echo's lap on the couch, Michael was smiling down at some girl I'd never seen before, and a few of my co-workers were in the hallway making out. I was going to have to rework the entire schedule to make sure they weren't on at the same time. *Dammit.*

I found Asa standing in the kitchen, laughing with a pretty girl with blonde hair that hung down almost to her ass. She was pretty, *really* pretty, but the minute she put her hand on his chest she looked like a haggard bitch from hell to me. I saw red.

I slammed the door behind me, causing most of the occupants to turn in my direction, but I only cared about one person's attention. His head swung in my direction, and he smiled huge until he saw the scowl on my face.

If I had been a cartoon, smoke would have come out of my ears as I swung my purse at Farrah. She caught it as if she'd anticipated the move, and watched with a smirk as I stalked across the living room and into the kitchen.

"You," I pointed to the girl with Asa. "Get the fuck out of my house."

She laughed uncomfortably and glanced up at Asa.

Oh. No. She. Didn't.

"Bitch, you look at *me*," I sneered at her, causing her head to whip back around. "He's not gonna help you."

"Calliope—" Asa's voice was a warning I didn't heed.

"Get. Out. Of. My. Apartment," I told her through gritted teeth. "Unless you want me to rip that pretty hair out of your head when I beat the shit out of you."

"I—"

"You—nothing," I cut her off, pretending to stutter. "It's *my* house and..." I pointed my finger to Asa, "*my* man. You put your hands on him, you deal with me. Now *go*."

She looked between the two of us, trying to calculate her odds—but when I took another step toward her, she scurried toward the front door, dragging the girl by Michael with her. I watched her go and then pulled my arm from Asa when he tried to pull me to him.

His face was tight in anger when I glanced up at him, and I scowled until I heard Farrah clapping from the living room.

"Bravo!" she called, giggling. "I was hoping she'd stay so we could beat her ass. I got your back, sister!" She was drunk and swaying, and I couldn't keep a smile off my face from her antics. *Fucking goofball.*

The room was still quiet, watching Asa and me closely, so I raised my hands in the air and shook my hips from side to side.

"Nothing to see here, folks!" I called out with a derisive smile. "Drink up and be merry! Happy fucking Birthday to me!"

I walked back to my room with Asa less than a foot behind me. When I got there, he slammed the door behind us and I spun around in surprise.

"What? I thought that's what we're doing now," he rumbled,

slipping his cut off his shoulders as he stalked me across the room. "Slamming fuckin' doors and having bitch fits when I haven't seen you in three goddamn months."

"She was all over you!" I sniped back as he pulled his t-shirt over his head. "What the fuck are you doing?"

"She wasn't all over me. The chick came with Michael and you just fuckin' cock-blocked him."

I stood next to the bed, stuttering as he slipped off his boots and socks. He was even bigger than the last time I'd seen him, and apparently he'd had a few of his tattoos touched up, too, because the one on his back was even bigger and creeping up his neck. I soaked him in with my eyes, not coming out of my stupor until he was right in front of me and pulling my work polo over my head.

"What the hell?" I gasped. "We've got like fifteen people in the living room!"

"I don't give a shit," he replied, leaning down to take my mouth in a wet kiss as he unsnapped my bra. "They know what's good for them, they'll stay out there... even when they hear you screaming."

He undressed me as I tried to squirm away, but I gave a halfhearted attempt at best. It had been too long since I'd felt him, and I couldn't truthfully make myself care that we had an apartment full of people.

He tossed me on the bed and I scrambled up and off of it as he undid his belt and pants. I started for the door like I was going to leave, but didn't make it far before he was lifting me by the waist and tossing me back—his jeans falling farther and farther down his hips as we struggled.

When he'd finally pinned me down, my hands were captured in one of his above my head, and I was in nothing but my underwear.

Somehow he'd even stripped off my shoes and socks. His pants had completely fallen down at that point, and he kicked them off his legs without moving from his position above my body.

"You miss me, baby?" he rasped, running his nose along my collarbone and neck.

"I did, until I saw you in my kitchen with that skank," I sniped back, pulling on my arms.

"Wasn't doing anything with her and you know it," he whispered, biting my lower lip gently. "Why would I want that, when I've got this?" he asked with a rock of his hips, the friction causing me to rock into him.

"Don't let them touch you," I whispered back. "I turn into a psycho."

"Yeah, Sugar." he told me with a chuckle, still rocking against me, "It's hot as fuck, too."

He pushed my hands into the mattress as he leaned down to kiss me, pushing his boxers off his hips as he bit and sucked at my lips. I used my toes to help him push them down, grabbing his lip in my teeth as I growled into his mouth. I could still see him laughing with that girl.

He pinched one of my nipples hard, making me gasp, and as soon as I let go of his lip, his tongue plunged inside my mouth in a quick thrust. His hand had let go of mine, but before I could grab him, he flipped me over to my belly. He leaned back on his knees and jerked my hips up, ripping my underwear down my thighs until they were stretched tight between my knees.

I didn't get a word out before he slapped my ass hard, making me screech in response.

"Shut it," he hissed at me, slapping my ass again. "You want your little friend running in here?"

He waited for a response, pausing to put a condom on before rubbing my ass firmly, causing me to gasp into the comforter.

"No," I moaned, and he slapped his hand down again.

"I get here, and first thing you do is cause a scene." *Slap.* "You start bitching and treating me like shit for no reason." *Slap. Slap.*

He leaned down over my body, which made my ass throb in response, and whispered in my ear.

"I love you. Don't want *anyone* but you," he rasped as he slid easily inside me.

I whimpered as he rocked back and pushed my body toward his. He'd never told me he loved me before, so I hadn't said it, either. All of a sudden, I was overwhelmed by all of the emotions running thorough me. Love, anger, annoyance, surprise, and lust flooded my brain like a tidal wave and I felt tears rolling down my face as he ground his hips into my sore ass.

"You gotta stop pushing at me baby," he whispered, kissing at my neck. "I love you. It's hot as fuck, but I wanna come home to you and not fight about the goddamn house or your piece of shit car."

I tried to focus on his words, but he ran his tongue down my back, making me shiver and lose my train of thought. He felt so good against me—surrounding me—that the throb of my ass was barely noticeable as I pressed my hips harder against him, my nails digging into the comforter beneath us.

"You have to tell me what's really going on, Calliope," he told me, resignation in his voice.

"No!" I gasped as he pulled out of me completely, but went quiet as he gently turned me over to my back. He rubbed away the tears on my face with his thumbs, and kissed me softly before pushing back inside.

His eyes met mine as he glided back and forth, and I didn't look away, even as he picked up speed and our headboard started slamming against the wall.

"Tell me you love me," he growled, before leaning down to suck hard on the side of my breast. "Tell me you're mine."

"I love you," I sobbed back, wrapping my fists in his hair.

His hips paused, leaving him only halfway inside me before he ordered again, "Tell me you're mine."

"I'm yours. I'm yours!" I pleaded, sliding one hand to his shoulder and digging my nails into his back until he slammed back inside me.

"That's right, baby. You're mine and I'm yours." He leaned down and kissed me deeply while one of his hands slid between us to pinch and pull at my clit.

"Okay," I responded, and then my voice broke as I moaned deep and long as I came.

"So beautiful," he rasped as he sped up inside me.

I lay there in a daze and watched him, the veins in his neck bulging and his thrusts becoming short as he reached his own orgasm.

He was the beautiful one.

Chapter 41

Grease

If she only knew what I'd been through over the past few months, I think things would've been different. Shit was happening in the club that I couldn't tell her about because I was scared as hell that it would push her right back to where she'd been when I'd met her—scared of her own shadow. So I'd been pissed as hell I couldn't see her, making the long-ass drive when I could—but it didn't seem to matter. She'd still seen it as abandonment, growing angrier with me at every visit, and I'd had to just take it because I wasn't willing to explain it to her.

She didn't know that being away from her had been like needles constantly stinging under my skin, and I'd had to work out like crazy so I could actually fall asleep at night.

I swallowed hard past my tight throat as Callie curled into my chest. For the first time in months, her whole body was relaxed against mine.

Thank fuck.

I had my girl back.

Chapter 42

Callie

We barely made it out of the bedroom that night. I didn't want to move away from him for a second—I was feeling too raw—but eventually we had to make an appearance. It was my birthday party, after all.

My face flamed in embarrassment as Farrah hooted with glee, but thankfully Echo said something into her ear that made her straighten her shoulders and glare at him, ending her amusement. I wondered what exactly they'd heard. I was strangely unembarrassed about the spanking and more concerned with the fact that they may have heard Asa tell me he loved me for the first time. Out of the entire episode, that was the one thing I fiercely wanted to keep private. Only one person made a comment after that, something about the thumping of the headboard, but the look Asa gave him was enough to make him stop mid-sentence.

The only people left in the house were Aces and their women, and I was glad that I didn't have to worry about socializing with a bunch of people I barely knew. I couldn't make myself leave Asa's side, and it reminded me of the needy girl I'd been the year before, but I refused to stop. I needed to touch him, and if his arm wrapped tightly around my shoulders was any indication, he was feeling that need, too.

I watched Farrah and Echo argue quietly for a while before she headed toward me, pulling me away from Asa as she marched into the kitchen. I didn't have a chance to say a word before she started speaking fast, almost manically.

"Are you okay? He did *not* seem happy. I couldn't believe that chick. What a whore. I can't believe he was pissed about that. I mean—

she was all over his ass. I swear guys are such idiots sometimes—"

"Whoa! Slow down," I interrupted her, pulling her in for a hug. "It's all good. We had some other shit to work out—but it's all good now."

She dropped her head on my shoulder and her arms tightened around my waist.

"Hey, you okay?" I asked gently, rubbing my hand down the back of her hair.

"Yeah. I'm sorry." She tried to pull away, but I held on tight, refusing to let her go.

"Something's up," I whispered in her ear. "You've been arguing with Echo since we got out here. What aren't you telling me?"

"It's nothing," she sniffled, pulling her head back and giving me a bright smile that looked gut-wrenching when paired with the sheen in her eyes. "Stupid drama. You know I don't have time for that shit."

She patted me on the back a few times before pulling away again, and that time I let her. I watched her closely as she walked to the fridge and opened it as if looking for something, but never grabbed anything before swinging it shut again.

"I think I'm gonna head home," she told me nonchalantly. "You had a hell of a party, even though you weren't there to witness it, and I'm tired as hell."

She looked tired. She also looked haunted, and I noticed for the first time how dark the circles under her eyes were.

"I'm sorry for not hanging out more," I replied, looking around at the drooping balloons and streamers. "You did an awesome job."

"No worries, sister. Anything for you." She walked over and gave me a sloppy kiss on the cheek, paired with a fake smile, before heading for the front door.

She hadn't been through it for two seconds before Echo was following, looking both pissed and worried.

It wasn't long before the others followed them out and we finally had the apartment to ourselves. If I hadn't come home to an apartment full of people, we would have stayed curled together in bed from the moment I got there. The minute the last person walked out the door that was exactly what we did.

Asa stripped me as we walked down the hall, and only seconds after I'd climbed into bed, he was climbing in behind me, naked.

"You have a good party?" he asked me quietly, his hand rubbing lightly over my belly.

"Yeah...Well, what was left of it," I sighed back with a smile.

His breath huffed against my neck and he gave me a squeeze, pulling my back tighter against his body. "I've missed you like hell, Calliope."

"It's been a long three months," I agreed, finding his hand with mine and patting the back of it gently.

"Been longer than that, sweetheart," he mumbled, lacing his fingers with mine.

"Yeah," I answered, sniffling once as my eyes filled with tears.

"I want you to move with me, Callie," he told me seriously, his arm tightening to keep me from bolting. "I want you with me. I wanna see you every day and start a family at some point. It's not gonna happen if we aren't in the same place. This shit is fuckin' with both of us."

"Okay," I whispered back.

I was startled when he pulled away and pushed me to my back so he could loom over me.

"What did you say?"

"Um... okay?" I replied, confused.

"Is that a question?"

"No, it's my answer," I snapped, exasperated with talking in circles. "You asked me to move with you and I answered yes!"

His face lit up with a smile so big it made my breath catch in my throat.

"I have to take care of things around here," I told him softly as he dropped down beside me so we were lying face to face. "I have to give notice at my job and have Gram to visit one more time."

"Okay, sweetheart. We'll make it work."

"I don't know how long it's going to take," I warned, "I need you to be patient with me and—"

"As long as you're making the move, I can be patient."

"—and I need you to come see me more often. I can't keep waiting on you for three months at a time."

"I'll do my best, sweetheart," he promised immediately, leaning in for a kiss.

We lay there a while, just watching each other. It had been so long since we'd done that, just spending time soaking each other in without arguments or sex between us. It was soothing in a way that I couldn't have imagined.

"You want to start a family?" I asked him quietly, reaching up to run my fingers lightly over his lips.

"Yeah," he cleared his throat, but his voice was still husky as he continued. "Doesn't have to happen tomorrow, or even in the next few years. But, yeah, I wanna see my babies growing in your belly."

"Okay."

"Yeah?"

"Yeah."

And that was that.

Apparently, I was moving to Oregon.

Chapter 43

Callie

It was almost four months after my birthday and there was no move in sight.

I'd started the process, giving notice at my job and packing boxes of little-used items in the apartment, but it seemed that one thing after another delayed my plans.

When I'd talked to my boss at the restaurant, he'd seemed sad to let me go but willing to give a good reference whenever I found a new job. Unfortunately, he'd asked me to take over hiring and training my replacement first. For a variety of reasons, I didn't feel like I could say no. He'd not only trusted me when he hired a kid with little experience to manage his restaurant, but he'd also been really good about giving me time off when I'd needed it during Gram's and Asa's visits. I felt like I owed him.

The applications didn't come flooding in. They came in more of a trickle, and it was three weeks before we had a pool of applicants large enough to start the interview process. Most of them had little experience and a few didn't even realize what the job was. It was a nightmare.

By the time we'd finally hired someone, a month had gone by since we'd started the entire process. I was anxious to train him so I could finally move, and I'd gone to work with a spring in my step, thinking the end was in sight… and the new hire had never shown up. He literally never showed. Not that day *or* the week following. Because the new hire had been the only valid option in the slew of applicants, I had to start all over again.

Thankfully, the second hire turned out to be perfect. She was an older lady who seemed a little down on her luck, but anxious to work. I'd spent the last two weeks training her, had just finished my last day, and was feeling pretty damn happy that I could finally pack up the rest of my things and make my way to Asa. I missed the hell out of him.

I hadn't seen Asa since my birthday, and I was trying not to resent the fact that he'd promised that he would visit and hadn't. I knew he wasn't staying away by choice. The same frustration I was feeling was in his voice every time we talked. We hadn't planned for such a long delay, and it was wearing on both of us.

Work issues weren't the only things that had me breaking out in hives on a daily basis. It seemed that everything was hitting me at once, and when Asa had opened the bottle of feelings that I'd closed up tight, I'd been unable to close it again.

Gram hadn't been able to visit because she'd picked up some sort of virus and it was kicking her ass. I paced the floor every time I talked to her, the only outlet I had that wouldn't make her worry, while she spoke to me in a raspy tone each night. She didn't seem to be getting better fast enough, and while I knew it was because she was older and it really couldn't keep her down for much longer, I still worried. I wanted to be able to take care of her, but it was impossible for her to drive, and even *more* impossible for me to go to her. For the first time in a long time, I hated the fact that I was no longer in San Diego.

Cody wasn't helping my peace of mind, either. He'd begun calling me a couple times a week, and though I couldn't put my finger on it, something was wrong. He never told me what was going on, but he wasn't the happy and teasing brother I'd known all my life. He was moody and acted like he didn't want to talk even though he was the one who made the call. I felt like I was walking on eggshells every time we spoke because anything could set him off, and when it did, he'd hang up and I'd have to wait almost a week for another call while he ignored all my attempts to contact him.

With both my remaining family members causing me to lose sleep at night, it took me a while before I noticed the change in Farrah. At first it was little things that could be easily overlooked—a day without makeup, or letting an extra week go by before she touched up the roots of her blonde hair. But soon, things were worse, and that's when I began to worry. She was showing up at my house at all hours of the night, high as a kite, just to pass out on the couch. The bones in her chest were becoming more pronounced and her boobs became almost non-existent as she lost more and more weight. Even with fully fixed makeup, she couldn't hide the dark sunken circles beneath her eyes.

She was scaring me, and she wouldn't let me help her.

I was thinking of all those things, driving home, and trying to decide how I'd pack the house when Asa called me.

"Hey, baby."

"Callie. How was your last day, sweetheart?" his voice never failed to cause a little dip in my belly.

"It went good! Rhonda seems to fit right in. Damn, I'm glad to be finally out of there."

"You and me both, Sugar. I hated you working at that place."

"Yeah, yeah," I snickered, pulling into my apartment's parking lot. "I'm not there anymore, so quit bitching."

Whatever he said next was completely lost when I looked toward my building and the noise of my heartbeat started thrumming in my ears.

"Asa, I have to go," I interrupted, slamming the car in park and fighting to get out of my seatbelt.

"The fuck is wrong, Callie?" he snapped frantically, his end of the line rustling with movement.

"Farrah," I choked out before stuffing my phone into my pocket and jumping out of the car.

She was sitting awkwardly, halfway up the stairs to my apartment, cradling one arm and staring at me through two swollen black eyes. Her clothes were clean, but her shirt was hanging haphazardly across her chest, with one arm through the sleeve and the other sitting on her shoulder, and yoga pants that she'd sworn she'd never wear out of the house sagging at her skinny waist.

I stumbled toward her, willing myself not to cry as she tried to stand.

"I have my key but I couldn't get up the stairs," she lisped brokenly, her split lips tilting a little in a grimacing smile.

"Oh my God, Farrah! Don't move!' I snapped, racing to her spot on the stairs as she swayed drunkenly.

When I reached her, I wasn't sure where to touch her to stabilize her. I threw my arms out around her, grabbing the railing to brace myself in case she started falling toward me.

"Can you make it down if I help you?" I asked her gently, searching her face for the truth. "We need to get you to the hospital."

"No hospital."

"What the hell are you talking about?" I screeched, causing her to startle and wince.

"Just get me inside, okay? I need to sit down," she mumbled back, turning gently until she was facing up the stairs. When she turned, I noticed bruises all over her back and her messy hair caked with dried blood.

Oh God.

I swallowed against the rising need to scream in horror and

followed her as she slowly made her way up the stairs, only swaying back against me once before she took another step. She shuffled to my front door slowly, using one arm to brace against the wall as I watched in silence.

I didn't know what to do.

When we got inside and I'd situated her on the couch, I rushed to the bedroom and called the one person I knew could fix anything.

"Asa?" I gasped, rifling through my toiletries to find first-aid supplies.

"What's going on, Calliope? Talk to me, Sugar."

His soothing voice broke a hole in the wall of my emotions and they all came pouring out.

"Farrah," I sobbed, trying to catch my breath. "She's—God. Somebody beat the hell out of her!"

"Who?" he thundered, his voice deepening in a way I'd only heard once before on the porch of my grandmother's house.

"I don't know!" I sobbed back, still searching in vain for Band-Aids or gauze. "I just got her in the house and called you. She won't go to the hospital and I don't know that to do!"

"Callie," he snapped back, "you need to get your shit together right now. You hear me?"

"Yes," I gasped, nodding as I wiped my nose on the shoulder of my shirt.

"You don't need to do shit. Okay?" he told me gently. "You just be there; make sure she's got anything she needs. Is she bleeding?"

"Her hair has blood in it, but it looks like it's all scabbed over." *Why the hell was I looking for Band-Aids?*

"Okay, that's good, baby. That's really good." He paused for a moment and I heard his breathing stutter as I imagined him running his hand down his face. "I'll make some calls. You make sure the door is locked and don't open it for anyone but my boys."

"Okay. I'll just—" I walked around my room with no destination, my mind running in a thousand different directions.

"Callie! Go check on your friend and lock the goddamn door."

"Okay. Doing that now," I told him calmly, squaring my shoulders before stepping out of the room.

"I'll call you back. I love you." He hung up before I could say anything back.

I checked the door first and then went to Farrah, who hadn't moved an inch.

"I'm not sure how I can help you," I whispered, kneeling at her feet. "Should I get an icepack?"

"Nah, I'm good," she told me cockily, her lisp belying the words. "I just need to sleep it off. It'll be like ten times better tomorrow."

"Farrah!" I snapped back, frustrated that even when she was sitting on my couch beaten bloody, she still refused to let me in. "I think your arm is fucking *broken*."

"Oh," she seemed bewildered as she gazed down at her arm and then back to my face, her eyes filling with tears for the first time. "Yeah, it might be."

"Yeah, baby girl," I told her gently, my own nose tingling with tears. "I'm pretty sure."

"Okay." She looked around the living room as if searching for something, and then her swollen eyes found me again. "What am I gonna do?"

I wasn't sure if she was in shock or just completely overwhelmed, but in that instant, she was a child—a broken and scared child—and she was looking at me like I'd protect her. My chest filled with purpose, and for the first time since my parents' death, I stepped into that role. It was an almost burning sensation—a fierce need that filled me.

From that moment on, I would kill to protect her.

I would die to protect her.

"You don't have to do anything," I reassured her, pulling off her dirty flip flops. It seemed her feet were the only things that had escaped the trauma. "I called Grease and he's going to send some boys over."

"No!" she screeched, her entire body tensing. "Nonononono."

"Why?" I asked firmly, my stomach sinking.

"Not Echo," she told me beseechingly. "Just not Echo, okay?"

My heart started to race at the implications of her request. *Holy hell.*

"Why not, baby girl?" I asked quietly, bracing for her answer.

She sniffled quietly for a few minutes before answering.

"I don't want him to see me like this," she whispered piteously, her eyes begging me to keep him away.

I wanted to sigh in relief that Echo wasn't responsible, but I couldn't. Someone had beaten her so badly that her arm was broken. There was no relief in that.

"He only sees me when I'm pretty," she whimpered, leaning toward me to get her point across. "He won't want me anymore. I'll have nowhere to go."

Her words were like a punch to the stomach. I wanted to argue, to tell her that he'd seen her getting skinnier and skinnier and it hadn't seemed to matter. I wanted to tell her that at my birthday party she'd had lipstick on her teeth, and he'd *still* watched her like she was the most beautiful thing he'd ever seen. Instead, I just shook my head.

"You stay with me," I told her, squeezing her feet in my hands.

"You're moving with Grease—"

"You. Stay. With. Me," I said again, my voice resolute.

She nodded her head, but didn't say anything as someone started pounding on the door.

"Don't let him see me!" she whispered frantically, like the men in the hallway could actually hear her over all the noise they were making.

I nodded and stood up, wondering how I was going to keep Echo out of my house. I shouldn't have assumed that I had any say in the matter.

I looked through the peephole and opened the door to Michael and Echo on my welcome mat.

"Where is she?" Echo asked frantically, crowding me as I refused to budge from the doorway.

"She doesn't want to see you," I told him apologetically, wincing when his panicked eyes came to mine. "You need to go."

His face turned bright red in anger, looking at me in disbelief.

"Callie, I know that you're looking out for her. I respect the hell outta you for that," he told me through gritted teeth, very obviously trying to hold his temper. "But that's my woman in there, and if you don't move, I don't care who you are, I'll knock your ass out."

I stood there for a moment weighing my options, but I must not have come to a decision fast enough, because soon he was literally picking me up and moving me to the side.

I was happy he hadn't decided to 'knock my ass out'.

I raced around the couch after him, anxious to be a barrier for Farrah if she needed it. But I would forever wish I hadn't.

Because I had a front row seat when he stopped in front of her, frozen.

And I watched as he dropped to his knees and roared in pain and anger.

I wanted to turn away, but the whole thing was like a beautiful train wreck. I couldn't take my eyes off it.

"Don't look at me!" Farrah cried, her breath coming in harsh sobs. "Don't look at me! I'm ugly. Don't look at me." Her voice quieted into a whimper as she held her uninjured hand over her face.

Echo made a choking sound and instantly scooted between her legs on the couch, whispering to her gently.

"Baby. You're always beautiful... I need you to look at me, Farrah." His voice was rough with tears as he pulled gently at her hand and Farrah dropped it to her lap in defeat. "Aw, baby. Shhhh."

She was crying in earnest, and the overwhelming sadness on her face had tears rolling down mine.

"I called you," she choked, searching his eyes. "I called you. Where *were* you?"

He made a sound like a wounded animal and dropped his head into her lap. Sobbing.

Farrah raised her head and met my eyes, her message clear. I nodded, walked completely out of the house, and sat next to Michael at the top of the stairs.

"I don't know what to do," I told him quietly.

He threw his arm around my shoulders and kissed the side of my head. "She's got her man and yours is on his way. Only thing you can do is wait."

Chapter 44

Callie

Echo convinced Farrah to go to the hospital, but she refused to let him take her.

I ended up driving her with Michael crammed into the backseat of my car for protection. They didn't want us going alone, but I didn't understand why Michael rode with us because I watched Echo ride behind us on his motorcycle the entire way there.

The doctors and nurses tried over and over to get answers from Farrah, but she wasn't talking. She wouldn't tell anyone. The scene with her and Echo stayed in my mind, though, and I wondered if he knew more than he was saying—not that I could ask him. I'd lost him in the emergency room parking lot and hadn't seen him since.

It took hours, but they eventually sent Farrah home with me because she refused to stay overnight at the hospital. She told me she couldn't afford to stay there, but there was an underlying reason in her eyes that I couldn't interpret.

We held hands and cried as they took photos of her naked body. She wouldn't let me go, and I was glad. I didn't think I could let go, either. She had bruises covering her legs and torso, and there were crusted-over welts on her small breasts that looked like cigarette burns. The blood in her hair had come from a small cut on the back of her head that didn't even need stitches, and both bones in her forearm were broken. The bruises on her back and bottom were even worse than those on her front, and to top it all off, she was emaciated to the point that I could count every single one of her ribs.

More than once during the whole documentation process I had to swallow back my urge to vomit.

They set her arm and bandaged her the best they could before we left, and I was thankful for the strong injection of pain medicine she was given. She'd fallen asleep in the wheelchair before we reached the outside door which was probably for the best because Echo was waiting for us. I watched him closely as he carried her like a baby to the car.

The guilt he felt was like a fog hovering around him.

By the time we got home, it was the middle of the night and Asa was due within a few hours. It drove me crazy that he was riding his bike through the night, but he would have laughed at me if I'd said anything. I trusted that he knew what he was doing and left it at that. I was selfish enough to need him with me, no matter how he had to get there.

I made Echo put Farrah in our bed for the night even though he argued that she should go home with him. I knew she wouldn't want that, even unconscious, and I found myself sneering at him that he had no way to move her. He'd done something. I didn't know what, but I knew that he was guilty. He wasn't taking her anywhere.

A few hours later, Farrah woke up moaning, and I was sitting on the edge of the bed with her when Asa showed up. There was no emotion on his face as he walked forward, looking at both of us closely before leaning in for a kiss.

"You okay, Sugar?" he asked softly into my mouth.

"Better, now that you're here."

"Good," he answered gruffly before turning to Farrah.

"Damn, girl. I hope the other guy looks worse," he teased her softly.

"Killed that bitch," she replied with a small smile.

"Yeah?" he questioned seriously, his voice still soft.

"No," she moaned back as her face crumpled and tears began running down her cheeks.

"Well, I'll take care of that for you," he promised with a nod, causing Farrah to nod back.

I gave Farrah her pain medicine and followed Asa out of the room, closing the door quietly. Before I could move down the hallway, he was in my face, pushing me against the wall and running his hands all over my body.

"Fuck, Callie," he whispered. "Fuck. Fuck."

"I know," I whispered back, putting my hands on his cheeks. "She's okay. I'm okay."

He kissed me long and deep, pressing my head into the wall until he was calm enough to pull back.

"She said anything to you?" he asked, locking his arm around my shoulder as he guided us toward the living room.

"No," I hesitated for a moment, "but I think Echo knows something."

His eyes shot to me in disbelief before nodding that he understood. Things were not going to go well for Echo if he had anything to do with what happened to Farrah.

We swerved toward the kitchen when we saw the guys standing by the counter, and Asa leaned against the wall across from them, pulling my back against his chest so he could wrap both arms over my shoulders.

"You got something to tell me, Echo?" he asked calmly, watching Echo with an unnerving intensity.

"No," Echo stuttered back, his brows furrowed in confusion. "What are you talking about?"

"Seems you know something you aren't saying."

Echo gulped and opened and closed his mouth a few times

before dropping his eyes to the floor.

"That stepdad of hers is a member," Michael cut in, his eyes swinging back and forth between the other men in the kitchen. "Echo came to us about him a few months back and said something wasn't right with the dude." He rubbed the back of his neck. "Farrah wasn't talkin', but shit, all of us saw the way she was fuckin' wastin' away. So we had a little talk with the man, tried to feel him out a bit without steppin' on any toes."

I scoffed, but went silent when Asa squeezed me in warning.

"So, everything's fine for a while, but Farrah's not coming around as often, and Echo here's getting worried. Then one night, outta the blue, she shows up on his doorstep, soakin' wet and wearin' nothing but her pajamas." He paused for a moment, glancing away from Asa's stare, and when he looked back his eyes were pained. "She'd locked herself in the bathroom at home and had to turn on the shower to hide the noise of opening the window... The whole story came out that night. Seems Farrah's mom was beating the shit outta her while her old man watched, and all the while, Gator's been eying Farrah like a prime cut o' meat."

I felt my legs lose all feeling, and Asa wrapped one arm around my waist to keep me standing.

"Some of the boys went and quietly taught the man a lesson. He's a brother, and in that he deserves some respect, but that's Echo's woman. Not to mention the fact that girl is about a hundred pounds soakin' wet and was getting smaller by the day. No way we could let that shit go—but we couldn't do anything *officially*, either."

Asa's arms grew so tight around me that it was a struggle to breathe, but still he kept silent, letting Michael finish the story.

"We thought it was over, man, we thought we made things

clear." He raised his hands in supplication, but I felt no sympathy as he finished. "No way that broken arm came from her mama."

I wrenched myself from Asa and flew across the room at a silent Echo, punching him over and over wherever I could reach. He stood there stoically, letting me pound him, with his jaw clenched and his chin raised until Asa yanked me away from him.

"He deserved respect?" I screeched. "She was being hurt and you did *nothing*? What the fuck is wrong with you!" I pulled at Asa's arms, my hair flying in all directions as I reached for Echo. "*Where were you? She needed you! Where the fuck were you?*"

I fought and screamed until Asa finally subdued me with a hand over my mouth. I watched Echo, my chest burning, and I could have gladly killed him and felt no remorse.

"She told me shit was getting better. She said that Gator wasn't around as much and she was spending most of her time here with you!" He looked at me accusingly until Asa growled in warning.

"This afternoon, we got in a fight because she wouldn't stay at my place and wait while I took a meet. She said she was coming *here*. She said she was coming here, so when she called me, I i*gnored* it. *She said she was coming here!*" He spun around and punched the wall over and over, mumbling to himself. "*I ignored it. She said she was coming here,*" he repeated over and over again until his shoulders slumped and he grew quiet.

"You did what you could, brother," Asa told him quietly, and my eyes shot to him in accusation. "You did what you could, there ain't no use looking back. But you got a girl in there that needs you to get straight so we can handle this. You with me?"

I couldn't believe what he was saying and my chest burned in betrayal. I didn't hear Echo's answer because I reached back and pinched

Asa hard, startling him into loosening his arms so I could escape.

"Don't touch me!" I hissed as he reached out to grab me. "You guys are disgusting! He did everything he could, huh? A little intimidation, because, hey, the guy is a *brother* and *deserves* respect? That's all he could do? You all make me sick."

I stormed into my room to find Farrah sitting up in my bed, crying softly.

Chapter 45

Callie

I lay in bed with Farrah after she'd cried herself to sleep, but I couldn't shut down my brain.

I was guilty—as guilty as the guys talking quietly in my living room. I'd noticed something was wrong with Farrah. I'd seen all the signs, but I hadn't pressed her for information because I'd believed that my life was so incredibly difficult that I couldn't handle *her* issues, too.

When I'd been screaming at Echo, I was also screaming at myself.

I should have done something.

I watched Farrah's chest rise and fall as I thought about how the guys had thought they'd handled things and how I felt about Asa's commiserating words. He'd acted like what they'd done was normal— that they were completely justified in keeping things quiet and not even going to the police.

I knew that Asa's world was different than the world everyone else lived in. I'd known it from the moment he walked brashly into the party where I'd met him. Everything he did was a testament to how he lived his life, from taking in a girl of sixteen to the tattoos that were slowly working their way up his neck.

So what he'd said wasn't surprising—not really. It was apparent that they lived under a code that I could never understand; I just hadn't seen the ugliness of that code until that night. Asa was still the same man I ran to if things were bad, the same person I called if I had good news, and even as I lay there in bed, I ached to touch him after being away from him for so long.

I had to make a decision, and I had no idea how I'd do that. If I chose to overlook what I'd heard in the kitchen, I felt like I was condoning their decision to leave Farrah to the wolves, but if I left Asa, I didn't think I would survive it.

When Farrah woke up late the next morning, she practically made the decision for me.

"Hey, Callie?" she called sleepily from the bed. "Can you go get Echo for me?"

I looked at her in confusion, but when she pushed herself up as if to get him herself, I scrambled out of the room. Asa wasn't in the apartment when I made my way to the kitchen, but Echo was. I nodded my head toward the bedroom, taking in his dirty clothes and messy hair before turning away as he left the room. I never found out what they said that day, and it really wasn't any of my business—but when I went to check on Farrah two hours later, the two were cuddled in the middle of the bed with Farrah tucked gently against Echo's chest.

Asa showed up after I'd showered and made myself lunch, and I had to force myself not to look at him as he grabbed a beer out of our fridge.

"You ignoring me?" he grumbled quietly, his tone implying that I was being unreasonable.

"Not ignoring you, just don't have anything to say," I replied, never looking his way.

"Yeah, okay," he scoffed, and my head snapped up in irritation. "Ah, *there's* my girl."

"I can't believe you said that last night!" I growled quietly, hoping to keep our conversation from Echo and Farrah. "He fucked up, badly!"

"Yeah, Sugar. I know that," he told me with a nod, moving forward to wrap his arms around my stiff body. "But those thoughts aren't gonna help anyone. He fucked up, it's over. Man's gotta get his head in the game—that girl in there needs him to be a man, not some pussy that can't get over the guilt he's feeling. She needs him to take care of shit—and there wasn't any way he was gonna be able to do that acting like he was last night."

I let his words sink in, deciding that they made a weird sort of sense.

"But what was that shit about respect?" I asked incredulously. "You really believe that?"

He sighed and was quiet for a minute before meeting my eyes. "I have never in my life agreed with a man putting his hands on a woman. I stop that shit when I can, and it burns me when I can't. But the club has a set of rules, Callie," he told me while I rolled my eyes. "No, don't do that shit. Let me finish. We have our own laws that we live by, that we *choose* to live by when we decide to become a part of this life. If we didn't, shit would be anarchy—brothers ratting each other out, stabbing each other in the back—no loyalty. You understand what I'm telling you?"

"I understand the words coming out of your mouth, but it still sounds like bullshit," I answered petulantly, crossing my arms over my chest.

He huffed in amusement. "It may sound like bullshit to you, but it's the way we survive. Echo beating the shit outta Gator could have got him in deep shit. He's got no claim on her."

"But they've been together for like a year!"

"Yeah, Sugar, but he never *claimed* her. Farrah didn't want that shit—told Echo that she didn't want that life." He shook his head. "His hands were tied."

"Okay," I replied softly, trying to process his words, "but what happens now?"

"I made some calls. Knew Farrah's mom sounded familiar, couldn't remember how. I remember now." He raised his hand to my face. "Farrah's dad is on his way here, Calliope. You need to brace because shit is gonna get worse before it gets better."

My eyes felt like they were going to pop out of my head at his revelation, and I opened my mouth and closed it again before I could find my tongue.

"What? She doesn't even know who her dad is! Why would you do that?" I gasped, scared as hell at what Farrah's reaction would be.

"Sugar, Echo's hands are tied." He leaned down and gave me a fierce kiss before raising his head again. "Slider's hands are *not*."

Chapter 46

Callie

The day passed slowly for everyone in the house, but especially for me as I worried about the imminent arrival of Farrah's dad. Apparently he was the president of Asa's club, the *married* president. The fact that he'd been married for over twenty-five years didn't endear me to the man, but I made myself hold all judgment until I saw how he treated Farrah.

He'd been gone her entire life, contributing no more than a sleazy orgasm with Farrah's disgusting mom, but the fact that he was coming to Sacramento for her gave me hope that he had *some* redeeming qualities. I just prayed that Farrah wouldn't completely lose it when he introduced himself.

I heard them before I saw them.

The apartment was filled with a loud roar of bikes, to the point of rattling a mason jar sitting on the windowsill. It startled me until I looked at Asa who wore a satisfied smile on his face. He opened up the front door before anyone could knock, and suddenly my home was filled with at least ten very large men. They weren't quiet in their greetings, and a sound from my bedroom had me rushing away from the group toward Farrah.

"What's going on?" she asked me quietly, as Echo rose from his place next to her.

"Grease called in reinforcements," I answered her with a grim smile.

"Why are you calling him Grease? You never call him Grease," she replied, her nose scrunched in confusion for only a second before she was wincing and raising her hand to her face.

"He's Asa to *me*," I told her ruefully, climbing into Echo's deserted spot. "But today, he's definitely Grease."

We sat on my bed as Echo wandered into the living room, and I grabbed her hand as my heart raced. It took them longer to make their way to my room than I thought it would, and by the time they did, Farrah was leaning heavily against my side with her head on my shoulder.

Asa led a man I'd never met into the room, and I braced, only to relax a little when I saw Poet come in behind them. It was nice to see a familiar face, and I couldn't help but smile when he winked at me from behind the others.

"Farrah—" Asa rumbled, but his words were cut off by the girl at my side.

"Hey, Pop. What are you doing in my neck of the woods?" she called out cockily.

I watched in awe as three pairs of eyes opened wide and the man in front cleared his throat nervously.

"You know who I am?" he asked, tipping his head to the side as he studied her.

"Mom has a picture of you," she answered flatly. "You look a lot older, your shit's gone gray, but yeah, I know who you are."

He looked at a loss for words as he stared at her, eventually taking steps closer to the bed. With every inch, Farrah's hand tightened on mine beneath the blankets at our hips, but she showed no other display of nervousness.

"I'm gonna make this right for you," he told her, his eyes intent on her face.

"Why bother?" she scoffed. "When mom was shooting up and letting junkies into our house, you didn't 'make things right for me'. You didn't do *shit* when she started whaling on me for no reason. And I'm pretty goddamn sure that you were nowhere to be found when her husband beat the hell out of me—" she pulled the neck of her t-shirt down,"—and used a cigar to burn me."

Slider's eyes went glossy for a moment, and Poet ran a hand over his face when she bared the insides of her breasts. When she turned her head away from them in dismissal, Slider pinched the bridge of his nose and rubbed his eyes with his fingers.

"I'm gonna make this right for you," he repeated, his voice hoarse. "I shouldn't have left you with your mama. I got no excuse except that I had a wife—"

"Yeah, I'm well versed in married men who fuck my mother," she replied in a bored tone, never looking his way. "*And* parents who put their pieces of ass before their children."

"I know you're pissed at me, and you got a right to that, but I don't *ever* wanna hear you disrespect my wife," he warned, looking at the back of her head where her hair was still matted and tangled.

"You don't ever have to hear anything from me," she answered quietly. "Get the fuck away from me. You're nothing."

He was scary, and he had a way of looking at you that made you think that he could kill you at any moment and not feel anything. But the tremble in Farrah's voice, and the knowledge that she'd hate them looking at her the way she was, had me squeezing her hand and jumping off the bed. I strode to where her dad was standing and stopped right in front of him while Asa looked on with his jaw clenched.

"Out," I ordered, pointing to the door.

"What?" he asked incredulously, his eyebrows lifting in surprise.

"Out of this room."

"Calliope—" Asa called in warning, but I waved him off.

"I get that you're scary, and you could probably snap me in half," I told him seriously, "but she isn't yours, she is *mine*. You gave up your rights. She wants you out of this room, and I don't care how you feel about that. I also don't care how I have to get you out of here—I may have to knee you in the balls and drag your crying ass into the hallway, but you *will* leave this room."

We stared each other down for a few minutes before he turned abruptly and walked out of the room, mumbling to Asa to control his woman. I flipped him off behind his back, and Poet covered his laugh with a cough as he strode out behind him.

"The fuck, Calliope?" Asa roared at me, as I started to push him out of the room.

"We're *not* having this discussion now," I informed him as I moved him to the doorway. "Your loyalty may be to him, but mine is to her." I pointed in Farrah's direction. "Now make sure that those men are in the living room or kitchen and out of the hallway. I'm gonna help Farrah take a shower. She looks like shit."

I closed the door in his face and swung around quickly at Farrah's laugh.

"I don't care if I have to knee you in the balls!" she snickered at me. "That was fucking classic."

"Yeah, yeah," I grumbled back at her as I tried to find some clothes that wouldn't fall off her thin frame. "You'd better be thankful. Asa likes to spank me when he thinks I've done something wrong."

She snorted with laughter and climbed gently off the bed. "Dude, I know. We all heard that shit at your party."

"Shut up," I griped back, my skin burning. "Grab a towel from the closet, would you?"

We made our way to the bathroom without interruption, but I

was helping her undress when there was a knock at the door.

"We're busy! Pee outside!" I called, causing Farrah to snicker.

"Yeah, I know," Echo's voice came through the door, causing both of us to freeze.

I looked at Farrah to get her permission and then opened the door a little to let Echo into the tiny bathroom. His gaze was locked on Farrah as he stepped inside, and I felt like a third wheel as I tried to scoot my way past him.

"Echo will help me, Callie," Farrah told me quietly, lifting her hand to his face.

"Okie doke! I'll just, you know, go." I scrambled to open the door and escape the intimacy I was witnessing. "Let me know if you need anything!"

After I closed the door behind me, I straightened my shoulders and made my way to the living room.

Chapter 47

Grease

I'd been half embarrassed and half impressed as I'd watched Callie stare down Slider and force him out of our room. It was a stupid thing to do, but hell if she didn't do it in a way that had both Slider and Poet looking at her with respect.

We were standing around the counter, quietly making plans, when Callie tiptoed into the kitchen. She tried to act like she was unaffected by the men in our home, but I could tell that old demons were surfacing by the slightly panicked look in her eyes. I met her gaze and lifted my arm for her as she scooted around the counter and slid in beside me, wrapping her arms around my waist and laying her head on my chest.

"Hey, Sugar. Farrah still in the shower?"

"Yeah, Echo is helping her," she answered me quietly. "She didn't need me in there."

"Yeah, he'll take care of her."

"Like he did before?" she scoffed lightly, before turning her face away from me.

I gave her that and didn't start an argument, no matter how badly I wanted to set her straight. The man did his best, and he was broken up about it. There was no use pointing fingers at people who weren't to blame, especially if Farrah had already forgiven him.

"You've got brass ones, girl," Slider called to Callie from across the table, a smirk on his face.

"My name is Callie."

"Know what your name is, but you threatened to kick me in the balls earlier, so I think I'll call you girl."

"Whatever." She looked away from him with her nose up, and I couldn't stop my lips from pulling into a grin. *Brass ones.*

"Girl," Slider's voice lowered, "I'm glad my daughter has you on her side. Ain't many people that would stand up to a man like me."

"I didn't help when it mattered," she confessed quietly.

"There was nothing you could do to stop it," he answered, leaning forward across the counter. "Girl like you might think she can take on the world, but she'd be wrong. Don't know her, but I have a feeling your friend is a whole lot like me—keeps her cards close to her chest. Doubt you even knew what was happening." His voice lowered to an intense whisper, "You ain't to blame for that."

He leaned back and turned to Poet who was watching the scene with a thoughtful look on his face. "Need a smoke."

As Slider left the room, Poet came to stand in front of Callie and reached down to run his hand along her hair in a soft gesture.

"Definitely not the same little girl I met a year ago," he told her tenderly. "You keep fighting back, Callie. Proud'a you." Then he followed Slider out of the house.

"Holy shit," Callie commented, looking up at me in wonder.

"Yeah, Sugar. Looks like you have the seal of approval from two of the scariest men in the United States."

Chapter 48

Callie

Asa and most of the men left the house that night around dinner time. I knew where they were going—all of us knew, but no one said a word about it. They just got up as a unit and started for the door at a certain time without any words spoken. Echo went with Asa, which didn't surprise me, but what *did* surprise me was that Poet stayed with us.

He sat on our couch, calm and relaxed, watching some motorcycle show on cable, and didn't pay any attention to Farrah and me when I brought her out for dinner so I could change the sheets on my bed. She was getting up and around more after her shower, but she hadn't left my room while Slider was there. I didn't blame her; he hadn't exactly endeared himself during their five-minute conversation.

I wanted to sit with Poet and ask him how he'd been, but I never got the chance. Farrah stuck to me like glue that night, jumping at shadows and any noise outside of the ordinary. She tried to play it off, and wasn't outwardly clingy, but when she stood outside the bathroom door while I did my business, I wanted to cry for her. She reminded me of myself, and it brought me back to a time I'd tried my hardest to forget.

The men were only gone a couple hours before I heard the roar of bikes outside. Farrah stood so close to me we were almost touching as Poet unlocked the front door, letting the men file in. I was watching for Asa, and the minute I saw his face, I took an involuntary step forward.

He looked wrecked.

He came right for me without pausing for a second, and knocked into me hard enough that I lost my balance and had to wrap my arms around his neck to keep from falling. He didn't stop there, though. He took another step, knocking my legs out from under me as he grabbed my thighs and wrapped me around him. Echo was doing the same thing to Farrah, though much gentler, and our eyes met over their heads.

Asa buried his face in my neck and took a long inhale as I pulled the rubber band out of his hair so I could run my fingers through it. I wasn't sure how to soothe him, but I tried my best as I tightened my arms and legs.

"Slider and the boys are heading to a hotel for the night," he growled into my neck, his voice husky and deep. "Echo's using your car to take Farrah home with him."

He lifted his head as I turned mine toward Farrah, preparing to argue.

"He needs his woman tonight and she needs him. Ain't nothing for you to protect her from." I nodded once, looking down into his face, and my chest burned at his next words. "He needs his woman and I need mine. You gonna give that to me?"

"Yeah, Asa," I murmured back gently, running my fingers into the hair behind his ear. "You can have whatever you need."

"Good," he growled, before setting me down and walking away.

I stood in the middle of the living room and watched the men around me. Their faces were drawn and their jaws were tight, but not one of them said a word about what had happened. Asa and Slider rounded them up, and when Slider was the only one left, I watched him walk to Farrah and put a hand on her shoulder. He whispered something to her that I couldn't hear, but I saw her nod into Echo's chest before Slider leaned forward and dropped a soft kiss on the back of her head. Then he was gone.

Echo and Farrah left right after everyone else, and as I locked the door behind them I felt Asa move in against my back.

"Need you, Callie," he mumbled into my neck, pulling my shirt over my head without letting me turn away from the door. His hands pushed and pulled roughly at me, stripping off my clothes efficiently, until I was standing completely naked. I heard his belt clink as he unfastened it, but I didn't move from my position.

He was riding a fine line of control, I could feel it in every one of his movements, and I knew that a single twitch could set him off. I was panting, resting my hands against the door when I felt him fall to his knees behind me, jerking my hips toward him so I was bent over at the waist.

"Fuck," he whispered against my skin, slowing his movements. "Didn't mean to scare you."

"You didn't scare me," I rasped, pressing my forehead against the door.

He didn't reply because he was pushing his face between my legs and capturing my clit between his lips, bypassing every other piece of flesh. He rubbed it slowly at first, warming me up, but the minute I started writhing against him he sucked. It took only a few minutes to come with him shoving me over the edge, and before I could come down from my high, he was standing and spinning me around.

His jeans and boxers fell to his feet as he lifted me up, and without pausing, dropped me onto him. He used his body to press me to the door, but instead of holding me with his hands on my ass like I was used to, he ran his arms under my knees until they were resting on the insides of his elbows. I wrapped my arms around his neck in a death grip, but the position left me with absolutely no control unless I wanted to fall to the floor.

"Lift your chin for me, Sugar," he ordered huskily as he pounded in and out, causing my back to slam into the door.

The second I tilted my head back, I felt his tongue and teeth at my throat as he bit down and then sucked strongly. When he was done, he pulled back to gaze at it and mumbled, "Better," before dropping his forehead to my collarbone. I let go with one hand, trusting him to keep me from falling, and ran my hand softly through his hair as his thrusts became fast and jerky and he came with a slow groan.

He held on to me and shuffled into our bedroom, falling to his back on the bed. I kissed him as I climbed off, and went to crouch at his feet when I felt something running down my leg.

We hadn't used protection.

I didn't say a word as I rushed to the bathroom to take care of the mess, and when I got back to our room, he was laying in the same position with his forearm resting over his eyes.

"You want to talk about it?" I asked gently as I pulled off his boots and socks.

"You don't need that shit in your head," he told me with a sigh. "It was a clusterfuck. Farrah's ma was there."

He didn't say another word, and I didn't press as I stripped away his jeans. I started for the dresser to get us some clean clothes but he stopped me.

"Don't get dressed tonight," he said wearily. "Want to feel you when I sleep."

I didn't reply, but turned back toward him and climbed back in the bed.

I bit the inside of my lip as he crawled under the covers, but couldn't stop myself from blurting out, "We didn't use protection!" before averting my eyes.

"That a problem?" he asked as if he didn't see one.

"What if I get pregnant?"

"What if you do? I've got a job, we're both adults, and you'd be a hell of a mother," he answered, closing his eyes as his head sunk into the pillow.

My mouth open and closed a few times, trying to decide on a suitable reply, but he reached out without opening his eyes and pulled me down next to him.

"Stop worrying about it, Callie," he told me simply.

His body was relaxed into the bed as if boneless, and for the first time that night his face wasn't drawn and tight. I could force him to have the conversation with me; he'd do it if I asked. But as I felt his arm tighten around me, and his breathing grow even, I couldn't make myself say anymore.

"I love you," I mumbled, my lips pressed to his chest.

"Love you, too, Sugar."

Chapter 49

Callie

The next few days passed in a blur as Asa and I argued about when I was going to move. He thought it made perfect sense to pack up the rest of my shit and move it when he left, so he didn't have to make an extra trip. I could see his logic, and in any other situation, I could have agreed with him.

But Farrah needed me.

I couldn't move to Oregon when she was still startling at every noise. She was staying with Echo, but driving to my house whenever he was working which meant she was at our house a lot.

I wasn't sure what was happening with the Aces, but the guys that came down with Slider and Poet still hadn't left. Something was brewing, something big, and I wondered what Asa wasn't telling me as he and Echo disappeared for meeting after meeting. For some reason, his insistence that I move to Oregon with him immediately had turned almost desperate, and he was snapping and snarling at me constantly.

"Farrah doesn't need you here!" he roared, continuing the argument the minute he walked in the door that night. "She's living with Echo! He'll deal with her shit!"

"She was there for me when you weren't," I told him calmly, refusing to get into another screaming match. "She sat with me the day of my parents' funeral. She came by every day to make sure that I wasn't alone."

"Don't throw that shit in my face again, Calliope!"

"I'm not throwing it in your face," I replied, "I'm trying to explain to you that I owe her."

"You *owe* her? That's what this is about? That's fuckin' ridiculous."

His automatic brush-off of something I felt so strongly about made my entire body tense with anger and I had a hard time controlling myself as I answered him.

"She was taking care of me while she was living through a nightmare, Asa," I seethed through clenched teeth. "*She* was taking care of *me*, and I was so caught up in my own shit that I didn't even notice that anything was wrong with her."

His face softened and his voice lowered as we came to the cajoling portion that ended each of our arguments.

"Sugar, you can't keep beating yourself up over that shit." He came toward me, putting his hands on each side of my face. "There was nothing you could have done and it's over now."

"Yeah, well, I'd feel a whole lot better if I could return the favor for a while without you on my ass all the time," I answered, trying to turn my face away from him.

His hands tightened on my head and he lowered his face to mine, his jaw clenching. "How am I supposed to keep you safe when you're hundreds of miles away from me?"

He didn't expect an answer, because he kissed me punishingly, not allowing me to pull away.

"You can't keep putting this off, Callie." He kissed me again, "It's one thing after another."

I bit him in frustration the next time he pressed his lips to mine, causing him to drop his hands from my head.

"You want an angry fuck, Callie?" he asked me, nostrils flaring as he took a step back. "'Cause I can give it to you. I'm done with your procrastination bullshit."

"Fuck you," I sneered, wiping my mouth with the back of my hand. "It's all about you, right? The whole world revolves around *Grease*."

I knew what I was doing. The anger, guilt, and frustration over our situation had me snapping at everyone I came in contact with, and I felt myself slipping into the same building resentment that had plagued me for months. I hated the club and everything it represented, but I was in the untenable position of loving one of its members. I'd somehow become a fighter, but there was nothing for me to fight against.

I needed him to snap me out of it before I ruined everything.

His eyes closed into slits, his chest heaving, and I froze for a moment, thinking I'd gone too far. Then suddenly, without any warning, he bent at the waist and shoved his shoulder into my belly before standing straight so I was hanging down his back.

I pounded against anything I could reach as I screeched, but he ignored me as he calmly made sure the door was locked before walking us into the bedroom. His lack of concern with my fit made me even angrier, so I pulled up his shirt and leather vest to dig my nails into his back in frustration.

"Knock it off, Calliope!" he growled at me, turning his head to bite my thigh as his hand slapped my ass hard.

He tossed me onto the bed and I scrambled off, expecting him to catch me at any moment, but he didn't. Instead, he stood in front of the door, my only means of escape, and slowly started undressing.

"You gonna make this easy and get undressed?" he asked in a bored tone that had my stomach turning in uncertainty. "Didn't think so."

I stood at the opposite side of the bed, watching him like a cornered animal, as I rethought my approach. I wasn't feeling fierce anymore. The only thing I could feel was a nervousness that didn't have anything to do with physical harm. What if I was too much? What if he decided that he didn't need my shit anymore and left me? The old fear of being too needy rose up until I felt tears stinging my nose.

"Come here, Sugar," he called softly.

I shook my head and backed into the wall, practically hyperventilating. I wanted to go to him, be accommodating and sweet instead of hissing and scratching, but I didn't know how to change my emotions. My heart was still racing with a frustration that made me want to scream just to let some of it out.

"I need to come get you, Callie?"

He wasn't interested in a stand-off because he started toward me, his steps measured but never faltering. When he reached me, I pushed at him, making low noises in my throat, but he stripped me anyway until I was standing naked with hands fisted.

"I love you," he told me gently as he pulled me toward the bed and sat down.

He pulled me between his knees and kissed me sweetly, rubbing his thumbs against my cheekbones until I melted against him. Then he wrapped one leg around both of mine and pushed me face-first on the bed so I was bent over one thigh, his hand heavy on the small of my back.

Smack.

I screamed, pissed that I'd been tricked into compliance.

"You call me *Asa*," he rumbled, smacking my ass again. "Though you know that, so I'm guessing this is what you were angling for." *Smack. Smack.*

"Get off me!" I bellowed, pushing as hard as I could with my arms but getting nowhere.

He rubbed my sore cheeks for a moment, quiet, and then started the spanking again.

"You need me to spank your ass?" *Smack.* "You can just fuckin' ask for it."

"I can't."

He paused for a moment, quiet.

"Why can't you ask for what you need?"

He waited for me to answer, then sighed deeply when I didn't, smacking me again.

"Answer me."

Smack.

"Because it's not the same," I sobbed, pulling my arms under me so I could cover my face with my hands. "I want you to be as mad as me! I want you to be frustrated! I'm afraid you're going to leave me if you aren't!"

"Sweetheart," he whispered tenderly, letting go of my back so he could rub it gently.

I scrambled away from him, hating the fact that I was naked in front of him with my words between us. I pulled the blankets to my shoulders, but didn't turn away from him as I watched him run his hand down his face.

"I love you, Calliope," he told me softly, crawling under the covers with me and pulling me into his arms. "I'm not going anywhere."

I was silent as I watched him, tears blurring my eyes.

"You're my family," he mumbled, kissing me and then rubbing his lips down my neck. "You're everything."

He took one nipple into his mouth and sucked gently, pushing the covers to our knees before grabbing the back of my leg and sliding it up his hip. He ran his fingers between my legs lightly, barely touching me before sliding it up to rest on my stomach. He let go of my nipple and ran his tongue around it once before raising his eyes to mine and leaning up on a forearm.

"I'm not going anywhere," he promised as he shifted his hips and pushed inside me. "You belong with me."

My back arched and I lifted my hand to his hair to pull his face to mine.

"I love you," I whimpered, my body feeling almost weightless in relief.

His jaw went tight at my words, and he leaned back so he could slide his hand between us, hitting the perfect spot with his thumb.

It didn't take long for me to come, taking him with me.

I barely made it to the bathroom to clean up afterward before dropping with exhaustion. He pulled me on top of him like a blanket when I made it back to the bed, and I pushed my face into his neck. I couldn't get close enough to him. Neither of us said a word about our lack of protection. We were forgetting as much as we were remembering the condoms, and I knew I needed to get on birth control, but every time I'd used it in the past it had been non-stop periods for me.

I wondered how long we could play with fire before getting burned—but I couldn't bring myself to care.

Chapter 50

Callie

I didn't realize that it would take almost a year for Farrah to come back to herself. I should've known. I should have guessed that years of abuse ending in a beating so bad she'd forever carry the scars would take a long time to recover from. But I'd optimistically thought that when things settled down, she would turn back into the snarky girl I loved like a sister.

That year was one of the longest of my life.

Gram brought Cody with her to visit a few times, but the brother I knew was nowhere to be found. He was quiet and intense in a way he'd never been before, and his body had changed so much since I'd seen him last that it was startling. His shoulders had broadened and his jaw was sharper, making him look more man than boy. But when he smiled at Gram, his eyes crinkling, I couldn't help but notice the little boy I'd chased around the house with a tube of my mom's lipstick when I was six years old.

I hadn't kept in touch with him the year before like I'd promised, but it was as much his fault as mine. We'd seen each other on his school breaks, but in between those times, it had almost seemed as if he was avoiding me. That all changed the year he graduated from high school.

He became a repeat visitor to the apartment in Sacramento, spending his time equally between Gram's house and mine whenever he was home. The minute he finished his classes each term, he'd be on the first flight to California, even refusing to attend graduation. I loved it. It made me feel like my family was back together, finally.

I was happy to be reconnecting with my brother, but the rest of my life seemed to be in some sort of limbo.

Asa had stopped asking me when I was moving, but he visited more that year than he had before, averaging about six weeks between visits. It had to have been exhausting, making that drive so often, but he didn't complain and he wouldn't let me drive north instead. He said he wasn't comfortable with me driving so far by myself, which I thought was ridiculous, but not worth causing an argument over.

Those visits were also different than they'd been before. In the past, every visit had become an event that I planned for, but I no longer had time to worry that the apartment was spotless or his favorite foods were in the fridge. Farrah took up all of my extra time, stopping by the house at all hours to do nothing but watch TV or help me make dinner.

I slowly watched her heal, and refused to allow myself to become impatient at her progress.

It was odd, but Farrah and Cody rarely crossed paths. She seemed to know that I needed time with my brother, and would make herself scarce whenever he was in town without my Gram. I hated that she was so weird about it, but I didn't push it until one summer night when she was almost back to normal and Echo called and asked me and Cody to go out with them.

The bar we went to was run by the Aces; I swear they had their hands in so many things I didn't know how they kept them straight. I wasn't complaining, though, because Cody and I walked in without one person looking our way. It was in a strip mall, one of the old ones built in the seventies, and the floor to ceiling windows in the front made me assume it had been a Laundromat at some point. It just had that look.

I greeted Chucky and Echo, introducing them to my brother while I searched for Farrah. She was standing near the bartender with a hand on her hip, the pose making me smile. I was so glad that she finally resembled the girl I'd met two years before, that I was grinning wide as she handed something to the guy behind the bar.

The music cut off with a screech as she made her way to the middle of the floor, and men around the room yelled out their annoyance as the music started again. It was some sort of Pop music that I hadn't heard before, but the beat blared out of the speakers so loudly that I could feel it in my chest. It wasn't something they wanted to listen to, and they were complaining loudly, but I couldn't take my eyes off Farrah, and soon everyone else was staring silently, too.

She was dancing.

Her hips shook as she put on a show for the guys at the bar, and I glanced across the table nervously, imagining how Asa would feel if I were shaking my ass in the middle of a bar.

Echo was relaxed back in his chair, a little smirk on his lips as he took a sip of his beer. He must have felt my eyes on him, because his eyes shot to mine for a moment, winking, before going back to Farrah.

"Holy shit," Cody sighed next to me, making me laugh.

"Close your mouth, little brother," I teased him as Farrah bent at the waist so her hair was brushing the floor.

His chair screeched across the floor as he ignored me and tried to stand, but a hand on his shoulder stopped him.

"That one's mine, son," Echo told him with a smile, standing up from his own chair. "Get your own."

My eyes had moved back to Farrah as Echo sauntered up to her, and I couldn't drag them away as she started dancing on him while he stood relaxed, still drinking his beer. He wanted her; I could see his struggle to let her dance instead of dragging her off. But the pride in his gaze was apparent as he let her do her thing.

"Why are you crying?" Cody asked, perplexed. "That's hot as hell."

"Yeah," I mumbled back, never taking my eyes off the couple on the dance floor as I smiled. "She's back."

Chapter 51

Callie

I loved it when Cody stayed with me. He not only did things around the house like take out the garbage, but it was nice to come home to *someone*—even if it was my stinky brother with his feet on the coffee table. Our shared history was like a security blanket for both of us, and we understood each other in a way that no one else ever would.

We were packing up my apartment, laughing over kitchen gadgets that looked like torture devices, and I couldn't remember the last time I'd felt so happy. I was giddy with excitement to be moving to Oregon after so long, one of my favorite people in the world was sitting on the floor of my kitchen, and my best friend was on her way over. It was bliss.

Some people go their entire lives without facing tragedy. They live every day as if nothing bad would ever happen to them, because they have no experience to draw from and no reason to be weary. Others are always waiting for the other shoe to drop. They don't assume that nothing bad was going to happen, but wonder when it would.

I forgot for a moment that I was one of the latter.

When I heard a bike pull up, I ran to the door and flung it open, racing down the stairs so I could walk Farrah up. I didn't *need* to do it, it's not like she needed the direction, but I wanted to say hi to Echo before he took off to take care of some club crap. Farrah smiled at me, pulling off her bright pink helmet, and I waved as I jumped down the last two steps of the stairs.

I didn't notice the car at first. I wasn't paying attention to the road, because even though it was a quiet street, cars passed by all the time.

It wasn't until Echo shoved Farrah at me that I realized something wasn't right. I caught her and we went stumbling into the stairwell, barely catching our balance before hitting the stairs. I watched over Farrah's shoulder, my arms wrapped tightly around her waist as Echo glanced over to where we were hidden by the wall of the stairwell and met my eyes.

Then his eyes shifted to Farrah's and he winked.

"Hey, Ace!" someone called out.

It's funny how the human brain works. Or is it the speed of sound that makes memories seem just a bit off?

Echo's body started jerking before I heard the gunshots.

Or maybe it was after.

I can't remember, because the minute he winked, I had to tighten my arms around Farrah and use all of my body weight to keep her from running to him.

I held back a scream and wrapped my legs around her hips, my back digging into the cement stairs as I fought her.

I managed to get one hand over her eyes as she gouged my arms with her nails, making me the only one who witnessed Echo turn his eyes to Farrah as he dropped to his knees and fell forward onto the pavement.

Neither of us made a sound.

And then, with squealing tires, it was over.

Chapter 52

Callie

I lost my grip on Farrah as Cody came barreling down the stairs.

"What the fuck?" he asked me, pulling me up as Farrah started scrambling toward Echo's body, not even taking the time to stand.

"I don't know," I whispered back, watching as he ran toward the couple only a few feet away.

I should've been screaming. I should've been running for Echo the way Farrah and Cody were.

But I wasn't. I was back in my crawlspace, and I knew not to make a sound. Instead, I pulled my phone out of my pocket and called Asa as I walked slowly to where my brother and Farrah were rolling Echo onto his back.

I wanted to scream at them that there was nothing they could do—that he deserved to keep a little of his dignity.

"Hey, Sugar," Asa answered lazily, completely unaware of the scene unfolding before me.

"Asa," I rasped, "I'm scared."

"Talk to me, Callie!" he ordered, all complacency gone.

"There was a car," I looked up the quiet street, but nothing was there. "Echo brought Farrah over."

"You have to tell me what happened, sweetheart," he prodded urgently.

"I don't know," I told him vaguely, the world becoming hazy as I watched Farrah push Cody's hands away so she could kiss Echo sweetly on the lips.

"Calliope, I can't understand what you're saying. Is your brother there?"

"Yeah. He's with Echo."

"Give him the phone."

"But his hands are all bloody…"

"Give your brother the phone!" he roared.

I lifted my phone in Cody's direction, and he must have been watching me, because he grabbed it right away.

"Grease, fuck! It's bad, man," he spoke into the phone softly, taking a few steps away from where Farrah and I were huddled over Echo.

The next few minutes felt like an eternity as we sat guard over Echo's body. Farrah was still surprisingly silent, but she reached out and grabbed my hand as we waited. I wasn't sure what we were waiting for, but the minute I heard the roar of multiple Harleys, my entire body sagged in relief.

As the men parked their bikes and came toward us, sirens began to fill the air.

"You call the cops?" a large biker I'd never seen before asked Cody.

"Nah," he answered, pulling the phone away from his ear to gesture with it. "Grease. It was probably the neighbors."

I watched the faces of the men around me as they took in the scene, and only a few were successful in maintaining their stoic expressions.

"You know who did it?" a man with tattoos on his face asked Farrah and me, kneeling next to Echo and pulling something out of the chest pocket of Echo's shirt.

"No," I answered, shaking my head a little.

"Good. That's *exactly* what you tell the cops," he told me ominously before standing back up and disappearing into the crowd.

I sat there in a daze as an ambulance pulled in with its lights flashing, and I didn't move a muscle when two policemen ordered everyone to put their hands up.

They treated me like a threat, and as they took Echo away, I lay handcuffed, face down on the ground, less than a foot from his blood.

The rest of the day and into the night was a blur of giving statements and listening to apologies from weary policemen. They'd eventually uncuffed me, realizing that I was a victim, though I didn't feel like one. I was just a bystander to something horrific that I was unable to talk about but would never forget.

Late that night, after the police had left the apartment and the place was quiet, Farrah finally spoke.

"I never thought that I could feel worse than the night I realized my mom would never love me," she told me quietly. "I was wrong."

"Things can always get worse," I told her seriously.

"I don't know what could be worse than this."

"Me, either," I answered, wrapping my arm around her shoulder.

We were quiet for a while, listening to Cody pace back and forth in the kitchen. After all of the trauma of the afternoon, there was nothing for us to do. There were no papers to sign, no questions to answer, just... nothing.

Eventually Farrah stood, pulling me with her, and headed toward the bathroom.

"We need to take a shower," she told me flatly, pushing the door open and ushering me inside.

She stripped down to her underwear, throwing her clothes out the door as she took them off, while I turned on the water. I assumed she wanted me to stay with her, so I made no move to leave, but was surprised when she came over and started pulling at my t-shirt.

"What are you doing?" I asked curiously as I let her pull it over my head.

"You need to take a shower."

"Okay, I'll take one when you're done," I told her gently, trying to pull her fingers from the front of my jeans.

"You need to take one now," she mumbled urgently, looking into my eyes. "You've got bloo—you've got bloo—you need to take off these clothes. You need to take a shower *right now!*"

I looked down in surprise, realizing for the first time that I was covered in dried blood.

"Okay, baby girl. I'll take a shower now," I answered her quietly, moving her hands so I could strip off my jeans. "Climb in."

The shower ran red when we climbed inside, and Farrah kept her eyes pointed toward the ceiling as she grabbed my body wash and started scrubbing. We passed it back and forth, washing our arms and torsos until the half-full bottle was completely gone. Then we started on our hair.

Farrah was rinsing her hair for the second time when Asa walked into the bathroom and slowly pulled back the curtain. I could see the questions in his eyes, but he didn't say a word as he reached out a hand to me.

"We need towels, baby," I told him quietly, ignoring his hand.

"Okay," he answered hoarsely, looking between Farrah and me before walking back out.

"Okay, Farrah, that's enough," I told her gently as she started to pick up the shampoo bottle. I reached behind her and turned off the water as her arms dropped down to her sides. I wrung out her hair while she stood quietly, her eyes vacant.

"Here's your towels, Sugar," Asa called, pulling open the curtain. "You need some help?"

"No, I've got her," I assured him. "I'm going to get her into some clothes and then I'll be out."

"Okay," he answered, searching my face as he put a hand on my wet cheek. "Call if you need me."

I gave him a nod and turned back to Farrah, wrapping one of the towels around me and using the other to dry her off. I held her hand as I led her to my bedroom, but her grip was nonexistent.

"Farrah, I grabbed you some clothes," I called out, rifling through my dresser for underwear and pajamas. When she didn't answer, I turned to find her standing exactly where I'd left her in the middle of the room. "You want some pajamas?"

She was looking at me—aware of everything that was happening—but it was like her body had just stopped working, except for the tears running down her face.

"I'm going to help you into these, okay?" I asked, hoping she'd push me away and ask if I was a lesbian. "Okay, well if you don't mind then neither do I," I told her with a shrug of my shoulder.

I unwrapped the towel and ran it over her head once, but she was beginning to shiver, so I dropped it on the floor behind her and started stripping her. I unclasped her bra and pulled the straps down her shoulders, leaving it stuck to her breasts with water as I pulled the oversized sleep shirt over her head. When that part was done, I finished stripping off her bra and pulled her underwear down her legs, thankful she stepped out of them with little prompting.

When I'd just finished getting my smallest sweatpants over her hips, there was a small knock on the door. As I turned toward it, a familiar head popped through, taking in the scene before walking completely into the room.

"Gram," I sighed in relief before rushing to her. "Did Cody call you?"

"Yep. Told me my baby needed me, so here I am," she told me gently, kissing my forehead before turning to Farrah. "Get some clothes on, Callie Rose, you're gonna catch a cold in that towel."

I hurriedly threw one of Asa's t-shirts and a pair of yoga pants on as I watched Gram lead Farrah to the bed. She'd grabbed my hairbrush off the dresser on the way over, and once Farrah was seated, she stood behind her and started brushing.

"Asa's out there climbing the walls, Callie," Gram informed me, running her fingers through Farrah's hair. "I've got things handled in here."

Oh, God. I'd forgotten how good it felt to have Gram take control of a situation.

"Thanks, Gram," I told her quietly, walking out the door and shutting it quietly behind me.

Chapter 53

Grease

"Give your brother the phone!" I yelled at Callie as I stomped into my boots and left my room.

I'd been lying on my bed in my underwear, looking at fucking apartment ads, when she'd called. I'd immediately scrambled into some jeans when I heard her scared voice on the other end of the line.

"Grease, fuck! It's bad, man," Cody hissed, his voice low. "Echo was bringing Farrah over and Cal went out to meet them. I didn't see it. I was in the bathroom when I heard the shots and came running."

"Is your sister okay?" I asked as I raced through the clubhouse looking for Poet or Slider. *Where the fuck was everyone?*

"Yeah, she wasn't hurt." He paused. "Echo's dead, though."

"What the fuck?" I roared, pausing in disbelief. "What the fuck happened?"

"I have no goddamn idea. When I came out of the apartment, Echo was fucking down, and Callie was wrestling with Farrah on the stairs."

I finally found Poet and Slider outside having a smoke. I wasn't sure why they did it, but if they were smoking together they always stepped outside to do it.

"Prez, we've got fuckin' problems," I yelled, practically running toward him. "Cody, I'll send some boys to you and call you back."

I hung up the phone as I reached the men and took a second to control my emotions.

"Some fucker killed Echo in Callie's parking lot, with Farrah and Callie fuckin' watching," I told them as I flipped open my phone. "I don't think they knew who it was."

"Are the girls okay?" Poet asked calmly, but the twitching of his fingers gave a different impression.

"Callie's brother says they're fine," I answered, listening to Michael's phone ring repeatedly before hanging up.

"We need to get some of our boys over there—Echo's fuckin' dead in her driveway," I told them both, but Slider was already on his phone.

"We'll get some men over there, boyo, calm down."

"Fuck that! Some fuck just shot down a brother in my woman's fuckin' driveway!" I roared back, completely losing my shit. "She fuckin' watched it go down, and she's not strong enough for that shit!"

"I think the girl will surprise you," Slider commented as he shoved his phone back in his pocket. "I'll head out with you and we'll take some of the boys. Be ready in ten."

He turned and walked back into the building as I gaped at his retreating back.

"Don't forget that his daughter was there, too. Don't matter how well he knows her, that's still his blood, yeah?" Poet warned me quietly, patting me on the back as he passed.

It didn't take ten minutes to leave—it took seven—and by the time we rode out, I'd talked to Cody and found out that brothers from the Sacramento Chapter had already showed up. I heard sirens in the background as he hung up, and I hoped that no one did anything stupid.

I was so scared out of my mind, wondering what shape Callie'd be in when we got there, that I couldn't focus on anything *but* that and ended up making the drive on autopilot.

It reminded me so much of another time I'd raced south to get her that it felt like déjà vu.

I just prayed to whoever would hear me, that when I got to her, she wasn't the girl I'd found hiding in a crawlspace.

Chapter 54

Callie

I walked into the living room to find Cody, Asa, and Slider talking quietly. Asa's back was to me, so I didn't say anything as I came up behind him and wrapped my arms around his waist. He spun around at my touch and immediately brought both hands to the sides of my head.

"You okay?" he asked fiercely, searching my face.

"Yeah," I answered seriously, comforted just from having him beneath my hands. "Farrah's a mess, though. She's practically comatose."

"That what the shower was about?"

"She pulled me in there and refused to get in without me," I told him with a shrug. "We had blood everywhere."

"Gotta say, that's always been a fantasy, but that shit was *not* what I thought it'd be," he said with a small shake of his head, causing me to choke out a small laugh.

"Yeah, nothing sexy about cleaning blood off," I told him, my mouth trembling for the first time that night.

"Christ, Callie," he whispered, leaning down to kiss me softly. "You scared the shit outta me."

"It scared the shit out of me, too," I answered as he lifted me and then sat down on the couch, setting me in his lap.

"How's Farrah?" Slider asked from his perch on the floor. He was sitting against the wall with his elbows resting on bent knees. His eyes were weary as he stared at me, and it was the first time I'd seen any emotion there.

"She's a wreck." I told him honestly. "I don't think seeing you will help."

"I know," he answered, rubbing the back of his neck as he looked down at the floor. "Couldn't stay in Eugene—even if she doesn't want to see me."

"I don't think she's thinking about you at all," I told him.

"That's enough, Callie," Asa growled behind me.

I nodded and shut my mouth. He was right. Slider was trying to do the right thing, as misguided as it was.

"What happens now?" I asked Asa quietly as I pressed my forehead into the side of his neck.

"Aces have an in with the local police, so it shouldn't be long before they release Echo's body," he rumbled, rubbing my back. "So we'll be able to have a funeral."

"What about his family?"

"Didn't have one, far as I know."

"I didn't even know is real name," I cried softly as I snuggled in closer.

"William."

"Oh," I sighed softly. "That's a good name."

"Yeah, Sugar, it is," he confirmed, kissing the side of my face.

"What about the guys who did this?"

"Think we know who it was, not sure yet."

"They called him Ace," I told him, pulling my face back to meet his eyes. "Did they think he was you?"

"No. No, Sugar. Is that what you've been thinking?" he asked gently.

I nodded, my chin trembling. It had been running through my head the entire night, even though I'd tried to ignore it.

"Baby, we're *Aces*. That's the name of the club. You know that." He ran a hand down my face. "Echo was on his bike, which meant he was wearing his cut. They knew who he belonged to."

"Oh," I sighed in relief and then felt horrible for doing so. "So you joined a club that has almost the same name as you? That's a weird coincidence."

Slider barked out a quiet laugh behind me, and I watched Asa's cheekbones flush.

"Uh. My dad was an Ace, too," he grumbled. "Wasn't with my mom for long, so when I was born, she named me Asa."

"In honor of your dad. That's kind of cool," I told him tiredly, laying my head back down.

"Ha. No. More like a reminder," he snorted, dropping the subject completely as he started talking to the guys.

I lay there silently, feeling his pulse against my forehead as the men spoke around me. A part of me was horrified that Cody had seen so much, but the other part of me thanked God that he'd been there. I didn't know what I would've done without his help, how Farrah and I would have handled the situation ourselves.

I grew more and more weary as I listened to Asa's voice, and soon I was drifting off to him whispering, "Sleep, Calliope. I've got you."

Chapter 55

Callie

They buried Echo in a cemetery near my neighborhood.

The funeral of an Ace was a thing of beauty. There was no other way to describe it.

Well over a hundred motorcycles escorted the hearse and a limo carrying Farrah, Cody, Gram, and me from the funeral home to the cemetery. Aces from all over the West Coast had showed up to pay their respects, and the roar of Harley pipes was heard from blocks away, rattling window panes and bringing entire families outside their houses to watch us go by.

Farrah had come out of her trance the day after Echo was shot, and I watched her intently for days, waiting for her to crack.

She didn't.

She was in mourning—there was no doubt of that—but she hadn't completely lost her shit the way she had a year before. It seemed as if that year with Echo had made her infinitely stronger, because once she was facing a life without him, she seemed to just… accept it.

I didn't think I'd be able to do what she did. It would have completely broken me if I lost Asa.

The thought that he could be taken from me at any time ran through my mind on a constant loop. I started to hate the club he belonged to, resenting every minute he had to spend there. It was the reason Echo had been gunned down, the reason Asa and I were living apart, and the reason Farrah had been abused for years. It became such a demon in my mind that I couldn't hear anything about it anymore without inwardly flinching.

I started having nightmares again for the first time in months. I'd wake up in a cold sweat, curled against Asa on the couch, and burrow into him, sometimes waking him up just so I could hear his voice. I no longer dreamed about my parents' deaths—I dreamed of Asa's. I barely slept.

A week after Echo's funeral, I woke up slowly, having gotten only an hour's worth of sleep the night before. The nightmares had plagued me every time I shut my eyes. They became so vivid that I hadn't been sure if I was awake or asleep, and had laid on the couch, terrified, as I listened to Asa's heartbeat.

"Callie Rose, get dressed!" Gram called from the stove. "Need to run a few errands this morning and you're coming with me."

I grumbled as I rolled off the couch and onto my hands and knees. "Gah! I feel like shit," I griped as I dragged myself to my feet.

"Umhmmm," Gram scoffed from the kitchen.

"Where's Asa?" I rasped as I walked toward my room.

"Took Farrah to some sort of appointment," she called back over her shoulder.

God, I was tired. It took me twice as long to get dressed as it usually did, and by the time I made my way back out, Gram was standing at the front door.

"I'm gonna brush my teeth and stuff—I'll be right out," I mumbled.

"No!" she snapped, and then smiled. "We're just doing a couple errands. Let's go."

I complained in my head as she asked me to drive her to a pharmacy a few blocks away from the apartment, but followed her out of the car when she snapped her fingers at me. Snapped her fingers—like I was a dog. It wasn't until we were in the tampon aisle that I started to get a little weirded out—she was *way* past the need for those.

"You need to pick a test," she told me, pointing to a plethora of pregnancy tests ironically surrounded by condoms. "It's been a long damn time since I've been pregnant, and we didn't use these things."

I gaped at her, shocked silent as she watched me through narrowed eyes.

"Well?"

"Um..." I looked back and forth between the tests and Gram, completely at a loss for words.

"I'm guessing you and Asa haven't been very careful," she commented, looking over her glasses at me. "I'm pretty sure you're pregnant."

"Why would you think that?" I asked, licking my suddenly dry lips.

"Because you're tired all the time, you're barely eating, and you look like you have four boobs under that shirt because your bra is too small," she told me matter-of-factly as I looked down at my four breasts.

"Oh," I sighed. "Yeah. Maybe we should grab one... since we're already here."

"That's what I've been telling you for the ten minutes we've been standing here, Calliope," she answered as she bent over and picked up a lime-green package of ribbed condoms. "Hmm, interesting."

"Oh. My. God," I mumbled, my face flushing as I reached out to grab the closest test. "This one will work!"

"Well, that one doesn't detect pregnancy early like that one right there," she argued, pointing at a test that cost twice as much. "You should probably get the early one."

"Okay, I'll get this one then." I picked up a different test.

"No, that one next to it has two tests in one box—in case you drop the first one in the toilet or something."

"Gram, do *you* just want to choose?" I asked her, frustrated.

"Oh, fine." She grabbed the box she wanted off the shelf and turned her back on me, walking toward the front of the store as I scrambled to put all the discarded tests back in their proper places.

We made our way to the car in silence as my mind raced. Asa and I hadn't been trying to get pregnant—but we hadn't been *not* trying, either. The condom situation had been pretty hit or miss for the past year, but I'd never gotten pregnant, so I'd just assumed that I wouldn't. Asa was only visiting once every six weeks or so, and I knew that the timing had to be just right for conception.

I couldn't decide if I was really freaked out or really excited.

Gram didn't have any more errands that day—she'd just wanted me to go with her to the drug store. *The sneaky old broad.* We drove straight back to the apartment while I held an almost transparent grocery bag in my hands with the pregnancy test's bright pink lettering mocking me through the side of the bag.

I really hoped that no one was home when we got there—I wasn't sure how I could hide it.

I breathed a sigh of relief as we pulled into my parking lot and Asa's bike was still gone. I only had to worry about Cody, who I'd assumed had been out on his morning run when Gram and I had left. I didn't know how he could stand to go running after sleeping on the floor all night.

My house was beginning to feel like a train station with all of the people staying in it—sleeping on every available surface.

When we walked into the apartment, my brother was sitting on the couch watching television, so I discreetly tucked the test into my armpit and called out a hello as I rushed to the bathroom.

"Where'd you guys go?" I heard him ask Gram, but I slammed the bathroom door before I heard her answer.

I had to pee so bad that I danced around the bathroom as I pulled the test out, not bothering to read the directions before plopping myself on the toilet. When I was done, I stayed where I was as I set the test on the rim of the bathtub and pulled out the directions.

So I was sitting on the toilet, my pants around my ankles, and my un-brushed teeth making my mouth taste like shit when I found out I was going to become a mother.

Chapter 56

Callie

Gram was standing outside the bathroom door when I opened it, her eyes wide in question.

"We need to go to the grocery store for supplies." I told her quietly, biting the inside of my cheek.

"You sure?"

"Yeah," I murmured, holding out the test.

"Okay, let me get my billfold and we'll go now," she told me with a nod, reaching forward to kiss my head. "But brush your teeth first."

I'd seen movies and read books where the main character would wait days, or even weeks, to tell her man that she was pregnant. She'd hem and haw about the right time, as if waiting would somehow lead her to a favorable reaction. I didn't feel that way. Not at all.

I was bursting at the seams to tell Asa. I wasn't worried about his reaction, or waiting until the perfect time to tell him. I just wanted him to know. I wanted to share it.

But there were a few things I had to do first.

There was a tradition in my family that had started with Gram. She was probably one of those women who prayed for a favorable reaction, and went out of her way to make sure the scene was set perfectly, before telling her husband she was pregnant. My grandfather had been an asshole. But when it came time for my mom to tell my dad about me, she'd followed in Gram's footsteps and cooked him his favorite dinner, setting the table with her best dishes and lighting candles, even though she knew my dad would be over the moon with excitement.

Asa's favorite dinner was my Gram's homemade spaghetti recipe with a side of green beans cooked with little bits of bacon, and I was going to make it for him.

Our trip to the grocery store took longer than I expected because Gram had wanted to look at all of the new gadgets in the baby department. I would've thought she'd be pissed that I was barely nineteen and having a baby, but if she was she didn't let on. She treated me like any other expectant mother, cooing at pacifiers shaped like butterflies and bitching about the price of diapers.

By the time we got home it was late afternoon, and I was worried about how I'd get everyone out of the house so Asa and I could have dinner alone. We hadn't had any time to ourselves in so long that dinner together felt like a novelty, and I'd begun to wish that everyone would go home and leave us alone. I also didn't want there to be an audience when I gave him the news. He deserved to be able to react however he needed to without having to worry about what everyone was thinking. Besides, the moment I told him the news should be just for us.

I'd just started unpacking the groceries when Farrah burst into the apartment with Asa following behind her. He looked tired and annoyed and I wondered what appointment had taken so long that they'd been gone most of the day.

"I got a tattoo," she told me bluntly, pulling a banana off the bunch and peeling it quickly.

"A piercing, too, I see," I commented, eyeballing the septum piercing that hadn't been in her nose the night before.

"Yup!" she answered around the huge piece of banana she was practically inhaling. "Goes with the tattoo."

I looked her over but couldn't see the tattoo anywhere. When she caught my gaze, she tapped on the back of her neck.

"It's on my neck. Hurt like a bitch, but it looks awesome. I'll show it to you later after I take the bandage off."

"Okay," I replied slowly, watching her carefully. I hadn't heard any mention of a tattoo before she went out and got it done, and I wondered what had led her to wake up that morning and permanently ink her body.

"Hey, Sugar," Asa murmured as he strode into the kitchen, completely ignoring Farrah as he stepped past her. "You making dinner?"

"Yep," I told him quietly, leaning up to kiss his lips.

"Callie, what are we having for dinner?" Cody called from the couch, making me clench my teeth.

"I'm making spaghetti and green beans," I called flatly, turning toward the counter as Gram walked out of my bedroom.

"My favorite," Asa mentioned with a smile, patting me on the ass.

"Cody and Farrah, we're going out to eat, get your shoes on," Gram ordered at the same time.

My brother, who had been leisurely strolling into the already crowded kitchen, stopped abruptly, his mouth dropping in surprise as his eyes narrowed. "Oh, *hell* no."

"Not another word out of your mouth, Cody Daniel," Gram snapped at him, stopping in front of him to push him toward the door with both hands on his belly. "We're gonna give them some time alone."

"I'm hungry as hell; I don't care where we eat," Farrah piped in, completely oblivious to the undertones in our conversation as she walked toward the front door. "Take your time, kids. I'll take Gram to the bar after dinner!"

I was strung tight as a wire by the time the door closed behind them, and I wasn't sure how I'd be able to keep my mouth shut until I had dinner at the counter. I really wished we had an actual kitchen table, but I was willing to improvise.

"Why don't you take a shower, and by the time you're done, I'll have dinner in the oven," I told him brightly as I poured noodles into water boiling on the stove.

"Don't need a shower, took one before we left, and I've been sitting on my ass all day while Farrah fucked around at the tattoo parlor," he grumbled, sitting down at the counter. "That girl is gonna lose it soon."

"What happened?"

"Nothing huge, she just seems like she's strung tight as hell, and she's trying to find a way to let off some steam." He shook his head. "You better watch out for that brother of yours."

"Gross!" I snapped, pulling hamburger out of the fridge. "Cody wouldn't do that. He knows Farrah's having a hard time."

"Your brother's got a dick," he answered seriously, looking down at his phone. "He'd do it."

"Can we not talk about my brother and my best friend having sex right now?" I asked, frustrated tears forming in my eyes. He was texting someone on his phone, talking about people that I'd just kicked out of the house so we could be alone, and I was having a hard time not just blurting my news out before dinner was ready. The night was *not* going how I'd envisioned it. "I just want to make fucking dinner for you and me without any other shit getting in the middle of it."

I sniffed once, turning back to the stove, and in seconds he was wrapping his arms around me from behind.

"What's going on, sweetheart?" he asked gently, kissing the back of my neck.

"I just want to finish dinner so we can sit down and eat your favorite meal. Alone. I want to eat dinner alone without worrying about anyone else's problems."

"Look at me, Callie," he ordered, pulling at my waist.

"I need to finish this," I told him desperately, dumping spices into the pan frantically. "The hamburger will burn if I don't stir it."

He reached past me and turned off both burners before spinning me to face him.

"You're going to ruin it!" I practically screeched, pushing at his hands.

"What the fuck is wrong?" he snapped, making the tears that had been stinging my nose well up in my eyes. "What's wrong?" he asked again quietly, searching my face as it crumpled.

"I just wanted to make your favorite dinner," I whispered, wiping off my face, "and now it's ruined and I don't have any more noodles."

I burst into gut-wrenching sobs and pushed my face into his neck as he picked me up and strode toward the front door, locking it before taking me to the bedroom. He set me down by the doorway and walked to the bed, pulling at all four corners of the sheets until he'd wrapped all of the bedding into a ball that he threw on the floor.

"What are you doing?" I asked hoarsely as he put a clean sheet on the bed.

"I'm stripping the bed, so I can fuck you without smelling Farrah's and your grandmother's perfume, and I'm leaving that shit in a pile so we can put them back on later and they don't have to smell us," he told me simply, making me cry again.

"What the fuck is wrong with you?"

"I'm pregnant." *Well, shit.* I guess I *was* going to just blurt it out.

"What?" he whispered, dropping onto the bed.

"I took the test this morning. I didn't realize..." I swallowed hard as I walked toward him. "Gram took me to the store this morning and pretty much ambushed me into buying a test. With all the stuff going on, I just didn't even—"

"Oh, fuck," he whispered, his eyes widening in horror.

"Not the reaction I was going for, Asa," I mumbled dryly, trying to disguise the panic rising in my throat. *Why did he look so horrified? It's not like he didn't know it could happen!*

"Are you okay?" he asked, dropping to his knees and lifting up my shirt. "Is everything okay in there?"

I sighed in relief as I ran my fingers through his hair. "I haven't been to the doctor yet. But I think so."

"You fell on the fuckin' stairs," he mumbled, unbuttoning my pants and peeling them down my legs. "They had you cuffed on the ground."

"I'm pretty sure something would've happened by now if I'd been hurt," I reassured him, "but I'll set up an appointment to make sure everything's good."

He pulled off my t-shirt as he got to his feet, staring at my breasts in amazement. "Whoa! Your tits are *huge!*" he gaped, reaching up to cup them in his hands. "How did I not notice this? They're popping out all over!"

"Probably because you haven't seen me naked in for-freaking-ever," I griped, pushing his cut off his shoulders.

He reached behind me to unclasp my bra and I took a huge breath of relief as it fell away. I hadn't noticed that my boobs were bigger, but I *had* noticed that the band had been digging into my sides for what felt like weeks. It left itchy little indents that I loathed.

"Shit, you're really pregnant," he mumbled. "Put some pajamas on. We need to find you a doctor."

I stomped my foot as he started to walk away. I actually stomped my foot.

"You haven't even kissed me!" I yelled, my emotions all over the place. "We don't need to call the doctor right now! I need you to kiss me and tell me you love me and then fuck me on our four hundred dollar bed that you insisted we have!"

My chest was heaving as he turned back around, the most beautiful smile pulling at his cheeks and crinkling his eyes.

"You're having our baby," he roared loudly, lifting me so high by the backs of my thighs that I had to lean forward or bump my head on the ceiling. I laughed hysterically as he spun in a circle. "I love you and you're having my baby."

"Yeah," I whispered, my smile trembling.

He carefully slid me down his body until my legs were wrapped around his waist and grabbed the back of my head.

"I love you," he murmured into my mouth. "Best thing I ever did—taking you outta that house. I'd change a lotta shit that came after if I could, but even if I did, we still woulda ended up right here where we are now."

He kissed me hard as he laid me down on the bed.

"You're so beautiful," he whispered as he softly rubbed his thumb back and forth below my belly button. "What'd I do to deserve you?"

"You saved me," I whispered back.

Chapter 57

Grease

If I'd thought leaving Callie was hard before, it was *nothing* compared to leaving her then. Shit was heating up big time with the Jimenez gang, and I had to get back to Oregon to deal with it. Stuff like that made me glad Slider was head of the club. He was able to see the big picture, where I would've flown off the handle a year before.

The Jimenez brothers had fucked up badly when they sent me into Jose's. Not only had they practically shoved me into a fucking trap, but they'd still owed us thousands of dollars when all was said and done. They'd played like they'd had no idea what was happening with Jose— that he'd acted on his own—but it didn't matter what they'd claimed. They'd successfully put themselves on Slider's radar which was *never* a good thing.

Over the past two years they'd continued to fuck up, talking shit to the wrong people and claiming an alliance with the Aces as they did it, leaving us to smooth shit over with clubs we'd never had a problem with before. It was bullshit.

The latest in a long line of shit was with a club out of Montana and we hadn't smoothed that one over. We'd thrown the Jimenez boys under the bus, breaking all affiliation instead. Slider hadn't been willing to overlook shit anymore and was somewhat friends with the club president up in Montana. He drew the line on fucking with the guy.

It burned me that my brother Deke was a part of those assholes, but there was nothing I could do about it. I'd given him more than enough chances to break with them with no blowback, but he hadn't taken them. I don't know which was his biggest issue: his loyalty to them or the meth they were supplying to him. I had to let him hang himself, which was *exactly* what was going to happen if Slider found proof that they'd put the hit out on Echo.

Slider would find out what happened, and God help the person who'd sanctioned the hit. They not only took one of ours, but could've killed his daughter. He wasn't going to let that shit pass, and the more we dug, the more we found that all signs pointed to southern California.

I'd taken Callie to the doctor and made sure everything was fine with her and our kid. They'd even done an ultrasound to see how far along she was. In the movies, they'd put some shit on her belly and then rub it with a little wand, but apparently she was too early for that shit. When they pulled out this fucking probe that they were going to stick inside her, I think we both went a little pale. Watching anyone, even a woman doctor, lube that shit up so they could put it inside a place that was meant for me made me sick. I'd had a hard time even focusing on the little screen they were showing us, my skin feeling too tight for my body all of a sudden, and I'd been happy as hell when it was all over. I'd made her take a bath when we'd gotten home, anxious to wash that shit off.

We'd also talked to the owner of her apartment and convinced him to let her move into the unit next door that had two bedrooms. I wasn't sure how long she'd be staying there—I was anxious to have her with me—but she couldn't keep sleeping on the fucking couch with Farrah and Gram in our bed. Cody'd gone to San Diego to make sure all was okay with Gram's house, but eventually he'd be back, and there were too many people for a fucking one-bedroom apartment. It was easy to move her, we only had to carry shit a few feet down the walkway, and I could see how relieved she was when we were all done. We'd have our own bedroom again. *Thank fuck.*

I was getting ready to leave, packing up my saddle bags, when Callie came stumbling down the stairs, rubbing the sleep from her eyes. She was wearing a little black tank top with no bra, and I thanked the pregnancy gods for the way her tits had grown. I'd thought she was perfect before, but holy shit, they seemed to be growing more by the day—I couldn't keep my hands off them.

When she was at the bottom of the stairs, she froze, her eyes opening wide. My body tensed and I searched the area for anything out of place, but couldn't see anything that would freak her out.

"Hey, Sugar," I called, smiling. "You okay?"

"Yeah, I'm just tired," she answered cautiously, watching the neighborhood carefully as she came to me.

"We've got boys keeping an eye on shit. Men will be around," I told her as I buckled my bag. "No need for you to worry."

"I know. I'm just a little jumpy," she mumbled, stepping into me and wrapping her arms around my waist. "You done here? Can we go inside?"

"Yeah, but I have to hit the road soon," I warned her, setting my hand on her lower back to lead her up the stairs. "You need to put some clothes on before you leave the house."

"It's like seventy degrees already!" she scoffed, walking inside.

"I know how warm it is, Callie, but your tits are huge and your tank top is really fuckin' small!" I practically shouted as I followed behind her.

"Can I please not hear about my sister's tits at nine in the morning?" Cody grumbled from the couch.

"Fuck!" I hissed as Callie gave me a snotty look and stomped toward the bedroom. "Shut the fuck up, Cody."

I followed her into the bedroom as she was whipping off her tank top and trying to stuff herself into a bra. I wasn't sure why she hadn't bought any new ones yet, but the old ones looked uncomfortable as hell.

"The doctor said at thirteen weeks they'd probably still grow a bunch, and I didn't want to buy new ones yet," she commented, snapping the bra straps over her shoulders angrily. "But they're really uncomfortable, Asa! And those tank tops are tight enough that I can wear them without a bra."

"I didn't mean to embarrass you, Callie," I told her, rubbing my hand down my face. "I just don't want other men seeing your tits everywhere you go."

She nodded her head, stripping out of her pajama shorts and underwear, and I couldn't help myself. I scooped her up against me and kissed the hell out of her. By the time I'd maneuvered her to the bed, I'd already undone my belt and jeans, and it took only a matter of seconds for me to shove them down and push inside her. I fucking loved grumpy morning Callie.

"I'm still annoyed with you," she gasped, pulling my hair loose with one hand. Every time she did that it was like a straight jolt to my dick. "You're gonna be back soon, right?"

"Yeah, sweetheart. Soon as I can. I'll be back down," I assured her, reaching behind her to unsnap her bra as her back arched. "I'm gonna leave some cash for you. You buy new bras."

She shook her head, her eyes growing dazed, but still following the conversation, "I'll just grow out of them."

I stopped moving, making her whine quietly. "Then I'll buy you more, yeah? Don't want you walking around uncomfortable for no reason when I can fix it."

She didn't argue so I started moving again, my belt clinking loudly as it hit the edge of the bed where I was standing.

"They'll be ugly," she told me softly, her eyes meeting mine. "The bigger they are the uglier they get."

I barked out a laugh that had her tensing, and I had a hard time not groaning when she clamped down on my dick. "Calliope," I gasped, moving harder against her. "I don't care what the fuck they look like as long as they're comfortable. I want what's *inside* them.... and why the fuck are we still talking about this?" I asked, running my hand down her belly so I could pinch at her clit.

"No idea," she whimpered back, arching her neck as I hit the right spot.

I felt her pulsing around me when she came, and I wondered how the fuck I was going to leave her in an hour.

Chapter 58

Callie

Once Asa left, I felt quite a bit more apprehensive about the whole 'baby' thing. I didn't really feel pregnant yet, mostly just tired, and the thought of ballooning and then pushing a baby out of my business had me breaking out in a cold sweat. I couldn't help being excited, though, especially after we'd seen our little bean on the ultrasound.

Farrah continued to live with me full time, but Gram stopped staying with me a couple weeks after Asa left. Thankfully, because Cody's scholarship had expired when he'd graduated, Gram was no longer tied to San Diego. She'd had Cody drive down to pack up her trailer and move her things north—right into the apartment I'd just vacated. She'd said she didn't want to be far away when I had the baby, which made the move to Sacramento seem odd to me. I was still planning on moving in with Asa as soon as Farrah got her shit together, and frankly, I was running out of patience.

It wasn't as though I'd put her on a time limit. I hadn't. But she seemed to be racing toward the edge of a cliff and everyone around her was just waiting for the fall. I sort of wished she would get to that point so we could deal with the fallout and she could start to heal. Everyone dealt with grief differently, and it seemed as if Farrah's grief was manifesting into a drinking, tattooing, piercing extravaganza. She reminded me of a coloring book; every time she came home she had something new drawn or stuck into her body. Unfortunately, Asa had also hit the nail on the head when he told me to watch out for Cody.

Something was going on with them even though neither of them were talking about it. It was almost a relief that Cody would be heading to Yale in the fall and I wouldn't have to worry about whatever fucked up thing they had going. The last thing Farrah needed was a new guy fucking with her life, especially if that guy was my little brother.

It was the third week after Asa'd left and I'd slipped back into preparing for his visit. Everything was so much more vivid now that we were starting a family. I missed him more, loved him more, wanted him more—it was like every emotion I felt was magnified by ten. I wanted everything to be perfect when he arrived, even going so far as to buy new sheets for our bed and cleaning the toilet.

"Honey, I'm home!" he bellowed from the front door, startling me into hitting my head on the top of the cupboard I'd been cleaning.

"I just talked to you three hours ago!" I yelled back, running to him so I could jump and wrap my arms and legs around him. "You said you were just leaving!"

"I lied," he replied smugly, grabbing my hair in a fist and kissing me deeply. "You surprised, Sugar?" he whispered into my mouth, walking us to our bedroom.

"Best surprise *ever*," I whispered back, smiling wide.

"I even stopped by your Gram's and let her know I was here so no one comes knocking."

"I get to fuck you without an audience?" I asked mischievously. "I won't know what to do with myself."

"How about you make all those noises I haven't heard in fuckin' forever," he told me with a groan as I bit down on his neck.

He carried me to the bed, never letting my feet touch the ground. When he set me down, I lay there lazily as he began to strip. His cut came first, sliding down his broad shoulders until he grabbed it with one hand and tossed it at the end of the bed, never taking his eyes off me.

When he reached behind his neck and could barely grasp the back of his t-shirt, I made a noise deep in my throat.

"You keep getting bigger," I sighed huskily.

"Not a lot to do except drink when I'm not on jobs," he told me with a grin. "Been working out so I didn't give myself blisters jacking off."

I snorted then laughed hysterically. "Been a little frustrated, baby?"

"Fuckin' understatement," he grumbled at my laughter as he stripped out of his boots and jeans.

"I can help with that," I murmured, my eyes widening as I realized he hadn't worn boxers.

"You think?" he asked, leisurely stroking himself as I watched.

"I'm pretty—" my voice came out sounding like Jessica Rabbit's and I had to clear it before continuing, "I'm pretty sure."

"Good," he answered, nodding his head. "Strip."

My heart was pounding as I climbed up to my knees, my hands going directly to the waistband of my shorts. I pulled them off slowly, watching his nostrils flare as my shorts and underwear hit the bed. I leaned back onto my ass to pull them off and gave him a good view, but he didn't take the invitation, content to watch as he stroked himself.

"The shirt," he commanded, his voice a deep growl that I'd come to know and crave.

I pulled my shirt off slowly. Once it was off, I remembered the bra I was wearing and raced to pull it off, fumbling and turning my body away from him as I tried to undo the closure on the back.

"Hey," he called, reaching out to grab my hands as I frantically tried to get it off. "What's up?"

"I bought a really sexy bra that I was going to put on when you were almost here," I moaned, embarrassed. "I was going to change out of this one before you got here."

"Why?" he asked, his brows furrowing in confusion.

"Because it's an old lady bra!" I huffed back, finally giving up on trying to unhook the three rows of hook-and-eyes holding it together.

"Sweetheart, it's just a bra," he told me, leaning down to run his lips over the top of my breasts. "It looks like it fits."

"It *does* fit," I told him softly, running my hand through his hair as he placed little kisses all over my chest. "But the other one is pretty, and this one isn't."

"If you don't like this bra, then why did you buy it?"

I grasped his hair and tilted his face up to mine. "This is one of my comfortable bras. The other ones are for you to see."

"You're saying I can't see most of your bras?"

"Just the comfortable ones," I said with a nod.

"You're outta your mind," he stated firmly, pulling my hips until I'd fallen back on the bed. "You're throwing all of those uncomfortable bras in the fuckin' trash."

"The hell I am!" I gasped, trying to sit up.

"Calliope, I want you," he told me seriously, running his fingers down the center of my belly until he'd reached the heat between my legs. "I don't give a fuck what kind of bra you're wearing as long as it's not digging into your ribs and your tits. You have uncomfortable bras, you throw that shit out."

His fingers started exploring as if they hadn't touched me a million times before, and my breathing hitched as he hit my clit.

"Now, take off this bra that you've been bitching about so I can see you," he whispered as he leaned down to kiss me softly.

I arched my back and easily undid my bra with one hand as he leaned back on his knees, his hands leaving my body.

"Jesus Christ, you're beautiful," he mumbled as I threw my bra as far across the room as I could. He knelt there staring for what felt like forever, and I wondered if he was noticing the thicker thighs and waist I was sporting. When he hadn't moved for over a minute, I felt myself growing embarrassed even though I knew it was ridiculous.

"Are you going to touch me?" I asked in a snippy tone, my insecurity coming out bitchy like it always did.

"Yeah, Sugar. I'm gonna touch you," he answered, running his hand down my leg. "I wanna look at your new body first."

"Cataloguing my fat, huh?"

"Shut it, Callie," he answered fiercely. "Don't *ever* say that shit to me."

My mouth snapped shut at his order, my face burning with embarrassment. I knew I wasn't fat, but insecurities were a bitch and it felt like I was gaining weight faster than I should have been.

"You were gorgeous when I met you," he told me quietly, running a hand from the top of my shoulder to my wrist. "But now? You're so fuckin' beautiful it almost hurts to look at you. Your tits are all full and round, your belly's got a little bump already, and *fuck me*, but I'm pretty sure your thighs and ass are gonna make me have a heart attack." As he detailed my body parts, he ran his hands over them lightly until my entire body was covered in goose bumps.

"Such a sweet talker," I murmured back, reaching up to run my fingers across his jaw as tears filled my eyes.

"I aim to please," he grunted back, leaning down to catch a nipple.

I sniffed once before getting my tears under control and arched my back as he tugged hard with his teeth.

"Careful!" I hissed quietly. "I'm super sensitive and they hurt."

"Aw, I'm sorry," he murmured back, licking over the offended nipple as if to soothe it. "You sore down here, too?" he asked as he slid down my body until he was looking between my legs.

"No," I gasped as he licked me gently. "Not sore."

I think he mumbled the word "good" but I wasn't sure because his lips pressed firmly into my clit and I keened low in my throat. He licked and sucked and bit at me until I was writhing on the bed, but right when I was about to come, he pulled back.

"Asa!" I snapped, pulling at his hair in an attempt to move his face back where I wanted it.

"That's right, Sugar," he hissed as he pulled my hands away from his head, trapping them above me as he moved in between my legs.

He paused until I was jerking at my arms and tilting my hips against him, then leaned down and whispered in my ear, "Now scream it for me," as he pushed inside with one powerful thrust.

"Fuck!" I yelled, shocked by the feel of him after three weeks.

"Not what I was looking for," he commented as he pulled out slowly and slammed back in.

"Asa," I whimpered, trying to follow his directions but unable to catch my breath enough to do it.

"Louder," he grunted, letting go of one of my hands so he could reach down and very gently twist my nipple.

I jerked off the bed in response, feeling myself start to shake as his pelvis rubbed against my clit with every slow, outward pull. We were quiet for a few moments, watching each other as my climax grew closer and closer, until finally, it hit.

"Asa!" I moaned loud and long as I came.

"Perfect," he gasped as his hand slid to my chin, tilting my head back. "So goddamn perfect."

Then he latched down on my throat and sucked strongly, marking me as he came.

After catching our breath, I cleaned up and crawled back into bed with him, content to do nothing but feel his skin against mine.

"You been feeling okay?" he questioned, rubbing his hand softly over my belly.

"Yep. No issues so far," I answered, planting my elbow on the bed so I could lean up and trace the tattoo across his collarbone.

"I hate being so far away," he told me seriously. "I wanna watch all this. Seems like you've already changed in the three weeks since I saw you last. This little curve is new."

"Yeah, it's kind of funny because people can't figure out if it's a baby or just fat," I told him with a laugh.

"When are you gonna let Farrah stand on her own two feet?" he asked with a sigh. "I know she's your best friend, but she doesn't seem to see anyone but herself, and you're not doing anything but giving her a free place to live."

"I know," I murmured, flopping onto my back on the bed. "But I can't just ditch her. Everyone in her life fucks her over. I don't want to be another person on that list."

"I think you're gonna have to have a 'come to Jesus' with her. We can't keep putting off our life for her, Callie. It's gotta stop at some point," he told me, playing with my fingers.

When I was silent, he changed the subject, "Why don't you paint your toenails? Fingers are always different colors, but you never paint your toes."

I slipped into a memory of leisurely painting my toes as I

listened for my parents and forcefully pushed it out of my head. It was a simple question and didn't require a long explanation, but I couldn't force the answer past my throat.

"Don't care if you paint your toes, Callie," he assured me, coming to the wrong conclusion about my silence.

"The day before my parents were killed, instead of talking things out with them, I sat in my room and painted my toenails," I told him with a shrug and shake of my head. "Because that was so fucking important."

"That had nothing to do with what happened," he told me quietly, leaning over me.

"I know that."

"You need to stop ignoring it, Callie."

"I'm not ignoring anything. I just choose not to remember."

"Sweetheart, it's just gonna keep popping back up, you can't hold that shit back forever," he stated seriously.

"Can we talk about something else? You just got home and I'd just like to revel in that for a bit," I answered, leaning up to give him a peck on the lips.

"Yeah, but we're gonna revisit at a later date," he warned.

"Fine," I pouted, then ordered, "Tell me how much you love me."

"More than my bike, less than my dick," he answered with a straight face.

"Ha! Asshole!" I laughed as he began to tickle me.

That weekend with him would become one of my best and most important memories.

Chapter 59

Grease

Callie was sending photos of her belly every day, and I swore I could see a difference in each of them. I was fucking *done* with having her so far away from me. She was already halfway through her pregnancy, and I was still dragging my ass to Sacramento each chance I got. It was insane—how long we'd waited to finally be in one place together.

As far as I was concerned, Farrah could deal with her own shit. She was still partying and doing fuck all to help herself, and I didn't see an end in sight. I hated it that Callie was down there taking care of her shit when she should be worrying about herself and our kid. She was tired all the fucking time because she was having a hard time sleeping, and I knew that having Farrah stumble in drunk as shit in the middle of the night wasn't helping.

The bullshit needed to stop.

I was packing up my bike to hit the road that morning when Tommy Gun came lumbering out of the clubhouse calling my name. I was standing right in front of him, and I shook my head when he bellowed my name again.

"What?" I snapped, anxious to get on the road.

"Slider wants to see you," he mumbled, raising his hands with his palms out.

"You know what it's about?" I questioned, stuffing the rest of my clothes into the saddle bags.

"Nope. I'm just the messenger!" he called almost a minute later as I was walking back inside.

Slider was sitting at the bar when I got inside, and he raised his chin at me as I headed toward him. He had a packet wrapped in brown paper on the bar in front of him, and he palmed it as I reached him.

"You heading south?" he asked, rapping his knuckles on the countertop.

"Yup. Callie's got a doctor's appointment that I'm gonna miss if I don't leave now," I answered impatiently.

His brows lowered in response to my tone, and I automatically took a step back.

"Not gonna hold you up. Just need you to drop a package in Sacramento when you get there," he replied quietly, sliding the package to me across the countertop.

"That it?"

"That's it. I'll see you when you get back," he responded, standing from his stool. "Check on my girl for me, would ya?"

"Yep. I'm outta here." I turned and strode toward the door, raising my chin at Dragon who'd been passed out on one of the couches and was looking blearily at me over the head of some blonde chick.

The first hour of the ride was uneventful. I'd taken the trip so many times I could probably sleep through it, and I had gotten complacent about watching for speed traps and highway patrol. I was thinking about the ultrasound, excited as fuck to see my kid again.

I know most people say some stupid shit about not caring if their kid was a boy or a girl as long as it was healthy, but I didn't think about it that way. Of course I wanted a healthy kid, which went without saying, but I wanted a fucking boy. I wanted a boy so badly it was like a weight in my gut, something I thought about constantly, no matter what I was doing. I figured Callie probably wanted a little girl that she could dress in frilly shit, but the thought of a little girl made me anxious as hell.

I wanted a boy that I could teach to throw a football and take apart a motorcycle. I wouldn't know what the hell to do with a girl.

I was flying down the highway, thinking about Callie's appointment and how the hell I was gonna talk her into moving and leaving that fucking weight around her neck, so I didn't see the police car under an overpass with a radar gun waiting for stupid fuckers like me.

When I noticed the lights in my mirror, I was annoyed as fuck that they were going to hold me up. It was getting later and later and Callie would have my balls if I didn't meet her at the doctor's office that afternoon.

I pulled over to the side of the road and shut off my bike, putting the kickstand down and taking off my helmet as I waited.

"You know why I pulled you over?" the cop asked as he walked up beside me.

"Speeding," I answered, running my hand over my beard. *Damn, I needed to trim that shit so I didn't look like a fucking mountain man the first time I met my kid.*

The cop looked at my beard and then down to my cut, his mouth lifting into a sneer.

"I'm going to have to ask you to step off your bike," he told me condescendingly, taking a step back and dropping his hand to the gun at his waist.

Fucking prick. He was going to mess with me and there was not a goddamn thing I could do about it. I climbed off my bike and stood with my arms at my sides as he spoke into the walkie-talkie on his shoulder before raising his eyes to mine.

"License and registration."

As I reached for my wallet inside the pocket of my sweatshirt, he pulled his motherfucking gun.

"Hands where I can see them!" he bellowed, pissing me right the fuck off.

"My wallet's in the front pocket of my sweatshirt," I told him, hands raised in the air. "Thought you wanted my license and shit?"

"One hand stays in the air, grab your wallet nice and slow," he ordered, watching me closely.

I followed his orders, slowly using both hands to give him the shit he needed. I didn't want some rookie cop shooting me in the chest because his balls hadn't dropped yet.

"Stay off your motorcycle, I'll be right back," he grumbled, taking my shit as he walked toward his car.

He took a long-ass time running my shit, and I seriously considered hopping on my bike and leaving his ass behind. If he hadn't had my paperwork, I would have taken off.

"You have anything on your bike that I should know about?" he asked, as he reached where I was standing.

"Nope," I told him with a smirk.

"I believe you might be under the influence. I'm going to need to search you and your bike."

"What the fuck?" I sputtered, completely fucking confused.

"Hands on the hood of the car."

"Fuck you."

"Are you resisting, Mr. Hawthorne?" he asked menacingly, one eyebrow raised. The fucker was just dying to get me on something.

I leaned over the car, pissed as hell but still relatively unconcerned as he searched me. I didn't carry a weapon when I was making the trip to Callie because I was on probation from shit that had happened years ago. I had a piece at her house that I carried when I was in town, but if I wasn't on a run I didn't bother to carry. It was more hassle than it was worth if I got pulled over.

"Keep your hands on the vehicle," he ordered as he headed toward my bike. Fuck, the guy was taking forever and I was counting the minutes that I stood there, wondering how the hell I'd make up the time so I wasn't late.

He was shining a light under my bike even though the sun was coming up, and huffed when he didn't find anything. Then he searched through my bags, pulling out mostly boxers because I'd bought ugly-ass new ones to wear around Callie so she wasn't so fucking worried about her bras.

He finished with the first saddle bag, finding nothing, but when he started pulling shit out of the second, he paused. He reached into the bottom of the bag and my stomach fucking dropped when he pulled out the package Slider had given me that morning. He glanced up at me, probably to make sure I hadn't moved, and then used both hands to unseal the package and open it up.

"Jesus Fuckin' Christ," I murmured, dropping my head in defeat when I saw what he'd sent.

I didn't watch the cop anymore; I just stared at the hood of his car as my heart raced. I was going to miss the goddamn appointment and who the fuck knew what else.

As the cop walked up behind me and pulled my hands behind my back, I knew before he started reading me my rights that I was going to jail.

Chapter 60

Callie

"Where is he?" I asked Gram as I paced the waiting room of my doctor's office. The ultrasound technician was running half an hour late, so it was twenty minutes past my scheduled appointment time and Asa *still* hadn't showed.

"Probably running late," she answered calmly, flipping through a magazine. "You know he can't call you when he's on the road."

"He would have stopped to call if he was going to be late," I worried, chewing the inside of my cheek.

"Or he's riding like hell to get here and won't take the time to stop," she told me firmly. "Now sit down and calm down."

I dropped heavily into the seat next to her and watched my phone. There were no incoming or missed calls, and the longer I went with no word from Asa the more anxious I became.

"Calliope?" I turned my head when the nurse called me from the doorway to the exam rooms but couldn't make myself stand.

"Well?" Gram asked impatiently. "Let's go darlin'."

I drug my feet as I made my way to the nurse, looking behind me a few times in hopes that Asa would be walking through the door.

"Can we wait a couple more minutes?" I asked her almost desperately as we met her in the doorway.

"Sorry, hun." She looked at me sympathetically. "We're already so far behind, you'd have to reschedule."

I looked at Gram for validation, hoping she'd assure me that we should come back, but her lips were pressed into a flat line. My mind raced as I thought it over, but Gram's hand on my back had me walking through the door and toward a room before I could come to a decision.

"No need to get undressed," the nurse told me as she set my chart on the countertop. "Just pull your shirt up and your pants down a little. The tech will be in soon."

She shut the door behind her as tears filled my eyes.

"Calliope Rose Butler, you look at me," Gram snapped fiercely, pressing both hands against the sides of my head and pulling me close until we were almost nose to nose. "I know you're disappointed, baby. I know you're worried and anxious and God knows what else. But seeing your baby on that screen and hearing them tell you if you're having a boy or a girl—that only happens once in a lifetime. *Once*, Callie. You'll never get this moment back."

I nodded and sniffed as she studied my face.

"You get up there and get ready to see that baby, and you leave everything else outside that door. It's got no place in here with you and me." She kissed me quickly and took a step backward, giving me a swat on the hip. "Crawl up there so you're ready when the guy gets in here."

I worked at pushing everything else out of my head as the female ultrasound tech came in and started chatting. I didn't hear a word she said because I was so busy trying to filter out everything happening outside the room. It hurt that Asa wasn't with me, but we'd known for weeks when the appointment would be. If he'd wanted to be there, he would have.

I watched intently as she used the computer to measure my little bean, tracing little lines over its head and torso and labeling different body parts. I was so intent on the baby that she startled me when she spoke.

"Do you want to know the sex?"

I looked at Gram who'd stood from her seat across the room to watch the monitor closely.

"Let's do it," she told me with a nod, grabbing my hand tightly.

"Yeah. We want to know," I answered, searching the tech's face for an answer before she spoke.

She turned back toward the monitor and started moving her mouse around again. "You see that right there? You, my dear, are *definitely* having a boy."

"Are you sure?" I asked, stunned.

"I've been doing this for five years, and I've been wrong twice. I'm reasonably certain," she told me with a smile as she stood from her seat and handed me a row of black and white photos. "The doctor will be here in a few minutes after he goes over the results." She gave a small smile before exiting the room.

"A son," Gram murmured quietly, running her hand down my hair. "There's nothing in the world like it."

I ignored her teary eyes, knowing she wouldn't appreciate if I made a big fuss about it, and cleaned the goop off my belly. The doctor came in a few minutes later, giving us the all-clear on all the test results, and I left the office in a daze, thankful that Gram had driven me to the appointment.

We were having a son, and Asa had missed it. How could he have missed it? I swung between worry and fury as we rode home. How *could* he? *Where the fuck was he?* I would have known if he'd been in an accident. I was listed as his next of kin on a little card in his wallet—someone would've called me.

I'd no sooner had the thought than my phone started ringing shrilly in my purse and my stomach dropped.

"No. No. No," I murmured as I fished it out and saw an unknown number on the caller ID.

"Hello?" I answered frantically.

"Hey, little girl."

"Poet? What's wrong? Asa was supposed to be here this afternoon and he never showed." My words were tumbling over each other in my panic as I stared blankly out the windshield.

"Asa's just fine—"

"Then where the fuck is he?"

"He ran into some problems on his way down this morning..."

"Why am I just now hearing from anyone? What the hell is going on?" I asked as Gram parked the car and I threw myself out of the car so I could pace.

"Just heard about it myself. Called you first thing."

"What. Is. Going. On?" I snapped back.

"Asa got arrested this morning, and he had to use his call to phone Slider—"

"Arrested?" I whispered, my stomach dropping. "What happened?"

"Not sure of the details yet, just wanted to let you know that he's fine. He was real insistent that I call you soon as I could."

I pressed my hand to my head, feeling dizzy all of a sudden, and I felt Gram wrap her arm around my waist, ushering me toward the stairs.

"Okay, well let me know..."

"I'll keep you updated. Don't worry, darlin', he'll be out before you know it."

I climbed the steps wearily as Poet hung up, and I couldn't even answer the questions in Gram's eyes, I was so bewildered. Why would he have gotten arrested on his way to me? It didn't make any sense and my mind was spinning.

"Baby daddy stood you up, huh?" Farrah mumbled around a mouth full of what looked like shredded wheat cereal. My heart sped up as I stared at her in disbelief. She looked like shit. Her hair was matted on one side and there were half-circles of mascara under her eyes. She'd probably just woken up after her bender last night, and she'd been passed out cold while I'd been freaking out for the last two hours.

"Fuck you, Farrah!" I screamed, throwing my purse at her and knocking cereal all over my couch. "You're such a fucking bitch!"

I felt Gram's hand on my elbow, but I was too overcome with emotion to pay any attention to her.

"What the fuck did *I* do?" Farrah yelled back, standing from the couch.

"It's all about poor fucking Farrah! Farrah has had such a shitty time that she treats everyone around her like total crap!" My hands clenched into fists as she stared at me in disbelief. "I should've moved to Oregon by now!" I screeched, the veins in my temples throbbing.

"Fuck you! I didn't ask you to stay! Move to fucking Oregon, then!" she sniped back, sliding her feet into shoes. "I didn't need you to stay here, Callie. I got along fine without your ass."

As she was finishing, Cody walked through the door, his face a mask of fury. "What the hell is going on? I could hear you yelling from Gram's."

"Your sister's got a stick up her ass because her boyfriend never fucking showed and now she's taking it out on me," Farrah replied, folding the blanket I'd thrown over her the night before when she hadn't made it to her bedroom before passing out. "Apparently, everything is *my* fault because I got the shit beat out of me and had the bad fucking luck of having my boyfriend killed, too. I'm such a fucking burden because she felt obligated to stay instead of starting her own fucking life."

At her words, I lost all steam and was suddenly exhausted. "I stayed because I love you," I told her, tears filling my eyes. "But you don't even care. You don't even care that I'm five months pregnant and went to my ultrasound today. You don't care that I postponed my entire life to make sure you were okay." I paused, hiccupping. "I needed you today and you were passed out on the couch, and the minute I walk in the door you make some stupid fucking comment without *once* asking if everything was okay, because it so obviously wasn't."

I shook my head and walked toward my bedroom. "I'm going to take a nap, Gram. Can you keep my phone in case someone calls?"

"Yeah, baby girl. I'm gonna run to my place and get some potatoes for dinner and I'll cook over here tonight," she told me gently. "You get some rest."

I heard Cody and Farrah start to argue as I reached my room, but they went silent as Gram's angry voice roared through the apartment.

I barely crawled into my bed before I began to sob.

Chapter 61

Callie

I woke up the next morning to Farrah sitting on the edge of my bed holding a plate full of toaster waffles.

"I'm here to grovel," she told me with a rueful smile, gesturing with the plate. "I'm not very good at it."

I gave her a small smile, scooting up in bed so I could lean against the headboard.

"I've been a dick," she said, handing me the food. "I know when I'm being a dick and sometimes it feels like I can't stop it."

"I'm sorry I yelled at you last night," I answered quietly, setting the waffles on my lap. "I was freaked out about Asa and you were in the line of fire."

"Yeah, but you meant what you said." She raised her hand when I tried to interrupt. "No. I get it. You've stayed here to help me and I've been an ungrateful asshole. I'll try to do better."

"I just want you to be okay." I reached out and squeezed her knee.

"Yeah, I'm running out of skin anyway," she told me with a shrug. "I need to get a job or something. I can't live off your food and other people's booze forever."

I snorted and started choking.

"Shut up," she laughed back at me. "I'll get a job. I'll figure something out."

"I know you will," I gasped, my throat still tickling. "I was more worried about the partying and pin cushion thing you've got going."

"Fuck!" she hissed, falling backward on the bed. "I'm gonna have to take some of these out or I'm never gonna get hired."

"Do you really care?" I asked seriously.

She raised her head to gape at me. "They hurt like hell and now I have to take them out!"

I started to giggle, my heart feeling lighter than it had in weeks.

"Well, maybe not *all* of them," she replied, raising her eyebrows up and down.

We sat on my bed laughing for a few minutes before reality came crashing down with the arrival of Gram at my bedroom door. "Poet," she mouthed silently, handing my phone to me.

"Hey, Poet," I answered cautiously.

"Hey, girl. I just wanted to give you an update. Looks like they've got Grease on a probation violation. The suit says he should be able to get him out on Monday."

"That's *days* from now!" I argued.

"Shit takes time, darlin'. Don't you worry; we'll have your man out soon. You have another phone number?"

"What? No, just this one," I answered, confused.

"He's not gonna be able to call, then. Can't make collect calls to a cell phone—has to be a landline."

"I can go get one!" I answered almost frantically. "I'll go today."

"Saturday, girl. Nothing's open. Just give it a few days and he'll be able to call. I'll let you know if anything else comes up."

He hung up again without saying goodbye, and I dropped the phone to my lap.

"Fuck," I whispered, raising my eyes to Farrah and Gram who were waiting. "Probation violation. I don't even know what that means!"

"Just means they'll hold him for a few days, maybe longer,"

Gram reassured me, sitting down next to me on the bed. "You just worry about you and that baby."

"I need to go to Oregon," I responded, flipping my blankets back so I could crawl out of bed.

"What the hell would you do that for?" Gram argued. "Nothing you can do up there that you can't do down here. You need to just wait until we know how long he's gonna be there."

"I can't just sit here. I feel like I'm going to crawl out of my skin knowing he's in there." My nose tingled with tears as I rifled through my dresser, picking out clothes. "I have to do *something*."

"Why don't we go baby shopping?" Farrah piped up from where she was laying, covered by the blankets I'd thrown off. "Plus, you need some new clothes, that shirt is way too small."

I looked down at the tee I'd put on and pulled at the hem to cover the sliver of belly I was showing. I'd gotten significantly rounder in the last month and I'd had to start wearing yoga pants and leggings constantly because I couldn't zip my jeans.

"I can wait a little longer before I buy maternity stuff," I answered, my nose crinkled in distaste. I'd seen some of the shit other ladies at my doctor's office had been wearing. *No, thank you.*

"Dude, you're like the Hulk; you're busting out of that shit. We need to at least buy you some bigger regular shit—people are already staring because you look like an after school special. No need to look white trash, too," Farrah told me seriously as she climbed off the bed.

"I'm not white," I commented drolly as I followed her out of my room.

"Half-white trash then!" she called as she walked into her room and slammed the door behind her.

"It's nice to have her back," I said quietly to Gram, putting my arm around her shoulder as we reached the living room.

"It is, but don't think that girl is all healed up just because she came in all smiles this morning. Nothing's *ever* that easy," she warned. "I'm going to go get my billfold from the house and let Cody know where we're going."

I brushed my teeth and hair, but didn't bother with anything else before sitting down on the couch to wait for Gram and Farrah. I needed a moment, just a moment, to let everything from the last twenty-four hours sink in. The pendulum of my emotions had swung widely the day before, from worry over Asa to complete awe of our son, and I felt like I couldn't catch my breath.

I hadn't realized how much I still depended on Asa to feel safe until Poet had told me that he was locked away from me. The entirety of my need for him had come crashing down and I hadn't known how to deal with it, so I'd picked a fight with Farrah. Our argument had been a long time coming, but I didn't delude myself into thinking that I'd been angry with her. She was just the tip of the proverbial iceberg, not the solid chunk below the surface.

I felt lost knowing that Asa was unavailable to me, and scared that he was in jail worried out of his mind. I knew he could take care of himself, he'd made that clear on several occasions, but I hated that he'd missed our appointment and was probably beating himself up about it. I desperately wanted him with me.

"Okay, I'm beautiful! You ready?" Farrah called cheerily as she came down the hallway, slinging her purse over her shoulder.

"Who *are* you?"

"Your cool-as-shit best friend. Now get off your ass and let's go," she answered with a smirk.

"Gram got to you, didn't she?" I asked suspiciously, narrowing my eyes at her.

"She ripped me a new one. It still hurts to sit down," she told me with a grimace as I laughed. "That old broad knows just how to twist the knife."

"Ha! You haven't seen *anything* yet," I told her as we walked out of the house and locked the door behind us. "She's a freaking virago."

"The hell is that?"

"Callie, stop jabbering and let's go," Gram called as if I hadn't just been waiting on her. I shook my head and smiled as she started down the stairs.

"You need to read more," I told Farrah teasingly as we jogged down the stairs behind Gram, only pausing slightly as we hit the bottom step. We'd gotten better about ignoring the spot where Echo had been killed, but I knew both of us still felt that jolt of fear whenever we reached the bottom. We could have moved into another place that didn't make us cringe, but for some reason those shitty-ass apartments made us feel safe. They felt like home.

"Shotgun!" Farrah called as she ran toward my car.

"Fuck you! I'm the pregnant one!" I bitched back as I waddled after her.

God, I'd missed her. Even with my mind swirling with worry over Asa, I was still almost giddy at the thought of shopping for baby things.

And I refused to feel guilty about it.

Gram had been right when she'd spoken her words of wisdom at the doctor's office the day before.

These moments would only happen once, and I could either let outside forces overshadow the joy I felt about my baby boy, or I could revel in the feeling despite those forces.

I was going to have a son. I chose to revel.

Chapter 62

Callie

Monday came and went with no word from Poet or Asa.

So did Tuesday and Wednesday.

On Thursday, I threw up twice from nerves, and still no word.

I finally got a call on Friday.

"Asa!" I answered the phone excitedly, feeling like I was taking a deep breath for the first time in a week. "Hello?"

"Hey, Sugar," he answered quietly.

"I missed you! Are you okay?"

"Yeah, I'm fine. How are things with you and baby?"

His voice sounded off, and my stomach churned.

"We're both fine. The doctor said everything on the ultrasound looks great!" I answered with false cheer.

"I'm sorry I didn't make it, sweetheart. I really wanted to fuckin' be there."

"I know, baby," I told him quietly. "I wished you were there, too. You want to know what we're having, or do you want to wait until I see you?"

"Better tell me on the phone, Callie. Not sure when I'll be able to make the trip down there." He paused for almost a full minute. "I can't leave the state."

"Well, I'll just come to you, then!" I promised, still hanging on to my false cheer. "I can leave now and be there by tonight!"

"That's not gonna work, Calliope," he answered vaguely, and as I listened to him, my legs started to tingle as if they were falling asleep.

"What? Why? I can be right there. I'll even take Gram with me, if that's what you're worried about. Or Cody! I can bring Cody!" I was racing through the words frantically, trying to convince him that it was a good idea.

"I love you. I love you so much," he told me seriously, and I fell against the wall as I heard his breath hitch, my legs giving way until I'd slid completely down to my ass.

"I love you, too," I whispered back. "I want to be with you."

"Sugar, things are worse than we thought. I wish I could explain it all to you, but the lawyer said not to talk about it on the phone, so you're just gonna have to trust me."

"Trust you with what? What's going on, Asa?"

"They think they found something on my bike that I wasn't supposed to have," he mumbled, pausing to sigh deeply, "I was coming from the clubhouse, and your friend's dad said to bring her his love."

Confusion set in and I sat silently for a few moments before I realized he was speaking in some sort of code.

"When I got pulled over, they took me in. Judge let me out on bail, but it's only a matter of time before they arrest me again. The lawyer thinks they're gonna make an example outta me," he told me quietly. "I don't want you driving all the way up here before the court date."

I inhaled on a sob, scared as hell. "I'll just come up and see you and then leave again. I won't be there long!" I pleaded.

"Not good for you to sit that long in a car, Sugar," he answered gently. "Round trip, that's almost twenty hours. You gotta take care of you and the baby."

"But I miss you," I whimpered, not willing to give up.

"Fuck, I miss you, too. But I don't want you driving all the way up here," he told me firmly. "I gotta go, Sugar. I'm sitting in the fuckin' parking lot of the jail, but I wanted to give you a call first thing. I'll call you back as soon as I get home, okay?"

"We're having a son," I replied quickly, in an anxious bid to keep him on the phone.

"A son?" he whispered.

"Yeah." I smiled, tears rolling down my face. "They even took a picture to prove it."

"They took a picture of our son's dick?" he asked, his voice rose at the end in disbelief.

"Chill out!" I giggled. "It's a grainy black and white photo. It's not porn!"

"A son," he muttered again quietly. "Thank you."

"I'm pretty sure you determine that, but you're welcome."

"I gotta go, Callie. I'll call you back," he muttered abruptly, shattering the moment we'd been having.

"As soon as you get there?"

"Yeah, Calliope, I'll call you the minute I park," he assured me. "I love you."

"Love you, too," I murmured and then listened to the click as he hung up.

Cody found me bawling on the kitchen floor only a few minutes later.

"What the hell, Callie?" he panicked, lifting me to my feet with his hands under my arms.

"Asa called," I told him dully as I grabbed a glass and filled it with water. "He's out."

"Then why the hell were you crying on the floor?"

"He said it's bad, Cody," I whispered, looking directly into his eyes. "He said they're going to arrest him again."

"What? Why?" he asked, bewildered.

"I don't know! He said that they'd caught him with something, and then said something about Slider sending his love to Farrah! He wasn't making sense!" I barked, running a frustrated hand through my hair.

"Wait, what does Farrah have to do with it?" he asked protectively, pushing out his chest and crossing his arms over it.

"I have no idea. I think he was trying to tell me something without really saying it."

"What exactly did he say?"

"That he came from the clubhouse and my friend's dad asked him to bring his love to her."

"Holy fucking shit," he mumbled, looking at the floor and rubbing the back of his neck. "He was carrying something for Slider."

"What?" I screeched.

"It makes sense. Think about it—they found something on him, right? And he said Slider sent his love to Farrah, but that would be a pretty fucking weird thing for him to do," he told me intently, his eyes boring into mine. "Slider sent something with him."

"You think he was making a drop for Slider when he was supposed to be coming down for our doctor's appointment?" I asked incredulously. "That would be so fucked up!"

"That's what it sounds like," he confirmed.

"No way," I mumbled, pushing past him. "Tell Gram I'll be over later. I need to take a shower."

I strode into the bathroom, effectively ending our conversation. I needed to think.

Asa wouldn't have made a drop when he was coming down for

something so important. I knew him. I knew he wouldn't taint our day with club shit. He knew how I felt about the club even though I'd never voiced it.

My mind ran a thousand miles a minute as I took a shower, and I tried desperately to find something else hidden in his words.

When I climbed out and dried off, I noticed a missed call from Asa, but I didn't call him back. I needed to get my head together before I talked to him and didn't want to accuse him of something that wasn't true. I was afraid that if I called, I'd demand he tell me that Cody was wrong—that he hadn't made his trip to see me into some sordid club errand.

I was not only afraid it was true, I was also afraid that if I asked him directly and someone was listening in, I'd get him into even more trouble. There were certain things that I knew he kept from me—things about what he did for the Aces. I wasn't sure if he couldn't tell me, or just chose to keep them a secret in some misguided attempt to shelter me, and honestly I'd never cared before. I'd deliberately chosen to ignore that part of his life that didn't pertain to me directly, as I did with most everything else in my life.

Was it self-centered? Probably, but I couldn't stop it. I'd been protecting myself for so long at that point that it was second nature for me to take things at face value and refuse to question them. I should've learned with Farrah that I needed to be more aware of the things happening in my peripheral, but I hadn't. And now, once again, the fact that I'd turned a blind eye was coming back to haunt me.

I got dressed and headed to Gram's slowly, loathe to answer the questions I knew she and Farrah would have. They were curious and worried, just like I was, and I knew I'd have to give a full accounting of what Asa'd said. I was still trying to convince myself that Cody had been wrong, and something else was going on, when I walked in Gram's front door.

"Hey, chickie!" Farrah called from the kitchen as I strolled in. She was helping Gram make dinner, and it gave me a warm feeling when I thought about how close they'd become. Farrah had basically grown up without any parents, taking care of herself from a young age, and it was beautiful to see how she soaked up Gram's presence.

Gram had stepped in, with little fanfare, and treated Farrah the same way she did Cody and me—loving with a touch of guilt when needed.

"Hey," I answered back, watching Farrah closely. "I talked to Asa."

"Yeah, Cody told us," she answered tentatively, turning from the stove to look at me.

"He said Slider told him to bring you his love."

"Yeah, right!" she scoffed, turning away again.

For some reason, those words confirmed to me what I had refused to believe, and a small flame of resentment started deep in my chest.

Slider had asked Asa to bring something entirely different to California.

Chapter 63

Grease

I was having a shitty week.

First, I got pulled over and arrested, then the club's lawyer told me the DA smelled blood in the water and it looked like the judge was going to make an example out of me, and finally, something was up with Callie. I wasn't sure what was going on, but when she'd called me back Friday night, she'd seemed off.

I wasn't sure if she'd fully understood what I was telling her when we'd spoken, but she didn't ask again to visit. I was pissed at myself that I'd told her no, because I missed her like hell, but I knew that the drive would be horrible for her and I wasn't good company anyway. I was on the fucking chopping block, waiting for the blade. The wait was worse than the punishment because I fucking *knew* I was going to see the inside of a cell again, and not knowing how long I'd be in was driving me insane.

We had a fucking baby on the way. A son. And I was pretty sure I was going to miss the first part of his life. There was a slim chance that I'd be out in four months, but I wouldn't even let myself think that it would be a possibility. No, I'd be locked up and probably miss a ton of shit.

It made me sick to think of Callie going through all that alone. I knew that her Gram would be with her every step of the way, but I wouldn't. I wasn't going to get to see her waddling around and complaining about how her back hurt.

I was going to miss the excitement of her water breaking, of the

339

contractions that would make her hate me, and the relief on her face when some doctor finally gave her the drugs she needed to take the edge off. I was going to miss her sweaty hair and tired face, and the way I knew she'd look at me—like I could make everything better.

I was going to miss the look on her face when she saw our son for the first time.

It hurt like hell.

I'd spent the week getting my shit in order. I made sure that someone would deposit money into my account periodically, checked and rechecked with Poet and Slider to make sure they'd keep an eye on Callie, and paid all of Callie's bills six months in advance so she wouldn't have to worry. I didn't want to leave anything to chance; I didn't want anything to worry her when I couldn't be there.

I'd also called my girl constantly that week. I had nothing to do while we waited, so I spent the time with her. Well, as much as I could with her being hundreds of miles away. We were spending more time on the phone than we ever had, discussing everything from politics to baby names. We even discussed what would happen while I was inside—how she'd need to deal with the accounts, how to shut off my cell phone once I didn't need it, the boys in Sacramento she could call if she was having car trouble. We talked about everything except whatever was bothering her and had her going silent for full minutes at a time while I wondered what the fuck was wrong. It went past the ache we were both feeling at the thought of being separated. Something was happening with her and I had no clue what it was or how to fucking fix it.

I was stuck in Eugene, waiting for the inevitable, while something ate at her in Sacramento—and there wasn't a damn thing I could do about it.

Over a week after I'd been released, it was time for my court date. I rode with the lawyer to the courthouse, but I didn't have anyone else with me. The lawyer had told Slider that his and Poet's notorious faces might hurt my chances and I didn't even mention anything to Dragon or Tommy. I didn't want them to see me looking like a chump, being cuffed by some fat fuck cop, so I was on my own. As soon as we arrived, the lawyer stepped out of the car so I could make one last phone call.

"Hey!" she answered calmly, a smile in her voice.

"Hey, sweetheart." I hated the fact that I was going to be wiping that smile away. "It's time."

"What? I thought you had a few more hours! I thought—"

"Sugar, we went over this. We knew it was coming," I corrected her gently as I slid my sleeves down my arms and buttoned them around my wrists. I couldn't hide the tattoos on my neck or the ones on my hands, but I didn't think my full sleeves of ink needed to be on display.

"I know," she whimpered dully, sniffing into the phone.

"Now, we went over everything so you shouldn't have any problems, okay?" I told her urgently as I heard car doors shutting and the lawyer tapped on the driver's side window. "I'll have one of the boys call you once we know what's going on."

"Okay." I heard her sniff again before her voice grew stronger. "I'm fine—*we'll* be fine. You just do what you need to do, and I'll wait."

A lump formed in my throat as I opened the door and climbed out of the car. Fuck, but she'd grown up since I'd met her as a scared sixteen-year-old girl.

"I love you," I told her fervently as the lawyer started ushering me toward the front doors.

"I love you, too—so much."

"Be strong, okay? This'll be over soon, I promise, and then we can finally move you up here and be a family," I promised frantically as we joined the line in front of the metal detectors and I patted down my pockets, making sure I hadn't accidentally dropped my pocket knife in there like I usually did.

"Don't hang up!" she sobbed hysterically, making my chest feel like it was imploding. "I'm not ready! Don't hang up!"

"I love you, Sugar. Stay strong," I answered calmly as I heard a rustling on the other end of the phone.

"Hey, Asa," Cody greeted while I heard Callie sniffling in the background. "I got her, you just worry about your shit. Take care."

The click of the phone call ending made me flinch.

I was standing with my hand over my face and my phone dangling from my fingertips when the security guard called for me.

Once the lawyer found the right courtroom, we walked in silently to find some seats, and my heart raced as I saw the back of a familiar gray head sitting two rows from the front.

"Rose?"

"Asa," she called back with a nod as she stood from her seat.

"What are you doing here?" I asked, confused. I thought she'd be in California taking care of Callie.

"I'd never let one of mine face something like this alone," she told me firmly, motioning with her hands so I'd lean toward her.

The minute my head was lowered, she pulled a blue checkered tie out of her purse and wrapped it around my neck.

"Get that top button," she ordered as the courtroom started filling up. After I'd followed her direction, her fingers started flying as she knotted the tie.

"There, now you don't look like a hooligan."

"I don't think a tie is gonna make a difference," I told her sincerely, afraid that she was envisioning a far different outcome than I was expecting.

"Doesn't matter. You know you did your best to put the right foot forward, that's what's important," she stated seriously, smoothing down the tie with her gnarled fingers.

"We need to take our seats," the lawyer interrupted behind me.

"My lawyer," I informed Rose with a motion of my hand.

"Yeah, the suit tipped me off," she replied wryly, scooting down the aisle so there was room for the three of us to sit.

When we got situated in our seats, I felt the walls start to close in around me. *Fuck.* Jail time wasn't shit; I'd done it before, no problem. But the thought of leaving Callie was like a lead weight in my gut. I was pulling at the collar of my shirt when I felt a small dry hand settle onto mine.

"Nothing wrong with your shirt. Stop fidgeting," Rose ordered quietly, facing straight ahead.

Her hand in mine and the no-nonsense tone of her voice had me instantly pausing, and I took a deep breath as I squeezed her hand.

"Thanks for coming," I whispered back.

"I wouldn't be anywhere else," she assured fiercely.

We had to sit through two other cases before it was time for mine, and she held my sweaty palm the entire time. When they called my name, she gave me a squeeze and let go as the lawyer and I stood.

"It's time, son," she murmured, looking intently into my eyes. "You ready?"

"Yeah." I looked down at her as my heart beat frantically and my head began to throb. "I'm ready."

Chapter 64

Callie

When we prepared for Asa to go away—that's how I liked to think of it—we hadn't envisioned the length of time that would entail.

They gave him twenty-five months. Twenty-five months because he'd broken his probation and it had nullified his suspended sentence for an assault charge from three years before.

Twenty-five months because Slider had asked him to carry a gun to Sacramento.

The first week he was gone, I barely got out of bed.

The second week, I raged.

The third week, I played the what-if game.

The fourth week, I realized that I had a baby growing inside me that didn't deserve a basket case for a mother.

The entire time I raged, wept, and pleaded, my resentment for the club he'd called home his entire life grew. It grew to such massive proportions that I couldn't bear to see the members of the Sacramento Chapter when they came to check on me. Even Michael was turned away at my front door, his confusion apparent when I shut it in his face.

Asa called as often as he could, but the calls were often stilted and awkward. He refused to talk about anything to do with his incarceration, and answered any questions I asked with yes or no replies that made me want to pull my hair out. Most of our conversations were carried by me as I spoke on and on about the baby.

As those first months passed by, I grew.

My belly became more and more prominent, becoming so large

that even maternity shirts left a little sliver of belly showing whenever I moved. As it swelled, I gained line after line of angry red stretch marks, beginning at my hips and wrapping around the lower half of my belly, making me look like I'd gone head to head with Freddy Kruger and his knife fingers.

My bump wasn't the only thing that grew in those months. My boobs became massive, so massive that Farrah would run around the house with my bra on her head like a yarmulke, spouting off random Hebrew words. My feet were so swollen that Gram made me spend hours each night with them elevated, though it never seemed to help. My cheeks, thighs, and ass grew rounder until I looked like a snowman with all my lumps.

And as my body changed and I recorded everything for Asa, my resentment grew.

One morning, almost five months after Asa went to prison, I woke up having contractions. It scared the hell out of me and filled me with so much adrenaline I was shaking. I climbed out of bed slowly, taking the time to shower and blow dry my hair before I woke Farrah up. When I was finally ready, I strode into her room, only to find her up and putting her shoes on.

"I heard you in the shower and you never get up this early. Baby time?" she asked me briskly as she pulled her hair into a high ponytail. She'd slowly but surely come back to the girl she was before, and I wondered how much of it was because of her need to take care of me. It seemed that both of us had broken at different times and the only thing that put us back together was the other's need. It was a hell of a cycle.

"Yep. Let's go over and wake Gram up," I told her as she passed me. "Wait for me!"

The bubble I was floating on at the thought of racing to the hospital and popping out my son was burst when we got to Gram's apartment.

"You don't need to go to the hospital yet," she stated matter-of-factly. "I'm gonna go get dressed. I'll be out in a minute."

I watched her walk into my old room with my jaw hanging wide open at her nonchalant reaction. I was having a baby! Did she not see the urgency in the situation? *What the hell?*

Farrah was pacing behind me when Gram finally came out of her room, wearing an entire set of jogging gear. She even had a sweatband on her head.

'What the hell are you wearing?" Farrah barked, bending at the waist as she burst out in hysterical laughter.

I glared at Gram, waiting for an explanation, but she just smiled cheerily back at me.

"Time to go for a walk!" she ordered, clapping her hands together.

"I'm in labor, Gram. We need to go to the hospital," I explained slowly, wondering if she'd finally lost her mind.

"Walking first, Callie Rose," she told me as she pushed me toward the door. "Trust me on this; go put some tennis shoes on."

She closed the door on Farrah's laughter as I stood on the landing, gaping.

I wished my brother hadn't left for school a few months before. He'd understand my need for the hospital. He wouldn't tell me to put shoes on, or laugh, or force me to walk.

I trudged to the house and put shoes on, meeting Gram and Farrah outside.

"We'll walk around the block first," Gram informed us, taking off before we could reply. I had to race to catch up with her, which wasn't helping my contractions or swollen feet one bit.

"First?" I practically yelled. "What the hell, Gram?"

"You're not even breathing hard, and I bet those contractions barely hurt," she said with a nod as she came to a stop on the sidewalk. "You don't want to be sitting in a damn hospital bed waiting for hours and hours before anything even starts happening. Walking gets things moving."

She gave me a squeeze on the arm before turning and stalking off again.

So, we walked.

And walked, and walked, and walked, until the sun was inching toward the middle of the sky and my contractions were coming hard and painful. Yet, we still didn't head to the hospital.

First, Gram helped me take a shower and braided my hair. Next, she made a small breakfast for me and Farrah. Then she called my brother to let him know that we were leaving.

After all of that, I was still barely dilated when we got to the hospital.

It took hours for me to reach the point where I felt the need to push, and I was exhausted. The anesthesiologist had come in around six that night and put a huge needle in my back, almost instantly providing relief from the pain, but I still didn't get any rest. It was impossible to turn my mind off long enough to get more than fifteen minutes of sleep at a time, and the pressure of the contractions wasn't helping the situation.

I wanted Asa so badly that it was hard to breathe at times.

I wondered what he was doing as I was laboring and if he knew that we were at the hospital. I wondered if he could feel somewhere in his gut how badly I needed him in those moments.

I pushed for over an hour, Gram and Farrah at my knees, bracing against them as I burst blood vessels in my cheeks and eyes. They encouraged, cajoled, and wiped my face with a cool washcloth—but nothing, and no one, was a substitute for Asa.

"I need Asa, Gram," I wailed, completely out of my mind with fear and exhaustion. "I'm tired. I want Asa."

"I know, darlin'. But he can't come so we're gonna have to make due." She wiped my hair back from my forehead with the palm of her hand. "Let's get your boy out. You can do this, Callie."

"I can do it," I answered with a nod, any reassurance giving me strength at that point. "I can do it. Let's get him out. I want him out."

"That's right. Push, Callie. Push!"

I grit my teeth and bore down, and within minutes, I felt him sliding from my body, screaming.

They laid him on my chest, covered in gross white crap and blood, and all I could think about was how much I loved him, and that he had Asa's nose.

"Why are his balls so huge?" Farrah gasped in fear.

The nurses started laughing loudly. "There's a lot of pressure on him in the birth canal, and he's got mom's hormones running through him. They'll go down in a few days," a nurse assured Farrah as she gently picked my boy up. "I'm just going to weigh him and test him real quick," she directed at me, giving me an understanding smile. "I'll bring him right back."

"Take pictures, Gram!" I called to her as she followed the nurse to the little bed on the other side of the room.

The next few minutes were a disgusting mess of delivering the placenta and getting stitches. Yes, stitches. The only downside to having children with Asa was his son's ridiculously broad shoulders.

"Here you go, mama," Gram called tenderly as she brought the baby to me and laid him on my chest again. "You might want to start trying to breastfeed. Good for him to start right away."

"Okay," I whispered, reaching blindly for the button to raise my bed as I watched him open and close his mouth. "He looks like Asa."

"Yeah, but he's got your skin, lucky little booger," Farrah commented quietly, reaching out with one finger to touch the side of his face. "What's his name?"

"William Butler Hawthorne," I answered, watching as her eyes widened before she schooled her features.

"Good choice," she replied with a small smile. "Hey, Will."

Chapter 65

Grease

Almost five months down and only twenty more to go.

I was trying not to count the fucking minutes, but it was hard as hell. Shit wasn't bad inside—if you didn't care about the nasty-ass food and complete lack of freedom. Thankfully, we had boys on the inside, so I'd rarely had to bust heads to make sure fuckers left me alone. Between the other Aces locked up for a variety of crimes, and my size, guys didn't mess with me much.

I picked up the phone and went through all of the shit I needed to do to call Callie, anxious to hear her voice after a night of barely any sleep. We'd passed her due date a couple of days ago, and I couldn't' sleep wondering if she was okay. After all our years of living far away from each other, I was used to not seeing her gorgeous face every day, but it fucking sucked that I couldn't call her whenever I had the urge. I had to wait until the fucking designated times, which usually meant I was waiting hours before I had the chance.

Her phone rang and rang, and when she didn't answer, my heart started thumping hard in my chest. I tried to tell myself that she was probably sleeping, or forgot her phone somewhere, but I knew in my gut neither of those were true. She *always* answered her phone, no matter what she was doing.

I hung up and started the process over again, calling Rose this time, but she didn't answer, either. My hands were shaking and my chest felt like it had a hundred-pound weight on it as I hung up and started again. The guy behind me in line started bitching about how he was

350

waiting for the phone, and it took all I had not to turn around and shut him up. All it would take was one fist to the jaw, but I knew if I started a fight, I'd have to wait God knows how long before I got to a phone again.

I took a deep breath in relief when Cody answered.

"Hello?"

"Hey, man, it's Grease," I told him quietly.

"Hey, how've you been?" I could hear cars in the background and wind blowing into the cellphone, making my gut clench for a second as I imagined life outside.

"I'm good. Livin' the dream," I answered flatly, causing him to chuckle.

"Yeah, I bet. What's up?"

"I've been trying to get a hold of your sister, but no one's answering. You know where she might be?"

There was silence on the end of the line for so long that I thought I'd lost him. "Hello?"

"Yeah, I'm here. I just—no one has gotten a hold of you?"

"Not sure how they could," I replied calmly, as I felt myself breaking into a cold sweat.

"Yeah, just a sec." I heard some shuffling, and Cody said something to someone before it was silent on his end again. "Had to go out in the hallway—class is starting." He paused while I held my fucking breath and clenched my teeth against the need to scream at him to just spit it the fuck out.

"Callie went into labor yesterday," he told me quietly. "It took a while, but she had him this morning. Gram says everything went well. She's doing good and so is the baby."

I locked my knees so I didn't fall to the floor and rubbed the back of my neck with my fingers. *Fuck me. Fuck. Fuck.*

I couldn't say anything. I knew he was waiting for a response, but my throat felt like it was swollen shut. She'd had our son and I'd missed it because I was rotting in a fucking shithole prison. I'd known that I was missing out on a ton of shit while I was in there, but what I'd lost had never been clearer.

I had to restrain myself as I heard the douche behind me complaining again.

"She's good, man. Gram said she was up and walking around right after she had him, and he scored high on all the tests they do."

"Do—" I stuttered and cleared my throat in an attempt to get it together. "Do you know how big he was, or any of that shit?"

"Uh, I think I wrote it down. I was writing all of it down when she called me because I knew I'd forget it if I didn't," he mumbled. "Had this hot as fuck chick in my room, I was a little preoccupied."

I waited silently as he searched, even though I wanted to tell him that I didn't give a flying fuck about his bang from the night before.

"Got it!" he called. "He weighed eight pounds and two ounces, and he was twenty-three inches long. Gram said that's a pretty good-sized kid. I didn't write down how big his head was, though—sorry."

I swallowed over and over, trying to get my shit together as I stared at the yellowing tile under my feet. *A good-sized kid. I had a good-sized son.*

"Need to make a fuckin' call!" the guy bitched behind me.

"Do you know what she named him?" I asked hoarsely, ignoring the douche—anxious to know anything Cody could tell me and irritated that I had to drag shit out of him.

"Yeah. William Butler Hawthorne," he answered proudly.

"Thanks, man, I gotta go." I hung up on him as he tried to say something else. I didn't know how much longer I would've been able to keep talking to him without losing my shit.

Hawthorne. She gave him my name.

As soon as I put the phone down, I spun and faced the fucker that had been on my ass since the minute I'd picked up the phone. His eyes widened in fear when he saw the look on my face, but I didn't give him a chance to apologize.

I swung my arm and punched him hard in the throat, following as he fell to the ground. I beat the shit out of him until the guards pulled me away, and even though I knew I was getting solitary for the fight, I wasn't sorry.

Because, if I hadn't used my fists, I would have sobbed like a fucking baby.

I had a son.

Chapter 66

Callie

I had to wait a week after Will was born to talk to Asa. Cody'd said he'd spoken to him the morning I gave birth, and I was frustrated Gram had silenced our phones so I could get some rest. I would have rather spoken to Asa than slept, especially when we didn't hear from him again.

"Asa!" I answered happily.

"Hey, mama, how's our boy?" his voice was gravelly and low, and I felt my eyes fill with tears. Dear God, I missed him.

"He's good. Eating like a pig right now."

"Yeah? You decide to breastfeed?"

"That's the plan," I told him ruefully. For something so natural, it sure wasn't as easy as I'd envisioned.

"You telling me your tits are hanging out right now?" he asked with a chuckle.

"Shut it. Your son's eating. It's not sexy."

"Sugar, you're always sexy *and* you're feeding our son. Can't think of anything more beautiful," he whispered softly.

"I miss you like crazy."

"You have no idea," he grumbled. "You doing okay?"

"Yeah, I'm sore, especially with the stitches, but it's not horrible. And my boobs hurt."

"Stitches?"

"Your son has broad shoulders," I answered dryly.

"Holy fuck."

I started laughing at the horror in his voice and startled Will who immediately popped off my nipple and started wailing.

"Sorry, give me just a sec!" I practically yelled, trying to get him latched back on. When he was finally calmed down, he started suckling loudly and I giggled. *Little piglet.*

"You still there?" I asked with a smile in my voice.

"Yeah, still here," he answered, clearing his throat. "Got a good set of lungs on him, yeah?"

"Yep. He's loud as hell, but it's usually if he wants something, otherwise he's pretty mellow."

"That's good, sweetheart. Real good." His words were mumbled as if his hand was covering his mouth.

"We wish you were here," I told him gently, my eyes starting to water. "I miss you so fucking much."

"I wish I was, too. I'll be home before you know it."

I knew he was trying to comfort me, and if the taut way he spoke was any indication, he was frustrated as hell that he couldn't. He wouldn't be home before I knew it. We weren't even halfway there.

I pinched my nose and pulled the phone away from my face so I could sniff and get myself together. When I felt like I could talk to him without sobbing, I put the phone back to my ear.

"So, I was thinking, as soon as Will's immune system is stronger, we could come up and visit you."

"You call him Will?"

"Yeah, William makes him sound like a banker."

"I like Will," he said with a snort.

"Did you just snort?" I teased in a deep voice, mimicking him.

"Shut the fuck up." I could hear the smile in his voice and it made my chest ache. I looked down at our son and gently pulled him away from where he'd fallen asleep with my nipple in his mouth.

"So, the visit?"

"You really want our son in here? You think that's a good idea?" He sounded skeptical, but underneath the worry lacing his voice, I could hear the hope.

"Yeah, I looked at the website and it said kids can come."

"I know that, sweetheart. Just not sure *our* kid should come."

"I want you to meet him," I answered softly.

"Fuck." He blew out a harsh breath. "Me, too."

"Okay, well, it'll have to be in a couple months. I don't think he's up for that type of drive yet anyway."

"I love you so fuckin' much, Calliope."

"I love you, too, baby. Everything okay with you?"

"My woman's bringing my son for a visit, everything's great," he answered seriously.

"Good."

"I gotta go, Sugar."

"Already?"

"Yeah. Don't get much time."

"I know. This one went fast, though," I grumbled.

"'Cause we got a lot of shit to talk about. I love you, kiss my boy for me."

"I will. Love you, too."

I listened as he hung up, and continued to hold the phone to my face as if keeping it there would keep him closer. The separation was harder than I'd imagined, especially with Will. He was an easy baby, and Gram or Farrah were always around to help, so it wasn't as if I were overwhelmed. The hard part was watching him change, which was happening at an alarming rate, and knowing that Asa would never get to see it. By the time we would be able to visit, Will would look completely different, he'd be more alert and active, and his cone-head would be gone. It was gut-wrenching to know that Asa would never see the sweet, cuddly, newborn stage.

I sighed and leaned my head into the back of the couch. Two months couldn't pass quickly enough for me.

"Callie!" Farrah whisper-yelled as she came through the front door. She'd been pretty good keeping the noise down since Will was born. We never knew when he'd be sleeping, and he hated being startled awake, hence the crying fit when I'd talked to Asa.

"What's up?"

"I have the best idea. Ever. In the history of the world."

She looked at me expectantly while I studied her, still feeling hungover after my phone call with Asa.

"Well? Spill it."

"We should go to cosmetology school!"

"The hell are you talking about?" I scoffed, standing from the couch to carry Will to my room. Usually, he'd sleep for a couple hours in the morning and I really needed a nap.

"It would be perfect! We're both orphans and you're a single mother—we could get all sorts of grants to pay for it and it only takes like a year."

"I'm *not* a single mother," I snapped back, hugging Will to my chest as I scowled at her.

"I didn't mean it like that, Callie," she replied softly. "I know you're not, but Asa doesn't live here. He's not gonna be around until after we get done with the school and have kickass jobs."

"I never said I was going to do it!"

"You will. You'd be good at it. Just think, you could handle the classy clients and I could take the Rock-a-Billy ones. It's a match made in heaven!"

"You're insane," I whispered as I laid Will in his portable crib. "I'm taking a nap."

"We're talking about this when you get up!"

"Fine. Now let me sleep." Grumbling, I crawled into my bed and pulled the blankets over my head.

Farrah was right. After listening to her cajole and whine for weeks while I came up with every excuse I could think of, she finally wore me down. I think the deciding factor was Gram. She was adamant that I go to some type of school so I could get a decent job. I was lucky that Asa was still supporting Will and me, even though he wasn't working, but I didn't know if that would last forever. I had to be able to support us if I needed to. It was time I stood on my own two feet.

By the time Gram and I headed for Oregon to visit Asa, I was enrolled and ready to start the following term. Farrah'd been right about the grants, too. We were attending school for free, which seemed crazy to me, but I wasn't going to complain.

The trip to Oregon took forever. Will was pretty easy, but he still wanted to eat every two hours, and we must have stopped at every rest stop on I-5 between Sacramento and Salem. I'd never felt so relieved to get out of a car in my life.

We stayed at a hotel in Salem the night before the visit, but it didn't matter how exhausted I was, I still didn't sleep. I lay next to Gram, Will sleeping peacefully between us, filled with apprehension. I hadn't seen Asa in seven months, the longest we'd ever been apart since we'd met.

My body was different, my face rounder, and I wondered what he'd think. I was afraid things would be awkward, that we'd have nothing to say to each other, that our connection would be forced or completely absent.

I also worried about the fact that I couldn't wear an underwire bra, which meant my boobs wouldn't be at their best. It was a stupid thing to worry about, I knew it was, but I wanted to look good. I wanted him to still want me even though my eyes had dark circles under them and my boobs were different.

I finally crawled out of bed when I saw weak sunlight peeking through the curtains, and after placing a rolled up blanket next to Will, took a shower. I took my time, shaving my legs and conditioning my hair twice. I went all out, putting on makeup for the first time in months and stuffing myself into pre-pregnancy jeans with a flowing top to hide where my chubby waist bubbled at the top. I had a freaking muffin top. It made me want to cry.

When I was finished getting ready, I came out of the bathroom to find Gram walking Will back and forth across the room.

"He's hungry, but I wanted to give you some extra time," she told me with a knowing smile. "He's not gonna wait much longer, though."

I took Will and settled in to nurse him on the bed, grimacing as my jeans dug into my waist.

"You can't wear those jeans," Gram commented as she rummaged through her bag for some clothes. "Inmates wear denim. You'll have to put on other pants."

"What?" I gasped. "How do you know that?"

"I called the prison. Didn't you look at the website?"

I had, but the only thing I remembered was the stupid rule about underwire bras. I was screwed. The only pants I'd brought were jeans for the visit and ratty leggings so I'd be comfortable on the drive. I felt myself starting to panic, opening and closing my mouth, and trying not to scream in frustration.

"I don't have any other pants!" I wailed, startling Will into screaming, and causing complete anarchy in our room.

"Calm down, Callie," Gram ordered sharply. "You have other pants. I doubt you were planning on driving home in your underwear."

"Yeah, but those are gross! They're all stretched out and they don't go with my shirt!"

"Don't yell at me because *you* didn't read the rules," she snapped, and I instantly felt like shit.

"I'm sorry. I'm a little nervous," I told, her my eyes watery and a half-smile on my face. "I just wanted it to be perfect."

"Not sure how perfect you're gonna get in the visiting room of the state pen," she mumbled, walking into the bathroom. I guess she wasn't ready to forgive my freak out yet.

When Will was finished eating, I changed into my unappealing leggings and started getting him ready for the day. I didn't want to give him a bath in the nasty hotel bathroom, so instead I just used a tiny bit of baby soap to Mohawk the small patch of hair on the top of his head. I wanted Asa to be able to smell it, that fresh baby smell.

I had less than thirty minutes before we had to leave for the prison, so I got him dressed, too. I put him in a black long-sleeved Harley Davidson one-piece outfit that Slider's wife Vera had sent when he was born. I thought it was a nice thing for her to do, especially since I'd never met her, but I figured it was more for Asa than me. It was the perfect outfit for him to meet his daddy.

When we pulled up and parked, I was a little startled when Gram didn't climb out of the driver's seat.

"Aren't you coming?"

"No. I'm just gonna sit out here and read," she told me, pulling a worn paperback with a half-naked couple on the front out of her purse.

"But I thought you were coming with me!"

"They have a point system. I go in there, that means he uses up points for the month. Don't want him to run out," she answered over the top of her glasses. "This time should just be for the three of you, Callie Rose."

"Okay." The word came out in a long exhale, and I shook my head as I pulled Will and a small blanket out of his car seat. I prayed that he wouldn't need to eat while we were there, because he wasn't taking a bottle yet and I was pretty sure they wouldn't let me breastfeed in the middle of the visiting room.

My anxiety built as I went through the necessary procedures, and the guards made me really nervous as they went through all of my stuff. I was terrified that I hadn't followed some rule and they were going to turn me away. By the time I was through the security, I felt my heart beating at the base of my throat and I had trouble catching my breath.

I didn't anticipate that when I saw him, all of the nervousness and worry I was feeling would just... melt away.

Chapter 67

Grease

My leg was bouncing nervously under the table. I was afraid she wasn't going to show for some reason, and I'd built it up in my mind so much that I'd fucking lose it if I didn't see her. I was anxious to see my son, too, but he was still more of an idea in my head. I hadn't had a chance to miss him yet.

When she walked through the doors, I stood up automatically and almost tripped over the bench I was sitting on. *Really fucking smooth, Grease.* She was wearing a loose purple top that covered fucking everything from her neck to her hips, but goddamn if I couldn't imagine everything underneath, even with our son resting against her chest.

My eyes moved from her chest down, and noticed her leggings; they had a hole in the knee and some sort of bleach stain on them. It made my gut clench for some reason, seeing those pants. When I finally made my eyes meet hers, I swear to God it was like the entire room went quiet.

She had a little smile on her mouth, like she wasn't sure if she should be smiling or not, and it made me fucking grin. She was so fucking beautiful. Her face was a bit rounder, and so were her hips, but to me—she'd never been sexier.

My grin got her moving, and she started walking fast until I met her at the edge of the table.

"Hey, sweetheart," I mumbled, swallowing hard.

I pulled her into my arms and hugged her around the baby as she sniffled into my neck. We could only hug for a minute—there were rules about that shit—so within seconds, I was tilting her face to mine so I could kiss her. I didn't wait until we were feeling comfortable; we didn't have time for that. I just tilted my head to hers and pulled her bottom lip into my mouth a tiny bit and ran my tongue across it before pulling back.

I couldn't kiss her like I wanted to. I couldn't put my tongue in her mouth, or pull hers into mine, and it fucking killed me.

The guard at the edge of the room cleared his throat, so I pulled away and grabbed her hand. She still hadn't spoken by the time we'd sat down, and I couldn't think of a fucking word to say.

I was just staring at her. Soaking it all in.

"Hey," she whispered, looking at my face and rubbing her thumb over my palm.

"This is fuckin' awkward, right?"

"A little." She smiled gently, and I wanted to pull her over the goddamn table. "You wanna meet Will?"

For a second, a fraction of a second, I'd forgotten he was there as I'd stared at her.

"Ye—" I cleared the nervous knot in my throat. "Yeah. I do."

She unwrapped him from a dark green blanket, and the first thing I noticed was a little fucking black Mohawk down the center of his head. He was sleeping—his fist by his face—and the sight of him was like a punch to the chest.

"You wanna hold him?" she asked, looking anxious. "I checked the rules and I think you can hold him."

Before I could answer, she'd leaned across the table and laid him against my chest so I had no choice but to put my arm under him. He was so fucking tiny; my empty saddlebags must have weighed more than him.

"Holy fuck," I gasped, trying to figure out the best way to hold him so his head wasn't flopping around.

My head snapped up when I heard her giggle, and when I met her eyes, something just clicked. We were parents. *Holy shit.*

"I'm not writing that in his baby book," she told me with a smile. "The first time your dad held you, he said, 'Holy Fuck'. It was a tender moment..."

I huffed out a laugh and felt my throat start to close up.

I reached my hand back to hers and she caught it instantly, watching Will and me with a soft look on her face. "He looks like you," she murmured.

"Naw, he's all you. Look at that hair!"

"I know, right? I couldn't believe he was born with it like that. Gram says it's pretty normal and it might even fall out."

"What color are his eyes?" I asked softly, looking down at his little face, his mouth smacking like he was trying to eat or something.

"They started out this dark grey color, and I thought for sure they were gonna turn blue, but he got your brown ones. They're getting more like yours every day."

"I can't believe we made him," I whispered softly to myself, but knew she heard me when her hand squeezed mine.

"Pretty cool, huh?"

"He's fuckin' beautiful," I told her seriously, lifting my face so I could focus on her again.

I was holding my son in my arms and holding hands with my woman, and it was the best thing I'd felt in months.

"I can't wait until you're home."

"Me either, Sugar."

We lapsed into silence again, but it was comfortable this time. I was soaking that shit in. I could smell her lotion from across the table, and I prayed that I'd be able to smell it on my clothes after she'd gone. She'd just arrived and I was already dreading her leaving so much that I was having trouble breathing.

I wanted to walk out that fucking door with her. I wanted to carry my son to the car, buckle him in, and then kiss the hell out of his mother. I wanted to hold her hand as I drove her home, watch her feed Will, give him a bath, and change his shitty fucking diapers. I wanted it all and it hurt so goddamn bad that I couldn't have it.

"I signed up for cosmetology school," she told me abruptly, biting the inside of her cheek. "Farrah and I are going to go together."

"Is that doing makeup and shit?"

"No, it's mostly cutting and coloring hair—stuff like that." She was looking nervous and I couldn't for the life of me figure out why.

"That's great, Callie. Are you excited?"

I watched her shoulders deflate in relief. "Yeah, I am. I'm excited to learn a bunch of new stuff and be able to get a good job."

"Then what's wrong? Why're you strung tight as shit?"

"I just wasn't sure what you'd think," she mumbled, looking down at the table.

"Hey, look at me," I whispered softly as one of the guards called a motherfucking ten minute warning. "I'm so happy for you, baby. You're gonna do so good."

"You think?"

"I'm sure. It's gonna feel good when you can get a sweet job, not have to work at a fuckin' fast food place forever, yeah?"

"Yeah, I'm stoked that I'll be able to support us."

I jolted in my seat at her words and instantly felt uncomfortable. "Why do you need to support yourselves? I'll always take care of you."

"That's not what I meant," she backpedalled, making my anxiety ratchet up a bit. "I just don't want to have to depend on you for everything. It's not fair to either of us."

"Don't hear me complaining, Callie," I rumbled, completely frustrated at the turn of the conversation. I looked away, trying to get my shit locked down, when she squeezed my hand.

"I love you and I know you'll always take care of us. I just want to be able to do my part, okay?"

"Yeah, Sugar. Okay." I could understand that; she'd been vulnerable for a really long time. I hated the thought of her moving on without me, but I wasn't going to fuck up our visit by being an asshole. I started feeling comfortable again just as the guard called for visits to be over, and I felt myself growing panicked.

"Can I hug you again?" she whispered as she stood up across from me.

"Fuck yes," I grumbled, following her up and pulling her close. "I love you both so fuckin' much."

"We love you, too," she whispered as she started to cry. "I wish I didn't have to go."

"I know, sweetheart. It's only for now, okay?" I whispered back fiercely. "Thank you for bringing Will."

I handed her our son and wrapped my arms around both of them.

That was where I was supposed to be. I was supposed to be holding my family, taking care of them. I wasn't supposed to be visiting them with people watching our every fucking move, analyzing the way I fucking held her hand or carried my boy.

She tilted her head up to me in invitation, and I fucking took it. I pushed my tongue between her pursed lips for just a second, tasting her, and then pulled away before the guards could fuck with us.

"I'll call you in a couple days. Send me some pictures of you and

Will, yeah?"

"Okay." She was crying hard then, sniffling, her makeup running down her face. "I love you."

"I love you, too. You better go," I told her, lifting my chin toward the entrance.

When she turned around to walk away from me, I almost dropped to my knees.

My chest was on fire.

I wasn't ready.

I wasn't done yet.

I needed more fucking time.

I was missing goddamn everything.

I wasn't fucking ready.

I just needed a little more time.

Just a few more goddamn minutes.

Holy fuck.

It couldn't be over already.

Chapter 68

Callie

That first visit with Asa was the hardest. I cried the entire way back to the hotel with Gram holding my hand. She didn't speak; she just wrapped my hand in hers the minute I sat down, and drove.

I didn't remember much of the next few hours, but eventually I got my shit together, and we left for Sacramento the next morning.

After that, both arriving at the prison and leaving again got—if not easier—at least bearable. I knew each time that Will and I would be back, and it gave me something to look forward to. Sometimes we'd bring Gram or Cody during school breaks, but mostly, it was just me and Will. We needed that time, just our little family.

Farrah and I started school and she was freaking fantastic at everything. While I had to study and practice until I thought my brain was going to ooze out my ears, she just seemed to pick up everything the first time, without even trying. It was frustrating, but I couldn't be too pissed about it—she loved it. She'd obviously found something that made her happy, and after all she'd been through, she deserved it.

Gram took care of Will, even though it left her exhausted by the end of the day. She never complained, but I was always relieved when Cody was home from school and could help her out. She refused to let me look into getting a different babysitter, but sometimes I felt guilty for leaving him with her all day. Leaving him at all was so much harder than I'd imagined, but the look of pride on Gram's face when we'd arrive home from school was like an affirmation that I was doing the right thing.

Will grew like a weed. His hair took forever to grow in, but he never lost the little Mohawk he was born with, and I freaking loved it. He was my little rocker baby, and some of my favorite memories are of Farrah and me dancing him around the house while he giggled hysterically, his little mouth pouring drool all over the front of our t-shirts.

He was a ham, grinning in almost every photo we took, and he looked like Asa more each day. His little body was sturdy, usually measuring in the ninety-fifth percentile at his appointments, and it was a chore just keeping the poor boy in clothes that fit. I loved it. Every minute of every day, I was thankful for the little person that got into my makeup bag and poured out all of my loose powder, then stayed up until all hours of the night when I had tests the next day. When I looked into his face I saw a perfect mixture of his father and me, and I couldn't imagine my life without him.

We recorded every milestone, no matter how small, with video and photographs and I sent the photos to Asa weekly, keeping him updated on what our son was up to. I knew that he hated missing so many things, so I tried to keep him as involved as possible. It wasn't easy.

Sometimes, I just wanted to enjoy the moment, without feeling panicked when I couldn't find the camera. But I never stopped the video diary. If *I* was feeling frustrated, I knew Asa was feeling a thousand times worse.

My resentment over our circumstances grew with every passing day, burning and churning inside me until I felt ready to erupt. It was the club's fault that our son barely knew his father. It was *their* fault that I was sleeping alone every night and that Asa was stuck behind bars in a prison full of murderers and rapists and God knew what else. My loathing for the Aces fed me, it kept me focused and calm when I felt the opposite, and it reinforced the wall between me and anything that I knew would be too much for me to handle.

It kept me safe from my memories by giving me something else to focus on while Asa was gone.

We were only able to visit Asa around my school schedule, which sometimes left us without face to face contact for months. Those were the hardest times. I lived for the moments that I could see him smiling at Will—watching as Will sat up for the first time on the little visitor's table, or seeing him stumble into the room for the first time on his own two feet. In those moments, we were like any other family in the world.

Will's first birthday passed with little fanfare—Gram's homemade pineapple upside-down cake, and a trip to the prison for a visit. That seemed to be our life in a nutshell.

Six months later, Farrah and I graduated from cosmetology school and found jobs in a little salon at the mall. The pay wasn't great, but they let us make our own hours and we were always able to work together, which helped when my car died for good and we had to carpool until I could get a new one.

We were riding in my new car, a cheap used Toyota that was easy to finance, when Will said his first word. He'd been mumbling and saying Mama and Dada, Fawa and Gram for months, but it was the first word that wasn't a name. He pointed out the window at the semi driving next to us on the freeway and said "truck" as if he'd always known how to say it.

I cried the entire way home, while I clapped and cheered him on, because I hadn't brought my camera with us to the grocery store and Asa had missed it.

Some days I didn't know how I would keep going without Asa, and others felt as if he'd never been there to begin with. I'd begin to feel as if I'd always lived without him, and it would scare me so much that I'd slide back into missing him to the point of madness. It was a cycle that repeated itself over and over again until I felt exhausted from it, but one thing was certain: there wasn't a minute that I didn't wish he were beside me.

Life passed slowly in some moments, and quickly in others, leaving a bittersweet sensation behind. As hard as I wished for time to pass quickly, I also begged it to slow down. I missed Asa, but Will was growing so fast that I could barely stand it.

And then, after twenty-five months of waiting, he was out.

Chapter 69

Grease

The air smelled fucking sweet on the outside.

The boys had brought my bike to the prison so I could drive it home, and I looked like an asshole in my fucking dress shirt, but I didn't care. I was so glad to be going home to Callie that I would have ridden in a clown suit.

I had to stop by the club on my way out of town to get a couple changes of clothes and check in with Slider, but I was planning on hitting the road the moment I got my shit together. I couldn't wait to see Callie, and my dick had been hard since the moment I sat down on my bike and knew for sure that I was out of there.

I promised Callie that I would head straight to her once I'd grabbed my shit—she'd been practically bursting with excitement for the last month as we waited for my release. I wondered if she'd have Will with her when I got there, or if she'd have Gram keep him so we could have a little time for ourselves first. I didn't care either way—I couldn't wait to see my son—but I was dying to be inside my woman again, too.

I'd worked it out so I could drive back and forth to Sacramento as long as I let someone know I was going, but I was hoping that I wouldn't have to be making that drive for much longer. I was beyond ready to be living with Callie and Will full time, and I wasn't going to deal with her putting that shit off. I'd waited four years for the chance to live with my woman and I wasn't going to wait any longer.

When I pulled up to the club, the place was fucking packed. When I parked and climbed off my bike, I turned to Dragon to see what the fuck was going on, but before I could say a word a wall of noise came thundering out of the front doors. Boys were yelling and cheering, and even a few old ladies were fucking screaming and clapping their damn hands. It was embarrassing as all hell.

"Welcome home, boyo," Poet told me merrily, wrapping his arm around my shoulders.

"What's all this?" I asked with a smile, I couldn't help it. He was swaying from side to side, taking me along with him, and I'd rarely seen him so plastered.

"It's a welcome home party, obviously," Vera called as she and Slider came to meet us. "It's good to have you home."

"Good to be back. Is Callie here?" I looked around the crowd, but couldn't see her anywhere.

"Couldn't get a hold of her," Slider grumbled.

"What? I thought you were keeping an eye on her?"

"We have been. Kept boys on her since you been gone, but she doesn't talk to any of them. Won't answer calls, won't answer the door—we did what we could."

"Why the fuck didn't someone tell me?" I snarled. "I've seen you once a month for two years!"

Vera's face was sympathetic, but Slider and Poet were expressionless.

"Did what we had to, Asa," Slider rumbled, his use of my real name startling me. "You didn't need to worry about that shit. Knew she was coming to see you still—didn't want to cause problems between the two of you when there wasn't shit you could do about it. Didn't want to take the chance that you'd stop getting those visits."

I was fucking stunned.

I was also pissed as hell.

What the fuck was Callie's deal?

"Come on, honey," Vera said forcefully. "Let's get you a drink. This is a celebration!"

I let her drag me into the clubhouse.

The next two hours were a blur of toasts made with any liquor we had on hand. Brothers were bringing me their drinks of choice—whiskey and tequila mostly—and they were so genuinely glad that I was back that I couldn't turn them down without feeling like an asshole.

I woke up the next morning, face-first on my bed, with my boots hanging off my feet, and no shirt.

Oh, shit. Callie was going to be fucking livid.

I rolled out of bed slowly, my stomach fucking churning as I got to my feet. I needed a shower and some coffee before I could even *think* about hitting the road.

It took me less than an hour before I left, but it felt like days as I tried to get Callie on the phone. She wasn't answering, and I knew she was pissed. Dragon followed me down, making sure we got to Sacramento without any problems, and it was annoying as fuck that they thought I needed some sort of babysitter. I didn't mind the company, though—it gave me something to focus on other than the fight I knew I was gonna have with Callie.

Dragon kept riding when I pulled into the parking lot of the apartments. I recognized Callie's new car from what she'd described to me, but I didn't see Gram's anywhere. Good. I didn't want to deal with other people when I was dealing with whatever shit storm I'd walk into.

The door was locked when I got to her apartment, so I reached up and grabbed the key I knew would be hidden behind the siding above the door. I'd told her and Farrah to stop putting that shit there—but I somehow knew they wouldn't. *Fucking idiots.* Anyone could just walk into their living room.

The place was quiet when I opened the door, but I immediately saw Callie sitting silently on the couch facing me. She was wearing a little black robe that barely covered her thighs, and the way it gaped between her tits had my heart thundering in my chest. Her back was perfectly straight, feet flat on the floor, and her hands were gripped tightly together in her lap as she watched me walk in.

There was no expression on her face.

"Hey, sweetheart," I called quietly, shutting and locking the door behind me and pocketing the key. "I know you're pissed, but I can explain."

She didn't say a word.

"Club had a welcome home party for me last night—planned to head out after a couple hours, but the boys were bringing me drinks and I didn't want to end up getting a fuckin' DUI on my way down," I told her as I walked slowly toward her, every part of my body begging me to rush. "I know you're mad."

"I'm not mad," she told me seriously. "I'm done."

"What?" I slammed to a stop just feet from her.

"I can't do this anymore," she answered quietly.

"Fuckin' explain, Calliope."

"Last night," she swallowed, squeezing her eyes shut, before she pierced me with them. "Last night, Will and I made spaghetti," she told me, searching my face. "I told him all about how his daddy was coming home and we had to make him a special dinner. So we cooked, and I helped him clean up his toys while he rattled on about his daddy, mostly shit that I couldn't understand because he's twenty months old and most of the shit he says is gibberish."

Her thumbnail started scratching against the skin of her hand as I watched, vomit building in my throat.

"Eventually, I had to make him eat dinner, even though he was adamant that daddy was supposed to eat the spaghetti." She paused and took a deep breath. "So, we ate, and we waited. Will finally crashed around one, after fussing and complaining for hours because he didn't want to go to bed, and then it was just me, waiting."

"I'm—"

"I waited right here, all night," she cut me off. "Because I *knew* that you'd be here. I knew you were as anxious as I was, and I didn't doubt that you were on your way. I didn't doubt it because you promised you were headed straight here. So I waited. And eventually, Will woke up and wanted breakfast. So I made him breakfast while he jabbered on and on about you, but you still weren't here."

"I got here as soon as I could," I told her anxiously, palms up.

"I waited while I was giving Will his bath, and lunch, and finally put him down for his afternoon nap that he fought me on." Her gaze moved across the room, gazing at nothing, and I immediately missed her eyes on me. "And now it's twenty-four hours later, and I'm still in the nightgown I bought especially for your homecoming, and I have absolutely no desire to show it to you. *None*. I'm done."

"Sweetheart, I know you're mad. And I'm sorry as hell that I wasn't here and didn't call..."

"It wouldn't have mattered if you did," she told me with a shake of her head. "I broke it last night."

I followed her gaze to the corner of the room and the cracked cellphone lying at the base of the wall.

"You went to the club instead of coming home," she whispered pitifully.

"You could have been there!" I snapped, felling like shit and lashing out in defense. "They tried to get a hold of you, but you've been ignoring them the entire time I've been gone!"

"Why would I want anything to do with them?" she sneered, making me take a step back in surprise. "That club has completely fucked up my life for four years! They were the goddamn reason you were in prison!"

"That club has fed you and clothed you for four years, too," I growled back, irritated as fuck.

"No. *You* supported me. *They* didn't give *shit* to me," she shot back, her face immediately smoothing out again. "And I don't even need you to do it anymore."

I stared at her, gaping. It was so much worse than I'd thought. I'd known she was pissed, but I'd had no idea how deep that shit went, and now I was fucked.

"Sugar, don't do this," I whispered, my entire life crumbling around me. I wanted to fucking shake her, to shove her down on the couch and prove that she was mine. But I couldn't. She was the mother of my child, and she was breaking apart right in front of me.

"Will's still sleeping," she told me dismissively. "I know you have your phone, since I hooked it back up, so I'll have Gram call you when he wakes up."

"I'll just stay until he does," I answered, moving toward the couch.

"No. You won't," she commanded, shaking her head as she stood, the silky robe falling down her thighs in a way that made my mouth water. "I've been paying for this apartment for months, Asa. It's no longer yours. Gram will call you when he wakes up and you can come for a visit—after that we'll work something out."

"You don't want to do this, Callie," I warned her, my muscles straining in frustration. "You don't want me to leave."

"I'll probably cry," she told me quietly, opening the door and motioning for me to walk through it. "I'll probably weep and lie in bed for hours and feel like my heart is being ripped from my chest." She searched my face as I reached up to touch her, but she pulled her head back before I could make contact. "But I won't change my mind."

Just like that, she completely shattered my fucking life.

Chapter 70

Callie

The minute Asa walked out the door, I wanted to take it all back.

I wanted to tell him that I'd just been angry, that I loved him and wanted him to hold me. It had been so long since he'd been able to just hold me without the threat of a time limit, or of it being thought inappropriate. I just needed him to fight for me, to tell me that the club wasn't more important and that he would put Will and me first from then on.

I dropped onto the couch, stunned that he had actually left. When I realized I hadn't heard his bike start yet, I jumped back up and ran to the front door. I raced to the landing and looked over to find him talking on his phone. I raced down the stairs barefoot, anxious to get to him before he left, and he didn't notice as I came up only a few feet behind him.

"Bitch fuckin' kicked me out," he hissed to whoever he was talking to. "Yeah, I'll be there soon. Nah, man. Take care of it for me, would you?"

I felt my nose start running even before tears hit my eyes, and thought vaguely that it was weird as I quietly backed away from him. I'd messed up. I'd gone too far, and even though that was my intention, I felt gutted.

I backed into the stairwell before he could hear me, and listened as he fired up his bike. Within moments he was gone, and the warm afternoon suddenly felt frigid in my tiny-ass robe. I made my way back to the apartment on silent feet and prayed that I hadn't woken Will up when I'd thrown the door open. I didn't know if I could handle being mommy, when I couldn't even feel my hands. Why couldn't I feel my hands?

I wasn't in the house long, sitting on the couch where Asa'd found me earlier, when someone was knocking on the door. *He came back!* I was so relieved that I freaking ran to the door, my fingers fumbling with the locks until I got it open.

"Hey, remember me?" a voice called jovially. "I'm Grease's brother Deke, we met once before."

My entire body slumped when I realized Asa hadn't come back, and then stiffened when I noticed how the man was watching me. I didn't move from the doorway, but he used my surprise and disappointment against me as he slid past me and into the apartment.

"Seems like he would have hooked you up better than this," he commented, shaking his head as he looked around the apartment.

"I'm sorry, I don't really remember you," I answered calmly as I placed myself between him and the hallway. "We've met?"

"Yeah, I was there the night Grease found you. Remember? I had a Mohawk then." He was watching me intently, taking in my skimpy robe, and it creeped me out big time. There was something wrong with his eyes. His pupils were too large, his eyes sort of glassy and bloodshot at the same time.

"Yeah, I remember you now," I told him with a fake laugh. "That night is sort of a blur."

"I bet. Jose always had the good shit at his place," he answered insensitively, as if I'd *chosen* to be drugged.

"Are you looking for Asa? He just ran to the store, he should be back pretty soon," I lied through my teeth.

"Oh, yeah? Well, I'll just sit down and wait then."

I watched him make himself comfortable on my couch as my stomach turned. Should I have told him that Asa wasn't coming back? It seemed safer to lie and say that Asa would be there any second, but now he was acting like he wasn't going to leave and I had no idea what to do.

"I'm going to go get dressed really quick," I mumbled, watching him closely.

"No need to do that for me, I'm enjoying the view," he leered, making my skin crawl.

I didn't reply as I turned and made my way to Farrah's bedroom. There was a basket of clothes from the Laundromat sitting on her floor, and I'd never been so glad that she refused to put anything away when it was her turn to do the laundry. I left the door open half an inch so I could hear what he was doing, and raced to pull on jeans and a two t-shirts. I didn't have a fucking bra in there, but I wasn't about to bring any attention to my room with Will sleeping inside.

I moved silently to Farrah's dresser, one eye on the door as I pulled out her top drawer. The dresser was tall enough that Will couldn't reach into it, and I breathed a sigh of relief as my hand wrapped around what I was looking for, hiding underneath a plethora of silk and lace underwear. The .45 was heavy in my hand as I checked the clip, finding six bullets. I was glad as hell that I'd found high-waist jeans in the laundry basket, because the thing was so big there was no way I could have hidden it at my back if I hadn't.

I pulled my t-shirts down over the waistband of my jeans before swinging Farrah's door open so I could slide through. He was still sitting on the couch when I got back to the living room, but his knee was bouncing in impatience.

"Can't say the view's any worse," he commented mockingly as he looked at my braless breasts.

"Why don't I just have Asa call you when he gets back?" I asked calmly, crossing my arms. "It's been a long night and I'm not really up for company."

"Well, we both know he's not coming back," he answered, shaking his head in mock sympathy. "You kicked his ass out, right?"

My throat closed up as he stood from the couch, and my fight or flight instinct kicked in for just a second, but there was no choice.

My son was sleeping peacefully in the next room. I couldn't go anywhere.

"If you knew he wasn't coming, why are you here?"

"Came to get his son for him," he told me sadly. "He didn't want to deal with the inevitable drama, so he sent me instead. But I'm thinking... me and you can work something out. I'll put in a good word for you and maybe he won't take your kid..."

"Get the fuck out of my house," I hissed, my heart pounding in my ears.

"No can do, sweetheart," he sneered. Asa's endearment sounded like a curse coming from him, and it made me feel like a thousand ants were crawling all over my skin.

"He wouldn't send you here," I argued as he backed me into the kitchen. "You're a goddamn druggie."

He pulled back his hand, and I noticed a weird tattoo on it before he punched me in the face, sending me stumbling into the fridge.

"You just call me a druggie?" he growled menacingly, punching me in the stomach so hard I bent at the waist as my breath left me.

"Huh?" he asked, using one of my arms to spin me around and press my face against the freezer door.

"N-no," I stuttered as he pulled my arm so far up my back that my shoulder was screaming in pain.

"I'm pretty sure that's what I heard," he whispered into my ear, yanking on my arm until I felt the searing pain of my shoulder dislocating. I bit through my cheek, trying not to scream, and felt blood pooling in my mouth.

He shoved me to the floor and kicked me twice in the ribs before he started pacing, mumbling under his breath to himself. I wasn't sure what he was on, but he was acting fucking crazy, and I knew it was only a matter of time before things got a whole lot worse. I slowly pushed myself with my legs to the cabinet doors, using one arm to pull myself up to a sitting position while my other arm lay uselessly by my side.

When my back touched the cabinets, I hissed in pain, and my head started going fuzzy.

"You know, I fucking *hate* him!" he complained loudly. "He thinks he's so much fucking better than me because he's part of the Aces, and that's just not true!" He walked around the kitchen as he spoke, waving his arms in the air. "All the Aces think they're such hot shit! Acting like we're nothing, sending piece of shit recruits down to shake us down for money—it's insulting!"

His eyes dropped to me and I groaned as he kicked me hard in the thigh.

"So we send him into Jose's to teach them a fucking lesson, and what happens?" He shook his head and started kicking my legs again between each word. "He—survives—it—and—kills—some—of—our—best—men!"

My legs were on fire as I whimpered and pulled them as close to my body as I could. He'd started to breathe heavily, and it scared me, because I could see in his face that he had no intention of stopping any time soon.

"You know, when we killed your parents, I thought for sure that they'd get the picture," he told me softly, as if in apology. "I saw the way he looked at you, so I knew that using you was the answer, but when we showed up, you were nowhere to be found."

I stopped breathing as the implications of his words sunk in. He'd been one of the men in my house. He'd been one of the guys searching for me.

"Your mama was one hot piece of ass. Mm mm mm," he whispered. "Too bad I was searching for you and couldn't take the time to appreciate it."

I felt like I was in a tunnel, sinking into that place where nothing could hurt me and I could just float away like I had in the crawlspace. I wanted that place. I didn't want to hear anything else he was saying, I didn't want to know anymore.

I'd almost reached it, that place in my mind, when two things happened simultaneously.

He drew his foot back, kicking me hard in the stomach, pressing the small of my back into the cabinets, and I heard a small voice yell, "Mama! Door!" as little fists pounded from inside my bedroom.

His head turned sharply toward the hallway, listening, and I thanked God for the distraction as I used my good arm to pull the gun from the small of my back where I'd forgotten it. *How could I have forgotten it?*

I clicked off the safety with my thumb, and his head turned toward me as I racked the slide back against the edge of the cabinets.

"Get out of my house," I warned him in a garbled voice, blood still pouring from my mouth as I pointed it at him.

My heart was racing with adrenaline, all the colors in the room sharp and vivid as he smiled menacingly and pulled his leg back again.

I didn't hesitate and I didn't think.

I just pulled the trigger, the gun recoiling so hard that it hit me in the face and broke my nose.

I was momentarily stunned by the impact, but he didn't fucking drop. He just stumbled and came at me again, his eyes wide and crazy.

I shot him again, but he kept coming.

As if two shots in the chest were nothing but bee stings.

I screamed as he got close again and braced my arms as I emptied the entire clip into his chest, the last one hitting his throat as he stumbled back against the countertop, finally dropping to the floor.

Chapter 71

Gram

Farrah and I got home from a trip to my sister's, eager to hear about the reunion. We'd left the day before so they could have a little time for themselves, but I wasn't willing to stay gone for longer than that. I knew that those things rarely went how lovers envisioned them, and when I couldn't reach Callie on her phone I'd decided to head north.

I didn't know why I had such an awful feeling, things had seemed fine when we'd left, but I'd learned over the years to never ignore what my gut was telling me.

It was almost dark by the time we parked, and I was worried when I didn't see Asa's bike.

"Farrah, you see Asa's bike parked at the curb?" I asked as I dragged my old bones out of the car. Those long trips were coming to an end for me soon if my sore body had anything to say about it.

"Nope. Looks like he isn't here."

We trudged up the stairs, and she headed to her apartment as I pushed the key in to unlock my door. The hair on the back of my neck was standing on end, and I listened closely as I pushed the door open.

I hadn't taken one step inside before Farrah's terrified voice drifted through the night.

"Gram!"

I spun around, hitting my shoulder on the doorjamb before I hurried down the landing, cursing my old body for not letting me move faster. When I got to Callie's door, I stopped abruptly.

Farrah was gaping at a dead man lying in a large pool of blood on the kitchen floor.

"Callie!" I whispered to myself, looking away from the dead man and making my way hurriedly through the apartment. "Where are you?"

I found her quickly, but I thought I was going to have a heart attack when I did.

I've seen a lot in my seventy-three years on this earth. I've stitched gaping cuts on my children and I've set my own arm after an incredibly bad fight with my husband. I've identified four of my children's dead bodies, two from knife wounds and two from gunshot wounds. But nothing on this earth, no experience in my life, could have prepared me, or hurt as badly, as what I found in Callie's bedroom.

She was sitting on the floor, and Farrah's .45 was resting within her reach on top of the dresser, surrounded by bloody bullets and the cardboard box they came in.

Her face was almost unrecognizable, her nose and eye so swollen that the latter was completely closed, and she had blood all over her body. One of her arms was hanging at her side, and the other—

It was running through Will's hair as he lay next to her, his head on her thigh.

For the first time in his life, the boy was completely still, lying on his side with one palm flattened near his face on Callie's leg.

I covered my mouth in horror as I realized they were both covered in blood.

Dear God.

"Mama? Owie," Will mumbled seriously, turning his head slightly so he could look at Callie's face.

"Yeah, son. Mama has an owie," she answered gently in a tone that indicated it was a conversation they'd had before.

"Will kiss," he told her softly, turning his head so he could kiss her thigh before he settled back against her.

"Thanks, Will," she commented, closing her good eye as she leaned her head against the wall behind her. "Mama feels so much better now."

Chapter 72

Grease

I was sitting at a diner a few miles from Callie's place, waiting for her phone call. I'd been imagining scenarios where she'd call and apologize and beg me to come back, and we could act like the past few hours had never happened.

I couldn't believe she'd kicked me out—and I wasn't sure how I should've reacted.

I went over it a thousand times in my head—different scenarios that may have worked to change her mind. If I'd fought harder, maybe she would have relented. Maybe she needed me to fight, needed that release that she used to look for when we hadn't seen each other for months.

I'd pussed out, leaving instead, because it had been so goddamn long that I couldn't read her like I'd been able to before. I hadn't been able to tell if she was serious, or just pushing like she'd done a million times before.

Christ.

My phone vibrated next to my coffee on the table in front of me, flashing Rose's number, and I snatched it up before the first ring was over.

"Callie?" I answered, hope and dread pooling in my gut.

"It's Farrah," came a monotone voice from the other end. "You need to get over here... and call your boys for a pick-up. We're gonna need a cleaner."

The phone went silent before I could ask any questions, and I stared at it for a moment in horror before I jumped up and dropped a five dollar bill on the table.

I was on my phone before I'd reached my bike, barking out orders to Dragon as I climbed on and fired it up.

I made it to Callie's in minutes and almost dropped my bike as I went to climb off. Once I remembered I hadn't let down the kickstand, I quickly set it, hopped off, and went running up the stairs.

Her door was wide open.

I took in the mess in the kitchen, my brother—

What the fuck?

I turned to Farrah as she came down the hallway, and I panicked at the look on her face. Even during the hardest times with her, I'd never seen her face the way it was then.

She looked defeated.

"Callie's in her room. Gram's on the bed," she told me dully. "Be careful when you walk in, and do it slowly."

My heart thumped loudly in my ears as I made my way to her room, and my eyes went blurry as I stumbled into the doorway and saw her.

I must have made some noise, because her head snapped to the doorway and she lifted her arm, pointing a huge-ass .45 at my chest.

She was covered in fucking blood, her face was so swollen it looked like it was going to burst, and there in her lap was my son.

"Don't come any closer," she ordered, sounding slurred.

There were used baby wipes all over the floor around her, and it looked like she'd tried to clean the blood off her and Will, but had only managed to smear it around.

I lost feeling in my legs and dropped to my motherfucking knees.

"It's okay, sweetheart," I assured her calmly, making her flinch.

"Don't call me that," she muttered as Will turned over, facing me with his head in her lap. He didn't look hurt or scared, but he also didn't get up.

"Okay, Callie," I murmured, sitting back on my heels and raising my arms out in front of me.

"Your brother's dead," she smiled nastily.

"I saw that."

"Killed him," she mumbled, glancing at Will and then up to where her Gram was watching her quietly, tears running down her face. "Killed him and he just kept coming, so I had to do it again."

I wasn't sure what the fuck she was talking about, but she was making me nervous.

"What happened?" I questioned softly, flinching when her eyes moved back to me.

"Said he came here looking for you," she told me sadly, her arm wobbling until she slid the gun back up on the dresser. I sighed deeply in relief, but it was short lived.

"Told him you were on your way home," she shrugged one shoulder, bringing attention to the arm I hadn't realized she wasn't moving. Her hand went to the top of Will's head as her eyes went glassy.

"He knew. He knew. He *knew* you weren't coming. Said he was coming for—" she didn't say his name, but tilted her head down to look at Will who was still staring at me. "Said you asked him to come."

Tears started rolling out of her good eye as it came back to mine.

"I'd never do that, Sugar. I'd never take him. You know that."

"I know," she whispered. "But it didn't matter."

I moved slowly to my knees when she was quiet, and started to scoot into the room, but stopped instantly when her hand rose off Will's head to the top of the dresser.

"You didn't tell me he killed my parents," she accused, her eyelid closing halfway in defeat.

"What? Sugar, what did he say?"

"He killed them," she mumbled. "Mom's a hot piece of ass. Mad at Aces. Kill me to get you."

I'd had no idea that Deke was a part of that. I'd known that the Jimenez brothers were pissed as hell when I'd killed their boys, but when Deke had called me, I'd assumed he'd had no part in it. He'd convinced me that there was nothing he could do to stop it, but he'd been in on it from the start. I felt rage like a massive headache hit the back of my eyes, but forced myself to refocus on what mattered. Callie and my boy.

"You got him, baby. It's over. You got him," I murmured as I moved further into the room.

The closer I got to her, the more clearly I saw that there was something seriously wrong with her arm.

"You protected our son, baby," I told her softly, relieved when I stopped less than a foot from her and she still hadn't grabbed the gun. "You did so good. Is Will okay?"

"He's fine," she whispered, glancing down at him. "He was in here."

"I had to make sure no one got him," her voice rose as she looked at me fiercely. "I made sure. I made sure."

"Yeah, you did. I love you so much, Calliope," I whispered, reaching out my hand to lay it softly on hers where it rested on Will's head. "But you're hurt, Sugar, and it smells like Will needs his diaper changed."

She looked like she was going to agree, she'd even started to slowly nod, when we heard men coming through the front door.

Her hand moved faster than I could catch, and in seconds, the .45

was resting against my sternum, her finger on the trigger.

She didn't look away as she called quietly to Will. "Go over to Gram, Will," she said gently. "Run on over to Gram."

He climbed up to his feet slowly, wobbling a little in a way that had my heart lurching in my chest, but he made it to Gram as she stood from the bed.

"Get him out of here. Lock yourself in your apartment," Callie ordered, never looking away from my face. "Go, Gram!"

Rose shot out of the room, and the moment we heard her front door slam, Callie's hand dropped to her lap.

"Get your brother and get the fuck out of my house," she mumbled tiredly as I heard someone small walk up behind me.

"We need to get you to a hospital, Callie," I whispered, as I gently pulled the gun from her fingers.

"I'll take her," Farrah argued at my back.

"I love you so much, Sugar." I ignored Farrah as I set the .45 back on the dresser and ran my finger up and down the top of Callie's hand, the only place I was sure I wouldn't hurt her. "Let me take care of you."

She turned her head away from me, not saying a word as she pushed her forehead against the side of the dresser.

"Go, Grease," Farrah ordered behind me. "Get your guys and get them out of our apartment. I'll take care of Callie."

"She's mine," I hissed, turning my head to Farrah. "Go make sure that Will's okay."

I started to turn from her when I noticed another gun, this time in her small hand.

"Will's fine with Gram," she told me seriously, her hand hanging relaxed at her thigh. "Now you need to get the fuck out of here before you make her worse."

"She needs me," I argued, my hand tightening on Callie's. "I'll take care of her. I always take care of her."

"Look at her, Grease," Farrah snapped sharply. "She doesn't fucking need you."

My head turned to Callie to see she was still facing the dresser, her swollen eye practically hiding the rest of her face from me.

"Callie?" I questioned gently, as her body started rocking in tiny movements.

"Please leave me alone," she whimpered, never looking at me. "Leave me alone. Leave me alone. Leave me alone."

I heard Farrah's revolver as she snapped it into place, and I turned my head to see her pointing it directly at my head.

"I'm not Callie," she told me calmly. "I'll pull the trigger."

I didn't think she would, but it didn't matter.

I nodded in defeat, knowing that she was right. I wasn't making anything better.

I couldn't stop myself from leaning forward one last time and kissing Callie lightly on the side of her head. "I love you. I'm not going far," I promised.

I made myself leave the room as Farrah kneeled down to help Callie to her feet.

Chapter 73

Callie

The doctors told me that the psychological scars of the attack would be much harder to heal, and they were right.

Farrah had informed the police that my attacker had fled and she'd found me in our apartment. I didn't dispute it. I didn't say anything. Not to the nurses or the doctors or the social workers or the policemen.

I didn't speak.

They grew frustrated with me, asking the same questions over and over, sometimes changing the words they used as if phrasing something a different way would make me answer. I listened to them argue as if I wasn't there, sometimes stating that they needed to leave me alone, and other times fighting that someone needed to snap me out of the fog I was in.

I would have liked to see them try.

No one had known what happened when they'd found me because the Aces had taken Deke's body instead of letting the police do their work. It was a clear case of self-defense, as my broken body could prove, but I was glad that I didn't have to explain to anyone what had happened.

I was in a fog, not making a noise as they set my shoulder and checked out the rest of my body. My legs and stomach were bruised, my nose was broken, and they were most worried about my eye that was swollen so much that if I looked across the bridge of my nose, I could see the eyebrow on the other side.

They took photos that I knew they'd never need, but I didn't fight them. I didn't do anything but move when they moved me, and stared blankly as they tried to get answers.

At some point, Cody showed up at the hospital, and I could hear him in the hallway arguing with Farrah, but I didn't care. I didn't care about anything.

Not even my son.

Because when Asa'd left me, I'd successfully retreated to that special place where nothing mattered.

They kept me in the hospital for a few days to make sure I wasn't going to lose my eye, poking and prodding, and asking question after question as I stared at them blankly. But even after they knew that I would keep it, they didn't discharge me.

Instead they moved me into the psych ward.

They sent in a nice psychologist who asked me questions while I stared at her, and even though I could see the frustration in her eyes, she kept coming back. I guess she was getting paid for it, though, so it wasn't surprising that she was tenacious. She had beautiful strawberry-blonde hair. I wondered how Farrah would look with hair that color.

Gram and Farrah rarely left my bedside, taking shifts with Will so I wouldn't be alone, but they didn't get through to me and neither did Cody when he showed up. Nothing was getting through—and sometimes I'd hear them quietly arguing about what to do.

Something had broken in me when Deke was talking about my parents. I don't think anyone understood why I'd just disappeared inside of myself, but I didn't expect them to, not really. Only *I* knew what I had tried to ignore, what I'd pushed back so far that I'd rarely thought about it anymore. Only *I* knew that I'd been building those walls between my memory and myself so that almost nothing could breach them.

No one had hidden with me inside that tiny space, listening to my parents die and their killers calling my name. Only *I* knew that horror.

Asa was the only one who could've guessed where my mind was, we'd had a vague conversation about it years before, but for some reason—he wasn't there. If I had been feeling anything, I think I would have been sad about that.

I lay there, listening to Gram yell at the psychologist as I thought about the water stain on the ceiling. I wondered if anyone noticed it or if it was only patients that ever had that view and they just never said anything.

"You've been doing it your way for three weeks and this shit isn't helping," Gram thundered. "I don't give a shit *what* you think. I'm going to do this my way, and if you've got a problem, I'll just take my granddaughter home with me!"

The pretty-haired psychologist murmured something soothingly that I couldn't hear.

"Oh fuck you and your fancy degree!" Gram shouted. "*I* know her! I've wiped her ass and bandaged her cuts. I'll do what I think's best!"

I didn't hear anything for a while after that.

"Callie," Gram snapped, hours later, pushing the button on the side of my bed until I was sitting up. "You look like shit and you're ignoring your son who's been crying for you for weeks."

I watched her, detached as she opened the curtains in my room, making me squint as the bright sunlight filtered through. She rearranged my bedding so it was lying flat on my lap, and brushed the hair back from my face as I watched her silently.

"You've got a visitor," she informed me as she strode out the door.

When she came back in, she was carrying my beautiful son in her arms.

His face lit up when he saw me, but it fell when I didn't react to his presence.

"You hold your son. He misses you," she told me firmly as she placed him in my lap.

He snuggled into my body, pressing his head against my chest, and all of a sudden I felt like I couldn't breathe. He smelled really good, like baby shampoo and chocolate, and the warmth of his body seeped into mine until I wasn't sure where he ended and I began.

"Mama," he sighed, reaching up to pat my breast like he'd done a thousand times since he'd stopped breastfeeding almost a year before.

"Come on in," I heard Gram call as I stared at Will, forcing my arms to move around him until I knew he wouldn't fall off the bed.

The emotions overwhelming me were too much. Hope and fear and love and horror and grief—so strong that I clenched my jaw against them, begging for my brain to send me back. I'd almost succeeded, my vision going gray at the sides, when I felt him reach the head of the bed.

"Hey, Sugar," he whispered gently, reaching out to run his hand down my hair. "We've missed you."

My entire body jolted and I raised my eyes to his, the tender look on his face opening the floodgates as I began to cry. I cried in loud, obnoxious, gasping sobs that made Will start screaming in fear, and even then I couldn't stop them. Gram came to get the baby, tears on her face as she kissed me on the head, and in the next minute, Asa was in the bed with me, wrapping his entire body around mine.

"You're okay, Callie," he murmured over and over, never once letting go as I let out years of pain by screaming at the top of my lungs and pummeling my fists against his back.

When I'd finally calmed down into sobbing quiet hiccups, he pulled his face away from my neck.

"If you ever scare me like this again I'm going to paddle your ass," he rumbled, his voice sounding gravelly and raw. "Our boy needs you, Sugar. *I* need you."

I nodded once as he rubbed my back, and stuffed my face into my favorite spot between his jaw and shoulder.

My emotions were all over the place, but I let him have that moment. Once my body had relaxed, I noticed that his was trembling, and some place deep inside me wouldn't let him go uncomforted. I loved him so much, and guilt piled on top of grief when I thought of all the things I'd put him and the rest of my family through over the month I'd been gone.

I didn't know where I could go from there. I felt too exposed, too overwhelmed to just go back to my day to day life. The walls I'd built to keep me safe, to keep my world sane and ordered, had shattered around me and it felt as if I was standing in the middle of a war zone with no help in sight.

I loved Asa. I loved him so much, and I reveled in the way his arms wrapped around me and held me tight against him. I loved the scruff of his beard against my chin and the way he always smelled like smoke, Armani cologne, and leather. I loved the way he looked at me and our son.

I loved him, but that didn't seem to make any difference, because the moment he crawled off my bed, I was going to tell him I didn't want to see him anymore.

I couldn't bear to look at him.

Chapter 74

Grease

Leaving Callie after her breakdown was the hardest thing I'd ever done. I wanted to protect her, to save her from whatever demons she'd been fighting.

I didn't understand how I could have been so stupid, how I could have thought that I'd saved her. That I could fix her.

She'd been slowly drowning for years, and I'd missed it. I'd missed all the signs because I'd believed that as long as I took care of her, she'd be fine. I'd fucking loved the way she needed me, reveled in the way she'd been so clingy in the beginning of our relationship.

And in the end, that had fucked her up even worse.

It killed me to think of the way I'd ignored her when I was pissed, the way I'd thrown her out of the house because she wouldn't go get groceries, the way I'd pushed and pushed for her to act normal when she was doing the best she could.

I hadn't seen it before, but I sure as fuck saw it as she held me off with a pistol bigger than her arm.

So when she'd told me that she didn't want to see me, I'd taken her at her word for once. I'd given her the space she needed as I watched her slowly get stronger and leave the hospital.

I'd given her space as she met with a psychologist three times that first week out of the hospital, and I'd waited. When no word came from her that I would ever be welcome again, I said goodbye to my son.

"You know you can come see him whenever you want," Gram assured me sadly. "She doesn't mean to keep you from him."

"I know, Rose," I told her with a nod as I watched Will drive his monster truck into a table leg.

"Told you years ago to call me Gram," she scolded, wrapping up banana bread for me to take.

"Shit's different now," I mumbled, my heart breaking as I watched Will's little diaper-covered ass shake to the low music coming from the stereo.

"Nothin's different for me," she scolded over the edge of her glasses. "You're still one of mine."

I nodded again, my throat feeling tight, and then jumped to my feet as Cody came barreling in the front door.

"You leaving?"

"Yeah, it's time I take care of some things and let your sister be," I answered, the words tasting like acid.

"You getting payback?"

"Payback?" I laughed a little. "You mean am I going to take care of it? Yeah."

"Take me with you," he demanded earnestly. "That's my sister. Those were my parents. Take me with you."

I stared at him for a moment and realized that the kid I remembered—all big feet and arms that were too long for his body—had turned into something entirely different. He was a man. *When the hell had that happened?*

He looked like a backroom brawler, cleaned up in Ivy League clothes.

"Your sister would kill me," I mumbled, aware of Gram's eyes on the back of my head.

"My sister isn't even talking to you," he replied bluntly, making me want to punch him in the fucking mouth.

"You okay with this?" I asked Gram, turning my back on Cody.

"He's an adult," she murmured, looking up at Cody and then back at the bread she was wrapping. "He can make his own choices. Don't put me in the middle of it."

How the fuck I ended up riding to Eugene with Cody following behind me in a piece of shit rental, I will never understand.

And once we were there, he made himself known. He joked with Slider and Poet like they were his best friends, and in doing so, bought himself the respect of every member in the clubhouse that night. It was insane, but I was too wrapped up in my own shit to give a fuck.

Missing Callie was like missing a limb. It still felt like she was there, and at times I'd reach for her as I slept, or pick up the phone to call her, and in a rush of clarity realize I couldn't. I'd spent so much time waiting on her and working toward our life together, that I didn't know what to fucking do with myself once she was gone.

The boys and I headed down to San Diego that week, using Cody as a sneak to find out what was going down with the Jimenez brothers. He had contacts all over the fucking place, and I had no clue how, because he'd been going to school out of state for the past ten years. However he found them, I couldn't argue that the guy wasn't effective. He knew shit before the rest of us did, and he could move in and out of places like no one I'd ever seen.

He just seemed to blend into the crowd, wherever we were, and fucking disappear. You could be looking right at him and still not see him. It was weird as hell.

We used his contacts to find out where the big dogs were having their weekly meeting, and sure as shit, we found them in a warehouse so far south that it may as well have been in Mexico. They didn't expect us, and not even one of them had the time to rise from his seat around the poker table before he was dead.

"Don't fuck with my family," Slider mumbled, leading us back out of the warehouse and onto our bikes. "Good work, kid."

Cody lifted his chin in reply, but I could tell by the wild look in his eyes that he was about to lose his shit.

"Lock it down, little brother," I warned him, grabbing the back of his neck and giving it a squeeze. "All over now. Callie's safe and you got what you came for."

He nodded a few times, climbed on the bike he'd bought from one of the brothers, and slid on his helmet. The little shit was going to keep his cool. *Thank fuck.*

"Hey," Poet called as he climbed on his bike and motioned toward Cody with his chin. "Name's Casper. Kid moves like a fuckin' ghost."

We headed home that night, not stopping longer than it took to refuel. I was surprised when Cody didn't take the exit when we rolled through Sacramento, but it wasn't like I could ask him about it. I'd wanted to stop and see Will on the way through, but I was afraid that it hadn't been long enough between visits, and I didn't want to upset Callie by stopping in when I wasn't expected.

The doctors had told Gram that they thought Callie had PTSD. They weren't sure what the cause was, she'd refused to talk to them about it, but the rest of us knew exactly when it had started. Thankfully, she'd found a doctor that week before I left that she liked enough to start telling her story. I only hoped that the guy would be able to help her, because time kept passing and I didn't know how long I would be able to live the way we were without losing my mind.

I spent the next months the way I had years before, working as much as I could and taking any time I had to drive to Sacramento. But those days, I was seeing my son. He was growing fast, and every time I saw him, he'd know more words that he'd recite to me like a little dictionary. It was cute as shit, and I wished that I could joke with Callie about it.

I hadn't seen her in months because anytime I went to spend time with Will, he was at Gram's when I got there, and Callie was locked firmly in her apartment until I was gone.

I'd promised to give her space, but that didn't mean I liked it, and one of the hardest days came almost nine months later. Poet's daughter Brenna had come home one day out of nowhere, and she'd brought a kid with her that looked exactly like Dragon. I tried to stay out of their shit—it wasn't any of my business how they chose to deal with things—but fuck if they didn't keep pulling me back in.

One afternoon, I stopped by the house and found Cody sitting outside while the house was quiet. He hadn't felt comfortable enough to check on Brenna that entire morning, but the silence had finally made him anxious enough to unlock the front door and step inside.

I was right behind him when we'd found her, and the swelling on her cheek took me instantly back to a different time and place, filling me with rage. She'd calmed me down as best she could, and proceeded to tell her pop, Vera, and me the entire story. I'd understood it. I'd understood how it could have happened the way she said it had, but I hadn't been able to clear the red haze from my vision. Dragon had hit a woman I'd thought of as a little sister, and I'd wanted to fucking kill him.

But the time I'd wanted to hold Callie the worst, the time I'd had to give my bike keys to Tommy so I wouldn't be tempted to climb on and drive to her, was the day we'd found Brenna beaten bloody by her ex-husband and Cody shot in the shoulder, lying in the doorway of her house. He'd been trying to protect her.

I'd thought they were dead when we'd found them. For a guilty second, I'd thanked God that it wasn't Callie—that she'd survived and was somewhere in Sacramento living her life—even if that life didn't include me.

I'd felt so guilty for bringing Cody into the mess he was in, that it took me three tries to get up the nerve to call Rose that night, letting her know what was happening. She'd taken the news well, like I hadn't just told her that her grandson had been shot, and I was amazed all over again at the strength of that woman. But even as I spoke to her, worried about her reaction, I was still fucked up enough to be disappointed when I didn't hear Callie's voice in the background as Rose thanked me for telling her and hung up the phone.

I'd wanted Callie so bad that night. I'd wanted her to come to me and run her fingers through my hair so I knew that she was okay. I'd needed to know that she was safe.

But I forced myself not to contact her—because if she was getting better, and she needed time away from me, I was going to give her that.

Chapter 75

Callie

It was almost a year after I'd told Asa that I couldn't be with him anymore, and I was finally ready to speak with him again.

My time in therapy had been the hardest thing I'd ever done, and I'd probably never be able to go without it. I'd had a lot of guilt hanging over me from my parents' deaths, and though it wasn't going away, with Dr. Howell's help, it was getting easier to understand and manage.

Dr. Howell was an old, grizzled war veteran, and I'd liked him instantly when we'd met. He not only told dirty jokes when he knew I needed to take a step back for a few minutes, but he also knew how guilt and blame could royally fuck up someone's life—he'd lived through it when he came back from Vietnam.

I learned to let things out, and we worked on facing my demons head-on in a way that I'd never let myself do before. He'd told me something, and I'm sure he'd stolen it from someone else because he was always quoting self-help calendars and coffee mugs, "Demons come out in the dark because they're afraid of the light. We need to smash those motherfuckers to smithereens with light." Okay, I'm pretty sure he paraphrased, but the result was the same.

We brought everything out into the open.

I was ashamed that I'd blamed Asa and the club for a lot of things that they couldn't have changed, but I finally understood that my jumbled emotions had been totally normal.

My life had been a series of unfortunate events for a long time, starting with my decision to sneak out of my house to go to a party and ending when I'd kicked Asa out of my life completely. Looking back, I don't know that I would have been able to get my shit together, knowing that he was there to protect me. It would've been too easy for me to slide back into old habits.

I'd wondered for a long time if my relationship with Asa had been a fluke. That maybe I'd felt so deeply for him because he'd saved me and for no other reason. It had become an almost unbearable fear— that our love wasn't real—and I hadn't been able to get it out of my mind until I'd worked on it for weeks with Dr. Howell.

I learned something during those weeks when we did exercise after exercise helping me discover and understand my feelings.

I loved Asa. Loved him. It had nothing to do with how he could protect me, or some sense of indebtedness.

Take everything else away, until there was just Asa and Callie, and I still loved him with an intensity that bordered on madness.

A few months after Cody had been shot, I found myself with just enough cash to drive to Oregon and I used it. I was pissed at my brother for refusing to come to California to see me, and worried that he wasn't taking care of himself. I needed to get him away from the Aces, back to the school he'd ditched, and away from a life that would get him shot.

I was also irrationally pissed that Asa hadn't come for me yet. I'd asked him for time, but he'd seemed content to give it to me, and as time passed, I worried that he wasn't coming back. I was livid that he wasn't fighting for me, angry that he'd given up so easily. Dr. Howell would've had a field day with that information, but we hadn't yet touched on the difficulties I had controlling my anger.

I got there and made my way inside with few problems, but within minutes of my arrival, the love of my life was walking out the front doors shouting at me.

And after a spectacular fight with Asa in front of close to thirty bikers and their old ladies, he threw me over his shoulder and stalked past everyone into his room.

He dropped me onto the bed and took a weary step back. "Where's Will?"

"I left him with Gram," I answered softly with a shake of my head. "I didn't think it would be a good situation to bring him into."

"What the hell were you thinking, Callie?" he asked dejectedly as he ran his hand through his hair.

I stared at him, up close for the first time in months, and I couldn't stop the words that came pouring out of my mouth. "I love you!" I shouted. "You don't call me baby. Why were you calling me baby? You call me Sugar."

His body went completely still. "What did you just say to me?"

"You don't call me baby. You call me Sugar."

"Before that, Calliope," he rumbled, his hands dropping to fists at his sides.

"I love you. I know that now."

"Oh, you know that *now*, huh?" he asked gently.

I nodded quickly, pulling myself up on my knees.

"Well, I knew it *before*," he replied, shaking his head as he ran his hand down his beard. "I can't do this with you, Sugar."

"I love you. I love you and I want to be a family." I reached toward him in frustration, but fell back and started to cry at the anguish on his face. He was backing away. He didn't want me. All of my anger left me in an instant, replaced by fear and desperation. "I'm better! I promise! I'll do better! I miss you so much."

"I know you're doing better," he told me softly, coming back to reach his hand out and wipe the tears off my face. "You're doing so good, Calliope. But I can't be the reason that you slide back into that shit."

"You won't!" I pleaded. "It didn't have anything to do with you!"

"Bullshit, Callie," he shot back, walking toward the door. "You couldn't even fuckin' look at me."

He was almost out the door when I desperately shouted the one thing I'd promised I'd never reveal to him.

"I blamed you!" I yelled, watching his back snap straight. "I blamed you, and that's what made everything worse."

"All this time?" He turned to me. "All this time I've been trying to build a life with you, wrestling with my own shit over what went down with your parents, knowing that there wasn't a goddamn thing I could change...All this time you've been blaming me and never said a goddamn word?"

His voice was shallow, and the pain in his eyes made me feel like I was going to vomit.

"I didn't think about it," I sniffled, and he turned to walk out the door.

"I didn't think about it, because if I thought about how I blamed you, I couldn't ignore how I blamed me," I whispered, scratching at one of my arms with my short fingernails.

It was silent in the room for long moments as I wondered how I'd managed to fuck up so badly. I'd used a Taser to make my way into a gated compound, shouted like a maniac for my brother who ended up not even being there, and convinced the love of my life that I blamed him for my parents' deaths.

I was scratching faster, tears blurring my eyes, when I felt a warm hand cover mine.

"Stop scratching, Sugar," he murmured soothingly. "Gonna break the skin, you keep doing that."

"I'm sorry," I sobbed. "I know it wasn't your fault. I know that now. I know it wasn't your fault. I was a mess, but I always loved you. I never lied about that. That was always true."

"I know, baby, I know," he murmured, sitting down and pulling me into his lap.

"Don't call me baby!" I wailed, making him chuckle a little. "Don't laugh at me!"

"Not laughing at you," he commented, pulling my face up to his. "I've called you baby before, you crazy broad. Just call you Sugar more. You don't want me to call you sweetheart, yeah?"

"No," I said forcefully, the memory of Deke still making my skin crawl.

"Okay, then you get Sugar or baby when I'm loving on you. Callie when I need to say your name and Calliope when I need to make sure you're paying attention," he told me with a smile, leaning down to run his nose along mine.

"Okay," I whispered into his mouth. "I love you. I'm sorry."

"We've both been blaming ourselves for shit that has no blame," he told me seriously. "No more telling me you're sorry, Calliope."

"I'm paying attention."

"I know you are. No more telling me you're sorry. No more saying sorry, period. You didn't do anything wrong." He leaned down a fraction of an inch to run his tongue lightly over my bottom lip. "We're moving on from here."

"Just like that?"

"I've been waiting for a year for you to come back to me. Not wasting any more time."

"I've been waiting a year to come back to you, too."

He groaned deep in his throat and kissed me hard, his tongue thrusting into my mouth.

"No more running, no more hiding," he ordered as he pulled back and lifted my shirt over my head. "We'll deal with shit as it comes—and you're gonna find a shrink up here."

"Okay," I whimpered as he pulled off my bra. "I promise."

He stood from the bed and ripped his cut and t-shirt off, throwing them across the room as he undid his belt buckle. "And you're growing your hair back out," he insisted, pointing his finger at me. "Your hair is goddamn shorter than mine."

I laughed a little, feeling lighter than I could ever remember. "Farrah wanted to try something new." I gasped as he pulled my pants and underwear down my legs, cursing when he couldn't get them past my boots.

"Next time, tell Farrah to fuck off," he mumbled as he tore at my boots, finally pulling them off my feet along with my pants.

"Fuck me, Calliope," he swore and paused with his hands at the front of his pants, staring down at me. "It's been so damn long."

"Over three years," I murmured back, scooting myself up the bed with a sultry smile on my face. "What are you waiting for?"

He was out of his pants and on top of me before I could stop giggling at the shock on his face.

"Your body's so fuckin' soft," he murmured against my breast before pulling my nipple into his mouth. "Your tits are bigger."

"Yeah, that and a few other things," I moaned as his hand ran down between my legs.

"Oh yeah, what else?" he asked seriously, his hand stopping right above where I needed him.

"My ass, my thighs, my waist," I answered in annoyance, moving my hips against his hand.

He leaned back on his heels between my legs, and I almost screamed in frustration at the break in contact.

"Don't look any different here," he murmured, running his fingers over my belly, "Except for these little marks that prove you carried my son."

He scooted back even further as I watched his face go soft.

"These too?" he asked, wrapping his hands around my thighs. He glanced up at me, and at my nod, gave them a squeeze. "Can still almost wrap my hands around them, Sugar. And they're unbelievable, because they point to my favorite place. You know where that is, yeah?"

I nodded again, my eyes blurry with tears as he catalogued my body with gentle hands and softer words. His hand ran up the inside of my thigh until his fingers were rubbing gently over my clit. "Favorite place," he murmured again. "Where were we? Right, your ass."

He pulled my leg over his lap and flipped me over before running his hands over my ass.

"Nah. You could never be too fat there," he told me with a chuckle.

I pushed up on my hands, ready for battle, but paused when he pulled me up so my ass was resting against his hips. "Look at how much cushion I have there, Sugar. Big enough to fit my hands, soft enough that I can grab you like this—" he placed his hands on both cheeks, "and pull you apart if I need to."

I moaned and dropped my head into his pillows, inhaling deeply as I smelled him there.

"You're so fuckin' sexy, Calliope."

"I'm paying attention," I muttered, pushing my hips against him.

"Yeah, baby, you are," he groaned, running his fingers through the wetness between my thighs. "Wanna see your face, though."

He turned me again, letting me bounce against the bed for a minute before coming back down until he was covering me completely.

"Wrap your legs around me, Callie."

I did as he ordered, but the moment he started to push inside me, I stopped him.

"I need to know that you'll put Will and me first," I told him quietly. "I need to know that I can count on you to do what's best for our family."

He growled deep in his throat and plunged inside me, making me arch off the bed as his teeth clamped down on the side of my throat, and he began sucking hard. He pulled out slowly and slammed back in over and over, until both our bodies were covered in sweat and I had three different hickeys peppering my torso and neck, and then suddenly, he stopped.

"Nothing's more important than you, Calliope. Don't you see that yet?"

I looked into his eyes, but I already knew what I'd find.

"Yeah, baby. I see it."

And there in his bed, with my fingers in his hair and his mouth at my neck, no guilt or blame between us, he loved me and redeemed us both.

Epilogue

Callie

We were lying in his bed, sweaty and exhausted, when my mind returned to the main reason for my visit.

"Where's Cody?" I asked, leaning up on my elbow so I could look down into Asa's face. "I haven't seen him in months!"

"On his way to Sacramento, I imagine," he answered distractedly, staring at my breasts as he ran a finger over one of my nipples.

"Why didn't he say anything?" I griped, smacking his hand away lightly and flopping back onto the bed in exasperation. "I've been begging him to come down for-freaking-ever and now he's there and I'm here!"

"Don't think he was going to see you, Sugar," he replied with a smirk.

"No!" I gasped. "Gram?"

"Nope. I doubt she'll even know he's there."

"Well holy shit, little brother," I whispered to myself.

"Gettin' shot can change a man's priorities, yeah? I'm pretty sure he's done letting her push him away," he mumbled, rolling on top of me. "Now stop worrying about your brother and his issues with your idiot best friend and fuckin' kiss me."

ACKNOWLEDEMENTS

No one reads these things do they?

My girlies: You are two of the kindest, smartest, most considerate kids on the planet. I'm not sure what I did to deserve you, but whatever it was must have been awesome. You'll forever be my greatest accomplishment. I love you like crazy.

Mom and Dad: I love you! I can't believe I'm writing the acknowledgements for my second book. Thank you for the coffee, shoulders to lean on, and taking care of the girls so I could have an hour of silence. Let's do this again soon, okay?

Sisters and Brothers: Thanks for listening to me complain, talking me down, and boosting me up.

Betas: Gina, Kimberly and Kenna- Craving Redemption wouldn't be what it is without you. Thank you for your patience, your insights, and your love for Callie and Asa.

Kara Reavis and Sommer Stein: Once again, you've taken an idea and made it into a beautiful cover. You two rocked it beyond my wildest imaginings.

Toni and Lisa: Dudes. I think we're built to last. Three girls from completely different parts of the country, with three different accents (though, mine is more of a non-accent), and three completely different personalities… but somehow we fit together. Like peas and carrots...and broccoli. I'm not going to write something mushy—that's Toni's domain. Love you guys.

Madeline: You've helped me from the beginning and I wouldn't be where I am without you. You listen to me complain, commiserate when

I'm having a hard time, and kick me in the ass when I need it. I would have lost my mind writing CR if it wasn't for you. Thank you.

Cindy: Our late night chats kept me from losing my mind. I thank God daily that you're three hours behind me so I can text you at 3am and you don't think I'm crazy.

Scandal: I know your real name and use it on a daily basis… but you'll always be Scandal to me—the blogger who agreed to pick up a book from an author that no one knew and give it a try. You opened so many doors for me—I don't know how I'll never be able to repay you… maybe I'll send you a fruit basket or something. Thank you a million times.

Natasha: You came through for me in a BIG way. I'll never forget that. Thank you so much.

Mia and Elle: Thank you SO much for saving my bacon.

Bloggers: Your excitement and support has blown my mind. I could have never imagined that there would be so many of you itching to get your fingers on this baby. Thank you so much for spreading the word and caring about what happens to my characters.

Babes: You know who you are. Thank you for the memories… for research purposes, of course.

Man with the beard sleeping on my couch: I couldn't have done this without you. Literally. Not only did you pretend to pay attention while I read scenes to you out loud, you also woke up with the kids, cleaned the house and made sure we all had clothes to wear when I was in the middle of my writing madness. Also—thank you for sleeping on the couch so I could write in my writing spot undisturbed…I'd feel bad about that if the couch wasn't so much more comfortable than the bed.

Readers: Craving Redemption would still be an idea in my head if you hadn't been asking for more. I'm able to do this crazy author thing because of you. Thank you. Don't worry—Casper's story is next.

Printed in Great Britain
by Amazon

53033923R00236